EX-WIFE MISTRESS AND LOVE INTEREST

EX-WIFE MISTRESS AND LOVE INTEREST

Written by

SHARYN PAIGE

Angel Girl Publishing
New York, New York

Ex-Wife, Mistress and Love Interest

Published by: Angel Girl Publishing

New York, New York

shaysensuals@gmail.com

Sharyn Paige, Publisher / Editorial Director
Quality Press.info, Book Packager

Cover photo design.
Annakellywrites@selfpublishingbookcovers.com

Angel Girl books are available at special discounts for bulk purchases, sales promotions, fund raising or educational purposes.

ISBN # 978-0-578-63610-8

Library of Congress Control Number: 2020902017

This book is dedicated

to the following people:

Ethan, Brieanna, Brittney, Monti, Autumn, Travis,
Daniel, Alyson, Aliyah and my little Diva "Symora"

To my mother Rest In Heaven…

ACKNOWLEDGEMENTS

First and Foremost, I must give Honor to my Lord and Savior Jesus Christ To Whom All Blessings Flow.

Special Thank you to: Rev. Dr. Sean P. Gardner, Sr.

To my God-Daughters Brieanna and Brittney, I am so proud of you guys, you are my heart.

To my Youth /Young Adults at East Ward Missionary Baptist Church, I love you all so very much. You guys are the best.

To these special ladies (my angels): Words cannot express the love that I have for each of you: Tye, Mona, Clark, Norma, Gwen H, Mega, Shareen, Jennifer, Ivelisa, Shirley, Tylie, and Anna.

Daren you're the best brother/friend that a girl could ask for. Love You Immensely.

Terrence thanks for your unconditional love and support. Love You Much.

Joyce, Stephanie, Tracey, Nicole, Travis and Autumn you guys have been a true blessing in my life.

My B.F.F. Mia I am so glad that you are in my life, I love you more than you know.

To my nephews: Ethan and Monti, you two are my heart, love you both always.

To my cousin Lina Poo, stay sweet and beautiful as always.

Jamal, I am so proud of you, God has greater things in store for you.

My handsome cousins, Eric and Wadius you guys are the best.

Antrone and Eric I'm glad you guys are in my life.

LuLu super proud of you my friend.

Candie Girl love you, Simona, Amber, Aja-rae and Nova.

And to anyone that I have forgotten, please charge it to my head and not to my heart.

CHAPTER ONE

It's eleven o'clock on a cool Saturday morning, in August. Tyrone Tyler is looking fine, as always. He walks, or shall I say, he slides into Desire's Hair Salon looking for his ex-wife, Vanessa. Tyrone sure can make a woman stop and stare. Even though he is a low-down dirty dog, I have to admit Tyrone is one fine hunk of a specimen.

Delicious immediately summons for Tyrone, "My my my, who do we have here?" Delicious says to Tyrone. "Are you ready to come to my side of town?"

Tyrone says to Delicious, "Brother… Please."

Delicious says to Tyrone, "I aim to please."

Tyrone says emphatically to Delicious, "Enough of your foolishness. I am looking for Vanessa."

Delicious asks Tyrone sarcastically, "Why in the world would Vanessa want to speak to you? She has moved on with her new man, or should I say her soon to be husband. You do remember him, Kevin Brown?"

Tyrone says to Delicious, "So, they aren't married yet?"

Delicious Responds, "Tyrone, please don't go there."

"Look Delicious, what time will Vanessa be here?"

"Tyrone, she should be here in about ten minutes."

Tyrone says to Delicious, "I'll wait."

Delicious says to Tyrone, "Suit Yourself."

Tyrone patiently awaits Vanessa's arrival, which is a lot longer than ten minutes. At that very moment, in walks Vanessa. She is looking more gorgeous than before, she has a smile on her face that can light up a room. Delicious meets Vanessa in the reception area; he is trying to keep calm and keep a smile on his face.

Vanessa can tell that something is wrong, but he plays it off and tells Vanessa that he is not feeling well. "How are you, Vanessa?"

Vanessa tells Delicious that she is good, and Vanessa is looking and feeling good, that is until Delicious tells her that her ex-husband is waiting for her. Vanessa wants to know why Tyrone is at Desire's. "Delicious, did Tyrone say why he is here?"

"No girl, all I know is that he is waiting for you and you know I love you Vanessa, but Tyrone does look fine."

"Delicious, I agree with you. Tyrone is one fine hunk of man; too bad he wasn't a fine husband. They both crack up laughing. Vanessa knows this is going to be the hardest conversation that she has had in a long time, but it needs to be done. She is thinking, *God let me be nice to this man, no matter what stupidity comes from his mouth. Okay here it goes.*

"Girl, Vanessa, you know that I have your back, especially when it comes to that trifling no good for nothing fine ex-husband of yours."

"Thank you Delicious."

Vanessa says sarcastically, "Hello Tyrone, and what do I owe the pleasure of this visit?"

Tyrone tells Vanessa that even though they aren't married he still loves her and that he is miserable without her.

Vanessa says to Tyrone, "You came all the way here to say that to me? There's something else that's on your mind, what is it Tyrone?"

Tyrone says to Vanessa, "Honestly, I'd rather not discuss it here; can we meet for dinner?"

Vanessa says to Tyrone, "I'm not sure that is a good idea, I have to talk to my husband about this first."

Tyrone is shocked by what Vanessa just said to him. Tyrone says to Vanessa, “Your husband! What, wait, since when? Vanessa, from my understanding you weren’t married.”

“Tyrone, yes I’m married. Wait! I take that back I’m not married…”

Before Vanessa could finish, Tyrone interrupts her, and says, “I knew it.”

“Wait a minute Tyrone. Slow your roll, you didn’t let me finish. As I said before, I’m not married. I am happily married to a very incredible man.”

Tyrone says to Vanessa, “I really don’t want to hear about your so-called marriage.”

Vanessa asks Tyrone, “Is there something else that you want? I am trying to get my hair done and from the looks of things, this conversation is done as well.”

Tyrone says to Vanessa, “So that’s the way it’s going to be?”

Vanessa replies “Yes it is. Goodbye and have a wonderful day.”

“Vanessa, have you lost your mind, talking to me like that? I think you forgot who I am?”

Vanessa says to Tyrone, “I know exactly who you are. You are the same old tired no good for nothing jackass that I married. The problem is that you don’t know who I am, Tyrone. Don’t let the nice girl personality fool you, I can definitely handle my own. Tyrone, like I said a few moments ago, goodbye and enjoy your day.”

Tyrone is pissed as all get up; he storms out of Desire’s with an attitude. He is mad because his plan didn’t work. It seems as though Tyrone is still trying to get out of paying alimony to Vanessa. Tyrone is a sneaky dog, but what Tyrone fails to realize is that Vanessa is not the same woman she was when she was married to him, she is much stronger and wiser, and she is not taking any type of nonsense from that ex-husband of hers.

"Delicious, I truly cannot believe that Tyrone would show up looking for me."

Delicious says to Vanessa, "I would really like to know why Tyrone wants to have dinner with you? Vanessa, that low-down dirty dog is up to something and I cannot wait to find out what it is."

Vanessa says to Delicious, "I really don't care. Tyrone is so nonexistent to me."

Vanessa is so bothered by Tyrone's actions that she almost forgets to pay for her hair.

Delicious tells Vanessa not to worry about Tyrone; once a creep, always a creep.

"You know what Delicious? Maybe you're right; but knowing Tyrone the way that I know him, this isn't over by a long shot. That Negro is definitely up to something, I don't know what it is, but I will definitely find out. Delicious, how much is my bill?"

Delicious tells Vanessa not to worry about it, this one is on him.

Vanessa says, "Thank you, Delicious. I appreciate you doing that for me. I've got to get home to my husband. I love the way that sounds."

Delicious lets Vanessa know that he is happy for her. "Girl, you are showing teeth that you don't have." They both crack up laughing.

Vanessa says, "Delicious, you are crazy."

Vanessa has a question for him. "Delicious, where is Shaniqua?"

Delicious says with a smirk, "On vacation, both mentally and physically."

"Now Delicious, you know that's not right."

"Vanessa, there is nothing about me that is right, How about that?"

"Delicious, I will call you later to set up my next appointment. Take care of yourself."

Delicious says, "Vanessa you do the same."

Vanessa jumps in her car, she is heading home to her husband. She is still bothered by Tyrone showing up at Desire's unannounced. On her way home, Vanessa stops at Carl's, a very exclusive men's store and buys something special for Kevin. After she picks up Kevin's gifts she decides to call Vikki. It's been a minute since she last spoke to her best friend, but she knows she can't let this go without speaking to her.

Vikki is so happy to hear from Vanessa that she almost breaks Vanessa's ear drum, screaming so loud on the other end of the phone. Vikki begs Vanessa to stop by her house for a few moments of girl talk. Vanessa willingly obliges.

Vanessa says to Vikki, "I'll be there in about ten minutes." Vanessa let's Vikki know that she has something to tell her.

Vikki says to Vanessa, "What is it that you want to tell me?"

Vanessa says to Vikki, "I will tell you when I get to your house. I will see you in a few." Vanessa and Vikki both hang up their phones.

As soon as Vanessa hangs up the phone, she calls Kevin.

Kevin picks up, "Hey Baby, how is my beautiful wife doing?"

Vanessa answers with a strange tone, "I'm good."

Kevin asks, "Are you sure?"

"Yes, husband of mine."

"Vanessa, something is wrong. I can hear it in your voice."

Vanessa lies to Kevin. "Honey, I am doing okay. I was calling to let you know that I am going to stop by Vikki's for a little while and then I will head straight home."

Kevin says to his wife, "Vanessa baby, now you know that you don't have to call me to say that you are going to Vikki's, you can see her anytime you like."

"Thank you honey, but I do it out of respect. Kevin, I love you so much."

Kevin tells Vanessa that not only does he love her, but he is madly in love with her. Kevin says to Vanessa, "I'll see you when you get home."

Vanessa smiling proudly, says to Kevin, "Okay honey, I can't wait to get home to you. I will see you in about an hour."

Kevin cracks up, laughing. Vanessa asks him why he is laughing. Kevin responds, "Because you know good and well, when you and Vikki get together you guys talk for hours and hours."

Vanessa arrives at Vikki's house. Just as Vanessa is about to ring the doorbell, Vikki slings the door open. "Girl get in here." They hug each other, they are so happy to see one another.

Vikki says to Vanessa, "Girl you look good, marriage or shall I say Kevin is doing you good."

Both women laugh. As they walk to the couch, Vanessa asks Vikki how things are working out for her.

She tells Vanessa, "It's hard because Antonio is on the road so much. He wants me to travel with him, but I don't want to be a bother to him."

"Vikki stop it, that's your husband and if he wants you to be by his side, then do it."

"Vanessa, I guess you are right, enough about me, how are you?"

"Well girl, let me tell you what happened today."

"Oh Lord, Vanessa, let me sit down for this one."

"Vikki, I had an appointment today at Desire's. As I entered the salon Delicious met me at the front reception area of the salon, which was a little unusual for him. So, I asked him why he was in the reception area, and he explained that he needed to tell me something. I asked him if it could wait, and he said no it couldn't wait. Well girl, we walked to the back of the salon and who do I see sitting in a chair?"

Vikki says to Vanessa, "Girl, who?"

"None other than Tyrone Tyler, in the flesh…"

"Vanessa what in the world was Tyrone doing at Desire's?"

Vanessa said to Vikki, "Chile he asked me out to dinner."

"Vanessa, Tyrone asked you out to what? I know good and well that Tyrone didn't have the nerve to say that to you. Vanessa, please tell me you went off on him."

"Girl, you know I wanted to, but I had to hold my peace and be classy. I couldn't let Tyrone get under my skin. Don't worry Tyrone doesn't have to worry about me going to dinner with him tonight, tomorrow, or any other time. Vikki, he is no good and I don't trust him, and I can't put my finger on it, but he is definitely up to something. Vikki, knowing Tyrone, he will try and see if he can get back his alimony. He is just that trifling."

"Vanessa, I really don't think that Tyrone would do that, but you know what? Come to think about it, you are right I wouldn't put anything past him. Tyrone would make his own mother give him back everything that she purchased for him throughout the course of his life. Vanessa, enough about your trifling no good for nothing ex-husband, we have better things to talk about."

"Like what, Vikki?"

"Like, are you ready to be a Godmother?"

"Vikki, are you kidding me? You're having a baby? I am so happy for you. I can't wait to go shopping. I know that Antonio is running up and down the field and I don't mean the football field."

"Vanessa, I haven't told Antonio yet, I was thinking about surprising him for his birthday, but I'm scared that he would hate me."

"Vikki, why in the world would Antonio hate you?"

"Because he just signed an eighty-million-dollar contract, and a baby would make things difficult. He won't be able to travel the way he would like to; and you know, with him being on the road with his team it will cause a lot of distractions and I don't want this weighing on him because he can't be there with me and the baby."

"Vikki, now you know that's how Antonio is, so you might as well get used to it. Vikki, you have a great husband. He thinks the absolute world of you and there isn't anything that he wouldn't do for you."

"And that's what I love about Antonio. I know that I have a good man and so do you. Vanessa. So, how does it feel to be married to a man who is not trifling, deceitful and vengeful, but who loves you unconditionally?"

"Girl, Vikki, it feels so so good. Kevin knows how to keep me smiling, if you know what I mean." Both ladies crack up.

"Now Vanessa, you know I know about being happy. If Antonio had his way we would be hanging from the chandeliers every night two and three times a night. Girl, he is like three rabbits in heat."

"Vikki, now you know you're not right. But girl, it does feel good. Let me see who this is calling me. Vikki I don't believe it. It's Tyrone and I don't understand why he is calling me. I am not going to answer his call, maybe he will leave me alone." But Vanessa is wrong Tyrone has called her again and again she is ignoring his call.

Vikki says to Vanessa, "Doesn't he get the message that you don't want to be bothered?" Tyrone is calling Vanessa again for the third time.

"Vikki, it's obvious that he doesn't understand that I don't want to be bothered with him. I am going to take this call because if I don't answer him he will continue to call me like he lost his mind."

Vanessa answers her phone with an attitude. "Tyrone, why are you calling me? You and I have absolutely nothing to say to each other."

Tyrone says to Vanessa, "I want to take you to dinner."

"Tyrone, and again, I ask, why are you calling me?"

"Look Vanessa, I can call you anytime I want, I just want to have dinner with you,

I need to talk to you."

Vanessa says to Tyrone, "I don't know who you think you are talking to, but I want you to know that you can never think you can call me on my phone anytime you want. You lost those privileges the moment you cheated on me. And for the last time, Tyrone, what do you want and why are you calling me?"

Tyrone is beyond irate right now. He says to Vanessa, "You know what Vanessa, go to hell. I don't know who you think you are, but you aren't all that." Tyrone tells Vanessa, "I can see that you have a lot going on, so I am going to hang up and call you tomorrow when you are in a better mood."

Vanessa says to Tyrone, "When it comes to you, I will never be in a better mood.

You can definitely call me tomorrow but see if you have a conversation with me."

Before she can utter another word out of her mouth, Vikki grabs the phone out of Vanessa's hand and hangs up on Tyrone.

Vanessa tells Vikki, "Now you know that Tyrone doesn't take kindly to people hanging up on him."

"Vanessa, who cares! He got what he deserves. Tyrone had everything a man could ask for, but he threw it all away for a piece of tail. Now he has to pay child support for another man's baby and alimony to you. I don't care how upset he gets. He can go jump in the river as far as I am concerned."

Vanessa says to Vikki, "Girl you know you ain't right, but it's the truth. You made my day." Vanessa looks at her watch and says to Vikki, "I have to get home to my husband. I don't like to be out too late."

Vikki says to Vanessa, "It wasn't that long ago that you were trying to work longer hours and finish your degree. Look at you now, running home to your honey bunny. That's what true love will do for you."

Vikki asks Vanessa, "When are we going to get together again?"

"Soon Vikki, I miss my friend. We have to go out so we can talk about baby names." "Vanessa, that would be so much fun.

Both the ladies say good night to each other they smile and give each other a long hug. Vanessa jumps in her car she takes the twenty-minute drive home; she puts on the soulful sounds of Terence the hottest rhythm and blues singers out.

Vanessa is so immersed in listening to one of his songs that she almost runs off the road. She is shaken up so bad that she has to stop and gather her thoughts. She gathers her bearings and drives home… she makes it home safe and sound.

She doesn't want to say anything to Kevin, but he can tell something is wrong when he hugs her; she is literally shaking. Kevin asks Vanessa, "What in the world is wrong why are you shaking?"

Vanessa tells Kevin that there is nothing wrong, but he knows better.

"Honey you are not okay. What happened?"

Vanessa knows that she can't lie to her husband. "Well, you know I was coming from Vikki's house, I jumped in my car and I turned on some music and I was listening to Terence and I was so into his album that I almost ran off the road."

Kevin is upset with Vanessa. "Baby girl you have to be careful. I need my wife around for a very long time. Vanessa I love you so much."

"Kevin, I love you more than you know. Here these are for you." Kevin is happy to receive gifts from his wife, but he is concerned, and he wants to make sure that she is okay.

"Vanessa baby, are you kidding me? I can't believe you would do this for me, I just want to make sure that you are alright."

"Kevin, I am alright, but there is something that I would like to know."

Kevin says to Vanessa, "you can ask me anything that you like."

"Can we go out to dinner tonight?

Kevin screams out with a loud and cheerful voice. "Heck yeah, we can."

Vanessa is so excited she kisses him on the lips. Kevin tells Vanessa that he will be driving. Kevin and Vanessa go to Danielle's, it's a small quaint soul food restaurant. Southern hospitality and cooking at its best. Vanessa is trying to enjoy herself. She doesn't want to tell Kevin what happened about the situation with Tyrone, just yet, so she is going to keep her emotions to herself and enjoy a good time with her husband.

After an hour of wining and dining at Danielle's, Kevin and Vanessa jump in their car and drive home… they are there within fifteen minutes. Each of them gets in the shower; they begin to wash each other, and Kevin says to Vanessa, "It is going to be a good night tonight."

Vanessa lovingly responds by saying, "I bet it is going to be a good night!"

Kevin can't wait to get his wife into bed; he is happy to spend some time with her especially after the day they both had. Kevin jumps into bed and he is excited to see what Vanessa has on. After about ten minutes of putting the finishing touches on her outfit she appears, and she is looking more stunning than usual. Kevin stares and looks lovingly in Vanessa's eyes and says to her, "Baby you look scrumptious! I am so blessed to have you as my wife."

They begin to kiss each other and then they get into grown folks' business. Both of them fall asleep. Kevin is snoring like a baby; he has his arms wrapped around Vanessa so tight that she couldn't get up to pee if she wanted to.

Tyrone arrives home. He is steaming because he couldn't convince Vanessa to have dinner with him. Tyrone says to himself, *I cannot believe that Vanessa got married to that bum, Kevin, and so soon. She messed up my plan. I have got to figure out how to get back the money she took from me, who the hell does she think she is?*

It's a calm and warm Monday morning. Both Kevin and Vanessa are getting dressed for work. Vanessa walks to the other side of the bed and gives Kevin a kiss on the lips. Just as she is about to walk away from him, he grabs her and pulls her closer to him and plants a long kiss on her lips. She is loving this, but she has to get to a meeting. So, she says to Kevin, "Husband, if you don't stop, we are going to get into a lot of trouble."

"Honey, don't you know that's what I'm trying to do?"

Vanessa says to Kevin, "Honey, I can't. You know I have an important meeting in an hour, and I have to be there." She rushes out the door almost forgetting her pocketbook. She runs back upstairs, grabs her bag and tells Kevin, "Honey, I love you and I will call you later and don't forget to take the chicken out for dinner tonight." Kevin promises Vanessa that he won't forget.

As Vanessa is in her car driving to work, Vikki calls her; she wants to know what time she will be in the office because she is going to stop by. Vanessa tells Vikki to come to her office in twenty minutes. Vikki tells her that's fine and she will see her then, both ladies hang up.

Vanessa and Vikki actually meet up at Vanessa's job at the same time; they are so happy to see each other. They make their way up to Vanessa's office and before Vanessa can put her bags down, she gets a phone call and of course, you know who it is. Yep you guessed right it's her ex-husband Tyrone.

"Hello Tyrone, why are you calling me this morning? Did I or did I not tell you yesterday that there was nothing more that needed to be said? Get off my phone and don't call me anymore, the next time you invade my time and my space I will have my husband step to you. I hope I have made myself clear. Goodbye and good day."

Tyrone is heated. *I know Vanessa didn't just hang up the phone on me. I will go to where she is and turn that place out. Now she has pissed me off, and she is going to have a fight on her hands. She really thinks that Kevin can step to me I will beat that Negro till the black comes off him. This is definitely war. I'm going after Vanessa hard, she nor that so-called husband of hers will know what hit them when I get through with them.*

Vikki says to Vanessa, "I can't believe that Tyrone would still call you, even after you had two conversations - once with him at Desire's and once on the phone yesterday. Something is really wrong with Tyrone." Vikki jokingly says to Vanessa, "Can you say "crazee"? Vanessa you need to watch your back because there is no telling what he will do."

Vanessa says to Vikki, "That is why I am going to let my husband know what's going on so that if Tyrone tries any of his stupidity, Kevin will be ready. Girl I could see it now. Brown versus…. Tyler husband and ex-husband fight for the right."

Vikki says to Vanessa, with a smile on her face, "I would definitely pay to see Kevin whip Tyrone's behind."

"Vikki, my husband does not get into fights so he would never brawl with Tyrone."

"You are right, Kevin doesn't seem like the fighting type, but I bet you if you get on his nerve one too many times, it will be on and popping."

"I'm sorry Vanessa, I thought you said pooping."

"What Vikki? Girl, get your mind out of the gutter."

"Vanessa, you wish my mind was in the gutter, but it is far from there. It's somewhere else."

Vanessa says to Vikki, "You are so nasty.

Vikki responds by saying to Vanessa, "That's what I'm trying to be with Antonio." "Vikki, I don't want to hear about you and Antonio and all of your nastiness."

"Why not Vanessa? That's what married couples do."

"Vikki, that's because I'm thinking about all the nastiness that Kevin and I will be doing." Both of them crack up laughing.

Vikki says to Vanessa, "Girl, I'm leaving. I'm going home to get my nastiness on with my husband. But I have to make a couple of stops before I go home."

Vanessa asks Vikki, "Why did you come to my job and bring breakfast if you weren't going to have breakfast with me?"

"Vanessa I got turned off from eating, after listening to the bull crap coming from your ex-husband's mouth."

Vanessa says to Vikki, "I do understand, because I feel exactly the same way. Vikki, I just have one question to ask you, if you don't mind."

"Vanessa, now you know I don't mind you asking me anything, so what is it?"

"Vikki, please tell me why you are making stops if you want to get home to your husband."

Vikki says, "Because I need to get a nightie some honey and Whip Cream."

"Now that's what I'm talking about, Vikki Anderson. You know what Vikki, you just gave me an idea. I have a meeting at nine-thirty and after that I am free. I am going to call my husband and tell him to meet me at home because I have something important to tell him. Vanessa says to Vikki, girl I am going to put it on my husband so good that we both will be hanging from the chandeliers."

Vikki tells Vanessa, "Sista girl, I am so glad to see that you definitely got your groove back."

"Vikki, I will have you to know that my groove never left."

"I hear you Vanessa, now go home and show Kevin what you are working with."

"Bye Vikki, talk to you tomorrow."

"Okay, Girl."

CHAPTER TWO

It's seven-thirty in the evening, Tyrone has just arrived home. As soon as he opens the door to his massive mansion, he drops his briefcase and his bag of groceries on the floor. Tyrone immediately plops down on his plush couch and just stares into space. He starts talking to himself. *I have got to get some rest; it's been a crazy and hectic day. Vanessa has pissed me completely off; I know she doesn't think that she is getting away with keeping my money, this isn't over by a long shot.*

Now is definitely the time for me to stick it to Vanessa and Kevin. I'm going to call one of my boys and see what dirt he can dig up on Kevin Brown and I will get my money from Vanessa. I can say that she embezzled money from me or that the alimony documents were forged, one way or another I will get every dime that Vanessa stole from me.

As Tyrone is sitting on his couch, he realizes that he left his groceries in the vestibule, so he jumps up and decides to cook. He doesn't usually eat this late, but tonight is going to be an exception. He takes a pack of chicken from the bag and begins to clean it off, he puts on the new album from Terence: "Are You the One for Me". Tyrone pours himself a cold class of ginger-ale and closes his eyes as he listens to Terence.

He realizes after a few moments that he needs to season the chicken, so he runs upstairs and changes his clothes while the chicken is soaking. Tyrone is actually a great cook, and he cooked a lot while he was married to Vanessa, not because she didn't know how to cook, it was because he loved to do it. He is all prepared to fry chicken. He puts a couple of pieces in the hot grease, after which he walks into his living room and turns on his eighty-four-inch television screen and is so completely enthralled in a basketball game that he forgets he has chicken frying. Not only was he five minutes away from some burnt chicken, but five minutes more and he might have had a burnt kitchen.

He runs into the kitchen, laughs at himself and almost swore. *I can't believe that I did that*, but he doesn't care because he is going to eat it anyway. Tyrone takes about three bites of the chicken, looks at his watch and realizes that it is getting late. He wraps up the leftovers and quickly runs upstairs and takes a quick shower and jumps in the bed. He has an early morning meeting with a potential new client.

It is eight o'clock in the morning on a crisp and cool Thursday morning in late August. Tyrone strolls into his office, he doesn't look the same since his divorce from Vanessa; and his attitude toward women has changed, since he found out that Kayla had another man's baby and he is still paying child support for the kid.

Tyrone is still the top Investment Banker and Investment Broker, and he is now the newly appointed Partner at his firm, Williams, Smith, Peterson and Tyler. Tyrone's professional life is going great, but his personal life is in shambles.

That is until Tyrone walks into his Midtown Office building near Grand Central in New York City. There stands Sheila. Sheila is five-feet-five inches tall; she is shaped like an hourglass, she has a honey-caramel complexion, long flowing hair and a pair of a legs that would make any woman envy her. Tyrone is so enthralled by Sheila's beauty that he forgets to press the button on the elevator, and almost misses his stop.

Unknowingly to Tyrone, Sheila gets off on the fourth floor, which happens to be that of his firm. He is so busy staring at Sheila that he didn't even notice that he was on the right floor. She is looking around to make sure she is on the correct floor. After a second, Tyrone snaps back to himself and says to Sheila, or shall I say he stutters, "uuuum isss tttt there something that I can help you with?"

Sheila responds, "I hope so." I am looking for Williams, Smith, Peterson and Tyler. Tyrone says emphatically, "You've come to the right place. I'm Tyrone Tyler. Please allow me to open the door for you." Tyrone says to Sheila, "Where are my manners, I never got your name."

Sheila says to Tyrone, "That's because I never gave it to you."

Sheila says with a smile, "My name is Sheila Smith."

Tyrone is trying to get his mack on. "Well Sheila Smith, can I take you out for a drink?"

Sheila says to Tyrone, "I don't know you from a hill of beans, I don't think that would be a good idea."

Tyrone says to Sheila, "You can't knock a brother for trying."

Sheila says lovingly, "You sure can't. By the way I'm here to see Mr. Peterson, is he here?"

Tyrone tells Sheila please have a seat. Even though Tyrone has been shot down by Sheila he is still captivated by her beauty, Tyrone tells Sheila that he will be right back. Tyrone heads down the hall to the office of one of the soon-to-be partners, Mark Peterson. Tyrone closes the door to Mark's office. Tyrone begins to ask a bunch of questions. He wants to know who Sheila is, where she lives and is there someone special in her life?

Mark asks Tyrone, man, why are you so interested in Sheila Smith?

"Mark, who said that I was interested in Miss Smith?"

Mark can't stop laughing, "Tyrone, please, it's obvious that you are interested in her; otherwise you wouldn't be in my office asking me a million and one questions."

Tyrone says to Mark, then answer the questions."

Mark let's Tyrone know that Sheila is not only a client of his, but that she is also a friend and that he and Sheila have known each other for well over twenty years. Mark lets' Tyrone know that Sheila is a sports agent, and that she has a lot of high-profile athletes with Antonio Anderson as one of them and she is one of the baddest female attorney's there is to know.

"My ex-wife's best friend is married to Antonio Anderson."

Mark says to Tyrone, "What a coincidence." He also let's Tyrone know that Sheila is single at the moment. "Tyrone, I really don't think that Sheila is for you."

Tyrone says to Mark, "Why would you say that?"

Mark then says to him, "Because Tyrone, you like your women to be at your beck and call, and Sheila is not that type of woman at all. Sheila will date you and file a lawsuit against you and represent you at the same time, and she will win. She is a force to be reckoned with."

Tyrone says to Mark, "That's not true."

"Tyrone, do I need to give you a refresher course? Have you forgotten about Vanessa; you had a fit when she wasn't home for you?"

Tyrone says sarcastically, "That was only because I was trying to get with Kayla, but I have changed. I am a one-woman man and I think Sheila can handle me and I can definitely handle being with just her. She is gorgeous."

Mark says sarcastically, "If you say so man, I don't believe it for a moment." Mark tells Tyrone that he loves women too much just to be with one woman.

"Tyrone, I think you need to chill for a moment. Look at what it cost you by trying to have more than one woman."

Tyrone says to Mark, "I know and I am mad as hell that Vanessa got my money, but you can best believe that I will get it back."

Mark asks Tyrone, "Man how in the world do you plan on doing that?"

"Mark, I really don't know, but I'm working on it. She got nerve thinking she deserves one penny from me, let alone twenty and one half million dollars. I don't think so, man Vanessa is messing with the wrong one."

Mark says to Tyrone, "Man, get over it, you have more than enough money,

Vanessa has moved on and so should you. Man, I have moved on. No, you haven't Tyrone, because if you had moved on you would concentrate on trying to get to know Sheila and how to win her heart.

"Man, Mark I guess you are right. Now I need your help to get Sheila."

"Tyrone, my brother, Sheila is a hard catch, but I will see what I can do. Peace Out."

Just as Tyrone and Mark slap each other five, who comes walking past Tyrone's office in a form-fitting dress? You guessed it. Sheila. Tyrone is so mesmerized that he can hardly contain himself.

Tyrone man, this is your chance to say something. Tyrone can't think of anything to say, he doesn't want to say the wrong thing and make a fool of himself, so he just stares instead.

Since Mark already knows Sheila, he is playing a great game and she is playing along with him. He decides to say "Hello" to Sheila; she says, "Hi there, how are you?"

"Sheila, I'm great, give me a few moments and we will start our meeting soon.

Sheila asks, "Who's your friend, Mark?"

"I'm sorry, Sheila, his name is Tyrone Tyler. I thought you two met a few moments ago?"

Sheila says to Mark, "Actually we did, I had nothing else better to do. Mark please answer a question for me, if you don't mind."

Mark says to Sheila, "I don't mind you asking me anything, so ask away."

"Why is he looking like that, Mark?"

Sheila wants to know if he is shy. Mark emphatically says "NO, he's just a little nervous around you." Sheila wants to know why.

Mark tells her that Tyrone thinks that you are absolutely beautiful. She says, "Oh, I see."

Mark says to Tyrone, "Man this is your time to say something, if you don't I will."

"Mark why would you try and talk to Sheila, isn't she a friend of yours already?"

"She is a friend, but I'm trying to help you out."

"Thanks brother, but I think I can do this."

Tyrone gets his courage up now. "I'm sorry for staring, but I think you are absolutely stunning."

Sheila smiles coyly, "Thank you for that compliment."

Tyrone stutters, "Cannn IIII pllllease take you to dinner."

Sheila says to him, "Didn't you try and step to me in the reception area, and I believe that I told you "No thank you" earlier, nothing has changed in the past fifteen minutes. It has been a pleasure to meet you Mr. Tyler." Sheila's attitude has changed because she can't stand a man who is too aggressive, and Tyrone is a man who doesn't take no for an answer.

Tyrone gives Sheila his business card. "As you can see, my home number, my cell phone number and my e-mail addresses are on here, so you can call or email me anytime." Sheila takes the card and says thank you and walks away, leaving Tyrone standing at the door of his office drooling with his mouth open.

Tyrone tells Mark that Sheila is going to be his wife. Mark tells Tyrone, "Slow your roll brother, don't you think you should get to know her a little better?"

"Mark brother, I got this."

"If you say so, look Tyrone I have got to go. I have to close on a deal. I will be out of the office for a couple of days signing deals. I should be back in the office on Tuesday or Wednesday, but I will call you; maybe we can go out for drinks one night."

"You are on, Mark." Tyrone slaps Mark five and gives him a brotherly hug and tells him later.

"Same to you, Tyrone."

Mark then turns to Sheila and apologizes to her because they were not able to meet with each other. As he hugs her, he whispers in her ear that he will make it up to her. They don't want Tyrone to know that they know each other intimately in more ways than one. She smiles and promises to call him and set up another appointment.

Tyrone closes the door to his office. Just as he is packing up to leave, he gets a call. "Hello, this is Tyrone Tyler."

Tyrone hears a sweet-sounding voice on the other end of the phone, "It's Sheila."

"Well, hello there, Sheila." He is trying to play cool, but he can't. Tyrone is so excited with joy that he puts on his so-called Barry White voice. "Hey Beautiful, I'm so glad that you called."

"It's not what you think, Tyrone. I believe that I lost my bracelet somewhere at your office. If you find it can you please leave it at the front desk, and I will be there about noon tomorrow to pick it up."

"Sheila, I have a much better idea. How about I leave it in my office, and when you come by to pick it up tomorrow I can take you out to lunch?"

"You don't give up at all, Tyrone, do you?" Tyrone says to Sheila, "Not at all, especially when I want something."

"Well, Mr. Tyrone Tyler, for the record I am not a something, I am a woman."

Sheila is so irritated with Tyrone that she changes her tone with him. Thank you for the invitation, but you can leave the bracelet at the front desk, if you find it. Have a wonderful evening. She basically slams the phone down in Tyrone's ear. He is surprised by her actions. Tyrone wants to tell her off, but he is so infatuated with Sheila that he can't go off on her, so he just grins and bears it.

He wants Sheila as a love interest, but he knows that he has to play it cool and leave the bracelet at the front desk like she asked him to. But of course, Tyrone is not the kind of man who will give up, nor does he follow directions that well, especially when he is trying to get his way; so, he decides to hold on to the bracelet instead of leaving it at the front desk, just so he can get the chance to see Sheila tomorrow afternoon. Tyrone has a smile from here to there. Tyrone packs his briefcase with great anticipation and heads to the firm's private indoor garage.

Tyrone is in his new black Mercedes 950 SLE, he is listening to the sounds of r and b sensation, Terence; and he is thinking about how he is going to win Sheila's heart.

Tyrone has the biggest grin on his face, as he is headed to his home in the Hamptons. As he pulls into his driveway, his mind is on Sheila; he steps out of his car and heads into his spacious mansion.

Tyrone's mood changes because he realizes that there is no one there to share his home with, but Tyrone hopes that this will change soon. *Ahh, Sheila Tyler, what a nice ring that has. I can't wait to see her tomorrow; but in the meantime, I still am going to get my money back from Vanessa. I don't care that she is married to that damn Kevin. The judge had no right to award her twenty and one half million dollars of my hard-earned money. How dare she! I ought to sue the judge, she totally lost her mind giving my money to that skank of an ex-wife.*

Vanessa could not have children, and she wasn't that good of a wife anyway, the only thing she had going for her was her figure and it wasn't all that, come to think of it. Vanessa will regret the day she married Kevin. I know she doesn't think that she is going to be married to Kevin and they are going to live off of my money. I really don't think so, she is playing herself.

Tyrone says out loud "Vanessa this isn't over! You have messed with the wrong one and I am coming for what is mine. Vanessa you will see who gets the last laugh, you are going to have hell to pay."

Let me call Mark, I am sure that he will be able to give me some good sound advice about some personal things that I am going through.

Mark picks up the phone, and says "Hey brother, what's up?"

Tyrone says to him, "I need some advice on a couple of things. Number one, I know that Sheila is your friend, but did she mention anything to you about me? Number two, how do I get back the money that the judge awarded to Vanessa from our divorce?"

Mark says to Tyrone, "Brother that is a losing battle, that is an iron clad settlement. Vanessa's attorney got you good. Tyrone, as my friend I just want to say, leave Vanessa alone and move on, she certainly has moved on. Tyrone, I thought you were interested in Sheila?"

Tyrone says emphatically "I am very interested in Sheila.

"So, Tyrone, then why in the world are you so eager to get back at Vanessa for something that you did."

"Mark please, I didn't do anything."

"Tyrone my brother, did you forget that you cheated on your ex-wife for five years, and you almost had a baby with another woman, and you don't think you did anything wrong? Man up, Tyrone. There is no way you can talk to Sheila and you are still trying to hurt Vanessa, make up your mind. If you want a chance with Sheila, then you need to let this go with Vanessa and realize you messed up and you have to live with what you did. You played a major role in this and if you had not cheated on your ex-wife and gotten another woman pregnant, then you would not have to pay alimony to Vanessa."

Tyrone says to Mark, "Kayla's baby wasn't mine."

Mark says to Tyrone, "You are right about that, brother, but by the time they found out that the baby wasn't yours, it was a bit too late, you were already divorced. Vanessa wasn't playing with you."

"Mark, as much as I don't want to hear this, man you are so right. What's done is done, and what am I thinking about? I have got to stop going after Vanessa. I want to get to know Sheila a whole lot better." They both laugh.

"Tyrone man, I have got to get off this phone, I have a woman who needs me. I will speak to you tomorrow."

Tyrone asks Mark, "What kind of man does Sheila like?"

Mark replies, "One who knows how to treat a woman like a queen, who will respect, and love her, and only her.

Tyrone is speechless because he knows that he puts the DOG in the word dog, but Tyrone also knows that it will take a special kind of woman to change him, and Sheila just might be the woman to do that, or at least that's what Tyrone thinks. "Well it's time for me to go, we will talk later Mark, and call me because I would like to go out for drinks. I'm in need of boys' night out."

Mark says to Tyrone, "I got you. Let me go and make some money for my honey."

Tyrone and Mark both crack up laughing.

Tyrone says to Mark, "Brother, I am with you. Let's do this." Tyrone packs up and heads out of the office for the rest of the day.

He has a very important deal to close, which is going to pull him away from the office for the entire day. Tyrone makes sure that everyone knows how to contact him. He gets on the elevator and as he is taking a ride, he is assessing his life and thinking about what it would be like to be with Sheila.

Tyrone summons for his car. As the security officer approaches him with his car, for some reason he abruptly decides to postpone his meeting. He makes up an excuse that he is not feeling well, so that he can push his meeting back for another day and time. Thank goodness his clients are very understanding people, otherwise it would have been a situation.

Tyrone decides to do something that he doesn't normally do; he jumps in his car and drives home for some good old rest and relaxation. After the last fiasco, Tyrone decides that it's better if he just makes a sandwich. After spending about ten minutes making his sandwich, he walks to his den and plops down on his ninety-inch plus sofa in his den, and chills.

Tyrone is excited because he got to enjoy himself; but he definitely doesn't like spending time alone and he is going to make sure that it never happens again.

Tyrone jumps in the shower, and as he is drying off getting ready for bed he decides that he will give it one more shot, so he decides to call Sheila. Her phone rings three times, Tyrone is just about to hang up when Sheila answers. "Hello, this is Sheila; how may I help you?"

"Well hello, beautiful woman. How are things with you today?"

"I'm doing just fine Tyrone. Can I call you back? I just walked into the house and I want to put my food away."

Sheila knows that she has no reason to call Tyrone back she is just making conversation with him to make him feel good.

Tyrone emphatically says, "I can't wait to hear from you." Tyrone is so excited to hear from Sheila that he can't go to sleep, so he decides to watch a pre-season game of football, and tonight he gets a treat because Antonio's game is being televised". Tyrone steps into the kitchen to get something to snack on. He looks at a pie that he has in the refrigerator, realizing that it looks good, but he doesn't like to eat this late and he just had a sandwich. But what the heck, Tyrone is going to eat the pie. *What harm can one piece of pie do?*

Time has gone by so fast that Tyrone realizes that an hour has passed. He checks his phone to see if Sheila called him while he was in the kitchen. Tyrone is hurt, there is no call from Sheila. He brushes it off that Sheila is busy and will call him. Tyrone goes back into the living room to finish watching the game and he eventually falls asleep. Tyrone is sleeping so hard that he did not hear the phone when it rang.

Tyrone is snoring so hard that he scared himself; he looks at his phone and realizes that he missed Sheila's call. Tyrone is so upset that he is mad at himself, he attempts to call Sheila; but then he realizes the lateness of time and decides against it.

Damn, I finally got Sheila to call me and I missed the call. I am going to take the chance and call her anyway.

Sheila answers the phone. "Tyrone, do you realize what time it is? Why in the world are you calling me this late?"

The only thing Tyrone can say to Sheila is that he just wanted to hear her voice.

Sheila says sarcastically, "You just heard my voice, now hear this!" Sheila slams the phone in Tyrone's ear. Normally Tyrone would be upset, and he would have probably gone off; but because it's Sheila he is going to let it go, at least for this time.

CHAPTER THREE

After a good night's rest Tyrone is at his office bright and early, he is dressed to kill, and waiting for Sheila to come through the door. Tyrone has summoned Michele the receptionist to buzz him, as soon as Sheila arrives. Tyrone is pacing back and forth like a hopeless little boy; he has called Michele so much that she had to put the "Do Not Disturb" button on. Tyrone is heated, he cannot believe that Michele has blocked him from buzzing her. Tyrone says with an upset voice I have a trick for Michele, watch this. He decides to call Michele from his cell phone, and he makes sure that the call is private.

"Michele, this is Tyrone is Sheila here yet?"

Michele replies, "She just got off the elevator" Tyrone please get off the phone so that I can take care of her."

"Hello Sheila, Mr. Tyler will be with you in a few moments."

Sheila asks Michele if Tyrone left a package at the front desk for her. Michele answers, "I am sorry, but Mr. Tyler did not leave a package here."

Just as she says that, Tyrone comes to the front area.

You have to admit, Tyrone does look good, the man always knew how to dress.

Sheila is definitely impressed by Tyrone's swag, but she will never let him know it. Tyrone is smiling so much that he forgets to greet Sheila and stands in front of her trying to get the words out of his mouth. Michele clears her throat so that Tyrone can get the courage to walk Sheila to his office. Tyrone says to Sheila, "I am sorry, where are my manners? Please come with me."

Sheila says to Tyrone, "When I called you yesterday, I asked you to leave my package at the front desk."

Tyrone says, "I know but I was so busy with my work that I totally forgot."

Sheila says sarcastically, "I bet you did." Tyrone promises Sheila that he will be a gentlemen and he didn't lie to Sheila; he was well behaved. Tyrone is still blushing from ear-to-ear, he is trying to keep his composure. He can't help but stare at Sheila.

What man wouldn't be nervous around her? Sheila is five-feet-two inches and shaped like an hourglass and she can wear the hell out of a pair of jeans.

Tyrone finally gets up the nerve to ask Sheila out for a date, but just as he is about to ask her out Mark walks into his office. Mark apologizes for interrupting their meeting. Sheila says to Mark, "No need to apologize I was just about to leave anyway."

Tyrone is stunned and mad at the same time, but he knows he has no other choice but to ask her out; and so, Tyrone asks Sheila if he can take her to dinner on Friday. Sheila replies Friday is not a good day. She lies and tells Tyrone that she promises to call him, when she knows that it ain't happening. "I will contact you when I have a free moment."

Tyrone says to Sheila that he looks forward to hearing from her.

Sheila gives Tyrone a kiss on the cheek and says goodbye.

Sheila thanks Tyrone for finding her bracelet.

Tyrone says to Sheila, "I'm glad that I was the one who found the bracelet, it gave me a chance to see you, even if it was for only five minutes." They both laugh. Tyrone asks Sheila if he can walk her to the elevator, just as Sheila is about to say yes to Tyrone, in comes Michele informing Tyrone that he is needed in the conference room for a meeting. "Damn," says Tyrone, "this is not my day." Tyrone says to Michele that he will be right there.

Tyrone says in his sexy voice "Sheila, I'm so sorry, but I have to go to this meeting."

Sheila tells Tyrone that she understands and walks down the hall to the elevators and what a walk she has. Sheila can stop a man dead in their tracks, she always leaves them speechless and Tyrone is no different.

Tyrone can't concentrate because all he is thinking about is Sheila. As Sheila gets into her car and drives away, she calls Mark. Sheila is Mark's ex-girlfriend. Sheila tells Mark that she feels bad for Tyrone because he is really trying to win her over, and she wants to at least go to dinner with Tyrone, once. Mark tells Sheila, "Tyrone is a dog, look what he did to his ex-wife, Vanessa."

Sheila tells Mark, "All a dog needs is a muzzle and some home training and they will act right. Sheila says to Mark that she doesn't feel right setting Tyrone up like this and hurting his feelings.

Mark tells Sheila that he is trying to teach Tyrone a lesson about dogging women out. "Now he will see what it feels like."

Sheila says to Mark, "I'm only doing this for you, but it's not nice to play with a person's feelings, no matter how bad they are."

"Sheila, you will understand why I am doing this to Tyrone. All I'm going to say is that payback will make you stay back."

"Look Mark, I will speak to you later." Just as Sheila hangs up the phone with Mark, Tyrone calls her. Sheila answers her phone in a sweet and sexy tone. "Hello Mr. Tyler, how may I help you?"

Tyrone responds, "I really would love to take you to dinner, I haven't dated anyone since my divorce."

"Tyrone, I told you before that I would think about it. Please don't ask me again, because if you do I will definitely turn you down."

The only thing Tyrone can say to Sheila is, "That's all that I can ask for. Sheila you have a good evening."

"And you have a good evening, as well, Tyrone."

As Tyrone hangs up the phone with Sheila, Mark decides to come back into his office. Tyrone says to Mark, "Sheila is a beautiful woman, what am I doing wrong? I have never had a problem with women."

Mark says to Tyrone, "Man, of course you never had a problem with women. Did you forget that you were married to Vanessa for twelve years?"

"Mark, you got me on that one, how in the world could I forget that."

Mark says to Tyrone "Man, I'm surprised that you want to talk to a woman so soon after your divorce."

"Man Mark, if Vanessa moved on, I have to at least try, but it's not easy, especially because she was awarded so much money, and then she got married so soon after the divorce. It's almost like Vanessa planned it."

"Tyrone, get that out of your head. Vanessa was faithful to you, even while you were dogging her out."

Tyrone asks Mark, "Can we please change the subject? The only woman I want to get to know better is Sheila."

Mark says to Tyrone sarcastically, "Yeah I bet."

Tyrone has an attitude and he asks Mark, "What do you mean by that?"

Mark says to Tyrone, "Now brother, you know good and well you are still in love with Vanessa, so how are you trying to make Sheila your one and only?"

Tyrone says to Mark, "My brother, you might not believe it, but I'm not in love with Vanessa and I haven't been in love with her for a long time; that's why I stepped out of my marriage and cheated on her. Truth be told I was just angry and wanted to get revenge on her, but I'm actually over that. I really want to get to know Sheila a whole lot better."

"Well, that is good to know, Tyrone."

Tyrone slaps Mark 'five' and says to him that they should go out for drinks. "Mark, I have not enjoyed a night out with the fellas in such a long time that I have forgotten what fun was."

Mark tells Tyrone that he will meet him at Club Force at eight o'clock. Tyrone tells Mark that he has a deal.

Tyrone finishes his work for the day, or so he thinks. Just as he is about to wrap things up, he gets a call from an unlikely source, Antonio Anderson, the number one athlete in the league.

"Antonio, what is it that I can help you with?"

"Tyrone I have about three million dollars and I need to invest it, and since you are a partner in your firm, and you do have an awesome track record who better to come to."

Tyrone is so excited to do more business with Antonio. "Antonio my man," whatever you need, it's been a long time". Tyrone invites Antonio out for drinks and to talk over business.

"You know Tyrone, Why not."

"Antonio, this is going to be great. I will see you tonight at eight o'clock at Club Force. Be there my brother or be square."

Tyrone packs his bags he finally gets to leave work, and he can't wait to hang with the boys, but his mind is totally on Sheila. Tyrone realizes the time and decides that it doesn't make sense to drive home, so he decides to buy some time and decides the best thing to do is to go shop for a shirt. Tyrone is in "Jordyn's Man" the most exclusive men's store there is. Tyrone picks out two of the most expensive silk shirts the store has, but he isn't sure which one to get, so he decides to call Sheila to see which one she thinks he should get.

Whenever Sheila answers the phone Tyrone gets turned on, he is like a young boy who has a crush on his teacher. To Tyrone's surprise, Sheila answers the phone. "Hello Mr. Tyler, how are you?"

"Sheila, you don't have to call me Mr. Tyler, Tyrone is absolutely fine."

"I prefer calling you Mr. Tyler, since I don't really know you that well."

"Sheila, I would love to get to know you much better."

"Again Mr. Tyler, why are you calling me?"

Tyrone is so nervous that he can barely get a word out. "Sheila, I am shopping for shirts and I am having a hard time deciding which one to pick, so I figured I needed a woman's suggestion, and so I thought that I would ask you."

"Tyrone please send me a photo of both the shirts, so that I would be able to give you my opinion. Before Sheila could get off the phone Tyrone had already sent the pictures to her. Tyrone they are both nice I really think that you should get both of the shirts. Sheila I'm glad that I called you because I would have never thought to get both of them. Sheila "thank you" so much for your help. You are welcome Mr. Tyler. Sheila here we go with the Mr. Tyler stuff again. Tyrone it's force of habit.

Tyrone I have to hang up now because I am expecting a very important phone call. Tyrone reluctantly says "Goodbye" to Sheila, he so much wants to stay on the phone with her as long as possible, but he knows that he must leave as well, so he tells Sheila until next time, and they both hang up.

Tyrone finds it hard to believe that he can't get Sheila off his mind. *What is it about Sheila that Tyrone likes so much? Is it that he needs someone to occupy his time because he doesn't have a wife anymore, or does he genuinely like Sheila?* Only time will tell especially when it comes to Tyrone, as long as he can play the field then he is alright because he is the true master at playing games with people, but he clearly doesn't like to be played. Tyrone realizes the lateness of time, so he jumps in his car and drives to

Club Force, he is a little early, so he finds seats for him, Mark and Antonio.

Mark is looking smooth as ever. He is one fine specimen of a man, and I do mean fine. Mark has had his fair share of women and on any given day, he might be out with one or two a day. Now don't get it twisted Mark is single and not ready to settle down, but if the right woman comes along, Mark will settle down but until then he is going to enjoy the single life. He calls Savanah his girlfriend for the month and lets her know that he is going out with the boys for a couple of hours, and he tells her that he promises to be on his best behavior. Savanah tells Mark to go and have fun, and that if he isn't on his best behavior he will be done in a heartbeat.

Mark assures Savanah that he is going to be a good boy, he tells her that he will call her later, and they both hang up the phone. Mark likes Savanah and can see a future with her, but he wants to get his playboy ways out of his system before he can settle down with Savanah if she is the one that he wants to be with now, next month it might be a different woman that he is interested in dating.

Mark arrives at Club Force about twenty minutes after Tyrone has gotten there, they both slap each other five and they begin to talk. Tyrone tells Mark that he invited another friend of his. Mark is okay with that the fact there is another person coming. He tells Tyrone man the more the merrier. Mark I have a friend that should be arriving soon. Mark I want to wait for my other friend to arrive before I start ordering drinks, Tyrone I really don't think that one drink will hurt either of us. Tyrone agrees.

Mark can't stand to be in the same room with Tyrone, but he is hanging out with him because he has an agenda. Mark hasn't gotten over what he did to him in college. Mark thought about bringing it up to Tyrone but he knows that an argument will ensue, and it will turn in to more than it should. The ironic thing is that they both are both partners in the same firm, well not quite Mark is a Junior Partner and Tyrone is an official partner, either way they are both bringing in the coins.

Antonio is home getting dressed he is a little concerned because Vikki isn't home yet, and he tried to call her on her cell phone on more than one occasion, but she hasn't answered, just as Antonio finishes getting dressed in walks Vikki, she looks fantastic. Antonio yells, "Baby, is that you?"

Vikki says jokingly, "You better not be calling another woman baby."

Antonio is a little bothered, so he asks Vikki "Where have you been, I've been calling you?"

"Honey, I went to get my hair done, and I was probably under the dryer, and my phone was in my bag. Honey, you look like nice, Antonio are you going somewhere?"

Antonio says, "By the way, I am. I'm going out with Tyrone and one of his friends, Mark."

Vikki asks with an attitude, "Tyrone who? I know you aren't talking about Tyrone Tyler. Antonio, please tell me your talking about a teammate named Tyrone."

"Yes baby, I'm talking about Tyrone Tyler." Vikki is shocked.

"Antonio, how can you hang out with Tyrone, knowing what he did to Vanessa?"

"Look baby, it's not what you think, it's really about business for me. Vikki you know that I didn't forget the way Tyrone treated Vanessa, and I'm still bothered by that, but I'm trying to make some business moves, and you must admit that Tyrone is the best in the business. I will be home soon; I won't be out long." Vikki has a sad look on her face. "Okay Vikki, what is that look for?"

Vikki comes out of left field. "Antonio are you cheating on me?"

Antonio says to Vikki, "Are you kidding me right now? No, I'm not cheating on you, and where did that come from?"

"Antonio, just forget I asked."

"Vikki, we will finish this conversation when I get back."

Vikki reluctantly says to Antonio "Yeah okay".

"I should be home by eleven thirty."

"If you say so, Antonio."

"Vikki, I say so and I have something for you when I get home."

"What is it, Antonio?"

"Just have on something sexy."

"Oh, I will Antonio, and you better make sure you can handle what I am about to give to you."

"Oh, I can handle it, and don't you ever forget it."

Antonio kisses Vikki on the forehead and heads to his car. Antonio stops by the florist and has flowers delivered to Vikki, with a card that reads to the most beautiful woman in the world my wife Vikki Anderson. Then he stops by Gorgio's the hottest and best jewelry store in the world and buys Vikki two of the most expensive pieces of jewelry he can find. Antonio says to himself, *I know that my best girl will love this.*

Antonio finally arrives at Club Force. Before Antonio can get inside Club Force he is met with women who are trying their best to get to know him in more ways than one. But Antonio is a one-woman kind of man and he is madly in love with his wife. Antonio is escorted to his table by security they stand by just in case someone wants to pop off.

As Antonio approaches the table, Mark is in shock because he can't believe that the hottest running-back in football is at his table hanging out with him and Tyrone. Tyrone introduces Mark and Antonio to each other; Mark says to Antonio, "It's nice to meet you."

Mark jokingly says to Antonio, "I could get used to this, look at the women that are in here."

Antonio says to Mark that there is nothing better than coming home to that special woman.

Antonio tells Mark that he wouldn't jeopardize what he has with Vikki for anyone in the world, no matter how many women throw themselves at him. Tyrone really doesn't want to hear about this because he jeopardized a good woman by being a greedy dog. And the one woman that he wants to be his love interest is playing him like a bad card game.

Tyrone immediately changes the subject. "So, Antonio how long will you be in town? By the way, that was a good game the other night you did your thang."

"Thank you man I appreciate that Tyrone. I will be home for a few more weeks then it's off to get ready for the season. So, I thought I would meet up with you about a business deal. You are one hell of an investment banker and broker. I made over twenty-five million dollars with you on one deal, so I'm back again. I'm only investing three million dollars this time around, but I'm sure you can turn it into some mean cash."

Antonio looks at his watch and realizes that he wants to get home to talk to Vikki before it gets too late.

Tyrone is a creep and he is loving the fact that the women are swooning over him and Mark and most of all Antonio. Mark is watching Tyrone's behavior he wants to see if Tyrone is really a changed man or if he is the same man that dogged out his ex-wife. Mark can't stand Tyrone and he wants to pay Tyrone back for stealing his first love Vanessa, and so Mark is going to do whatever it takes for him and Sheila to bring the dirtbag down.

Mark is adamant about getting revenge on Tyrone because Vanessa was pregnant with Mark's baby when she met Tyrone. Tyrone didn't want Vanessa carrying another man's baby, so he made her get an abortion. Mark was livid when he found out what Tyrone had Vanessa do. It tore Vanessa and Mark apart. And to top it all off, Tyrone blatantly lied to Vanessa and told her that Mark had cheated on her with her roommate and that was the end of their relationship. Vanessa found out later years later in their marriage that Tyrone had manipulated her and lied to her because he wanted to be with her so bad.

Tyrone was a dog and a manipulator back in the day and nothing has changed since then. If it weren't for all the things Tyrone did and said to tear the two of them apart Mark and Vanessa would be happily married with children and Tyrone would be a figment of their imagination, and he acts as though he doesn't know what he did to Mark. Mark is too much of a man to bring it up now but there will come a time that he will approach Tyrone about it.

Mark wants to get Sheila involved to prove his point and to pay Tyrone back, revenge is bad but sweet revenge is a mother. Tyrone doesn't even know Sheila like that nor does he know that he is a pawn in Mark's takedown, but when a man's pride and ego are in the way he will do what he thinks is in the women's best interest, or in this case Mark is doing what he thinks is in his best interest. So, Mark is playing this game of stringing Tyrone along. Grown men playing stupid childish games. Funny thing Mark is a player himself, but Mark thinks that he is better than Tyrone because he deals with one woman at a time. Mark cheated on Sheila a long time ago while they were in graduate school. Mark did apologize to Sheila after he cheated on her and that's when they both realized that they were better off as friends.

Mark drank a little too much; he knows that he can't drive home, so he excuses himself from the table and calls Sheila and asks her to pick him up.

She agrees to pick him up. "Mark, don't forget that I can't park in front of Club Force because we don't want Tyrone to know that you and I are actually closer than we are pretending to be." Sheila gets to Club Force in record time.

By now Antonio has headed home to find out what's going on with Vikki. Tyrone is flirting with the women in the club as he is heading out the door to his car. Surprisingly Tyrone has not tried to take any of these women home, but then again Tyrone is a snake and he likes to sneak and do things.

Tyrone slaps Mark five and tells him that he has to get up quite early in the morning, and that he has a long day ahead of him. Mark tells him peace out and Tyrone leaves Club Force without a woman on his arm. Poor Tyrone he just knew that he had it going on and that all the women were just going to throw themselves at him, he feels dejected, that is until a cute petite young lady walks over to him an introduces herself as Candace.

"Well hello, Candace, it's a real pleasure to meet you, you are a gorgeous woman. My name is Tyrone."

"Thank you for the compliment, I'm tired and I need a ride home." Tyrone is a bit hesitant but Candace is a very fair complexion woman with long hair she is definitely Tyrone's type of course any woman is Tyrone's type.

Sheila spots Tyrone coming out of Club Force, she ducks down in her car she doesn't want to take the chance of Tyrone seeing her, once she thinks that Tyrone is not in her eyesight she sits back up. Sheila can't believe that Tyrone is actually talking to this woman, and he is trying to get with her. Sheila decides to take a few pictures of this. She texts Mark and tells him to come outside now, and of course Mark leaves Club Force but not before he gets a few numbers he spots Tyrone talking to Candace he can't believe that Tyrone is trying to hit on a woman and he still wants to get with Sheila.

Mark is going to make sure come hell or high water that Tyrone won't get a chance to kiss Sheila let alone get involved in a relationship with her. Mark so desperately wants to punch Tyrone in the face.

Mark is about to question Tyrone about this situation when Sheila texts him again and tells him to mind his business and get his butt in the car. Thank goodness for Sheila because there is no telling what Mark would have done if Sheila hadn't been there.

Mark racked up the numbers as he left Club Force but that's Mark he is a player but he is fine as all get up. Mark is six feet tall two hundred pounds of pure muscle, with caramel skin and naturally wavy hair. Mark carries himself in a way that no one would expect that he is thirty-eight years old. Although Mark is fine as all get up his most attractive qualities is that he is a successful businessman with no children. Mark gets into Sheila's car and thanks her for driving him home.

"Mark what are you going to do about your car?"

"Sheila, I have no other choice but to leave it here and I will just have to come and pick it up sometime on Friday."

"Mark, did you forget that tomorrow is Friday?"

"Sheila, don't antagonize me, you know exactly what I mean."

"Mark, you have had a bit too much to drink and I am very surprised at you, especially because you are not the kind of person that drinks this much."

They finally arrive at Mark's condominium Sheila not only helps Mark inside his condo, but she puts him to bed. Mark asks Sheila to spend the night, but Sheila emphatically tells Mark NO. She says, "Good night Mark. I will talk to you tomorrow." She closes the door behind herself, makes her way to her car and drives home. She gets back in her bed and tries to get some much-needed rest.

Sheila wakes up bright eyed considering the night she had before, but she doesn't do this too often so this is an exception for her but trust she will not do this again not even for Mark. Just as

Sheila is about to jump in the shower Mark calls her, he is really out of it, he tells Sheila that someone has stolen his car.

"Mark, you are really gone. Did you forget that you went out with the boys last night and you got so drunk that you called me to come and get you from Club Force? I had to take you home last night I guess you also don't remember that your car is parked near Club Force. Do you remember that I had to put you into bed?"

"Sheila you did all of that then how come you didn't spend the night."

"Mark now you know that I am not that kind of woman. I would never sleep with a man that I am not married to."

Mark says, "You are so right, Sheila, but I had a spare bedroom so you could have slept in there until the morning. Well I think that I have a hangover."

"Really Mark! You think? Mark you need to go back to bed and when you get up make sure you drink a lot of coffee before you go to work, otherwise you need to stay home and sober yourself up and make sure that you pick your car."

Mark tells Sheila that she is a good friend, "and I am grateful that you are a part of my life."

"You are a good friend, as well Mark, now go get some rest and let me go. I have to get to work, I will call and check on you later to see how you are doing."

"Thank you so much, Sheila, for everything."

"You're welcome, Mark, now get off the phone."

"Okay, bye Sheila." Mark hangs up the phone and realizes at that moment how much he blew it with Sheila. He knows that there is no way in hell she will ever take him back, but Mark also knows that Tyrone will never stand a chance with Sheila, if he has anything to do with it. "I am going to drink some coffee before I head to the office."

CHAPTER FOUR

Vikki is upset with Antonio because he went out with the creep currently known as Tyrone Tyler; she still can't believe that Antonio would do that. She immediately calls Vanessa. Vanessa picks up the phone she can tell by Vikki's voice that something is wrong. "Hey Vikki, what happened?"

"Vanessa "It's so strange that you know me so well, that you know when something has happened before I tell you"

"Vikki we have been best friends since college, of course I'm going to know when something has happened to my best friend… now spill the tea."

"Okay Vanessa, here it goes. I came home from the doctor's office and Antonio was getting dressed to go out, which I didn't mind at all, but it was who he was going out with that bothered me."

Vikki, who is the person that Antonio went out with that has gotten you so worked up?"

"Vanessa, Antonio went out with your ex-husband."

"Vikki, why in the world would Antonio do that? He knows that Tyrone is nothing but a jerk. Vikki, I just don't understand Antonio, something is definitely wrong with that picture. Vikki did you ask Antonio why?"

"Vanessa, of course I did, he said that he was only meeting him for business purposes." "Oh then, Vikki that's okay."

"Vanessa why would you say that's okay, it's not okay."

"Vikki, if I know anything about your husband, he has never lied to you, so if he says it's business, then believe him, it's business; especially if Tyrone's name is attached to it., "Did you forget that Tyrone made him loads of money last year?"

"Vanessa, I guess you are right."

Just as Vikki is about to say something else to Vanessa, her doorbell rings. "Who in the world is this ringing my bell? I'm not expecting anyone."

"Vikki, the only way you will know who's at your door is to go look and see."

Vikki peeps through her custom-made blinds and realizes it's the florist. Vikki asks him to hold on, she runs to the back of the house and gets a bat to bat him upside the head if he tries something funny. Vikki opens the door with hesitation, "Can I help you?"

The delivery man asks, "Are you Vikki Anderson?"

Vikki reluctantly answers, "Yes, and why do you ask?

"I have a delivery for you." The florist hands Vikki two dozen blue roses, she gives the delivery man a fifty-dollar tip. Vikki closes the door; she is smiling from ear-to-ear. She proudly lets Vanessa know that she has received two dozen blue roses, and she reads the card aloud. "To the most beautiful woman in the world, my wife, Vikki Anderson."

"Aww, Vanessa, I have the best husband in the world."

Vanessa says, "no I think you have the second best one in the world." They both chuckle.

"Vanessa girl, I have to get off the phone because Antonio just pulled up in the driveway."

"Bye girl, talk to you later."

"Later Vanessa, love you."

Vikki is upset because she didn't have the chance to put on something nice for her husband, so she hurries up the stairs trying to look sexy for Antonio, but it's too late, he is already in the house.

Antonio yells, "Hey Vikki! Baby, where are you?"

Vikki responds, "Baby, I'm up here in the bedroom, give me a minute."

Antonio yells, "I'm coming up!"

Vikki yells back at Antonio, "Don't come upstairs, I need a minute."

Antonio yells back again, "You have exactly one minute and then I'm coming upstairs."

"Alright!" yells Vikki. It takes Vikki less than thirty seconds to get ready for Antonio. Vikki has taken some of the rose pedals and spreads them across the bed. Vikki texts Antonio. "You can come upstairs now; I am waiting and ready for you".

Antonio smiles when he reads the texts and makes his way to the master bedroom.

Antonio is all smiles when he opens the door, he can't believe what he sees.

"Vikki baby, I am more in love with you now, just as much as I was the first time that I laid eyes on you. Vikki I knew from the first day that I met you that you were the one that God had made just for me, and me only." Tears are streaming down Vikki's face. Antonio says romantically, "What's wrong baby, why are you crying?"

"Because I am so blessed to have a man like you in my life. Antonio I didn't realize that you loved me like you do until I read the card that was inside of the roses that you sent me."

"Guess what baby girl, I have something else for you."

Vikki laughs out loud, "I bet you do have something else for me."

Antonio grins sheepishly and says, "Yes, I have that as well, and something else to go along with that… actually they might work good together. Close your eyes and don't peek."

Vikki lovingly obliges, and Antonio places the jewelry boxes on the bed. "Okay, now you can open them."

"Oh, my goodness, Antonio, you didn't have to do this."

"Baby, yes I had to do this, when my wife is feeling sad I need to make her happy. And when I left the house this evening, I knew that something was on your mind, so let's talk about it."

Vikki is hesitant to say anything to Antonio, so she just says, "Forget about it.

Antonio I don't want to bother you in any way, I'm okay."

Now Antonio is steamed at Vikki, "baby something is upsetting you and I want to talk about it. You are not bothering me you are my wife."

"Antonio, do I make you happy?" Vikki asks.

"Excuse me, Vikki why in the world would you ask me a dumb question like that?" "Well, you are a handsome man and a super successful athlete and women throw themselves at you all the time, and I know you are tempted to get with one of them."

"Vikki, let's get a few things straight. Number one I know that I am a successful athlete, and yes I do have women throw themselves at me, but I also know what I have at home and I won't mess that up for anything in the world. And I told you before, baby, that I wanted you to travel with me, all the other wives travel with their significant others."

"Antonio, are you sure?"

"Vikki, I'm sure and that way when you are with me all the other women will back off, not only will they see the ring, but they will see my wife up close and personal."

"Antonio, that's why I'm in love with you. God couldn't have blessed me with a better man."

Antonio says to Vikki, "now come here and give me some of that sweet suga."

Antonio turns out the lights and they both head to bed. It's about to be on and popping in the Anderson household.

It's seven o'clock in the morning. Vikki is up and getting dressed, she is still blushing at the events from the night before. Antonio turns around and stares, Vikki asks, "Honey what's wrong?"

"Hello Antonio Baby, "Absolutely nothing, can't I look at my beautiful wife?"

"My handsome husband, you can look at me anytime you want."

"By the way Vikki, where are you going?"

"Antonio, I have a business meeting."

Antonio responds, "Oh really, what business?"

"Antonio, I can't tell you right now, it's a surprise." Vikki walks over to the bed and gives Antonio a long kiss. As she is about to get up, Antonio pulls her back down on the bed and they begin to kiss even more, and they are about to get into some more real grown folks trouble, when she stops Antonio and tells him that she has to leave, and that she can't miss this business meeting. Antonio moves, but he is very curious as to what business meeting his wife is attending. Vikki kisses Antonio on the forehead as she rushes to get up and leave, she tells him that she loves him, and Antonio says that he loves her as well. As soon as Vikki is in her car Antonio calls Vanessa. Antonio will definitely get to the bottom of this.

Vanessa is surprised to hear from Antonio. "Hello Antonio, how are things with you? Antonio is something wrong?"

"Vanessa, why would you ask that?"

"Because Antonio, since I have known you, you've never called me."

"You are right about that Vanessa, and to let you know there is nothing wrong. I need to ask you a question, but you can't let Vikki know that I am on the phone with you?"

Vanessa says hesitantly, "Oooookay, what is it?"

"Vanessa, is Vikki cheating on me?"

"Antonio, why in the world would you ask me that? You know good and well Vikki is in love with you and there is no other man for her."

"Then, if that's the case, Vanessa, why is she on her way to a business meeting?

My wife doesn't work."

"Antonio, I really don't know about a business meeting. I know that she has a doctor's appointment, but I will find out and I will let you know. I will speak to you later and, Antonio, rest assure you have absolutely nothing to worry about." Vanessa hangs up the phone, she is so mad that she had to lie to Antonio, but what else could she do. Vanessa immediately calls Vikki.

Vikki picks up on the first ring. "Hey Diva, how are you this morning?"

"Vikki, you know I'm feeling awkward right now."

"Vanessa, why in the world are you feeling so awkward?"

"Because your husband called me wanting to know if you are cheating on him." "What did you say to him, Vanessa?"

"Vikki, I assured him that there is no other man for you but him, and I think he believed me when I told him that I didn't know about a business meeting, but that you had a doctor's appointment."

"Vanessa thank you for keeping Antonio at bay, I have a few last-minute things to do, for his surprise party."

"Now Vikki, you know I don't like to lie to your husband, but it's for a good cause."

"Thanks Vanessa, I love you. Here comes Nicholas now. I will call you later, Vanessa." "Vikki, who is Nicholas?"

"He is the event planner who is helping me with Antonio's surprise birthday party."

Vikki and Nicholas are having a very productive meeting, they are finalizing everything for Antonio's party when Vikki decides that she wants to go to Hotel Mystique's Grand ballroom and go over some last-minute details with Nicholas. As she and Nicholas approach the hotel, of all the people in the world, Tyrone spots both Vikki and Nicholas entering Hotel Mystique. He decides to take a picture of them entering the hotel as they are at the Front Desk. He can't wait to call Vanessa and tell her what's going on, but he realizes that Vanessa won't believe him anyway. What Tyrone doesn't know is that Vanessa already knows what Vikki is doing.

Vikki and Nicholas leave Hotel Mystique separately. Vikki is on her way to see her doctor, she hasn't been feeling the best lately and she doesn't want to alarm Antonio until she knows exactly what was going on. Vikki arrives at the doctor's office, but she doesn't have a long wait at all Dr. Black begins a series of tests on Vikki immediately. Dr. Black tells Vikki that he will have her test results back in about two days. She is concerned that it could be serious, so she asks Dr. Black, "What do you think could be wrong with me?"

"Vikki, I am not sure. It could be a number of things, but as soon as we narrow it down you will receive a call from my office."

Vikki is about fifteen minutes from home when she receives a phone call from Dr. Black. Vikki is troubled because she just left Dr. Black's office and they said the results would be back in two days. *What could it be?* Vikki reluctantly answers her car phone, "Umm hello, Dr. Black, is there something wrong?"

"Quite the opposite, Vikki. I wanted to let you know that I got the results back from one of your tests, Vikki."

"Already Dr. Black? Okay, give it to me straight, how sick am I?"

"Vikki, you are not that sick and depending on how your body reacts, you may or may not have morning sickness."

"Run that by me again, Dr. Black. Did you say morning sickness?"

"Yes, I did."

Wait Dr. Black, I need to pull over, so I won't get into an accident. Are you saying that I'm going to have a baby?"

"Yes, Vikki, you are going to have a baby. I'm going to run all the tests again, but it looks that way."

"To be honest, Dr. Black, I thought I was pregnant. I had taken a pregnancy test earlier and the results were positive, but now you confirmed everything for me. Oh, my goodness, Dr. Black, I don't know if I can do this… I'm scared."

"Vikki, there is no reason to be scared. You are going to be a great mother, and I'm sure that your husband will be so happy."

"Dr. Black, I'm sure that he will. I don't know if I can keep this a secret until Saturday."

"Vikki, why in the world would want to wait until Saturday to tell him, instead of telling him immediately?"

"You see, Dr. Black, Saturday is Antonio's birthday, and I am throwing him a surprise birthday party, and I thought that it would be a wonderful time to tell him."

"I do understand Vikki, congratulations once again."

"Thank you, Dr. Black."

Vikki has so many emotions running through her head that she can't think straight right now, but one thing is for sure she can't tell Antonio anything right now, and she knows that she can't keep anything from him; this is going to be the hardest thing for her to do.

Vikki calls Vanessa. Vanessa answers on the first ring, "Vikki what's wrong?"

"Nothing is wrong Vanessa."

"Vikki you can fool other people, but I know you better than everyone else and something is definitely wrong with you."

"Vanessa, I will call you tomorrow and we can talk about it then. I just want to go home and get some rest."

"Vikki are you sure that you are okay?"

"I'm good girl, I gotta go."

Vanessa doesn't like the way Vikki sounds, but she is not going to push the issue.

Vikki arrives home. She thinks that Antonio isn't home, but to her surprise he is there. She has got to play this part and not let on that she and Antonio are having a baby.

Antonio says to Vikki, "Hey baby, how was your business meeting?"

Vikki tells Antonio that it was great.

Antonio is skeptical because he knows that Vikki is hiding something from him.

He can't put his finger on it, but he is going to let her tell him what's going on. Vikki dares not spill the beans, she realizes that Saturday is only two days away, but it seems like an eternity.

"Antonio, my wonderful husband, I'm tired. I'm going to sleep." She gives him a kiss and heads upstairs.

"Vikki, are you okay?"

"Yes Antonio, why would you ask me that?"

"Because you have been acting a little strange the past few days."

"Antonio honey, I'm okay, just had a stomach virus, but I'm feeling a little better, love you Antonio."

"Same to you, honey." They both go to sleep.

Antonio is definitely not happy, and rest assured he is going to get to the bottom of what's going on. *Vikki should not be having any type of business meeting without his knowledge; something just isn't right.*

CHAPTER FIVE

It's a cool early Friday morning. Tyrone is at work; he just can't stop thinking about Sheila; but he is in total disbelief by the photos that he has of Vikki and this random guy going into Hotel Mystique. He doesn't know how to tell Antonio, but his big mouth doesn't know how to shut up and mind his own business either. *Boy I can't wait for Antonio to see these pictures he thinks his wife is on the up and up, when I get finished with Vikki she is going to wish that she never sided with my ex-wife Vanessa about anything. Sweet revenge.*

I'm about to drop a major bomb and I can't wait for this bomb to explode. Tyrone decides that it is better for him to tell Antonio about what his wife is up to, and then to let Vanessa in on this. Tyrone can't wait to see the look on Vanessa's face. *Antonio is my man and I hate to bring him this drama, but I can't stand Vikki and I'm going to give it to her real good.* Just as Tyrone is scheming on when he is going to let the drama unfold he gets a phone call from Sheila.

Tyrone is sweating because he is excited that Sheila is calling him, but what Tyrone doesn't know is that Sheila is scheming on him with Mark to prove a point that he is a low-down dirty creep.

Tyrone answers the phone in his Barry White voice, "Hello this is Tyrone, how may I help you?"

"Hello Tyrone, this is Sheila. I was trying to see if you were available for lunch tomorrow?"

Tyrone says without hesitation that he sure is.

"Is twelve o'clock okay with you?"

"Sheila, that's perfect, my meeting for that time was canceled."

"Tyrone that's great, I will see you tomorrow."

Tyrone is excited about his lunch date with Sheila, but he knows that the icing on the cake is to let Antonio in on this little secret that he has on Vikki, so he decides to call Antonio.

Antonio is surprised to hear from Tyrone. Antonio has Tyrone on speaker phone.

"So, what's up brother, how are you today?"

"Antonio, my brother, I am great, but I need to speak with you about something that is very important."

"Antonio, can we meet tomorrow about eleven o'clock?"

Antonio looks at his calendar and tells Tyrone that he is available to meet. They both hang up the phone. Tyrone is excited, because he thinks that he is tearing up a marriage, when in fact the tables are going to be turned on him.

Tyrone realizes that he has a business meeting in about twenty minutes, but he has Sheila on the brain because he is thinking about having lunch tomorrow with his love interest or so he thinks.

Sheila has decided that she needs to get her hair done, so she heads over to the salon that everyone brags about, Desires. She walks in looking as fierce as can be and she asks for Delicious. Delicious greets Sheila with a smile. She tells him that she was referred by a friend.

Delicious escorts Sheila to the back of the salon where all the magic happens, after an hour of washing, drying and getting snatched, Sheila decides that she must come back again while she was under the dryer she asked Mark to pick her up; and he, of course, obliges.

Just as Sheila hangs up the phone in walks Mark, and Delicious is definitely on the case. "How may I help you?"

Mark says, "I am looking for someone."

Delicious replies that he is too. "You are a fine piece of dark chocolate" and he says that he would love to have some of Mark's Baby Ruth.

"Woo, slow your roll. I'm here looking for Sheila."

"Well, I'm here looking at your Almonds and I'm full of Joy."

"Negro Please…"

Delicious says, "I don't mind pleasing you."

By this time, Mark is so disgusted he almost leaves Desire's without Sheila, but she comes to Mark's rescue, thank God.

"Mark, what's wrong?"

"Sheila, who is this?" Mark looks at Delicious like he is going to beat the living hell out of him.

"Mark, this is Delicious."

Mark says, "D' Who? I'm not going to ask. Let's just go."

Just as Mark and Sheila are about to leave Desire's, Delicious stops and says wait.

They both turn around and Delicious walks over to Mark and asks him if he can dip his ice cream into Mark's Almond Joy. Mark says, "let's get the hell out of here."

"Sheila, check this. The next time you come here, don't call me to pick you up and I mean that."

"Mark, honestly speaking, Delicious is harmless."

Just as Sheila and Mark leave Desire's in walks Vikki. She and Delicious give each other a kiss on the cheek. "Well, well, well, Vikki. So, what brings you to Desire's? You don't have an appointment until Saturday morning."

"Delicious, I am desperate. I need to get a massage, and get a pedicure because I won't have time to get it done on Saturday. Delicious I really look forward to seeing you at Antonio's surprise birthday party."

"Vikki girl, now you know I cannot wait to come to Antonio's birthday party, I get to have plenty of Milk Chocolate, Caramel,

Dark Chocolate nuts all in the same place at the same time. Honey that is my fantasy."

"Delicious, I can't with you right now, stop it you, are so crazy." They both laugh.

Vikki decides to call Antonio while she is getting her pedicure." Hi honey, how are you? I'm at Desire's getting a pedicure, I will be home as soon as I am done."

"Okay baby, I will see you when you get home. And Vikki I love you."

Vikki hangs up the phone and immediately says to Delicious that she has the best husband in the world. Delicious lets Vikki know that he is happy for her. As Vikki looks around the salon she notices that something, or should I say someone, is missing.

"Delicious where is Shaniqua?"

"She is on an MHV."

Delicious What in the world is an MHV?"

"Shaniqua was mentally affecting my health, so I punched her out and now she is on a vacation." They both crack up laughing.

"Delicious, you need some serious help. Delicious, that is not nice."

"Vikki, it may not be nice, but it is true."

"Delicious, by the way, thank you so much for squeezing me in."

"Vikki, the way your feet were looking, you better be glad all I had to do was squeeze you in."

"Ha ha, very funny, Delicious. I will see you Saturday Delicious, I love you."

"Same to you, Vikki."

Vikki hops in her car and heads home to her husband. She can't wait to jump into his arms, she is driving like there is no tomorrow. She is excited to see Antonio, but she still can't tell him that she is pregnant, this is going to be the best birthday gift Antonio ever received.

She walks into the house and there is soft music playing, the lights are low, and Antonio walks over and grabs her hand and says follow him.

"Antonio, what in the world are you up to?"

"Vikki, please do not spoil the moment, just go with the flow." He has cooked dinner for her, which is surrounded by one dozen red roses, a rose for each month they have been married.

"Antonio honey, you did this for me?"

"Vikki, of course I did this for you, who else would I do this for?"

Vikki begins to cry.

Antonio asks her, "What's wrong?"

"Antonio, there is nothing wrong, I'm just so blessed to have a man who cares enough about me to do something as great as this. I am a blessed woman."

He gently wipes the tears from her eyes. They both sit down, and dinner is being served by their own personal chef Juan Carlo. Then, out of nowhere, Antonio drops a bomb on Vikki.

Antonio knows that Vikki doesn't want to hear what he has to say, but he is going to tell her anyway. "Vikki I'm meeting Tyrone for lunch tomorrow."

Vikki is steaming, "Antonio Anderson, how in the world can you have lunch with a creep like Tyrone again?"

"Vikki baby, I understand that you don't like Tyrone; but you have to remember, Tyrone and I aren't friends. He probably wants to fill me in on our business meeting that we had the other day. Vikki, it's a business lunch, that is all, I promise."

"Antonio, I don't like this one bit. Wait a minute....Didn't you just have a business meeting a few days ago and now you want to meet up with him again? Antonio is there something you're not telling me, what else does he want?"

"Vikki, stop worrying, everything will be fine… and don't forget, I don't even like Tyrone. Baby, if Tyrone wasn't good at what he does I would have no contact with him. Vikki, look enough about Tyrone. I am tired and I have a busy day ahead of me tomorrow."

"Me too Antonio, I have to meet a friend about a business meeting."

"Okay Vikki, you have been having quite a few business meetings lately. What's up with that?"

"Honey, you are making more out of it than it needs to be."

"Vikki, believe you me, we are definitely going to talk about this."

"Antonio that's fine, but we won't be talking tonight. I love you Antonio, now let's get some rest."

Antonio is feeling some kind of way right now, because he knows that Vikki is hiding something from him.

"Good morning beautiful, how are things with you?"

"Antonio I am fine, but who is beautiful?"

"You are Vikki, you know lately you seem to be a little down, and sometimes I feel as though you are not focused and that you are losing confidence in yourself."

Well Antonio, it's just that... I'm sorry Antonio, I have to take this call."

Antonio grabs the phone from Vikki, he says hello to the caller which happens to be Nicholas; but Nicholas dare not say anything to Antonio, so he politely hangs up.

"Vikki Anderson, who was that on the phone?"

"Antonio, how would I know, you grabbed the phone from me before I could say anything."

"We will definitely have a talk when I get back from my meeting with Tyrone."

"Antonio, I really don't like this at all; but if you have to meet with him I guess it will be okay. See you later."

"Baby, I will be back before you know it. How about this? After I meet Tyrone for lunch I will come back here, take you to dinner tonight and after that you can have your way with me."

"I love the way that sounds, Mr. Anderson.

They both smile. Antonio gives Vikki a kiss on her forehead before heading out to meet with Tyrone.

As Antonio gets into his car, Tyrone calls him on the phone. He wants to be sure that Antonio is still going to meet him for lunch. Antonio lets Tyrone know that he is on his way.

"Antonio, I'll be waiting. By the way Tyrone where are we meeting?"

"We are meeting at Bella's." Tyrone can't wait to ruin Antonio's marriage, or at least that's what Tyrone thinks. Tyrone says to himself, *this negro must be crazy if he thinks I really want to meet him for lunch. When I get finished embarrassing him he won't have a choice but to pay me. This is going to be good blackmail and I am the best at it*, at least that is what Tyrone thinks, but what he doesn't know is that the script is about to flip on him in more ways than he knows.

Antonio arrives at Bella's, one of the best restaurants in Manhattan. He slaps Tyrone five upon his arrival. "So, what's happening, Antonio?"

"Nothing at all. Tyrone I am surprised that you want to have lunch with me."

Tyrone asks, "why wouldn't I want to have lunch with you, Antonio, you are a cool brother… and by the way, Antonio, how is Vikki?"

Antonio answers by saying that she is fine and that he is in love with the best woman in the world.

"So, you really think that she is the best woman in the world?"

"Tyrone, my brother, I know for a fact that she is the best woman in the world. One thing that I do know is that I never ever have to worry about her cheating, I'm secure in my marriage.

Tyrone says to Antonio, "I hear you…" Just as Tyrone says, "I hear you" he whips out his cell phone, and he says to Antonio, man I have a picture of this woman I want you to see. Tell me if you know her and what you think."

Tyrone hands the phone to Antonio, and of course, Antonio is shocked by the picture; but he doesn't let Tyrone know this. "Tyrone, where did you get picture from?" "Man, you won't believe it, I was at lunch and I was driving back to work when I saw Vikki and this man going into Hotel Mystique. I was surprised to see her there with this man. I tried but I couldn't hear the conversation. Tyrone." so, you decided to show me this nonsense the day before my birthday."

"Antonio, so tomorrow is your birthday?"

"Tyrone, that's what I just said, so why are you trying to play like you didn't just hear what I said? Tyrone, you know you are a creep and I don't believe for one second that Vikki is cheating on me and I know that there is a good explanation for this."

"Antonio, it sure is, while you are away enjoying your career your wife is enjoying her extra-curricular activities."

Tyrone doesn't show it, but he is laughing on the inside. He is thinking that Vikki and Antonio's marriage is about to tank, and he is definitely going to make sure of it.

"Well, look here Antonio, if you don't want it to get out that your wife is sleeping with another man, here's what you need to do. Give me fifteen million dollars, and I won't take this to the papers."

"Man, Tyrone if you don't get the hell out of my face with your foolishness, I will beat you like you stole fifteen million dollars from me. I'm not giving you a dime."

Tyrone threatens Antonio or so he thinks that he is threatening him by telling him he has forty-eight hours to get the money, or this will be on the news. "Please don't test me, Antonio."

Antonio walks away from Tyrone and he is on fire. "I wish you would and that would be your first and your last time, now try me if you can, Tyrone. Have a good day Tyrone!!!!"

Tyrone screams out, "forty-eight hours, Antonio! …And oh, by the way, just thought you might like a copy of your so-called faithful wife." Tyrone has a sneaky look on his face, he is the worst type of human being there is. An animal is nicer than Tyrone, but as always, every dog shall have his day and that day will come sooner than later for Tyrone.

Antonio rushes out of Bella's and jumps into his car. Antonio is so upset that he almost crashes his car, trying to get home. He realizes that he has to slow down, otherwise he might land himself in the hospital. A fifteen-minute drive home took Antonio nearly forty-five minutes because he couldn't get that image of Vikki and another man out of his mind. Antonio finally arrives home, but he doesn't get out of his car right away. He sits pondering what he is going to do and say to Vikki… whatever it is it won't be pretty. After about five minutes of contemplating his next move, Antonio gets out his car and slams the door behind him. At this point, he is beyond heated, but he is going to play it cool. He wants Vikki to confess about her so-called affair and if she doesn't, there is no telling what Antonio will do and there will definitely be hell to pay.

Vikki is so happy to see Antonio, but she notices that something is wrong with him. "Antonio are you okay?" Vikki asks.

Antonio is steaming. "Vikki, I want you to be honest with me, are you having an affair?"

Vikki is extremely upset. “Antonio how can you ask me such a question? “No, I am not cheating on you.”

Antonio screams at the top of his lungs, “then who the hell is this man?!” Antonio shows Vikki a picture of her and the mystery man that is on his phone; but unknown to Antonio, Nicholas is assisting Vikki with his surprise birthday party.

Vikki knows that she has to convince Antonio that she is not cheating on him and she needs to say something to him now, otherwise this will definitely be the end of her marriage to Antonio and they have only been married for a little over a year.

She cannot allow Antonio to think that she doesn’t love him and that she is cheating on him. She has got to play the role of a lifetime. *Oh well here it goes,* hopefully, this will be the first and only time that she will have to lie to Antonio. Hopefully, he will understand once his birthday party is over why she had to lie to him.

CHAPTER SIX

"Antonio honey…"

Before she can get the rest of the sentence out of her mouth, Antonio says, "Don't honey me!"

"But Antonio, listen to me. That is a co-worker of mine, we were having a lunch welcoming him to the office."

Antonio says to Vikki that would be okay, but you forgot one thing you don't work. I want the truth and I want it now."

Vikki knows she has got to think quick, fast, and in a hurry, and again she needs to make it believable. But just as she is about to lie to Antonio, his phone rings; it's his mother Cassie. Vikki is so relieved because this will give her more time to make up something. Antonio puts his mother on hold, and he tells Vikki that this conversation is not over with.

"Antonio, as far as I am concerned it is."

Now Antonio is heated so much so, that he screams at his mother without realizing it. "Mother what did you call me for?"

"Young man, don't you take that tone with me, can't I call and see how my son is doing?"

"Mother, I am so sorry. I was in the middle of a heated discussion with my wife and you caught me off guard."

Mother Cassie is surprised, she wants to know if everything is okay with Antonio and Vikki. Antonio lies to his mother, "yes mom, you know how couples get, we will be okay."

Vikki is hoping that Antonio stays on the phone with Mother Cassie as long as possible, she knows that Mother Cassie loves to talk to her son. Antonio is engaged in a conversation with his mother, so Vikki figures this would be the perfect time to sneak out of the house, but Antonio knows this isn't over by a long shot. "Mom I have to go. I love you and I will call you tomorrow."

Antonio sees Vikki and blocks her from leaving, "Where do you think you are going? You are going to answer my question, Vikki, who is this man? And don't lie to me again."

"It's a friend of Delicious he is in town to surprise him and we don't want Delicious to know, so I was just taking him on a tour and getting him settled into his hotel until Sunday."

Antonio asks Vikki, "What's happening on Sunday?"

"That's when I am going to surprise Delicious for his birthday." Vikki seems a little nervous, but it's the best she could come up with.

"Vikki, then why didn't you say something before?"

"Because I didn't think it was that serious, until you showed me this picture."

"Antonio, where did you get this picture from?"

"Tyrone showed it to me and then that Negro had the nerve to send it to me, and now he is trying to blackmail me."

Vikki is stunned by what she is hearing. "Antonio, why in the world is Tyrone trying to blackmail you? Antonio baby you have to be kidding me. Tyrone Tyler is lower than scum, why would he do something like that to you Antonio, as much business as you have given him."

"Vikki, I am so ready to slap the taste out of his mouth."

"Antonio, do you want me to talk to him for you?"

"Vikki, you should not be anywhere near that man and I do not want you going to his job, calling him or having any type of contact with him. Do I make myself clear?"

"Antonio, I promise I won't do or say anything to Tyrone."

"Now I am going to ask you one more time, Vikki, are you sure that you are not cheating on me?"

"Antonio, I already said that I am not cheating on you, I would not lie to you.

You are my husband and I love you so very much." Just as Vikki begins to finish her conversation with Antonio, her phone begins to ring… it is Nicholas.

He is excited to fill Vikki in on all the details, but she knows that she has to be careful about what she says. "Hey Vanessa, I am having a discussion with my husband, can I call you later?"

Antonio can tell something is wrong, so while Vikki pretends to be on the phone with Vanessa, Antonio decides he needs to get some air. He jumps into his car, he is so angry at what he just saw, coupled with what he heard from Tyrone.

Antonio is at a point where he is going to go off on any and everyone, including his wife. Antonio is still feeling uneasy about the photos and now Vikki is acting strange on the phone, but Antonio isn't going to call Vikki out just yet. He decides that he is going to wait for the right time to catch Vikki in the act of lying.

He cannot believe this. Vikki, the love of his life, is cheating on him and she is basically lying about it to his face. Antonio drives off, but he is sitting on the side of the road contemplating his next move with his wife. He doesn't want to rush and make a move too fast. He knows that something will be done, but he also knows that he has to be cool until he has enough evidence to prove that Vikki is cheating on him.

Vikki hangs up with Nicholas. She races to meet him, but she didn't realize that Antonio was sitting on the side of the road. Antonio wants to follow her, but right now he has to figure out what he is going to do about Tyrone, the blackmailer. He has the option to kick his behind or ignore him; but one thing is for sure, Tyrone will not get a dime from Antonio, at all.

Vikki meets up with Nicholas to tell him about the drama that is going on in her life. "Boy oy boy, Nicholas, Saturday can't get here any faster. I am getting sick to my stomach lying to my husband; if he knew that I was with you he would kill us both dead. Nicholas, everything looks great. Nicholas, what time will you be here to decorate tomorrow?"

"Vikki, I have to stop and pick up a few last-minute things for the party, then after that I should be here about one o'clock."

"Nicholas, that's perfect, I will meet you here at one o'clock Nicholas, I have to pick up Antonio's mother from the airport and then I will bring her back here."

"Vikki, I think Antonio is going to love his surprise party."

"Nicholas, I really pray that he does, because right now I am Antonio's least favorite person. Antonio thinks that I am having an affair on him with you." Vikki says in a laughing way to Nicholas, "You know that might be a good way to get him here is to make him think that. Thank you Nicholas you gave me a great idea, see you tomorrow."

"See you at one o'clock, Vikki."

Vikki leaves the hotel, hoping that no one spots her. She cannot have any more drama or this party won't happen. Just as Vikki is getting into her car, she suddenly feels a cramp. *Oh no this can't be happening right now. I think I need to sit in my car before I drive back home.* Vikki begins to pray like never before. *Lord please do not let me lose this baby. Please cover the both of us.* Just as Vikki finishes praying, the cramps subside, and she is able to drive home without any complications or pain. When she arrives home, the first thing that she says is, "Thank You God, you kept me and the baby in perfect peace."

Vikki opens the door hoping that Antonio is home; but to her surprise, he isn't there; so she decides to call him on the phone. "Hello, my handsome husband, how are you?"

He answers her in a very soft tone. Vikki asks, "Where are you Antonio?"

"Vikki, I'm about to step to Tyrone."

"Antonio baby, come home, he is not worth it; and you know that Tyrone is full of crap. Antonio, you have more important things to worry about."

"Vikki, right now, I am not so sure about that."

"Antonio, what in the world are you talking about?"

"Baby girl, you are going to find out later. Vikki I am hanging up the phone now, I will talk to you soon." After Antonio hangs up the phone with Vikki he realizes that she is actually right, he shouldn't be wasting his time on a jerk like Tyrone. He has more pressing things to deal with, like the man who Vikki is cheating on him with.

As Antonio gets into his car and he begins to head home he has just made a decision. When Antonio arrives home, he finds Vikki is home waiting for him she is so excited to see him she meets him at the door. "Honey, I am so glad you are home."

"Vikki honey, you are so right. I thought about what you said, Tyrone isn't worth me fighting with, plus I have something more pressing to deal with. Vikki, I have decided to move out."

"Antonio, I need you to repeat what you just said."

"Vikki, I said that I am moving out."

Vikki is steamed. "Antonio, please stop with your foolishness."

"Vikki, for some reason, you seem to take me for a fool. Where were you earlier today? And before you say that you were in the house, that's a lie."

"Antonio, I went to meet a friend for lunch. His name is Nicholas and I told you before that he is a friend of Delicious and we were going over last-minute details for his birthday. Look Antonio I am not going to take much more of this question and answer game."

"Really Vikki, do you actually think that I am going to fall for that nonsense?

You are having an affair and I am out of here."

"Antonio, where are you going?"

Antonio looks at Vikki. "I am getting the hell away from you and I am going to start the divorce proceedings."

Vikki screams with a loud voice, "Antonio, I am not cheating on you!"

"Vikki, I never thought that in a million years you would cheat on me."

"Antonio, how many times do I have to tell you that I am not cheating on you?"

"Vikki, right now I don't want to hear anything that you have to say. I will come back tomorrow to get the rest of my things. Vikki, you and I are officially done."

Vikki is crying and upset about what Antonio is doing. Vikki knows that she has to tell him the truth, but he wouldn't believe her, even if she told it to him. Vikki says in a sad voice, "Antonio baby, I love you so much and I don't know what I can do to convince you that I am not cheating on you."

Tears are streaming down Vikki's face. She is about to say something else to Antonio when he says to her, "I don't want to hear anything you have to say, I'm gone."

Antonio is so mad at Vikki that he slams the door as he is leaving. Vikki doesn't know what to do, but she knows one thing for sure Antonio is going to look crazy when he finds out that she isn't cheating on him.

Vikki is angry at Antonio because in some strange way, she thinks that Antonio believes that the picture that Tyrone has showed him is real. But she is going to let Antonio have his way, it is actually better for her because now she can get a good night's rest and put the finishing touches on his surprise birthday party.

Vikki heads to her room. She tries to go to sleep, but that isn't working so she just stays up. She actually thinks it's better that her husband isn't around. She knows that Antonio is the only man for her, and she feels strange not having him in the same bed with her. She finally cries herself to sleep.

It is bright and early, and the sun is shining on this Saturday morning. Vikki gets up excitedly because she can't wait to throw Antonio his surprise birthday party, and to give him the best birthday present any man can get; but it is bittersweet because she wasn't able to greet Antonio with a birthday kiss. *I know what, I will call him.*

Antonio answers on the first ring. "Hello."

"Hey baby, Happy Birthday, Antonio. I love you and I want you to enjoy this day, and even though you are mad at me, and I am not cheating on you, I would love to take you out for your birthday is that alright?"

"Vikki, I need to think about that, I don't know if I can get over this so easily."

Vikki angrily says, "You know what Antonio, never mind. You can go to dinner by yourself. I am done with this pity party you are having right now."

Vikki hangs up from Antonio and jumps in the shower. After getting herself together, she grabs her car keys and rushes to the airport to pick up Mother Cassie, her mother in-law. She knows that this moment is bittersweet because she has to tell Mother Cassie that she and Antonio are living in separate places because he thinks she is cheating.

Vikki arrives at the airport and happily meets her mother-in-law. However, Mother Cassie immediately senses that something is wrong with her daughter-in-law. As they are driving from the airport to Vikki's house, Mother Cassie says, "Vikki, I'm not trying to be in your business but what is going on with you? And do not tell me nothing is wrong, because I can clearly tell that something is wrong."

"Mother Cassie, I don't want you to worry."

"My wonderful and beautiful daughter-in-law, it's too late, now give me the tea."

"Okay Mother Cassie, as long as you promise not to be mad."

"Alright already, Vikki, I promise that I won't get upset."

"Well Mother Cassie, here it goes. Antonio walked out on me last night, he says he wants a divorce because he thinks that I am cheating on him."

"Vikki, don't worry, I will talk to my son. I'm going to call him in a little while and when I finish with him he will be back home."

"Mother Cassie, that's great but can we do that later? I need to go to the hotel so that I can put the finishing touches on everything; then we have to get to the hair salon and then home to get dressed. Mother Cassie, I cannot wait to see the look on Antonio's face tonight."

"Vikki, I'm not concerned about this situation with you and Antonio, once he sees what you have done. I guarantee you that he will be home tonight, believe that."

"Mother Cassie, I'm so glad that you are here, and I am sure that Antonio will be happy when he sees you."

The ladies head to Hotel Mystique. They have arrived, but Nicholas is not there.

Vikki does what she can to start decorating, but she knows that with her pregnancy she can't do anything strenuous. She is a wreck and she reaches out to Nicholas. "Nicholas, where are you?"

"Girl, I am at the bakery, making sure that the cake is ready and delivered on time. As soon as they put the finishing touches on it, we are going to load in into the truck and we will be on our way, just hold tight."

"Mother Cassie, since Nicholas is not here yet, we are going to run to the house so that you can put your bags down and then we will come back." As they are driving to the house, Antonio calls Vikki.

"Hey Antonio, what's up?"

Antonio asks Vikki if she is home. She tells him no, but that she is on her way there and she will be there in about fifteen minutes. "Okay, I am on my way there to pick up some clothes."

Vikki says sarcastically, "Do you Antonio" and slams the phone in his ear.

Mother Cassie is very upset with this situation. My beautiful daughter-in-law, I don't like how Antonio is treating you."

"Mother Cassie, it is perfectly okay. I can deal with it because I know that I'm not cheating on him. He is only making himself look crazy. I am going to play along with the game." Just as Vikki says that, she yells out loud, "Oh my Lord!"

Mother Cassie is getting nervous... "Vikki what's wrong?"

"Mother Cassie, I just remembered, I can't take you to the house because you will spoil the surprise if Antonio sees you there. I know what I am going to do I will call my girl Vanessa. You can stay with her until Antonio leaves." Vikki proceeds to call Vanessa. The phone is ringing, and Vikki is surprised that Vanessa hadn't picked up the phone.

Finally, Vanessa picks the phone, "hey there doll, how is my best friend?"

"Vanessa, I am fine. I don't mean to bother you right now, but I need your help." "Sure, what is it Vikki?"

"Antonio's mother is in town and Antonio is on his way to the house to pick up the rest of his things, and he can't see his mother because it will spoil his birthday surprise."

"Vikki, bring her over now; but I'm confused Vikki."

"Vanessa, you're confused about what?"

"Vikki, what do you mean that Antonio is coming to get the rest of his things?"

"Vanessa, I will tell you when I get to your house, see you in five minutes."

"I will be waiting, Vikki."

Vikki arrives at Vanessa's house in less than five minutes. Vikki's mind is all over the place. *Antonio left, he thinks she is cheating; she has to get her outfit and get back to her house to get dressed and lure her husband to the hotel so that he can stop all of this foolishness and come back home.*

"Hey Vanessa, how are you?"

"Vikki I am great. Miss Cassie how are you? It is so great to see you again."

"You too Vanessa, and you are looking more gorgeous than ever."

Vikki tells Vanessa that she has five seconds to tell her what's going on. "Antonio thinks that I am cheating on him, so he moved out."

"Vikki, where in the world would Antonio get such a stupid idea like that?"

"Vanessa, you wouldn't believe me if I told you, but on the other hand you just might. Your ex-husband Tyrone is blackmailing Antonio with some pictures that he saw of me and Nicholas while we were going inside Hotel Mystique to finalize everything and do a little decorating for Antonio's surprise party. So, Tyrone decided to take a picture, invite my husband to lunch, show him the picture, and then blackmail him for fifteen million dollars."

"Vikki, how much money did you say that Tyrone is trying to blackmail Antonio for?"

"Vanessa, I said fifteen million dollars."

"Vikki, I wouldn't give Tyrone fifteen cents. What is Antonio going to do?"

"Vanessa, I think he is going to pay him, but I don't think that it is a good idea. "Well Vikki, I think it is."

"Vanessa, my husband should not be paying that miserable ex-husband of yours anything, not even one dime."

"Vikki listen, tell Antonio to pay Tyrone, arrange it so that when Tyrone shows up at the party, he is going to look like a total fool, when he realizes that the man you were with was Nicholas, who happened to be the event planner. Then, Antonio should turn around and counter sue Tyrone for trying to blackmail and extort money from him. Then watch the stupid look that Tyrone will have on his face."

"Vikki, I'm not married to him anymore and I am so sick of the nonsense. I am embarrassed that I even know Tyrone. I don't want people to think that I approve of the foolishness with him. I don't want that stigma associated with my name."

"Vanessa, everyone knows that you are not a part of Tyrone's dumb antics. Remember he is your ex and that's the key word. There was a reason for you and him not being together. Girl, you have nothing to worry about. Vanessa I hate you because you are so brilliantly devious, and I love every bit of it. I have to go, but can my mother-in-law stay here until I finish getting everything together?"

"Vikki, I will do you one better. Since I have to get my hair done, Miss Cassie can go with me and I will bring her to the party. Is that okay Miss Cassie?"

"Vanessa, it's fine with me. It will give us the chance to catch up and I get the chance to be beautified. I am all for a beauty makeover. I have waited for this for a long time. Antonio deserves this party and I think he will be happy to have it."

"This is so true Miss Cassie."

"Vanessa can you please do me a favor?"

"Sure, what is it Miss Cassie?"

"Please stop calling me Miss Cassie, Mother Cassie will do just fine. You are like another daughter to me. Then Mother Cassie it is."

"Vanessa, thank you so much for letting my mother-in-law stay with you. I will see you both in a few hours."

CHAPTER SEVEN

After spending all day getting hair and nails done everyone is on fire at the party.

Gorgeous women, good looking men, everyone is mingling and having lots of fun. All of Antonio's teammate are at his party, every top newspaper, magazine editors, sportscasters, some of the hottest athletes in the league. And, of course, the hottest R and B singer, Terence, is in the building and he is looking like royalty. Delicious is in the building, he is on his best behavior for the moment.

In walks Vanessa, every head turned when she walked in the room, men everywhere stopped and looked. Vanessa is gorgeous and she can definitely have her fair share of any of them and they are all trying to make a move on her, but she is not interested, at least not for the moment. Vanessa is married to an incredible man, Kevin, and he is the only one who makes her heart skip a beat. She still has it going on. She is more confident in herself than she was when she was married to you know who. One of Antonio's teammates tries to reach out and talk to her, but she lets him know that she is spoken for, she can't wait until Kevin arrives.

Vikki had a hard time getting Antonio to come out, so she had to use trickery, she asked Antonio's best friend and teammate, Marcus Cole, to help her get him to Hotel Mystique.

Vikki tells Marcus about her plan, but by the time she finishes Marcus is almost convinced that she is cheating on Antonio, but Marcus is willing to help his friend. Marcus calls Antonio.

"Hello, this is Antonio how can I help you?"

"Hello birthday boy."

Antonio says, "Marcus, is that you? What's up brother?"

"Well, I'm in town at Hotel Mystique, and I thought you might like to stop by for a drink."

"Thank you Marcus, but I'm not in the mood." Just as Antonio says that, Marcus turns it up.

"Oh, my Lord, Antonio I see your wife, Vikki, and she is here with another man." "Marcus are you sure?"

"Antonio, I know your wife when I see her, you need to get down here."

"Marcus, can you stall her for me? I am on my way. I will be there soon and thank you, Marcus."

"It's nothing but a gee thang, Antonio."

After Marcus hangs up the phone, he and Vikki both share a hearty laugh. "Vikki, I can't wait to see the look on Antonio's face when he sees that all of his family and friends are here to help him celebrate his birthday."

Antonio gets dressed and jumps in his car; he is in such a hurry to catch Vikki in the act of cheating that he almost gets into an accident.

He is so angry that he calls Marcus and lets him know that he will be at Hotel Mystique in fifteen minutes. Marcus tells him great. After Marcus hangs up the phone, he lets everyone know that Antonio will be arriving in about fifteen minutes or so. Before Marcus could get the words out of his mouth, Antonio is at Hotel Mystique, he is dressed to the nines. Antonio calls Marcus on his phone and asks him to meet him in the front of the hotel. Marcus tells Antonio that he will be right there.

Marcus tells everyone to prepare to yell surprise. As Marcus greets Antonio he says to him, "for someone who didn't want to celebrate his birthday you are looking mighty sharp."

Antonio tells Marcus that he wasn't going for that look but that it happened that way.

Antonio asks, "so where is Vikki? I am so ready to catch her cheating behind in the act. Marcus, you don't know how much I appreciate this."

Marcus says, "Right this way." They are walking closer to the banquet hall.

"Wait Marcus, what in the world is Vikki doing in this banquet hall?"

"Antonio, how in the world would I know what they are doing here, but what I do know is that I saw both of them come in this banquet hall together."

Marcus tells Antonio that he needs to open the door and bust Vikki and her mystery man together. As Antonio reaches for the knob he is trying to get the door open, but he can't seem to open it up right away. The second time Antonio turns the knob, he opens the door, but it's dark and that's when one of Antonio's teammates turns the lights on and everyone screams, "surprise!"

Antonio doesn't know what to do, he is stunned by all the love, he is almost in tears. "Oh my God, who put this together?"

Marcus says to Antonio, "Your lovely wife."

"My wife?"

Marcus says to Antonio, "Man you act like you don't have a wife or that you are surprised that she would do something like this for you.

Antonio says to Marcus, "No man, it's not like that at all."

Antonio immediately calls Vikki; he wants to apologize to her for listening to Tyrone and all his nonsense. "Vikki, this is your husband, baby. I really need to talk to you; can you meet me at Hotel Mystique?"

"Antonio, I am already here."

"Where are you baby?"

"I am standing by your birthday cake."

Antonio cannot wait to walk over to his birthday cake. He has treated Vikki terribly the past few days, listening to the foolishness of Tyrone. When Antonio sees Vikki, he plants a kiss on her that almost sets a record.

Antonio apologizes to Vikki for not believing her, and believing Tyrone and his trickery. Just as Antonio says that, in walks the creep of the year, Tyrone Tyler in the flesh.

Antonio cannot wait to light into him, but for right now he is going to leave it alone.

Antonio decides that he is going to go along with Tyrone's game and Vikki is in total agreeance with her husband, one hundred percent.

"Antonio, let's do this."

Both Antonio and Vikki act like they don't see each other, this charade goes on for most of the night, then about twelve midnight Nicholas asks everyone to gather around for gift opening time. Antonio is truly humbled by the gifts that he has received thus far.

Antonio was brought to tears when he saw a special person come and stand before him. It was his mother "Cassie". He held her in his arms. Antonio is very close to his mother. There isn't a dry eye at the party. The best gift of all is Vikki's news, but she decides that this news should be told in private, so she is going to hold it until Antonio is back at home where he belongs.

Marcus says loudly, "Is there anything else anyone would like to say?"

Tyrone says that he has something to say. He announces in front of everyone that Vikki Anderson is cheating on Antonio with a mystery man and Antonio moved out of their mansion and that he wants fifteen million dollars or you partygoers won't be the only ones who know about this.

Antonio is about to step to Tyrone and break his jaw, but Marcus grabs his hand, just as he is about to hit Tyrone. Marcus reminds Antonio that Tyrone isn't worth it, and that Tyrone looks like a fool. Marcus reminds Antonio that this is not the time nor the place to step to Tyrone.

Vikki has had enough of Tyrone, so she decides to come from behind the crowd to let Tyrone know that she has never cheated on Antonio and the man that he saw her with was the party planner Nicholas. "And for the record, Tyrone, Nicholas is gay; so, there is no way that he is interested in me. So, the next time you want to break up a happy home, get your facts straight you butt hole. Now turn around and say hello to the cameras because you are on Sports Addicts, and national television."

Tyrone is so mad and embarrassed. At the same time that he tries to flip over a table and some chairs, he is screaming at the top of his lungs. "I want my money, Antonio, you have twenty-four hours."

But that didn't work, so security escorted him out of the party. One of Antonio's teammates, Victor Sams, asks Antonio "Who is the clown that tried to ruin your marriage? That clown embarrassed himself to the fullest." They laugh at Tyrone behind his back.

Vikki asks Antonio if he is okay. Antonio says, "Baby as long as I have you by my side I am great."

"Antonio Anderson, I love you more and more each day."

"Vikki, I love you more than words can express, but can we get this party started?" Just as Antonio says that to Vikki, in walks Delicious.

Delicious makes it known that the party has not started until he arrives. Delicious looks better than most of the women at the party. Delicious is scoping out the room, "boy oh boy." He spots a handsome caramel-colored young man named Charles.

Delicious glides over to Charles and introduces himself, Charles is stunned. Charles asks, "How can I help you?"

Delicious replies, "Sometimes you feel like a nut, sometimes you don't, and I truly don't mind feeling your nuts."

Charles says to Delicious, "If you don't get the heck the out of my face..."

Delicious says to Charles, "I am sorry, I didn't get your name."

Charles says, "That's because I didn't tell you my name."

Just as Charles says that, Lydia, a friend of Charles' walks by and calls out his name. "Charles, I like the way that sounds."

Charles tells Delicious, "This conversation is done."

Delicious says, "Just for the moment, I will be back."

Charles says, "Not this way."

It's two o'clock in the morning and it's time for everyone to leave, especially Vikki, she is extremely tired due to her pregnancy. Delicious has decided to make his way over to the birthday boy. Delicious walks over to Antonio and screams as loud as he can, "Happy Birthday Antonio Anderson! I love you and this gorgeous wife of yours, Vikki. Congratulations to you both."

Vikki and Antonio both say, "Thank you, but it is weird for someone to say Congratulations at a birthday celebration... don't you think, Vikki?"

"Honey, you know how Delicious is."

"Yeah, I guess he is different in more ways than one." Antonio and Vikki crack up.

Antonio gives a final goodnight speech. He says, "I want to thank everyone for coming out to celebrate my birthday with me, before I head out to training camp. But most of all I want to thank my incredible and gorgeous wife for throwing me this awesome party. I am honored and truly grateful that so many family, friends and teammates came out for me. You guys are the best. Goodnight. Enjoy... we are leaving."

As Antonio finishes his speech, all the guests in attendance begin to leave the Celebration, as well. Everyone compliments Vikki on a job well done. Vikki reminds everyone to take a piece of cake or two on their way out. "We love you all."

Vikki, Antonio, Vanessa and Cassie walk over to Antonio's car. He is still amazed by all the love that he has been shown tonight.

Mother Cassie decides to ride home with Vanessa because she doesn't want her to ride home alone. Antonio and Vikki follow behind to make sure that Vanessa gets home safe, and to take Mother Cassie home. As they arrive at Vanessa's house, Mother Cassie and Vanessa both decide that she will stay at Vanessa's house; they want to give Vikki and Antonio some private time together. Both ladies tell the couple goodnight and that they will see them both tomorrow.

Antonio thanks both his mother and Vanessa. Antonio realizes that he has a lot of making up to do to his wife. Antonio is happy that his mother is in town, but he is even happier that he gets to spend some quality time with Vikki. As they are driving home Antonio is caressing Vikki's head. Before they go home Antonio let's Vikki know that they have one stop to make on the way home.

Vikki asks Antonio where they are going. Just wait and you will see. They stop at Luxury Suites where Antonio was staying, he is picking up his belongings. He says lovingly to his wife Vikki, "it is time for me to come back home." It is about a twenty-minute drive to the Anderson estate. Vikki couldn't be happier that Antonio is back home where he belongs. Vikki can't wait to tell Antonio the good news. She knows that timing is everything and now is not the right time, but she knows that she has to tell him before he leaves for training camp.

Antonio and Vikki finally arrive home Antonio takes a look around to make sure that everything is still the same. "Antonio honey, what in the world are you doing?" Vikki asks.

"I'm looking at my house, I can't believe that I let Tyrone's foolishness drive me away from you."

"Antonio, I am tired and all I want to do is get in the shower and get a good night's rest." So, they both decide to take a shower together. Antonio plans on making up for lost time. Antonio and

Vikki are both so tired that they fall asleep in each other's arms. Oh well, lost time won't be happening tonight.

CHAPTER EIGHT

It's about six thirty Sunday morning. Vikki is up bright and early; she didn't get much sleep, but she is rearing to go. Just as Vikki gets out of the shower, Mother Cassie calls to find out if she and Antonio are going to church. Vikki tells Mother Cassie that she is going, but that Antonio is going to stay in the bed and sleep. Vikki lets Mother Cassie know that she will stop and pick her and Vanessa up, so that they can all attend church together.

Vikki can't wait to tell Vanessa and Mother Cassie that she is having a baby. Vikki kisses Antonio on the forehead. She tells him that she is going to church and that she will see him later. Antonio smiles and goes back to sleep. Vanessa is dressed and ready to go. Vikki picks the ladies up and they head to church for a spirit-filled time. After the message has been brought forth and the benediction has been said, the ladies decide that they want to go to lunch. They find a quaint little hide-a-way called Modesa, it is where people go to get a good meal on a Sunday afternoon.

Vikki decides that she wants to sit on deck with Mother Cassie and Vanessa.

After they have ordered their food, Vikki decides that she is going to break her baby news to Vanessa and Mother Cassie. Mother Cassie asks Vikki how she is doing. "Mother Cassie, I am glad that you asked. I have something that I want to tell you, but I need you to keep it a secret from Antonio."

Mother Cassie tells Vikki that she doesn't like to hide things from Antonio.

Vikki says, "I understand, but after what I have to say, I think you will keep this secret."

Vanessa asks Vikki, "So what is this good news that you have?"

"Guess who's going to be a Grandmother and a Godmother." All the women scream out loud. They are so excited about the news.

"Vikki, congratulations again. I would be honored to be your child's Godmother."

Mother Cassie tries and throw some shade at Vanessa, "so Vanessa, you already knew."

"Yes and no, Mother Cassie. Vikki did mention it before, but she wasn't sure, and she didn't want me to say anything until she was one hundred percent sure, and so I guess now she is definitely sure, and I couldn't be happier."

"I want to tell him next week right before he goes to training camp."

Vanessa tells Vikki that she thinks it's a great idea for her to tell Antonio then. The food has finally arrived. Vikki doesn't have much of an appetite, but she knows that she has to eat for the sake of the baby.

"Vanessa, I am so scared."

"Vikki, what are you so scared about?"

"Vanessa, am I going to be a good mother? Is Antonio ready to be a father? Will he leave me once he finds out that he is going to be a dad?"

"Vikki, you don't have to worry, rest assure Antonio will not leave you and you are going to make an awesome mother."

Mother Cassie reassures Vikki by telling her that all Antonio talks about is being a father one day. "He won't know how to act."

"Thanks, Mother Cassie, I just want everything to go well."

"My beautiful daughter, you will have nothing to worry about."

After about two hours of lunch and conversation, all the women head to their perspective destinations.

Mother Cassie and Vikki arrive at the Anderson's estate to find Antonio lounging in the living room, watching sports. Mother Cassie is tired from the lunch, so she decides to take a nap. Just as Mother Cassie falls asleep, Antonio gets a call from Tyrone. Tyrone tells Antonio that he needs to meet with him tomorrow at his office, and he tells Antonio that he wants his fifteen million dollars, or he will be going to the press.

"Tyrone, I don't care what you do, you can go to the press, television, paper, magazine or your office. I don't care who you talk to, I will not give you fifteen million dollars. Tyrone, you are crazier than I thought you were, negro get off my phone now."

"Antonio baby, there must be something wrong with Tyrone, he is still trying to extort money from you."

"Honey, it is time for you to contact an attorney and I mean now."

"Vikki, I am just going to ignore Tyrone."

"Honey, this is not the time to ignore him. Tyrone will not stop until you make him stop. Antonio baby if you won't call the attorney, I definitely will call."

Vikki calls Vanessa, seeking an attorney. When Vanessa questions her, she tells Vanessa that her trifling ex-husband is still trying to extort Antonio for fifteen million dollars for a picture of me and the event planner, Nicholas, who happens to be gay. Maybe Tyrone is interested in him."

"Vikki, didn't Tyrone get enough of being embarrassed at Antonio's birthday party? I guess some people will never learn. Here is the number for a great attorney, she will help you out. Her name is Sheila Smith, she is one of the best attorney's there is. Vanessa how do you know her? I know her because she has handled some cases for my firm. Call her now."

"Vanessa, I will and thank you."

"By the way, Vikki, have you told Antonio that he is going to be a father soon?"

"Not yet Vanessa, I will tell him later, this isn't really the time. I have something planned out. I will call you once I speak with Sheila."

Vikki proceeds to call Sheila; but Vikki gets her voice mail. Hello Miss Smith, my name is Vikki Anderson I am calling because my husband Antonio Anderson needs legal representation please give us a call back as soon as possible so that we can discuss further.

Vikki goes back into the living room to snuggle up with Antonio she lets him know that she has contacted an attorney, but then she totally changes the subject. She asks Antonio how many more weeks until training camp.

"How many weeks, don't you mean days? I will be leaving on Tuesday."

"Antonio, I thought we had more time together?"

Vikki asks, "Antonio honey, how did it go from a matter of weeks to a matter of days? Well Antonio, I guess I have to deal with it."

"Vikki, that is why I want you to travel with me so that we can spend more time together."

Vikki realizes that now is the time to tell Antonio. "I wanted to tell you something, but I guess now is definitely not the time."

"What does my beautiful wife want to tell me?"

Vikki says to Antonio, "It is not important, so forget that I bought it up. I am going to get dinner started."

Antonio can tell that something is on Vikki's mind, so he decides to follow her to the kitchen. "Okay Vikki, spill it. What is on your mind?"

"Antonio, it is nothing. Just forget about it." Just as she says that she feels a cramp in her stomach, "Oh no, this cannot be happening."

"Vikki baby, what's wrong?"

"Antonio, I am okay. I just need to sit down. She is praying and crying that she isn't having a miscarriage… not now.

Antonio grabs his car keys and grabs Vikki and rushes her to the hospital. Vikki doesn't want to go to the hospital, but Antonio is not having it. "Baby girl, you are going to the hospital, whether you like it or not."

Antonio is driving so fast that he doesn't realize that he got pulled over by the police. Officer Scott approaches Antonio's car. Antonio begins to apologize for speeding, he informs Officer Scott that his wife is in pain and he was trying to get her to the hospital. It takes a minute, but Officer Scott realizes that he has a famous athlete in front of him. He is so in awe of Antonio that Officer Scott tells him that he will escort him to the hospital personally.

With the presence of Officer Scott, Antonio and Vikki arrive safely to the hospital. The pain has stopped, but Vikki is taken in to see a doctor immediately. Vikki is checked thoroughly she and the baby are okay, but the doctor wants to make sure that she is not stressed; so, the doctor lets her know that she needs to stay off her feet for the two months of her pregnancy. Vikki assures Doctor Jackson that she will not let anything stress her out and that she will stay off of her feet for the entire two months, but only if Doctor Jackson will do something for her. "Doctor Jackson I need you to lie to my husband. I have not told my husband yet that I am pregnant; please do not mention this to him. I am going to surprise him with the news tonight.

"Vikki, I promise not to tell your husband, under one condition. You must follow these instructions."

"I promise to adhere to all of your orders, Doctor Jackson."

"Vikki, then your secret is safe with me."

Doctor Jackson leaves Vikki's room and tells Antonio that everything is okay with his wife and that it was just a mild case of food poisoning and that Vikki has to watch what she eats and take care of herself and she will be up and at it in no time.

Thank you, Doctor Jackson, I will make sure of it."

Antonio and Vikki leave the hospital and head home. Vikki knows that she cannot hold this news anymore, she has to let Antonio know that she is pregnant.

As they are riding home, Sheila calls Vikki.

"Hello this is Sheila Smith; may I speak to Vikki Anderson."

"Hello Ms. Smith, this is Vikki Anderson."

"How may I help you, Mrs. Anderson?"

"I am in the car with my husband, you are on speaker phone. I will let him fill you in on the situation."

"Ms. Smith…" Before Antonio can get one more word in Sheila tells him and Vikki to please call her Sheila, not Miss Smith.

"And you don't have to call us Mr. and Mrs. Anderson, Vikki and Antonio will do just fine."

"Good, now that we have that out of the way, please tell me what happened."

"There is a person who is trying to blackmail me for fifteen million dollars because he has a picture of my wife entering Hotel Mystique with a man named Nicholas who happens to be an event planner. Nicholas and my wife were planning an awesome surprise birthday party for me, and the person snapped a picture of the two of them in the hotel together, and this person suspected her of cheating, and the way she was acting at the time, it almost made it seem as though she were."

"Is this true, Vikki?"

"Yes, it is true; but I would never cheat on Antonio… this man is my world. Plus, Nicholas isn't interested in me, I'm not his type, if you know what I mean."

"I do understand, Vikki."

"Okay, let's cut to the chase. At my party this person embarrassed himself because he finds out in front of people that Vikki and I are not getting a divorced and that she never cheated on me. He stormed out of my party and I thought that was the end of the situation, that is until about a couple of hours ago when he left a message, still demanding fifteen million dollars. So, I want to countersue this person."

"Antonio, is there anything that you have that can help me with the case to show you are being blackmailed?"

"Yes Sheila, I have the voice mail and text messages."

"Great, now I need to know the person's name, so that I can send them a cease and desist. Don't worry, when I get finished with them they will never try to blackmail money from anyone else again. What is the person's name?"

"Sheila, his name is Tyrone Tyler."

Sheila is stunned. She can't believe this, and this can't possibly be the same Tyrone Tyler who is trying to push up on her. *Tyrone Tyler, the Partner at his firm, William Tyler and Peterson. Tyrone is a multi-millionaire why in the world is he trying to extort money from Antonio Anderson he is a multi-millionaire himself. There definitely has got to be more to the story than this.*

"Thank you for the information, I will get right on it." Sheila can't let Tyrone know that she is handling Antonio's case, but she has to get to the bottom of this; there has got to be an explanation for this and who better to give her the answer but his ex-wife, Vanessa Tyler.

Sheila gives Vanessa a call. "Hello, my name is Sheila Smith. May I please speak to Vanessa Tyler."

"Hello, this is Vanessa how can I help you?"

"I am representing Antonio and Vikki Anderson, they are counter-suing your ex-husband Tyrone Tyler; can I ask you a few questions?"

"You sure can Ms. Smith."

"Great, is there somewhere that we can meet?"

"There is a quaint little restaurant that not too many people know about called Modesa's, we can meet there in about an hour."

"I look forward to meeting you, Ms. Smith."

"The same here, and please do me a favor?"

"What is it, Ms. Smith?"

"Can you please call me Sheila?"

Vanessa laughs, "I will do."

Both ladies hang up the phone, but Sheila can't shake the fact that Tyrone is trying to extort money from Antonio Anderson. Sheila knows one thing for sure, Tyrone will not get away with this and she is sho' nuff going to play Tyrone at his own game. And no one can play the game better than Sheila.

As soon as Sheila hangs up the phone with Vanessa, she notices that Tyrone is calling. Sheila says to herself *what in the world does this character want? He will never get anything from me. I do not want to talk to him.* Sheila lets the phone go to voice mail. She gathers her documents and gets in her car for the forty-minute drive to meet Vanessa at Modesa's. Sheila walks in looking as gorgeous as ever in a white fitting dress. Five minutes after she sits down, in walks Vanessa; she is looking as fierce as always. Vanessa is smiling from ear to ear. Vanessa introduces herself, "You must be Sheila." The ladies shake hands.

"Vanessa Tyler, it is nice to meet you."

"I am divorced, and my name is not Tyler anymore. I am happily a Brown now.

My husband's name is Kevin Brown, that's why I continue to have this smile on my face; because he has brought so much joy and happiness into my life. I truly thank God each and every day for him."

"Vanessa, why do you look so familiar?"

"You might not remember me, Sheila, but you handled cases for my firm. Bryant and Brown are a beast in the courtroom, I am so glad that you are not trying to sue me." Both ladies laugh it up.

"Now tell me how I can help you Sheila?"

"Vanessa, your ex-husband is rich beyond rich, he is worth well over seventy million dollars, so why in the world is he trying to extort, blackmail, call it what you want; but why is he trying to get fifteen million dollars from Antonio Anderson?"

"I am not really sure, Sheila, but if I had to guess, it really has nothing to do with Antonio."

"Okay Vanessa, now I am confused, what are you talking about?"

"Sheila, truth be told, Tyrone is mad that I was awarded twenty and one half million dollars in the divorce settlement and that his baby mother Kayla Jones was awarded about fifty thousand dollars a month in child support for a baby that is not his. Tyrone wants revenge on anyone that is close to me or that is happy, and Vikki is my best friend. Sheila sue him for everything he has, maybe this will teach him a lesson."

"Vanessa, thank you so much, I appreciate you."

Sheila apologizes to Vanessa for running out so soon on their meeting, "I am sorry, but I am running late I have a hair appointment and I can't keep Delicious waiting."

"Girl, he is good."

Sheila is stunned. "Wait a minute, Vanessa, Delicious is your hairdresser?"

"Yes, Delicious is the best in town."

Sheila says to Vanessa, "That he is."

Vanessa says to Sheila, "No one can do hair like Delicious."

"Tell me about it, Vanessa." I went for the first time and he had me looking simply marvelous. There is none other like Delicious or Desire's salon."

Just as Vanessa is about to leave the restaurant, Kayla arrives at Modesa's.

Vanessa is stunned to see Kayla, but she is a forgiving woman, so she walks over to her, says hello and asks how she is doing.

Kayla lets Vanessa know that she and the baby are holding up, considering. Vanessa notices that Kayla's eyes are watering up. "What's wrong, Kayla, do you want to talk about it?"

Kayla tells Vanessa that she doesn't want to disturb her.

"Kayla, I have an appointment to get my hair done, but I am going to call the hairdresser."

Vanessa calls Delicious but he isn't answering his phone so, she leaves a brief message and lets him know that she will be running a little late." This seems important, let's have a seat."

Kayla is trying hard to hold it in, but she cannot take it anymore and she lets Vanessa know that Michael, her child's father, passed away a few months earlier; and it has been hard trying to raise her child on her own, but she is going to do what she has to do.

Vanessa is genuinely concerned, so she says to Kayla, "If you don't mind me asking what happened to Michael?"

"Vanessa, I don't mind letting you know that Michael was recently killed in a car accident."

"Kayla, I am so sorry for your loss, and if there is anything that I can do, please let me know."

Kayla says to Vanessa, "I will do that and thank you so much."

"By the way Vanessa, how is your husband Kevin? That is his name am I correct?"

"Kayla, Kevin is fine."

"I can tell by your smile. Your smile is big enough to put a family there." Both ladies chuckle.

Kayla and Vanessa leave Modesa's restaurant and they both go their separate ways. Vanessa rushes over to Desire's. Of course, Delicious is somebody mad. "Vanessa, where in the world have you been? I have been waiting here for an hour without a phone call, a man, or anything else for that matter."

"Delicious, what does a man have to do with me running late? By the way, I called and left you a message that I would be late."

"You got this one, Vanessa, but do not let it happen again."

"I promise that I won't do it again, Delicious."

"By the way, how is that fine husband of yours, Kevin Brown?"

"He is fine, Delicious, and he is not the problem, but my ex-husband is."

"What do you mean, Vanessa?"

"Tyrone is trying to blackmail Vikki and Antonio."

"Vanessa, for what?"

"He is trying to get fifteen million dollars".

"Tyrone is super-duper rich, why in the world would he blackmail Antonio Anderson, of all people?"

"Delicious, who knows?"

"Vanessa, I know one thing for sure, Tyrone is a male who is black just the way I like it. Send him my way."

"Delicious, eww, you are just too nasty."

"I know and I will never change."

Just as Vanessa is about to say something else, in walks Vikki. She kisses Delicious on the cheek.

"Hey Vikki and Delicious, I am so glad that the both of you are here, now guess who I ran into today?"

"Vanessa, please don't tell me that you ran into that trifling ex-husband of yours again?"

"Vikki, it wasn't him, but you would never guess who it was."

"Vanessa, you are so right. I won't guess who it is, so tell us now."

Vanessa shocks the both of them when she tells them that it was Kayla that she ran into. Delicious says sarcastically to Vanessa, "You mean Kayla, the one who slept with your ex-husband and who slept with Michael her business partner turned lover, the Kayla who did not know who the father of her baby was… that Kayla?"

Vanessa answers him emphatically, "Yes Delicious, that's the one."

"Vanessa, what in the world did that trick want?"

"Now Delicious, that is not nice, especially because she isn't doing well."

Vikki and Delicious both ask Vanessa what she means. "She told me that Michael passed away a couple of months ago, he was killed in a car accident."

Vikki is feeling bad, "Aww Vanessa, that is really horrible."

"Vikki, I know it is horrible. I don't know what I would do if anything happened to Kevin. Now Vikki, on the other hand, if it were Tyrone and he were killed in a car accident, I think I would have to come to the scene of the crime and kill him dead again."

"Vikki jokes, "Now girl, you know that ain't right; but believe me, I do understand."

"Guys, I gave her my number and told her to call me if she needed anything, even if it were to babysit for her."

Delicious says to Vanessa, "Girl, I don't know how you do it. If I found out that a trick was messing with my husband for five years, knowing that he was married and almost ends up pregnant with his child and doing the nasty shasty with him, she wouldn't have to worry about being a trick anymore, because I would have a treat for her that she would never forget." Vanessa, Vikki and Delicious all crack up.

Vanessa is styled by Delicious and she is looking as fierce as always. He tells her,

"Vanessa girl, you make a guy want to go straight."

Vanessa tells Delicious, "You always outdo yourself. I love this look. Delicious that is what I love about you, you always make me smile. Thank you for always making me look good. I will see you in a week. Goodbye Vikki, I will call you later."

"Bye Vanessa, love you sis."

Vikki says to Vanessa, "Wait, I want to go shopping and pick up a few things before I go home. I would like you to wait for me so we can shop together."

"Okay Vikki, let me go take care of something and I will meet you back here."

Vanessa says goodbye to Delicious and he says "Ditto," to both of the women.

"Okay Vikki, spill it. Did you tell Antonio about the baby?"

"Delicious, I have not had the chance with everything that is going on. I figured that I wanted to do something cute, so this is why I'm getting my hair done and I want to go pick out some lingerie and sweet-smelling perfume; and with a dozen blue roses and some of me. Then I will tell him tonight over a romantic candlelight dinner."

Delicious says to Vikki, "Now that's the way to do it."

Vikki emerges from Desires looking fabulous; she is on her way to give Antonio the best news of his life and she cannot wait to tell him. Vikki is thinking that Antonio is going to have a fit when he finds out that he is going to be a father.

CHAPTER NINE

Vikki arrives home and calls out for Antonio, "Baby, are you home?" She is so glad that he's not home, now she can set everything in motion. Just as Vikki is setting things in order, Antonio calls to tell her that he and Mother Cassie are on their way back to the house. Vikki is pleasant and says okay, but deep down she is bothered because she wanted to spend this time with her husband alone, so that she can break the news to him and have some extracurricular fun afterwards. That won't be happening now.

Vikki has a short amount of time to get it together, but she manages to get it done.

In walks Antonio and Mother Cassie. Mother Cassie says, "What smells so good in here?"

Vikki responds by saying, "Oh, it's just a little something that I whipped up."

"Mother Cassie, where is Antonio?"

"Vikki, he went upstairs to take a phone call; he will be down in a moment."

Mother Cassie whispers to Vikki, "So, have you told Antonio that he is going to be a father soon?"

"Not yet, that's why I whipped up this dinner. I know that he has to get to training camp in a few days, so I think tonight is the best time to let him in on the secret."

Just as Vikki says that in walks Antonio and he says, "What secret"?

Vikki plays dumb and says to Antonio, "What in the world are you talking about?

No one said anything about a secret."

Antonio says in an upsetting voice, "Vikki don't lie to me now come with me, in the living room. I need to talk to you, what are you keeping from me?"

"Honestly Antonio, I have a birthday gift for you that I have been holding and I didn't want to give it to you because you might be just a little upset with me."

Antonio tells Vikki that she better tell him. "I am upset because you are keeping things from me and I don't like that. Spill the beans now".

Vikki hands Antonio a small box, inside of the box is a blue piece of paper that says congratulations. "Congratulations for what?" Antonio asks.

Vikki tells Antonio to flip the paper over and on the other side of the paper it says, "Dad."

"Are you kidding me right now, Vikki?"

"Antonio I am sorry, I know that you do not want to be a father and the timing is wrong, I didn't mean for this to happen."

"Vikki, what in the world are you talking about? I could not be happier; I am going to have a Junior in the family."

Vikki asks Antonio, "How do you know that it's a boy?"

"It could very well be a girl; all I know is that I want a healthy baby. Mom, get in here my baby is going to have a baby."

"Son, I know, that is why I am here."

Antonio realizes that he must tell Vikki that he has to go to training camp earlier because he is a veteran. "Vikki, remember the phone call that I took upstairs earlier? That was my coach."

"Antonio, what did your coach want with you?"

"Baby, he wanted to let me know that I had to report to camp earlier."

Vikki asks Antonio, "Why?"

He explains that the veterans must be there earlier to prepare and to also be there when the rookies hit the field. Just as Antonio tells this to Vikki, she starts to cramp and she is crying, "No please, I do not want to lose the baby. Antonio help me sit down."

"Vikki, what is wrong Antonio asks?"

"Nothing, I don't want you to worry about me."

Antonio raises his voice. "Vikki, I am going to ask you one more time, what is wrong?"

"The doctor told me that I have to be careful and not let anything stress me or I could lose the baby." She wouldn't dare tell Antonio that she has to be on bedrest for the two months or longer, especially if she doesn't take care of herself during her pregnancy.

"Baby, I never want to stress you; sit down, put your feet up and just relax. Let me rub that baby boy of mine."

"There you go again Antonio, thinking it's a boy. Antonio when do you leave for training camp?" Antonio tries to avoid the question. "Antonio Anderson tell me the truth."

"Well Vikki, I leave tomorrow."

"Tomorrow, can't they let you come later?"

"Vikki, I wish I could, but I can't."

"Look, my mother is here to help you and I will be home for a couple of days before the season starts."

"What about your case with Tyrone?"

"Vikki that's a no brainer, I am going to win hands down, that fool is crazy."

"Antonio, can I talk to your mother privately?"

"Sure baby, I will be upstairs." As soon as Antonio hits the top of the stairs, Vikki tells Mother Cassie that she has to help her keep another secret. Mother Cassie doesn't like to keep anything from her son, but Vikki tells her that if she doesn't, things could get even uglier. I am supposed to be on bed rest, or I can risk losing the baby; but I can't stay on bedrest because I am about to open up a boutique and I need to make sure things are going okay."

"Vikki, I can handle things for you with the boutique. How long are you supposed to be on bedrest?"

"Umm, for an two months, or more of my pregnancy."

"What?" Antonio is going to kill you if he finds out that you are jeopardizing yours and the baby's safety for a boutique."

"Mother Cassie I know he will be upset, but I want to do this."

Mother Cassie tells Vikki that she cannot keep something like that from Antonio, "You have to tell him. Antonio is going to make you travel with him, just so he can keep an eye on you."

"This is between us girls. Love you Mother Cassie." Before Cassie can respond, Vikki is making her way upstairs to the bedroom to talk to Antonio.

Mother Cassie is downstairs preparing for a date. That's right a date. Vikki comes downstairs and to her surprise, Mother Cassie is getting dolled up. She has on a fancy black dress that is hugging her shape. She is almost dressed when the doorbell rings. Vikki walks to answer the door, standing outside is an extremely tall, handsome and debonair and distinguished older man named Wallace. Wallace is looking for Mother Cassie. Vikki invites Wallace in.

Antonio comes downstairs and ask who the stranger is. "Antonio this is Wallace, Wallace this is Antonio my husband."

"You look familiar, wait, are you Antonio Anderson? I like you Antonio, I hope you don't mind me calling you Antonio."

"I don't mind at all, sir."

"You are number one in the league and headed for MVP again. Keep up the good work."

"Thank you, Wallace and how can I help you?"

"Antonio, Wallace is here to see Mother Cassie."

Antonio asks, "Cassie Who?"

"Your mother, Cassie, that's who."

"Wait a minute, am I missing something, my mother is going on a date?"

"Yes, she is Antonio, and I think that's nice and it's about time she enjoys her life. This necklace is absolutely stunning, Mother Cassie let's go, we don't want to keep Wallace waiting too long." both women head toward the door.

As Mother Cassie reaches the bottom of the stairs, Wallace says with a loud and confident voice, "My, you are a vision of loveliness."

"Wallace, please wait here." Vikki follows Antonio into his mother's room. He is very upset. Antonio tells his mother she can't go on a date with Wallace. Cassie asks her son, "And why can't I go on a date with Wallace?"

Antonio says something so dumb, "because you are my mother."

Vikki is confused, "Antonio, what does that have to do with anything? I think Wallace and your mother make a wonderful couple, now leave her alone and get back to me, your wife."

"Vikki, I said that she can't."

Mother Cassie lovingly says to Antonio, "I understand that you don't think any other man can take your dad's place, but it's been five years since your father passed away. I am entitled to have a friend."

"I guess you are right, mom."

Vikki tells Antonio that he has to stop being so protective. Vikki goes back downstairs to talk to Wallace. "Cassie will be with you in about five minutes."

Vikki walks back to her mother in-law to check on her and to make sure that she is getting it together. "By the way, you look good Mother Cassie, but something is missing from this outfit. Come with me, I have the perfect thing to make this outfit pop."

Mother Cassie follows Vikki upstairs to her bedroom. Once they arrive, Vikki pulls out a pair of black diamond earrings. Vikki proceeds to put the earrings on Mother Cassie. Vikki looks at Mother Cassie in the mirror and says, "Wow! You look stunning."

Mother Cassie turns to her daughter-in-law and says, "I am so blessed to have you in my life. These are absolutely stunning. Let's go we don't want to keep Wallace waiting too long."

Both women head downstairs, and as Mother Cassie, Wallace can't help but to stare. "Beauty at its best."

"Thank you for the compliment, Wallace"

"There is no need to thank me, Cassie, it's all true."

Wallace asks Vikki if everything is okay. "Yes, it's fine. It's just that my husband has to get used to his mother going on a date. Trust me, Wallace, it might take some time, but Antonio will get over it."

Before Vikki can finish saying another word, Antonio tells Wallace to make sure to have his mother home by ten o'clock. Vikki interrupts Antonio, "Please leave them alone, you two go and enjoy yourselves and have a good time. Bye, Wallace."

Mother Cassie gives Vikki a kiss on the cheek and whispers thank you in her ear.

Vikki says lovingly to Antonio, "Honey I am so glad that Wallace is a part of your mother's life. I actually think they make a good couple."

Antonio says Vikki, "only you would think that they are a good couple. I don't like that my mother is seeing another man."

"Antonio, I understand what you are saying. You have to understand your mother still loves your father, but she can't stop her life. I'm sure your dad is smiling down from heaven because she found a friend. Antonio instead of you being concerned with your mother and who she is dating we need to start talking about baby names."

"Baby doll, you are so late. I already have that taken care of and since we already know that it's going to be a boy we are going to name him Antonio (AJ) for short."

"I beg your pardon and what if it is a girl? I think we should name her Antonia India Anderson."

"Vikki, I love the way that sounds."

CHAPTER TEN

It's about seven-thirty on a beautiful Monday morning. Kayla is back in town and she has decided to stop by Bella's for a quick breakfast before she goes to the office.

As she is eating, in walks Tyrone. He is surprised, but happy to see his former mistress. "Kayla, what in the world are you doing here?"

"Tyrone, I live here now."

"Kayla, you mean to tell me that Michael is man enough to let you live in the same city with me. I can't believe it."

"For the record, Tyrone, Michael and I aren't together anymore."

Tyrone sarcastically says, "I knew you would come to your senses, Kayla, and come back to the only man who ever really loved you."

"Tyrone, enough of your lies, you never really cared about me; come to think of it, if we hadn't gotten caught by your ex-wife Vanessa, you would probably be still lying, telling me that you will leave her. And not that it's any of your business, Tyrone; but the only reason that Michael and I aren't a couple anymore is because he died tragically a few months ago in a car accident, plus I miss my home."

Kayla is shocked by Tyrone's concern because he usually cares only about himself, and maybe for the first time Tyrone is sincere. "Kayla, I am truly sorry I know this must be hard on you. If you need anything and I do mean anything please don't hesitate to call me. My house is your house."

"Tyrone, you haven't changed a bit, once a dog always a dog. Thank you, but no thank you."

Kayla angrily tells Tyrone, "I have to leave, I have clients that need me."

"By the way, Kayla, how is that pretty baby of yours?

"She is fine, Tyrone. She is a year old now, but not that it's any of your business."

"Kayla, you know that baby is mine and I am going to prove it."

Kayla is pissed off. She is about to cuss Tyrone out, but she thinks otherwise and tells Tyrone, "Go to hell, you wish she was yours, stop the nonsense and leave me alone."

Tyrone grabs Kayla by the arm as she is leaving the restaurant, "I am going to sue you for custody, you better hope for your sake it isn't my child."

"Tyrone, you are not smart enough to sue me, now get your hands off me, and get your stink breath and your no good for nothing behind out of my face." Kayla screams, "You Creep!" as she is leaving the restaurant. Not only is she beyond pissed, she actually throws water in his face. She is in a hurry to get away from Tyrone, she leaves quick, fast and in a hurry. Kayla jumps in her car, she is so mad that she calls Michael, forgetting that he can't answer the phone anymore. She is doing everything in her power to keep from crying, she says to herself, *who can I call` so she decides to call an old friend of hers, Sheila Smith.*

Sheila answers on the second ring, by now Kayla is steamed. She says, "Girl, I need to talk to you. I'm so mad right now and if I don't talk to someone right now, I am going to beat the hell out of him."

"Hold on Kayla, where are you?"

"I'm sitting in the parking lot at Bella's getting ready to drive back to the office."

"Kayla, I really don't think that it's a good idea for you to drive anywhere, calm down and I want you to just sit in your car and wait for me. I will be there to meet you in about ten minutes."

Just as Kayla hangs up the phone with Sheila, Tyrone walks over to her car and begins to bang on her window; she slowly rolls the window down. "Tyrone, what the hell is your problem?"

"Kayla, get ready for a fight, because I am getting my baby."

As Kayla rolls the window up, her parting words to Tyrone are, "You're a butt hole and you need Jesus. Tyrone, you know good and well that Kendra is not your baby; but if you want a fight, then a fight is what you will get. Now get away from my car."

Tyrone walks away, but he is still running off at the mouth, screaming, "This isn't over Kayla, this isn't over not by a long shot."

Sheila spots Tyrone walking to his car, so she decides to sit still until he gets in his car; but Tyrone doesn't drive off right away. He is pondering what Kayla just said to him, so he screams out loud, "Kayla, you played yourself and now I'm going to play you!" Tyrone starts his car and just as he pulls off Sheila drives up.

She spots Kayla's car and parks next to hers. As Sheila and Kayla both get out of their cars, they hug one another and walk to the restaurant. The Maitre'D seats both ladies. As the ladies sit down, the manager comes over to ask Kayla if she is okay, considering the incident that happened earlier.

"Yes, I am okay, thank you so much for asking."

Sheila emphatically asks, "Kayla, girl, what in the world happened?"

Kayla explains that she was in the restaurant having a quick bite to eat for breakfast and along comes her mistake.

Sheila is confused and she is wonders what in the world is Kayla talking about, so she says, "Your mistake?"

Kayla responds, "Yes, my mistake in the form of a loser by the name of Tyrone Tyler."

Sheila is in shock; she does not want to believe that this is the same man who is trying to hit on her. All of this time, Tyrone is pretending that he is someone special, but every time Sheila turns around someone is telling her that Tyrone is trying to do something to hurt them in some kind of way. First, it was Antonio and Vikki Anderson, and now it's my girl Kayla.

Kayla opens up to Sheila and tells her that she had a five-year affair with Tyrone, and he kept telling her that he was going to leave his wife. "I got fed up with all of his lies and when I finally decided that I wanted to break it off, his wife showed up in the middle of the day and saw both of us together in their house; actually I was glad because I got sick and tired of playing games and sneaking, creeping and peeping. Tyrone panicked, and right in front of his wife at the time, he admitted that we were having an affair and that I was having his child. For years I wanted to leave him because I knew that it was wrong, and of course one day after everything was out in the open and I stopped playing with Michael's feelings, I eventually fell in love with Michael and the rest is history. Tyrone is the most successful investment broker in East Hampton. His wife divorced him, and she received millions on top of millions, and to top it off, Tyrone is paying child support for my child."

"Wait a minute, Kayla, please tell me you did not get pregnant by him?"

"Sheila, I was not pregnant by Tyrone and my Kendra is not his, the idiot forgot that the one time we slept together he had protection through the entire time, as a matter of fact we didn't do anything because, at the time we were going to get intimate, his wife came into the house and I hid in his bedroom and he told me not to move or say a word because he was afraid that Vanessa would find us in the house and he didn't want her to find out like that."

"Sheila, believe me when I tell you that Kendra is Michael's daughter. Two paternity tests were done and they both were ninety nine point ninety nine percent that Kendra is Michael's daughter and Tyrone knows that; but somewhere in his twisted mind he believes that Kendra is his daughter and now all of a sudden Tyrone is trying to sue me for child support because he thinks that I kept my daughter from him. He upset me so bad that my nerves are spent. Sheila I am so sorry to bother you with this foolishness."

Sheila is steamed and it is at this very moment that she realizes that she definitely cannot have anything to do with Tyrone, not even a friendship; and now she wants to make him pay for hurting her friend.

Sheila says to Kayla in a calm and soothing voice, "You are my friend and I am so glad that you told me about Tyrone."

"Kayla, I wasn't going to say anything to you. Since you are my friend, I can't keep this from you, but you have to promise me that you won't say a word."

"Sheila, I promise… now what is it?"

"That's the same Tyrone who has been trying to hit on me".

Kayla angrily says, "Sheila, he what?" Kayla is beyond pissed right now, she can't believe what Tyrone is trying to do.

"Sheila, that jerk, I cannot believe that. So, he wants to take me to court to get custody of my child and all along he is trying to hit on my friend. Sheila, I'm not a person who gets back at people, but Tyrone deserves everything that is coming to him and then some. I want you to stick it to him. He messed with the wrong woman, Sheila mark my word, Tyrone is going to have to pay for all that he has done."

Sheila says to Kayla in a firm but angry tone, "You have absolutely nothing to worry about, we are going to get him good. I cannot wait to pay Tyrone back for all the things he has done to people, including his ex-wife Vanessa. Kayla, now you know when I get finished with him, he won't know what hit him. Not only am I going to hit him below the belt, but I am going to hit him below and under the belt. I didn't realize how disgusting Tyrone was, but I know now."

"Oh Lord, Sheila, what is Tyrone trying to do to Vanessa?"

"Kayla, you wouldn't believe me if I told you, but since you asked me I will tell you. Tyrone is trying to get back the alimony that he had to pay her as part of her divorce settlement, and on top of that he is trying to blackmail my client Antonio Anderson."

"Kayla says to Sheila, wait you cannot be serious. Antonio is very nice. Why is Tyrone trying to black mail Antonio?"

"Kayla, the reason why Tyrone is trying to blackmail Antonio is because he swears that Vikki was cheating on Antonio with a guy named Nicholas who is an event planner. I found out that it was all false information; but Tyrone doesn't care, he is trying to hurt everyone in his path. When I get finished with Tyrone, the only person he will ever try to hit on will be himself."

"Sheila, now you know that Tyrone is going to be livid when he finds out that you are representing Antonio, there is no telling what Tyrone will do to get revenge."

"Kayla, I am ready for whatever Tyrone tries to throw at me, you can believe that. Kayla, it is like taking candy from a baby and you know that I am the best at whatever I do, especially when it comes to revenge."

"Sheila, just make sure you keep me in the loop. Oh, believe me, Kayla, I will definitely let you know what's going on." The ladies finish their dinner, they both pay for their food and both drive off separately in their cars.

Just as Sheila pulls up to her house, Tyrone calls her. She sucks her teeth when she realizes that he is on the phone; but she is professional, so she answers it in her sweetest and sexiest voice ever.

"Good evening, Mr. Tyler, and what do I owe the pleasure of this call?"

"Sheila, is there something wrong?"

"Tyrone, why would you ask that?"

"Well you have never asked me a question like that before."

"Tyrone, I just asked a question, you are making it into a big deal for no reason."

"Sheila, well excuse me for asking."

"Goodbye Tyrone." Sheila politely hangs up the phone on Tyrone.

Tyrone says out loud to himself, "I know that she did not just hang up on me. Who the hell does she think she is? I am Tyrone Tyler no one talks to me like that. I need to let Sheila know exactly who I am and that I am not the one to play with; but not just yet, I am going to wait until the right time to show Sheila just who I am."

Just at that moment, while sitting in her car, Sheila realizes that she has an appointment with Delicious and she knows how he is about people canceling and not calling; so she immediately calls him and tells him that she will be at the salon in less than fifteen minutes.

Somehow, Sheila and Kayla both end up at Desire's. Delicious is happy to see Sheila, and shocked and surprised to see Kayla.

"Kayla girl, get over here how have you been?"

"I didn't really get the chance to speak to you the other day, how long has it been since you dropped the bomb about you and Tyrone and your pregnancy?"

"It's been about a year; it has been a very trying and traumatic year."

"Delicious, in case you didn't know Michael died in a car accident a few months ago. Yes, I know, Vanessa had already informed me. Kayla, I want you to know that I am very sorry for your loss."

Of course, Delicious makes light of the situation, "Too bad I wasn't able to get ahold of those nuts!!!"

"Delicious, you are not right, but thank you for making me smile."

"Kayla, that is what I do, now let's go to the back of the salon and let's make you look good because, chile, you really need it."

Delicious looks at Shelia, "Girl run, because you look like you stuck your finger in two sockets, what in the world is this?"

Sheila is laughing now. "Delicious, you know that there isn't anything wrong with my hair."

Delicious says with a smirk, "Sheila, if you say so."

Kayla asks Delicious, "Where is Shaniqua?"

Kayla, I am going to tell you like I have been telling others, "She is on a mental health vacation."

Kayla asks, "Well, when is she coming back, Delicious?"

"When Hell not only freezes over and turns into ice-water, but when I get a glass to hold the ice water in."

Kayla looks at Delicious in shock and says to him, "That is way too much information, Delicious."

Delicious asks inquisitively, "So Kayla dear, have you met anyone since you've been back?"

"Yes, I did go out the other day. I met one of Sheila's friend's, Lawrence, and we went out for drinks after Sheila and I left the salon..."

Delicious says to Kayla, "I didn't know that you drink."

Kayla responds, "Delicious, I don't drink, but I went out and I had a nice time."

"So, is there a love connection between you and Lawrence?"

"Delicious, I really don't think so; he is nice, but he is not for me. Delicious, check this out. Tyrone is up to his old tricks again."

Delicious says, "An old trick is playing old tricks. Kayla, send Tyrone to me and I will definitely show him some new tricks."

Delicious sends Kayla to another room to get a pedicure, while she is waiting for her to finish drying. They both laugh.

"Sheila, while you are getting your hair done, you also need to get those boxes together because girl they look like defense weapons."

"Delicious, what in the world are you talking about?" He immediately points to her feet. They crack up laughing. After they finish talking about how bad Sheila's feet look, Sheila tells Delicious that she has a plan to put in motion.

Delicious asks Sheila, "Girl, what are you scheming up?"

Sheila tells Delicious, "Just wait and see."

Sheila calls Mark on the phone. "Hello! hey there, how are you?"

"I am good, and how are you?"

"Mark, can you come and get me please."

"Sheila sure, where are you?"

Sheila tells Mark that she is at Desire's. Mark tells Sheila that there is no way in hell, that he will ever step foot in that place again.

"Now Mark, I know good and well that you aren't scared of the owner, Delicious. He is harmless, plus he will be in a meeting by the time you get here."

"Sheila, the only reason I will come to that place is because that person by the name of Delicious will be in a meeting when I pick you up. I will come, I will see you soon.

"Okay, thank you Mark."

"So, Kayla what are you doing after you leave here?"

"Girl, I am going to go home, and I am going to cuddle up with a good book. Kendra is with her grandmother and grandfather for the week."

Sheila wants to go out to dinner with her. Kayla has a puzzled look on her face, "Sheila didn't we just have dinner?"

"I know we did, but I should have said let's have drinks."

"Sheila, now you know I don't drink, but I will go with you and hang out for a little while. Sheila, as a matter of fact, you don't drink either."

"Kayla, I'm glad that you decided to go out; and even though we are cornballs who don't drink, it should still be fun. I know it's been hard for you since Michael passed away, but you have to live."

Delicious tells the ladies that he will be in a brief meeting. Five minutes have passed and Mark is at Desire's waiting in his car for Sheila, so he decides to call her on the phone. "Sheila, you can come out now, I am here."

"Mark, don't be rude. Aren't you going to come inside and say hello? Mark, Delicious is still in a meeting, you will be gone before he gets out."

"Okay, I am coming inside, just for you, Sheila."

As soon as Mark walks inside to the front of Desire's, Delicious comes from the back and says seductively, "I smell some sweet chocolate caramel nut candy."

Mark is so mad at Sheila because he thinks that she lied to him about Delicious. "I thought you told me that "he" would be in a meeting?"

"Mark, Delicious was in a meeting, he just walked out as soon as you walked inside." "Well, well, well, I think I am hungry; I am in the mood for chocolate caramel and nuts."

"Sheila, let's get out of here right now." Sheila and Kayla are both cracking up.

"Sheila, let's go and I mean let's go now."

Before Sheila, Mark and Kayla leave the shop, Sheila decides that she wants to introduce Mark to her very good friend. "Mark, this is Kayla Jones. We grew up together and were best friends in high school and roommates my freshman year of college, until she transferred to another school, but we remained best friends throughout the course of our lives."

Mark kisses Kayla's hand, "it is truly a pleasure to meet you."

"Thank you Mark, and the same here. Here comes trouble."

Delicious walks over to Mark and says to him before he leaves, "I have something for you."

Mark says to Delicious, "No thank-you!"

"Oh, so you think that you're too good to get a gift from me? I only give gifts to special people."

Mark apologizes and tells Delicious that he will accept his gift. Delicious hands Mark a small cup of chocolate ice-cream with a lot of nuts inside, Mark asks, "Why are you giving this to me?"

Delicious says, "Because when you eat this and the ice-cream melts in your mouth, I want you to think of me."

Mark angrily throws Delicious back the ice-cream; it just missed spilling on Delicious.

"Sheila, for the last time, let's get the hell out of here."

"And for the record, Mark, I would love to eat some of your ice and your cream."

Mark screams at the top of his lungs, "Ladies, let's go now and this time I mean right now." Mark runs out the door so fast he didn't realize that he dropped his phone. Sheila picks up his phone, the ladies crack up laughing; they pay Delicious for his services and leave.

Both the ladies tell Delicious that they will see him next week.

"Okay, you two, I look forward to seeing you both next week."

Sheila rushes over to Mark's car, hands him his phone, and tells him, you dropped this on the floor at Desire's. I wanted to return it to you because I know that you would be looking for it."

Mark is thankful to Sheila, but he is so upset by what happened that he cannot wait to get away from Desire's. He drives off so fast, that he doesn't give Sheila enough time to tell him to meet her and Kayla at Lighthouse Grill.

Sheila tries to call Mark again; he finally picks up on the third ring. "Hi Mark, where are you?"

"Sheila, I was so mad that I am on my way home." He asks Sheila, "Why, what's up?"

Sheila says, "Oh, remember my friend Kayla that I just introduced you to? Well, she lost her husband a few months ago and I thought that she could use another friend besides me. She and I are going to Lighthouse Grill. I wanted you to come and join us, we won't be long, just needed a break from the hustle and bustle of everything."

"Sheila, I passed by the Lighthouse Grill already; but only because I love you, I will make a U-turn and come back."

"Great, Mark, and thank you for doing this for me."

"No problem, Sheila, I will see you and Kayla in about twenty minutes."

"Mark actually got to Lighthouse Grill in record time. He spots the ladies and walks over to their table, looking incredible as always. Mark turns heads wherever he goes, and tonight is definitely no different. Mark kisses Sheila on the cheek and before he can sit down, Kayla apologizes to him about what happened at Desire's earlier. "Mark, I want you to know that Delicious is really cool; he just likes to have fun and one thing is for sure, he will always have your back."

"Thank you for that, but Delicious is not who I want to have my back." Mark definitely likes what he sees.

Marks says in the deepest and sexiest voice he can, "What an incredible beauty, Kayla."

"Thank you for the kind words, Mark."

Mark tells Kayla, "It's all true."

Mark takes a seat and begins to converse with Kayla, so much that he totally forgets that Sheila is at the table. Sheila becomes bored and decides that she wants to leave, she can clearly see that she is the third wheel.

"Hey there, you two, I am leaving because I have a big case that I'm working on and I must prepare for it."

Just as Sheila is about to leave the restaurant, Tyrone calls. Sheila answers the phone with a stank attitude, "Hello Tyrone, I can't talk I'm out with some friends."

Mark clearly sees where this conversation with Tyrone is going, and he motions to Sheila to hang up the phone. Tyrone does not want to get off the phone; so, Mark disguises his voice, "Sheila baby, we have got to go."

Tyrone angrily asks, "Who is that?"

"Tyrone, not that it's any of your concern or any of your business, but I told you that I was out with friends. I will speak with you tomorrow."

Again, Mark disguises his voice. He says to Tyrone, "Now get off her phone," and he tells Sheila to hang up on the old dude. And that's exactly what she does. Mark tells Sheila to wait and not to leave just yet.

Mark can't stand Tyrone, but he knows that Sheila is his ace in the hole to bring Tyrone down. Kayla doesn't know what it's like to go out and have a good time. Since Michael has passed away all she does is work and take care of Kendra, this is very different and nice for her. Mark wants to talk to Kayla all night if he could, but he realizes that the hour is getting late and he has to be up early.

"Okay ladies, it's been good, but I have to get out of here. I have a very important meeting at seven thirty in the morning. Let me walk you both to your cars." Mark asks Kayla for her number and she gives it to him, without hesitation.

They all get in their cars and drive home. Mark calls Sheila to make sure she made it home alright. But when he calls Kayla to make sure that she made it home okay, they talk for so long that Kayla falls asleep while talking on the phone with him. Mark politely hangs up. So much for getting home and going to bed early… that's what happens when you have good conversation.

CHAPTER ELEVEN

It is eight o'clock in the morning on a Friday in late August. Tyrone is already at the office; he is readily preparing for a meeting with some new clients. Tyrone is thinking about Sheila and how he still wants to get with her, even though she has been treating him like a stepchild lately.

Tyrone says to himself that he needs to call Sheila and take her to lunch to find out what's going on with her and see if they can take the relationship to the next level.

Tyrone stops preparing for his meeting for two minutes and calls Sheila. *Hello this is Sheila leave a message and I will return your call as soon as possible.* Tyrone is upset that Sheila didn't answer her phone, but he has no choice but to leave a message on her phone.

Sheila is listening to the message that Tyrone left for her. "Hello Sheila, this is Tyrone. I want to know if we can get together for lunch today. I really need to talk to you, please call me back. Thank you again."

Just as Tyrone finishes leaving a message for Sheila he hangs up the phone and Mark walks into his office; they both slap each other five. Mark asks, "Tyrone man, why are you smiling so much?"

"Man, Mark I just called Sheila and I'm waiting for her to call me back. I want to take her to lunch, I think it's time that we take the relationship to the next level."

Mark says to Tyrone, "I didn't know that you and Sheila were dating."

"Now I know that you know, Mark, we aren't dating just yet, but remember friendships are relationships and so I want to move past a friendship and into a relationship."

"Tyrone, are you really sure that you are ready to be with just one woman?

Because I know how you are when it comes to women."

"Mark, I want to be with Sheila and only Sheila."

"Tyrone, ain't no way. I don't believe that for a second, but okay, Tyrone, if you say so."

The phone rings right in the middle of the conversation, it's Sheila. "Tyrone, I am returning your call. Yes, I am free, and I would like to go to lunch with you today. Is twelve-thirty okay?"

"Sheila, anytime is good for me, as long as I get to spend some time with you."

"Tyrone, where are we going?"

"Sheila, can you meet me at the Lighthouse Grill?"

"See you then, Tyrone."

"Sheila, I cannot wait."

Sheila hangs up the phone. She is still disgusted by Tyrone and what he is trying to do to her best friend, but she cannot let him know that she is representing Antonio Anderson in his lawsuit, or that she knows what went on between him and her friend Kayla. Sheila immediately calls Kayla to let her know that she is planning to go to lunch with Tyrone. Kayla tells Sheila that she wishes her the best in dealing with Tyrone.

"Don't worry, Kayla, it will work out okay, I'm just trying to get information from him, and remember, it's only lunch. I know how to handle Tyrone."

"Okay Sheila, just call me when you are finished."

"You got it, girl." Sheila and Kayla both hang up the phone. Sheila jumps in her custom-made black on black Mercedes 900SE

SUV and drives to Lighthouse Grill to meet with the Andersons, when she realizes that she has just about an hour to meet with them.

Sheila is dressed to the nines, she has a form-fitting royal blue dress with matching shoes and bag, which compliments her cocoa skin. As she hangs up the phone with Kayla she sits down to meet with her clients, Antonio and Vikki Anderson. "So, guys here is an option, think about it and let me know if you like it. You can sue Tyrone Tyler for Defamation of Character. I believe that I can get you somewhere in the area of six million dollars or more, plus attorney fees and I can get a cease and desist against him."

Vikki asks, "What in the world is a Cease and Desist?"

"That means the case cannot be discussed by anyone or to anyone by any means."

Antonio and Vikki both crack up laughing, because they know that Tyrone has a problem shutting up, especially when something bothers him.

Antonio says, "This is going to get crazy."

Sheila tells Antonio and Vikki that they have nothing to worry about. "I am sure that you will see Tyrone at some point, if and when you run into Tyrone please do not say anything to him. I don't want the two of you speaking to him for any reason. He will eventually find out about the lawsuit."

Sheila thanks both Antonio and Vikki for meeting her on such short notice. She lets them know that right after she meets with them she is meeting with Tyrone.

Vikki yells "What! How can you go to lunch with that jerk?"

Sheila tells them in a confident voice, "Vikki, it is all a part of my plan, trust me. I can't stand Tyrone, but I can get him to spill the beans without him even knowing that I am representing you. Go home and relax. I promise I will let you both know what is going on."

Vikki is bothered by what she just heard from Sheila; she tells Antonio that something does not seem right. "Antonio, why in the world would Sheila have lunch with Tyrone, and she is representing us?"

Antonio lovingly responds to Vikki. "Baby, I don't know; but you have to trust her. I don't think that she would put her job on the line for that jerk Tyrone, so let's go home and finish the baby's room."

"I guess you are right, Antonio."

As Antonio and Vikki are leaving Lighthouse Grill, Sheila calls her office. She tells her assistant to call her if there are any urgent matters and to postpone her one-thirty meeting to another day. Mark isn't happy about Sheila going to lunch with Tyrone, but at the same time he can't wait for Tyrone to get what's coming to him. Mark so desperately wants Sheila to stick it to Tyrone, but he knows that he has to wait until the right time to get him.

Tyrone is so anxious to meet Sheila for lunch at Lighthouse Grill that he arrives a few moments earlier. He thinks that he has gotten there before Sheila, but unknown to him Sheila was already there to meet with Antonio and Vikki for lunch. Somehow, she has to play like she just arrived right before Tyrone got there. Sheila decides that, since the ladies' room is on the opposite side of the actual dining area, she is going to pretend as though she is coming from the ladies' room and she approaches him. Tyrone is so engrossed in the way Sheila looks that he can't speak, so he just stares. Tyrone is not tongue-tied; he is tongue stuck. He is in awe of Sheila's beauty.

Sheila realizes that Tyrone is stuck, so she breaks the ice. Sheila asks, "Well Tyrone, aren't you going to pull my chair out for me?"

Tyrone snaps out of his daze and apologizes to Sheila for having bad manners. The waiter comes over and asks Sheila if she would like a glass of wine. "I don't drink alcohol, but I will have a ginger ale on the rocks."

"Sure thing," says the waiter. He asks them both if they are ready to order. Tyrone asks the waiter to give them a moment.

Tyrone is looking at the menu trying to decide what he wants to eat, but while he has the menu in his hands, he takes a peek at Sheila and she sees him looking at her, so she asks him, "Do you like what you see?"

Tyrone says with a slick smile on his face, "Yes, I do."

Tyrone just hit a strike with Sheila, she is not pleased with Tyrone's answer. By the time Tyrone can get anything else out the waiter has come back to the table and once again he asks if they are ready to order.

Sheila says, "Yes I am ready to order, I would like a large Caesar Salad and a bottle of water."

Tyrone says, "I would like to order the Filet Mignon with a baked potato and a side salad and a glass of Chardonnay."

The waiter takes their orders and tells them both that he will be back soon with the meals.

While they are waiting for their food, Sheila questions Tyrone's motives so she asks him in a stern tone, "Tyrone why did you invite me here?"

"Well, Sheila you know that I am ready to be in a committed relationship."

Sheila knows that Tyrone is lying through his teeth, but she is going to make him feel special. Sheila asks, "Are you really ready to be in a committed relationship with just one woman, Tyrone?"

"Yes, I am, and Sheila and you are the woman that I want to settle down with."

"Were you married before?"

"Yes, I was married for twelve years. But my wife and I are divorced."

Sheila wants Tyrone to tell her what happened with his marriage. She hopes that he will tell her the truth, but she knows that Tyrone is full of crap. Tyrone tells Sheila that he and his wife just grew apart. Sheila is livid that Tyrone just lied to her, but she knows that she has to play it cool. Sheila has a blank expression on her face. She has really tuned Tyrone out, but she is going along with the crap that he is saying.

Tyrone tells Sheila that he has never met a woman as gorgeous as she is. Sheila immediately changes the subject, she acts as though she didn't hear what Tyrone just said to her.

"Tyrone, I have a very important question to ask, and I need you to be honest with me."

"Sheila, you can ask me anything that you want to ask."

"Okay here it goes, Tyrone, have you ever cheated on your ex-wife?"

Tyrone lies through his teeth, like there is no tomorrow. Tyrone proudly tells Sheila, "I would never cheat on my wife or any woman that I deal with, I am not that kind of man. Sheila I do have women who are attracted to me, but I am definitely a one-woman man."

Sheila almost chokes on her food because she knows that this Negro is lying to her.

"Sheila, is everything okay? Do you need any water?"

"No Tyrone, I am alright." Sheila tells Tyrone that she is glad to hear that he is "a one-woman man," but she is going to play right along with him. Sheila can't stand the sight of Tyrone and she wouldn't be on a date with him if both of their lives depended on it. But she is trying to gather up as much information on Tyrone as she can, so that she can use it when she presents her case against him; the more evidence she has, the better it is for Antonio and Vikki. Sheila has lost her appetite.

Sheila realizes the longer she sits at the table with Tyrone, the sicker she is getting. She can't stomach his foolishness anymore; she has got to leave, so she makes an excuse to get the hell away from him. Sheila proceeds to tell Tyrone that she has a headache and that she is ready to leave. Tyrone asks Sheila if there is anything else that she wants, and she adamantly tells Tyrone, "Thank you, but no thank you, Tyrone!"

Tyrone is not leaving, so he asks Sheila, "Do you mind if I finish my coffee and my drink?"

Sheila says in a low voice, "Tyrone, I would never tell you to leave after you paid for your dessert, so please eat." Sheila is upset now because she has to sit at the table with Tyrone longer than she actually wants to. Tyrone is trying to convince himself that Sheila is the woman for him; but what Tyrone doesn't know is that Sheila has already had enough of his lies. At this point, he can say what he wants, she really doesn't care what he says or does; she was finished with him when he tried to sue Kayla for her daughter. She can't wrap her mind around the fact that not only does he want to try to take Kayla's daughter from her, but he wants back the child support that the judge awarded her. Sheila is thinking about going shoe shopping and what she is going to have for dinner.

Sheila is so steamed that she pretends that someone texted her, just so she can tune Tyrone out. This is a disaster in the making. Sheila is thinking to herself, *why am I still sitting here with this tired Negro? Is it because I have manners and no matter what, I won't walk away in the middle of a free meal. I can drive myself home. It's time for me to get out.*

Sheila is making her way out of her seat, when all of a sudden, Tyrone asks her not to leave. And just as Tyrone is about to say something else to Sheila, of all the people in the world, in walks Antonio and Vikki. It seems strange because they just had a meeting with Sheila, no more than an hour ago. They actually want to see for themselves if Sheila is really going to take Tyrone down. They spot Tyrone and Sheila having dessert, well, at least Tyrone is. Sheila just wants to make dessert out of Tyrone, and I don't mean that in a good way. Antonio is not pleased because he knows that Tyrone tried to break up his and Vikki's marriage.

Antonio wants to step to Tyrone, but he plays it cool for the sake of Vikki and his unborn child. Antonio remembers what Sheila told him earlier, so he is playing the game just like Sheila is playing Tyrone, like a pawn in a chess game.

Although Vikki has nothing to say to Tyrone, Antonio decides that he is going to make nice and say hello. Vikki is trying to convince Antonio not to say anything at all, but Antonio tells Vikki that, if they don't speak, Tyrone will get suspicious and they don't want the plan to fall apart. Vikki understands, and although she doesn't agree with Antonio, she is going to support him one hundred percent. Antonio has to do what he has to do to make Tyrone feel comfortable, so he won't suspect anything so, Antonio starts the conversation. He is very nice and soft spoken. "Hello Tyrone, how are you doing? Who is this lovely lady?"

Tyrone says to Antonio, "I am so sorry, where are my manners? This is Sheila, my date."

Antonio gives him some shade. "I am surprised at you, Tyrone. I am so used to you juggling more than one woman at a time."

Sheila asks Antonio what he means by that. Antonio begins to tell Sheila that Tyrone would have lunch with you and will be texting another woman telling her to meet him in twenty minutes and tell you that he has to go to a business meeting, all the while pretending to like you.

Antonio says to Sheila, "Do you see where I am going with this?"

Tyrone cuts Antonio off with a swiftness, because he is afraid that Antonio will tell the truth about why his marriage really ended in divorce. And Tyrone doesn't want Sheila to know what really happened, otherwise he won't have a chance with her. In his mind, he thinks that he can have a chance with Sheila, but she absolutely knows better.

Tyrone asks Antonio, "What brings you and the wife here?"

"Well Tyrone, I just wanted to sit down and have a wonderful meal with my beautiful wife, before I leave for training camp."

"That's right Antonio, I forgot all about that. I am looking forward to some season tickets."

Antonio laughs so hard at what Tyrone just said to him that he almost chokes.

Antonio is livid that Tyrone thinks that he would get tickets to see him play. Antonio wants to tell Tyrone that he wouldn't give him tickets to see him play around the corner, but Vikki stops him in his tracks and tells Antonio to be nice.

Antonio knows that he has to be cool. He is so disgusted right now that he changes his mind and decides that he wants to go elsewhere to eat. Vikki is puzzled so she asks Antonio, "Why are we leaving?"

"Baby girl, I have to leave, or I just might slap the taste out of Tyrone's mouth."

"But Antonio, I want to stay. I'm pregnant and I'm hungry. Just ignore him, Antonio."

"Vikki, you know what honey, I am so glad that you are my wife; you always seem to know what to say to make it better. I will stay for you, this is our night and I will not let anyone spoil it, especially Tyrone Tyler."

Unfortunately, the only seats available in the restaurant is within ear shot of where Tyrone and Sheila are sitting. Sheila is so steamed with Tyrone and his antics that she wants to knock him a few times, but she plays it cool, and of course right at that precise moment, Tyrone gets a phone call. He says to Sheila, "excuse me, while I take this call."

Tyrone answers the phone in a sexy voice, "Well hello my love Kayla, I was wondering when you were going to call me. So, what are you doing later this afternoon?"

"Nothing at all Tyrone, why are you asking me?"

Tyrone says to Kayla, "Then how about joining me for a late lunch? I hear there is a nice cozy restaurant called the Lighthouse Grill, can you meet me there in about an hour and a half?"

"Sure Tyrone." Kayla hangs up. She is mad as hell at Tyrone, but she wants to bring him down, just like Antonio, Mark and Sheila. Kayla says to herself, *I don't know why this Negro thinks that everything is peachy keen between us. I can't stand the sight of him, but I am going to be his best friend until the big demise of Tyrone Tyler happens.*

Tyrone walks back to his table. As soon as he sits down and opens his mouth, he lies to Sheila and tells her that he just received a business call, but Sheila knows better. She and Kayla are in cahoots, she already knew that Kayla was going to call Tyrone. Sheila is letting Tyrone hang himself, one lie at a time. Sheila asks Tyrone if everything is okay.

Of course, Tyrone tells her that everything is okay; but in his mind, he is trying to figure out how he can get Sheila out of the restaurant before Kayla arrives. He definitely doesn't want them to run into each other.

Sheila asks again, "Tyrone are you sure that you are okay?"

"Yes, Sheila, why do you keep asking me that?"

"Excuse me Tyrone, I am asking because you seem like you have something on your mind."

Tyrone immediately changes the subject. He summons the Maitre'D. Tyrone asks him to find out from the waiter if he can bring him the check. The Maitre'D obliges. Before Tyrone can get another word out of his mouth, the waiter arrives with the check in hand. "Boy, you guys are fast. I like service like this."

Tyrone seems okay on the outside, but inside he is saying thank you because he knows that if Kayla sees him having lunch with Sheila World War Five will break out.

Tyrone has already set his plan in motion to get rid of Sheila, so that he can have his lunch date with Kayla.

Things seem to be going okay, and Sheila is making conversation. And she is about to touch a nerve with Tyrone. Sheila asks a question that he doesn't want to hear. "So, Tyrone, you told me earlier that you were married for twelve years. What happened that you and your wife did not want any children?"

Tyrone lies again. "Well Sheila darling, it's not that we didn't want children, my wife was unable to have children. I was all for her adopting children, but she wasn't cool with it, so it ended up being the reason we divorced."

Sheila has definitely heard enough of the bull crap from Tyrone, she knows that she has to make an excuse to get out of this lunch date. Tyrone forgot that Vikki and Antonio can hear the whole conversation. Vikki is so mad that she wants to pour a cold glass of water all over Tyrone, but she knows that she has to be cool because of the lawsuit.

Antonio pays the bill and he and Vikki say good-bye to Sheila, they both barely have anything to say to Tyrone.

Tyrone says to them both, "Aren't you guys going to say goodnight to me?"

Antonio turns around and says, "Hell No!"

Tyrone says loud enough for Antonio to hear him call him a "Punk."

Antonio turns around and steps to Tyrone and says, "I Got Your Punk."

Antonio says to Tyrone, "Negro, you better be glad that you are here with your date because I might have to take you outside and show you how much of a punk I am."

Tyrone says to Antonio, "Let's do this."

Antonio says to Tyrone, "You are not worth me losing my job. I have better things to do, like take care of my wife, what about you Tyrone? Oh yeah, that's right, you don't have a wife." That's when Vikki steps in and tells Antonio to walk away. Antonio is so mad that he tried to break a glass over Tyrone's head, but Vikki grabs his hand and tells him not to do anything stupid. She screams, "Antonio, please don't! He is not worth the time or the effort."

Antonio and Vikki both turn to leave, but before they leave, Antonio apologizes to Sheila for his behavior. Sheila accepts his apology and tells Antonio that she understands why he did what he did, and of course Tyrone disses both Antonio and Vikki.

Sheila is beyond disappointed; she is totally embarrassed by Tyrone's behavior. She can't wait to bring Tyrone down, he deserves it. Enough is enough. Sheila asks Tyrone why he did that to them.

Tyrone says, "Because I don't like them."

Sheila asks Tyrone "What did Antonio, and Vikki do to you, to make you react this way?" And all Tyrone could say is that since his marriage didn't work out, he doesn't want to see them happy.

Tyrone asks, "Sheila, why are you so worried about what I did to them, you are supposed to be on my side. I don't believe that you said to Antonio that you understand his actions towards me."

Tyrone tells Sheila that Vikki is his ex-wife's best friend. Little does Tyrone know that Sheila already knows why Tyrone was divorced, but she is playing along with the nonsense.

Tyrone looks at his watch and realizes that he needs to make sure that Kayla and Sheila do not bump into each other, so he has to figure a way to pretend to leave.

Then, Tyrone tells Sheila that he doesn't want to finish his dessert anymore, that Antonio made him lose his appetite, and that he wants to leave because he has a long day ahead of him. Sheila obliges and leaves Lighthouse Grill without saying a word. She is texting Kayla as she is leaving the restaurant to let her know that their plan is in motion. Tyrone pretends to leave with Sheila, but instead he puts her in her car. As soon as Sheila sees Tyrone walk away from her car she immediately contacts Kayla and tells her to be calm and listen to his lies and record whatever she can.

Kayla tells Sheila, "Girl I got this."

Tyrone pretends like he is going to get in his car and leave the restaurant; instead he goes back into the Lighthouse Grill and sits at the same table where he just had dinner with Sheila.

Just as Tyrone sits down, in walks Kayla. She is dressed in a Page Townes original two-piece blue pantsuit with blue four-inch stiletto's; her petite frame is just what any man would desire. Kayla has already called Sheila and told her that she is at Lighthouse Grill with Tyrone. Kayla puts on a fake smile as she sits down to have lunch with Tyrone.

"Kayla, this has been a long time coming, I knew you could not wait to get back with me."

"Tyrone, you are definitely beside yourself, we are just two people having lunch together. That's all that it is."

"Woman, don't be so sure of yourself. You know that you are the only woman for me and I was lost, and I am still lost without you and my daughter. Kayla, my heart was hurt when you picked up and got together with Michael."

"Tyrone, I am sorry that you felt that way, but that is the past. Tyrone why did you call me for this lunch; and I wish you would stop saying that we have a child together, the only thing we have between the two of us is distance, that's it."

"Tyrone, do you mean to tell me that all this time you have not found a woman that you like? I'm sorry Tyrone, I meant to say that you haven't found any women that you are trying to get with."

Tyrone lies to Kayla and tells her that she is the only woman for him, and he will do whatever it takes to win her back.

"Tyrone, do you really take me for a fool?"

Kayla is so sick that she feels like throwing up, and she hasn't eaten anything. Tyrone summons for the Maitre'D, and when he walks over he is shocked because he just saw Tyrone with Sheila, now he has a different woman sitting at the table with him. The Maitre'D is disgusted by what he is seeing, and says in a somewhat angry demeanor, "How can I help you, sir?" Tyrone asks the Matire'D, "can you bring us a pitcher of ginger-ale?"

"I sure will, and would you guys like to order now?"

Kayla says, "Yes, I would like to order a salad to start."

Tyrone said, "I will have what the lady is having."

The Maitre'D is so disgusted with Tyrone's reckless behavior that he almost throws Tyrone's food in his lap.

"Tyrone, how is your day at work going?"

Tyrone tells her that he cleared his calendar for the afternoon so that he can have lunch with her. Kayla already knows that Sheila was just with Tyrone and that they had lunch together, but she is going to act like everything is peachy keen between her and Tyrone.

"Kayla, I know this might be a little premature, but I want you to know that I still have feelings for you and I was really hoping that maybe we could start from where we left off. You know that you were the love of my life, and I am not married anymore, and this time we do not have to hide how we really feel about each other. I want everyone to know that I want to be with you exclusively and that I want to make you the next Mrs. Tyrone Tyler."

Kayla cannot stomach the lies anymore. She has had enough and enough is way too much for Kayla. "Tyrone, I have a child that I have to take care of, so I am not really looking to be in a committed relationship with anyone, especially not with you."

Tyrone is shocked by what Kayla just said; but he dismisses her and says to her,

"Kayla, let me change that for you. I want to be in a committed relationship with you, my feelings for you have never changed."

By now, Kayla has tuned Tyrone out; she has made herself sick on purpose, to the point that she can't eat her food. Kayla knows that Tyrone is going to lie, but she wants to record everything so that Sheila will have evidence against him. "Tyrone, I know that there has to be someone that you are interested in."

Tyrone tells Kayla that she has been and will always be the only woman for him.

Kayla wants to flip the table on Tyrone, *this fool must really think that she is stupid.* She is going to be classy and not let him get to her; she only has to listen to his lies for fifteen more minutes, then she has to get back to work.

Tyrone is thinking about Sheila, as he is having lunch with Kayla. Tyrone removes himself from the table so that he can call Sheila. Sheila already knows that Tyrone is going to tell her some crazy mess, but she is going to listen and then hang up on him.

Sheila answers the call, but she is totally disgusted, "Hello Tyrone, why are you calling me?"

Tyrone answers in his deepest voice, trying to impress Sheila, "How are things with you? I enjoyed having lunch with you today. Really Tyrone? Sheila says."

"Really Sheila, I did. I love it when I can spend time with you."

Sheila is on the other end of the phone, gagging at the nonsense. Mark is with Sheila and he is listening to the entire phone conversation.

Sheila asks, "Where are you now Tyrone?"

Of course, Tyrone lies and tells Sheila, I'm headed back to the office now."

"Wait a minute, Tyrone, you mean to tell me that you haven't gotten back to the office in all this time?"

Tyrone is feeling himself now and says to Sheila, "Honey, I had a few stops to make before heading to the office. I should be back in about twenty to thirty minutes or so. So, what are you doing Sheila?"

"First and foremost, Tyrone, please do not call me honey. I am not your honey and I would appreciate if you call me Sheila. And not that it's any of your concern I am about to head into a meeting with a client of mine. As a matter of fact, they just walked into my office. I have to speak to you another time Tyrone."

Before Tyrone could say "Goodbye" Sheila hung up the phone. Tyrone wants to say something, but he already caused a scene earlier in the day; so, he knows that he'd better play it cool, or he will never be able to come back to the Lighthouse Grill. But Tyrone doesn't care what happens because he can buy the Lighthouse Grill.

As Tyrone walks back to the table where Kayla is he has to smile, and he has to figure out what lie he is going to tell Kayla now. Tyrone apologizes to Kayla, for taking a phone call, but it was business and when business calls...

Kayla pretends that she understands, but she could care less because she already knows Tyrone would call Sheila right in the middle of them having lunch together. The game has not changed with Tyrone, he is predictable as usual.

"Tyrone, I need to leave I have to get back to the office. I have a client that I am meeting in about an hour and I want to get things in order before my meeting."

Tyrone asks Kayla if they can meet again.

Kayla tells Tyrone that she does not think that's a good idea. Tyrone is persistent and he is not going to give up on Kayla.

Kayla rushes out of the restaurant so fast that she almost knocks down a patron, trying to get away from Tyrone.

Tyrone looks at his watch and realizes that he must head back to the office to take care of some unfinished business that he has with a potential client.

On the drive back to work, Tyrone can't help but think about Sheila. Tyrone thinks that he wants to be with Sheila, but he also can't help but think about Kayla. He thinks that he wants to be with her as well. He is trying to see two women at the same time. Tyrone knows that he should not do that, but he doesn't care. All Tyrone wants to do is to have his cake and eat it too.

Tyrone does not care about anyone but himself, so he is going to continue to see both of the ladies… or so he thinks. Tyrone thinks that these women are strangers and that neither knows about the other. So, what harm could it do? It can do more harm than Tyrone thinks.

Tyrone makes it back to the office, just in time enough to meet with his new client. Tyrone is on cloud nine because he is about to pull in another two and a half million dollars for commission.

Kayla reaches her office and is about to prepare for her meeting when Tyrone calls. She answers, with an attitude, "Yes Tyrone!"

Tyrone asks Kayla, "What's with the attitude?"

Kayla says to Tyrone, "I just walked in and I am trying to get ready for my new client. Did you forget that I told you that at lunch this afternoon?"

Tyrone says in an angry tone, "So what! I called you and you can take a minute to talk to me! I could care less about your client."

Kayla realizes that this conversation is going nowhere fast, she knows that she has to think of something fast to get Tyrone off the phone. Just as Tyrone is about to say something else, Kayla informs him that her new client has arrived. Tyrone I have to go my client just came through the door, and I have to greet him.

Tyrone is shocked by what he just heard Kayla say, "Excuse me Kayla what do you mean by him?"

Kayla is an even-toned woman when she speaks, so for the mere fact that she has to raise her voice, it's not good, and she lets Tyrone know that she is upset. "Tyrone, have a good day. I have business to take care of." Kayla hangs up on Tyrone with a swiftness.

He is pissed off. He says to himself, *Kayla better hope for her sake that I'm in a better mood the next time I see her, otherwise it's going to be a situation.*

Kayla takes a moment to regroup, and immediately calls Sheila to spill the tea. Sheila answers and says hello, but just as Sheila is about to say something else, Kayla remembers that she needs to call her new client.

"Sheila I'm sorry, give me a minute. I have to call my new client, and push our meeting back can I call you in a few?"

Sheila says to Kayla, "Sure you can. Talk to you soon."

Sheila reminds Kayla not to forget to call her back. "Sheila I will call you back, I promise you; but I must take care of this call. This is a new client and I need to keep this client; your girl has to make the coins."

"Okay Kayla, take care of what you need to take care of. I will be waiting."

CHAPTER TWELVE

Kayla calls Reginald, her client, and asks him if she can move their meeting back and of course, Reginald tells her yes. Kayla tells him to meet her at Desire's and they can go back to her office from Desire's to discuss business. Reginald obliges. I will text you the address in a minute. See you soon, Reginald. Kayla has decided that she needs to get over to Desire's; she is due for a touch up from the neck up. Delicious is surprised to see Kayla but he is glad at the same time.

It has been a while, Delicious, I know I need a whole new me. Delicious agrees emphatically, "Yes girl, you sure do. I'm almost scared to touch your hair, but you have come to the right place, I will do my best to work some magic. Now what brings you in today Kayla?"

Well Delicious, there isn't anyone who can do hair like you, and I can always count on you to make me look my best for my business meetings. Delicious points Kayla to the back of the salon and says, "come on, let me wash and set you under the dryer. By the way Kayla, how is your day going thus far?"

"Hmm Delicious, where do I start? It has been a little eventful. I had lunch with a person of the opposite sex, and it went totally left; but I didn't let him know that. He wants to get together again, but I am not interested in him anymore."

"Kayla you said *Anymore.* Do tell, who is it?"

"Delicious, I will tell you, but you have to promise me that you won't pass any judgment if I tell you who he is."

"Kayla, I promise not to judge or throw you any shade."

"Delicious, it's Tyrone."

"Tyrone Who? Kayla, please tell me you are not talking about Tyrone Tyler."

Kayla is almost embarrassed to say anything, so she whispers, "Yes it's Tyrone Tyler."

"Kayla, why in the world would you want to have anything to do with Tyrone?"

"Delicious, there's a method to my madness. I can't stand Tyrone he is the worst of the worst. He was my worst mistake; I wish I could tell you what's going on. I have to keep quiet for now, but you will find out everything that's happening, sooner than later. Delicious to be quite honest, I am so over Tyrone, but if he wants to spend money on me who am I to stop him? So, I will let him spend as much money as he wants to on me."

"Kayla, I do agree, and I hear you girl."

"Delicious, my only problem is that somewhere in his delusional mind he thinks that he and I are in a relationship." Just as Kayla finishes talking, in walks a fine piece of specimen by the name of Reginald.

Reginald is six feet two inches tall; he is one fine man. Reginald approaches the reception area at Desire's and says, "Hello, I'm Reginald and I'm looking for Kayla Jones."

Phylecia tries to say hello to Reginald, but she is so tongue-tied that all she can do is just point to the back of the salon. She can't help but to get out of her seat and stare. Once Reginald arrives at the back of Desire's he greets Kayla with a kiss. Reginald tells Kayla that she looks great. Kayla thanks him for the compliment, she definitely likes what she sees.

Delicious tells Reginald that he is the best piece of dark chocolate he has seen in a very long time.

Reginald is feeling a bit uncomfortable, so much that he asks Kayla, "Who is This?"

Delicious says to Reginald, "I am your tasty man."

"Excuse me, I don't want you as my tasty man. Brother, please leave me alone." He is feeling a little irritated. "Kayla, are you finished getting your hair done, because I am ready to go."

Delicious asks Reginald if he can go with him.

Now Reginald is mad as all get up and with an angry tone he says to Delicious, "No, you can't go with me anywhere."

Delicious says to Reginald, "I will take you to a place you have never been before."

Reginald is desperately trying to ignore Delicious, so he says to Kayla, "How about dinner?"

Before Kayla could respond to Reginald, Delicious has put his two cents in the conversation. "Reginald, that is your name right? Well, I wouldn't mind being your dinner and you can be my dessert."

Reginald is so infuriated that he does not want to spend another minute in Desire's, so he quickly summons Kayla, "Let's go now." Reginald is a gentlemen and even though he is uncomfortable being around Delicious, he won't let that stop him from paying for Kayla's hairdo. They are at the reception area and he asks Phylecia how much Kayla's hair costs. Kayla tells Reginald that he doesn't have to pay for her; she has money and she can pay her own way. Reginald tells Kayla that he doesn't mind paying for her at all, but he has to get out of Desire's before someone gets hurt.

"Delicious, I love you, but I have to go I will see you in two weeks."

"Okay girl, but the next time you come here to get your hair done, please make sure you bring dark chocolate with you."

Delicious says seductively, "Goodbye Reginald, you fine piece of chocolate." Reginald leaves behind Kayla, without saying a word. As they are walking towards Reginald's car he tells Kayla that he will never come to Desire's again.

"Reginald, I would like to know why you won't come here to pick me up again. I think that it's unfair, if I am in trouble and I happen to be there, you would not come and get me? That's really not nice, Reginald. Give me a reason and it better be a good one."

"Kayla. it's because of him / her, you know who I am talking about."

"Do you mean Delicious?"

"Yes, I mean Delicious."

"Reginald, his name is Lavell and he is totally harmless."

"Kayla, like I said, I will never come here again. Find another spot for me to pick you up and I will definitely get you."

Kayla chuckles at Reginald. He tells her that it's not funny. Kayla tells Reginald to get inside the car and she apologizes for putting him in that situation without warning him. Kayla asks Reginald, "Do you have a car and if so where is it? And by the way, Reginald, how did you get here?"

To answer your questions Kayla, "I do have a car, but I decided to drive to your office and park my car and then I took a cab here."

"Reginald how much did it cost you to take a cab from my office to Desire's?"

"Kayla, it cost me about seventy-five dollars to take a cab from your job to Desire's."

"Reginald, that was a lot of money. If I had known that it would have cost you so much I would not have asked you to pick me up at Desire's."

"Kayla, money is no object and it was definitely well worth it. I like what I see, and the conversation is not so bad either."

So, after a twenty-minute drive they arrive at Kayla's office. Little does Kayla know that Tyrone has decided to stop by her office, unannounced. As she and Reginald head inside, there she finds Tyrone sitting in the reception area waiting for her to come back from lunch.

Tyrone is disgusted by what he sees. "Kayla, so this is the business meeting you were having? Kayla, who the hell is this?"

"Tyrone, not that it's any of your business, but this is my client, Reginald. He just picked me up and we are about to go into a meeting. Tyrone, what is it that you want?"

"Kayla, is everything is okay?"

"Kayla, I really feel insulted that Reginald is asking questions as though you aren't alright."

Kayla says sarcastically to Tyrone, "I don't know why you feel insulted, Reginald is only doing what a man is supposed to do he is looking out for me. Now I need to get back to my client, otherwise I won't be able to eat. I do have a child to support."

"Kayla, all I know is that there better not be anything else going on between you and Reginald except the client relationship, otherwise you and Reginald will both have to answer to me." Kayla pushes Tyrone so hard that he almost falls, she is embarrassed and upset by Tyrone and his shenanigans.

Tyrone tells Kayla that he is angry because she is choosing Reginald over him.

"Tyrone, for the record, you and I are not together, and we will not be together now or in the future. You can bet your last dollar that I won't make the same mistake twice; and when it comes to my business, I will always choose my clients and my business over you any day. Now get out of my office Tyrone and I mean now and don't bring that foolishness around me anymore."

Kayla is so pissed off that she slams the door so hard that when Tyrone walks out of her office the door hits him on the foot. Tyrone is too upset to say something right then; but knowing him he will say something to her later. Actually, he is about to call Kayla out of her name, but he realizes that he can't at the moment. Tyrone will make sure to have this conversation later. As a matter of fact, Tyrone decides that he isn't going to wait, so he calls Kayla while he is in the lobby of her building. The phone rings three times but Kayla has not answered, so Tyrone dials her again, and again the phone rings; but this time, Kayla reluctantly picks up the phone.

"Good afternoon, this is Kayla Jones. How may I help you?"

"Kayla, this is Tyrone. Stop acting like you don't know who it is."

"Tyrone, why are you calling me? You know that I am with a client."

"Kayla, the next time you disrespect me by trying to push me out of your office and slamming the door on my foot, it will definitely be a situation between the two of us, and you don't want that."

"Tyrone, I don't know who the hell you think you are talking to, but you have the wrong woman. Don't call my phone with any of your foolishness ever again or there will be a situation between the two of us. How about that? Goodbye, and get the hell off my phone."

Kayla steps back into her office, she apologizes to Reginald for Tyrone's erratic behavior.

Reginald asks Kayla, "Who is that bozo?"

"He was someone that I used to be deal with, he was the biggest mistake of my life."

"Kayla, enough about him. Can we talk about something else?"

"Well Reginald, here you go. Here is the contract that I drew up, I am sure that once you see the numbers you will realize that I am the best contractor around."

Reginald tells Kayla, "I love what I see and I'm not only talking about the contract."

"Reginald, was that a compliment and are you flirting with me?"

"Yes, Kayla, it is a compliment and yes, I am definitely flirting with you; and is there a problem with me flirting with you?"

"No Reginald, there isn't a problem with you flirting with me at all. I am actually flattered, but it's just that I'm not ready to jump into anything right now."

"Wait a minute Kayla, who said anything about jumping into anything? Kayla, I am your client; and yes, I do like you a whole lot; but right now, it's a conflict of interest. I just happen to think that you are a beautiful woman, and when the time presents itself, and it will present itself for us to take it beyond a client relationship to something else, I want it to be right."

"Reginald, thank you for that. I have a confession as well, Reginald. How do I say this?"

Reginald tells Kayla, "Just say it."

"Well Mr. Reginald, I think you got it going on."

Reginald lets out a loud chuckle. Kayla asks in a low and dejected voice, "Reginald, why are you laughing at me? I just gave you a compliment and you laughed at me, instead of saying ***thank-you.***"

"Rest assured, Kayla, that I am not laughing at your compliment, I'm laughing because that was corny as all get up. I got it going on, woman who says that?"

Kayla begins to laugh as well. "I guess you're right, Reginald. Okay then, let me rephrase that compliment. Reginald, I think you are fine."

"Kayla, now that sounds so much better and thank you for the compliment. I appreciate it."

Just as Reginald finishes saying that he appreciates the compliment Kayla gave him, he catches her off guard and pulls her close to him and begins kissing her. Kayla tries to pull away, but she realizes that she has not felt like this in such a long time. The only other man who has made her feel this way was Michael.

"Reginald, what are you doing? You are my client."

Reginald apologizes to Kayla. "I'm sorry, but it's just that I have been attracted to you since the first time I met you."

"Reginald, I have to admit that I feel the same way as well, but I don't want to mess up a friendship and a great client relationship."

Reginald stuns her by saying, "Kayla, then I think maybe it is best that we do not have a client relationship and work on having a personal relationship."

"Reginald, that's fine with me but are you absolutely sure?"

"Kayla, I am definitely sure about this."

"Reginald, please be patient with me. I don't know what it's like to be in a relationship, since my husband passed away a few months ago."

Reginald assures Kayla that he will be patient with her and that he really understands and that he is in the same boat. Reginald tells Kayla that he can't wait for them to be in a relationship with one another. "Kayla, I think I am going to enjoy being your man."

"Reginald, it's going to be so great calling you my boyfriend."

Reginald laughs. "There you go with the corny line again, Kayla."

Kayla is baffled, "What corny line are you talking about Reginald?"

"I am talking about the boyfriend line, who uses that these days?"

"Reginald, you have to realize that I was married for a little while and I haven't dated in years; so, I am not accustomed to what the 'cool' or 'in' sayings are. Let me rephrase that, Reginald, "I think it's going to be great calling you my man."

Reginald says, "That sounds more like it."

"I have a great friend; her name is Sheila. She is an attorney. I will ask her if she would be willing to handle your case as far as the legal matters go."

Reginald rips the contract up and tells Kayla that he is leaving, but that he will pick her up later for dinner. Kayla is stunned and excited at the same time, but she tells Reginald that she can't because she needs someone to watch her daughter. Reginald is hurt but he understands. He kisses Kayla on the forehead and tells her that he will call her later.

Just as Reginald walks out of the office, Kayla motions to Reginald to wait a minute. Kayla's mother Diana calls on the phone, she is calling to see how Kayla is doing. Kayla tells her mother that she is okay, but the sound of her voice says differently and her mother senses it.

"There is something wrong with you, Kayla. What is it? You know a mother knows."

"Mom, I don't want to bother you with my problems."

"Kayla, I am your mother and you are not bothering me. Now what's wrong?"

"It's just that a friend wanted to take me to dinner, but I can't go because I don't have anyone to watch Kendra."

Diana is upset with Kayla and she tells her that she is totally offended. "Kendra is my granddaughter and you felt that you couldn't ask me to look after her."

"Mom, you already do enough."

"Kayla, go and enjoy yourself; as a matter of fact, bring her clothes and I will watch her for the week. Kayla you can't stop living because you have a child, plus that's what family is for."

"Okay mom… and thank you."

"Kayla, there is no need to thank me, just bring my granddaughter to my house and enjoy yourself tonight. By the way, Kayla, what's his name?"

"Mother, how did you know it was a man?"

"Kayla, a mother knows these things."

"I love you so much, mom."

"By the way, Kayla, I like how you ignored my question; but it's okay and I love you more."

Kayla hangs up the phone and just looks at Reginald. She wants to break a smile, but she is playing it cool. He steps back into her office and asks her if something is wrong. She doesn't answer him right away.

Now he is getting worried. "Kayla is everything okay?"

She shakes her head and begins to cry. Reginald walks over to Kayla and hugs her; he tells her that everything is going to be alright.

"Reginald that was my mother, she called to check on me, she's going to watch Kendra tonight and she said that she would watch her for the entire week. I don't know what I would do without her. They don't make mothers like her anymore, she is indeed one of a kind."

"Kayla, I can't wait to meet her. And baby you were worried for nothing. I'm glad that everything worked out for us."

"Reginald, what do you mean, us?"

"Kayla, from this day forth, it's the both of us. You don't have to go it alone; I will be here for you, always."

"Aww that was so sweet, thank you for making me smile. It makes me feel so good to know that I have someone special in my corner. Reginald, now get out of my office so I can finish my paperwork."

"So, by the way, what time are we meeting for dinner? Kayla, is seven-thirty is okay with you?"

"Reginald, seven-thirty is perfect, here is my address. I look forward to seeing you, then Reginald." Kayla is blushing from ear to ear. She knows that Reginald is a welcoming addition, since Michael passed away.

As soon as Kayla sits down at her desk, her phone rings and of course it is Tyrone again. Kayla knows that she doesn't want to take this call, but if she doesn't Tyrone will keep calling her; so, against her better judgment she answers the call.

She is in a good mood not because of Tyrone, but because of Reginald. Tyrone has the audacity to think that because he has called Kayla that the excitement in her voice is because of him.

"Kayla, that's my girl. I knew you would be happy to hear my voice."

"Tyrone, I am happy, but it has nothing to do with you at all."

"Kayla, now you know that I am the only man who can make you happy."

"Tyrone, only you believe that."

"Okay Kayla, what's his name?"

"Tyrone that is none of your business, I am not your woman."

"So, if you are not my woman or you are not interested in me, why did you have lunch with me today?"

"Tyrone, you invited me to lunch, even though I told you that I didn't want to go. Tyrone what is it that you want? I am trying to wrap up my work and I don't have time to talk to you."

Tyrone has a major attitude. "You know what, Kayla, I don't know what your issue is, but I don't like this attitude of yours."

"Tyrone you have the nerve to talk about someone with an attitude, did you forget the embarrassing way you acted at lunch; and not to mention how you acted in front of my client, this afternoon. Tyrone, please, like I said before, I am busy, and I don't have time to talk to you or deal with any of your foolishness. Goodbye!"

Before Tyrone could get another word out of his mouth, all he hears on the other end of the phone is a dial tone. Tyrone is upset. I know this skeezer did not just hang up on me, she must not realize who she is talking to. She must have forgotten that I can make her life miserable. Tyrone is disgustingly fake and a dog, because, as soon as he hangs up the phone with Kayla, he immediately calls

Sheila thinking that she is going to be excited to hear from him, as well.

"Hello Sheila, this is the man of your dreams." Sheila answers with an attitude, she is trying to brush Tyrone off as best possible.

"What in the world is going on here? I call to say *hello* to you, and you act like you have your underwear in a bunch."

"Tyrone, I don't have time for your foolishness. I have two meetings back-to-back, one of which is about to start in about ten minutes. Tyrone is there something that you need?"

"Well I called to see if I can take you to dinner to make up for the fiasco that happened at Lighthouse Grill. Sheila, I promise you that I will be on my best behavior."

"Tyrone, I have to go. My clients will be here any minute. I will let you know later, good-bye Tyrone."

All Tyrone hears on the other end of the phone is a tone, a dial tone to be exact. Now he is really pissed off, first it was Kayla who hung the phone up on him and now Sheila just slammed the phone down in his ear. *These chicks need to watch themselves... they don't know who they are disrespecting. I can and I will shred them to pieces. No one and I mean no one disses Tyrone Tyler and gets away with it. I don't care who it is.*

It has been five minutes and Tyrone is stunned about the attitudes of Kayla and Sheila, but there is nothing that he can do at the moment. Mark walks into his office. Sheila has already filled him in briefly on how Tyrone acted at lunch. She told him that she will tell him the rest later. Mark can't wait to hear what lies Tyrone has to say. "So, Tyrone how was your lunch date with Sheila?" And being the liar that Tyrone is, he is not going to disappoint Mark at all; so of course, he tells him that everything went well and that he thinks Sheila is finally digging him.

"Oh really, Tyrone?"

"Yes, really Mark. I guarantee you by this time next week, all Sheila will be talking about is me and wanting to become the future Mrs. Tyler."

"Tyrone, you seem sure of yourself, how many dates have you and Sheila been on? Maybe one at the most, and you know that she is into you already?" Mark knows Tyrone is lying and he can't stomach him anymore, so he tells Tyrone that he has a meeting and that he will be back in the office in about two hours. They slap each other five and Mark leaves Tyrone's office and heads out the door for his meeting; then he is going to head home after that. Mark decides to call Sheila before her meeting with Antonio and Vikki. Sheila picks up and Mark spills the tea like never before.

"Sheila, I had to leave the office for a couple of hours. Tyrone made me so mad that I wanted to bust his lips open for lying."

"Mark, what did Tyrone say that made you so mad?"

"He had the nerve to say that things are going good with you and him; and that by next week, you are going to talk about becoming the future Mrs. Tyrone Tyler."

"Mark, he said what?"

"Tyrone better hope for his sake that I don't see him, because if I do, I am going to give it to him, and he won't like the way that he gets it. That Negro has lost his cotton-picking mind."

"Mark, please don't tell me anymore. I am actually about to start a meeting with my clients, and I cannot have my nerves upset. I will call you later."

"Okay Sheila, I will talk to you later."

Meanwhile Sheila is meeting with Antonio and Vikki to talk about the fiasco with Tyrone that happened earlier at Antonio's birthday bash and at Lighthouse Grill today. She wants to update them on the lawsuit. "I just wanted to let you guys know that we are moving forward with the lawsuit."

"I can't wait to see Tyrone in court."

"Antonio, listen to me. We have a court date in one month and I need you to stay away from Tyrone, you can't have any contact with him."

"Sheila, I don't think I will be able to be in court for the case. Football season is starting in a week and I am a veteran player. I need to be on that field."

"Sheila, I am available to go to court if my husband can't make it."

But Antonio is totally against it. "Vikki, I don't want you anywhere in the courtroom with Tyrone. I don't want him upsetting you and you miscarry our baby, I will kill that Negro if that happens."

"Antonio, I got this. Tyrone is a coward and I'm not scared of him."

"Vikki honey, I know that you aren't scared of Tyrone; but he is a sucker and he will try to get under your skin… just think about how he acted today."

"Honey, I understand what you are saying; but I'm a big girl, Antonio, and I can handle Tyrone."

"Sheila, will you please talk some sense into my wife."

"Antonio, it is highly unlikely that Vikki will need to be there, so you have nothing to worry about. Look, you two, I want to be there. I want to see Tyrone try and squirm his way out of this."

"Vikki, we will talk about this later at home."

"So, you two, I want to apologize for the behavior of Tyrone this afternoon. I was highly embarrassed for everyone, including the workers at Lighthouse Grill; and Tyrone has the nerve to think that I want to be in a relationship with him."

Vikki tells Sheila that's the funniest thing she has heard all day.

"Vikki, there is nothing funny about that comment at all, he is totally besides himself." Tyrone had the audacity to tell a friend of mine that, by this time next week I will be telling everyone that I will be the future Mrs. Tyrone Tyler. Vikki, now *that's* funny. Tyrone wouldn't know what to do with a woman if she came and beat him over the head with a broomstick."

"Antonio and Vikki, I need you both to listen to what I am saying to you. Whatever you do, stay away from Tyrone. Don't say anything to him, no matter what it is, and try not to be in the same places he is. I can win this case and I don't want him and his crazy antics to get in the way of that, and also do not mention that I am your attorney. He will find out when the time is right. Your case is on the calendar in about a month, but I am hoping that I can get an earlier date… if not, then so be it. But I'm prepared for a fight with Tyrone and his attorneys, I can win this case. Go home enjoy your time together and I will keep in touch."

"Thank you so much, Sheila, for everything."

"You two are welcome."

As soon as Antonio and Vikki leave the office, Sheila takes off her shoes and just takes a moment to reflect. As soon as she gets a good moment to relax, her phone rings. She is praying that it isn't Tyrone. And this time her prayers have been answered, it is Kayla. She called to tell Sheila what happened at Lighthouse Grill. "Sheila girl, let me tell you…, Tyrone acted a complete fool, he went ballistic on me and the Maitre'D… I have never been so embarrassed in my life."

"Kayla, that is nothing. He almost got into a fight with Antonio Anderson and his wife Vikki, for no reason at all."

"Sheila, that's Tyrone's ex-wife's best friend."

"Kayla, that Negro looked me in my eyes and lied to me. He told me that he was a good husband and that the only reason he and his ex-wife divorced was because she couldn't have children; and that he wanted children and she felt that she couldn't give him the children that he wanted, so she thought it would be better for them to get divorced."

Kayla is shocked by what she is hearing. "Sheila, you have got to be kidding me. Tyrone needs some serious help. Vanessa was faithful to him through all the dirt he was doing. I bet you he won't tell you that he never wanted to have a child with Vanessa. Vanessa was able to have children but because of all the stress he put her through she didn't get pregnant until she married Kevin. Now what does that tell you."

"Sheila, I can't stand Tyrone; he is the biggest liar I know, what a joke. Thank God, I am not interested in him anymore; because it would be on and popping, and I really don't mean that in a good way."

"Sheila, I have a new friend. His name is Reginald and I want you to meet him soon. Girl, now you know I can't wait to meet him, so that I can interrogate him. Sheila I hope that you don't give him the fourth and the fifth degree, because you can be hard on people."

"Kayla, I promise to be nice when I meet him face to face and I am sure that he will make you happy; but as of right now, I have to call Mark so we can figure out how we are going to bring Tyrone down. He needs to fall off his high horse."

"Sheila, I have to go. That's Reginald, he's taking me to dinner tonight."

"Kayla, I hope it works out for you."

"Thanks girl, no one can be worse than Tyrone Tyler."

"Kayla, my phone is ringing, call me later."

"Okay Sheila, we will speak later."

Sheila grudgingly answers her phone; it's Tyrone. She is going to play it cool and get him off the phone as soon and as quickly as possible. She doesn't allow Tyrone to say anything, she is doing the talking. "Tyrone, I will have to call you back."

"Sheila, I just want to know if we can go to dinner."

"Tyrone, I have to call you back." Sheila hangs up the phone in Tyrone's ear, he is steamed. He is tempted to take a drive to her job. The problem is that he doesn't know where she works, so he decides that he is going to call her back.

"Sheila, I don't appreciate you hanging up the phone in my ear."

"Tyrone, once again, I will have to call you back… please get off my phone."

Sheila hangs up in his ear.

Tyrone is beyond pissed. He wants to step to Sheila, but for now he is going to try and play it cool. But one thing is certain, he is going to make sure that the next time he speaks with her, he is going to let her have it.

Sheila calls Mark so that they can strategize their next move when it comes to Tyrone. Tyrone is becoming the talk of the town, and not in a good way. "Mark, have you spoken to Tyrone about our lunch date the other day? It was the worst, can you believe he tried to fight Antonio Anderson and his pregnant wife; and he called Kayla while at the restaurant and set up a date with her while I was there, not knowing that we planned it that way. He actually thinks that he was getting over, he also went ballistic on the restaurant manager."

"Mark, Tyrone has stooped to an all-time low. And he tried to justify his behavior."

"Sheila, it's only a matter of time before Tyrone loses everything piece-by-piece. He is going to be livid when he finds out that you are the one representing the Anderson's. I am surprised that Tyrone hasn't talked about it, yet he is good for broadcasting things like this."

"Mark, I haven't sent him any paperwork."

"Sheila, why haven't you sent the papers? What are you waiting for? Please tell me you aren't interested in Tyrone."

"Mark Peterson, I am not interested in Tyrone at all. Are you kidding me? I just got finished speaking with both Antonio and Vikki. I am going to file the papers first thing tomorrow. He is going to receive them in a couple of days."

"Okay, as long as you don't procrastinate."

"Can we change the subject, Sheila, how about dinner?"

"Mark, I can't, but you are on for tomorrow night."

"Sheila I want to see you;, it seems like we haven't seen each other in weeks."

"You are right, Mark, we haven't… so tomorrow is your time."

"Okay, let me go, here comes Tyrone. I will let you know what lie he comes up with about your lunch date."

"I will call you later tonight. I want to wrap up this paperwork, then I have to go to my hair appointment." Mark and Sheila hang up the phone.

Tyrone knocks on Mark's office door. "Come in."

"Hey Mark, how are you?" They both slap each other five.

"I'm good brother, have a seat. So, how was your lunch date with Sheila?"

"Man, it was good except for the interruptions."

"Tyrone, what interruptions?"

"While Sheila and I were sitting at the table enjoying each other's company, in walks Antonio Anderson and my ex-wife's best friend, Vikki. And they had the audacity to sit at a table across from Sheila and me, so you know that we weren't able to be intimate with each other."

"Tyrone, I can't believe that nothing happened."

"Mark, what are you trying to say?"

"Tyrone, there is always drama anytime you go somewhere."

"Mark, I am going to let that one slide."

"Tyrone, whether you want to accept it or not, it's the truth."

"Mark, I'm leaving now. I am working on getting a new client."

"Good for you, Tyrone, have a great day."

As Tyrone is about to leave Mark's office, he yells, "Don't be mad, Mark, you can become a partner one day."

"Tyrone, I know you don't think that I'm mad because you are a partner. Brother I don't want the responsibility I am glad to be a junior partner."

Mark pretends that his phone is ringing, just so he can get Tyrone out of his office. "Tyrone, can you leave so I can take this call?"

Tyrone tells Mark that he is out. Mark politely slams the door behind Tyrone, that the door actually hits Tyrone on the bottom of his foot. Tyrone is about to say something else to Mark, but he realizes that he can't go off on him at the office. However, he is thinking of a way to give him a piece of his mind.

CHAPTER THIRTEEN

Kayla is excited about her date with Reginald, it has been a while since she has dated. Reginald is the only man she has gone out with since Michael passed away. Kayla reminds herself that she did have an affair with Tyrone; but that does not count because Tyrone isn't a real man.

Kayla excitedly calls Sheila and tells her the good news. "Girl, this is that night for my big date with Reginald. I am so nervous, maybe I should call him and cancel."

"Kayla, you better not, go out and enjoy yourself."

"Girl, I guess you're right. He is kind of cute. So, you really like this guy?"

"I guess you can say that, and he is actually a client of mine."

"Kayla, do you think that it is a good idea to date your client?"

"Honestly, we talked about that and he decided that he no longer wants to be a client of mine; so now we are going to try and see if we can work it out and have a committed relationship. Sheila that's where you come in, I need you to look over his contracts please."

"Kayla, give him my information and I will definitely assist him in whatever he needs. I am really happy for you and I do hope things work out for you and Reginald, but please be careful. I don't want to have to cut him if he hurts my friend."

"Sheila, it does feel weird. Michael was the only man I was with for the past two years."

"Kayla, it's okay to move on with your life. Do you need me to watch Kendra for you?"

"Sheila, you are a good friend, but my mother said that she is going to watch her for the rest of the week, so I will be okay. I wish you were here to help me pick out something nice to wear; because you know me, I will put on anything."

"Kayla, I will be there in about ten minutes; just wait until I get there before you pick out your outfit."

"Okay girl, I will see you when you get here."

Kayla hangs up the phone with Sheila and immediately jumps in the shower she knows that time is of the essence, so she is going to make sure that she is smelling good, as well as looking good for Reginald. Kayla is so happy to go on her date that she is in the shower singing the song, *What a man, What a man, What a mighty good man.*

Kayla excitedly jumps out of the shower, rushing to wipe herself off. She lays out everything that she is going to wear, except for her outfit. Just as Kayla is about to sit on her bed to get ready, the doorbell rings. It's Sheila, they both greet each other with a kiss on the cheek. "Alright Kayla, let me see what you have in your closet."

They both run upstairs to Kayla's bedroom, Sheila is going through Kayla's closet and she finds a black body shaping dress that she thinks would be perfect for Kayla. "This is the dress, Kayla."

"Sheila, don't you think that is a little too revealing?"

"Girl, it's going to show all your curves, that's the best kind." They both chuckle.

"Kayla girl, you look amazing. My job here is done, it's time for me to go."

"Wait Sheila, aren't you going to help me with my hair?"

"Girl, it looks fine just the way it is. Just call me when the date is over, I want to hear all the details."

"Look, if things go well, you aren't the person I will be calling."

"That's what I'm talking about Kayla, you better get your groove on."

Kayla is five feet three inches with a body that everyone woman who sees her is envious of and makes the men swoon, at first sight. She steps into her four-inch stilettos. Kayla has naturally long black hair. She is a natural beauty. Kayla is ready as can be for her date. She is about to leave her house and get into her car to meet Reginald, when there is a knock at her door.

Who in the world can this be? I am about to leave. Kayla is thinking in the back of her mind that Sheila must have left something. Kayla opens the door, thinking that it's Sheila; but to her surprise, it's not it is Tyrone. "Tyrone, why in the world are you at my door ringing my bell? I am on my way out."

"Out where, Kayla?"

"Tyrone, that is not any of your business, now please step aside. I just told you that I am on my way out. Dressed like that you must be going on a date."

"And, so what if I am, Tyrone? That's none of your concern. Enjoy your night, Tyrone because I will definitely enjoy mine."

Kayla walks away leaving Tyrone standing at her front door, looking stupid. "Kayla I want to talk to you."

"Tyrone, I do not have time to talk to you about anything, I'm leaving." Kayla gets in her car and drives off, leaving Tyrone standing in the street with his mouth hanging down. "What just happened here?" Tyrone jumps in his car and tries to follow Kayla to see who she is going out with and where they are going. Tyrone is speeding, but not enough to get a ticket. All kinds of thoughts are racing through his sinister mind, he cannot believe that Kayla just shut him down and left him standing in front of her house, wide mouth and dumbfounded.

Tyrone is driving so fast that he is in close proximity to Kayla's car, but not close enough for Kayla to see that he is following her.

Kayla pulls up to Lighthouse Grill, the valet immediately parks her car. As soon as Kayla walks into Lighthouse Grill, Reginald is waiting with two dozen blue roses. Kayla is speechless. "Reginald, this is so wonderful and thoughtful of you."

"Kayla, you deserve this and more."

As Kayla and Reginald are escorted to their seats, Tyrone is roaming around the restaurant trying to get a good look at who Kayla is on a date with. Tyrone is steamed, he can't believe that Kayla is with someone other than him. Tyrone wants to break up this date so bad he can taste it; but he knows that would not be the wise thing to do since he is a partner in his firm.

Tyrone can't believe that Kayla is smiling and enjoying Reginald's company. Tyrone decides that he is going to interrupt this date, so he calls Kayla on her phone, but he gets the surprise of his life. "Hello, how may I help you?"

"I'm looking for Kayla, this is Tyrone." Reginald immediately hands Kayla the phone.

"Kayla, who is that man you are dining with? I don't know why you are trying to play me."

"Tyrone, you are crazy, you need to have your head examined. I am not in a relationship with you, now get the heck off my phone and don't ever call my phone again and I mean that."

"Kayla hear this…,"

"No Tyrone, you hear this!" Kayla slams the phone down so hard that the people can hear it at the next table. She makes sure to turn her phone off so that they won't be interrupted by Tyrone Tyler again.

And of course, Tyrone is scheming to try and find dirt on Reginald and he doesn't even know the man. Tyrone is going to do whatever it takes to make sure that Reginald has nothing to do with Kayla. Kayla has moved on from Tyrone, but for some reason he cannot seem to move on. He drives away, seemingly defeated by the thought that another man is in Kayla's life. Tyrone drives back to work. He arrives for a meeting, but his mind is still on Kayla; he won't rest until he finds some dirt on Reginald. *I don't like him, there is something fishy about this Reginald character and if anyone can get the dirt, I am the one. Reginald must be out of his mind if he thinks that he will ever have a chance with Kayla. He will never ever have the opportunity to even kiss Kayla. I don't want that man anywhere near my child. I will hurt him if he is going to replace me in my child's life. This war has just begun.*

Meanwhile, Reginald and Kayla are enjoying a candlelight dinner. Reginald is infatuated with Kayla. He can't help but notice how gorgeous Kayla is. "You are so fine, and I am going to do whatever it takes to make you my better half."

"Reginald, what are you talking about? Reginald don't you think that it's weird to say that I am your better half, and this is only our first date?"

"Kayla, there is nothing weird about me calling you my better half. I fell for you the moment that we met, just give us a chance to be together."

"Reginald, I have a daughter."

"Kayla, that's okay. I fell for Kendra the moment you mentioned her name."

Kayla is shocked by what Reginald is saying. "Boy, are you for real?"

"Kayla, I am a man who believes that action does speak louder than words. So, I'm going to show you how I feel about you and Kendra. You deserve to be happy and that's what I want to do, make you happy for the next thirty years."

"Reginald, what do you mean the next thirty years? I was thinking more like fifty years." "That sounds good to me. "They both chuckle.

Kayla is listening, but she is very hesitant in believing what Reginald has said to her because of the craziness that happened between her and Tyrone. Tyrone has made it very clear that he thinks Kayla's child is his, even though DNA has proven that he is not the father. *I have a nice man who likes me and my daughter and who wants to be with me. Tyrone can go suck a few lemons.*

"Kayla, did you just hear what I said?"

"Yes, Reginald, I heard everything you said."

"Kayla, is something bothering you, or am I bothering you? Because you seem like you are in another world."

"Reginald, I want you to know that I like you, but I don't want you to get mixed up in my drama."

"Too late, Kayla, I'm already in it. So, tell me what your drama is so that we can handle it together."

"I was dating a married man for five years he promised me that he was going to leave his wife, he claimed that she couldn't have any children. I knew it was wrong and every time I tried to leave he would make false promises; and I would fall for the lies time and time again until his lies caught up with him and his wife spotted me in her house. At the time, I thought that I was pregnant with his child; but eventually I learned that it was not his child. At the same time, I was also dating my business partner, who eventually became my husband. I ended up becoming pregnant with my husband's baby, but for some reason, my married ex-lover thinks that the baby is his; even though we had every test in the world to prove that he isn't the father. He is the worst of the worst and I regret ever knowing him, but sometimes you cannot help who you fall in love with."

"Do you mean Tyrone Tyler? I knew who you were talking about without you ever mentioning his name. I met him through a mutual friend Antonio Anderson. Kayla how in the world did you get mixed up with a character like that? Tyrone doesn't know the meaning of what a real man is or how a real man is supposed to treat a woman."

"Reginald that's a bit scary that you know Tyrone. I am almost scared to talk to you. I don't know about this, Reginald, this changes things."

"Kayla, what are you talking about? I don't think you heard me correctly. I said that I met him, I don't know that much about him, except for what I've been told about how he treats women. I hope that you don't hold that against me. I have strong feelings for you and I really want to see where this goes."

CHAPTER FOURTEEN

Antonio is so upset at the way he acted at the restaurant; he cannot believe that he let Tyrone take him there. Vikki is very quiet on the drive home; she is trying not to let this situation get to her because she could lose the baby and if that happens Antonio will lose his mind. He will never forgive himself for putting her in a position to miscarry his child.

Vikki has to tell Antonio what the doctor said about her being on bedrest, because if he finds out any other way she knows that it will definitely be a situation, and that won't be fun at all.

"Wife of mine, why are you so quiet?"

"I'm just thinking, Antonio. Do you think I will make a good mother?"

"Vikki, where in the world did that come from? I don't think that you will make a good mother…" Before Antonio can finish the rest of his sentence, Vikki has caught an attitude because she can't believe that Antonio would say that to her. "Vikki, would you let me finish. I don't think that you would make a good mother, I know for a fact that you will be a great mother to our children."

"Antonio, what do you mean our children?"

"Wife of mine, I know that you don't think that AJ is going to be an only child."

"There you go, thinking that it's going to be a boy."

"Vikki, I feel it in my spirit." They both laugh at his comments.

"Antonio, you are funny… you have jokes."

Antonio and Vikki arrive home; but to their surprise Cassie is not home. Antonio immediately calls her cell phone. "Antonio, what are you doing?"

"I'm calling my mother; she should have been home from her date already."

"Antonio, leave your mother alone, let her enjoy herself. I happen to think that she and Wallace make a wonderful couple."

"Vikki please, it is eleven o'clock at night."

"So, what is that supposed to mean Antonio? Your mother is a responsible adult, and if Wallace makes her happy then I think that she should be able to date whom she wants."

"I have a problem with that, Vikki."

Just as Antonio says this, he hears a car pull into the driveway. "Well look who's here." Antonio flings the door open and angrily greets his mother and Wallace. "Mother where have you been? Goodbye Wallace I need to speak to my mother. Come inside mom, so that we can talk."

"Antonio, Wallace is my friend and that is no way to talk to him, and I am not going anywhere with you until you change that tone of yours."

"Antonio, will you leave Wallace and your mother alone, they are grown adults and they are enjoying each other's company. Sorry about my husband's behavior, Wallace." Vikki grabs Antonio's hand and escorts him back into the house; she closes the door behind them. "Antonio, what is your problem? Your mother seems to like Wallace and he really likes her, so why don't you just let it go."

"Vikki, I know that, but I do not want him thinking that he is going to take my father's place."

"Antonio, I don't think that Wallace is trying to take your father's place. He is just a friend to your mother, and she is enjoying the friendship. You need to let it go."

"Vikki, I want to believe that, but I believe that there is a motive to this Wallace dude, and believe me, I will find out sooner than later."

"Antonio baby, please leave Wallace alone. You need to get over this. I know you love your mother and you were close to your father. I know that they had a wonderful marriage, they were married for thirty-five years, and all of us are still reeling from his death. She has moved on, and I know you think there is no one who can replace him; but you have to give Wallace a chance and by the way I think your mother is smart enough to know whether or not Wallace is authentic. Wallace would you like something to drink?"

"Vikki, I think he had enough to drink. The only thing he should be drinking is a cold glass of water and he needs to finish that as quickly as possible so he can leave."

"Antonio, in case you didn't get the memo, Wallace is a friend of mine. I know you miss your father and I do as well, but I have to live my life. I need someone in my life."

"Mother, that is why you have me and Vikki and your soon to be grandchild."

"I get that Antonio, and I am happy that you are concerned about me, but I am entitled to have some enjoyment in my life. I like Wallace and I am going to continue to date him and if he and I decide that we don't want to be together we will be the ones making the decisions, not your or anyone else for that matter. Now give it a break and let it go."

"I am going to leave it alone for now, mother; but if he does anything to hurt you he will definitely be answering to me. Vikki I'm going in the kitchen to get a bite to eat, would you like something?"

"Just some ice-cream, thanks honey."

"You're welcome."

"Vikki, you looked tired."

"I am, Mother Cassie, it's been a draining day for me; way more drama than I can handle, but I will be okay once I get some rest."

"Have you told Antonio what the doctor said?"

"Not so loud, I don't want Antonio to know anything yet. I will tell Antonio when the time is right."

"So, what is it that you want to tell me, Vikki?"

"Nothing, Antonio."

"Oh, it's something. You have been whispering to my mother, and when I come into a room you get quiet. Okay Vikki, since you won't tell me, maybe my mother will tell me what it is that you are holding back from me."

"Antonio, that is something that you need to discuss with your wife."

"Mother, I am trying to discuss whatever it is that she is hiding, but she isn't saying anything to me. Now, one way or another, one of you is going to tell me what's going on. So, this is what I am going to do; I am going to give you both fifteen minutes to think about what you are going to say to me and then I will be back."

"Wallace, I do want to apologize to you. It seems that my mother likes you and she should be able to have a friend or two so as long as she doesn't get hurt."

"Antonio, you have my word. I will not do anything to hurt your mother, she is a wonderful woman and I love her company."

"Wallace, how come you aren't married?"

"Antonio, young man, my wife passed away three years ago. It took me almost two years to finally start dating. If it weren't for my children I would probably still be in the house."

"How many children do you have?"

"I have three adults and I would really like for them to meet your mother; she is very special to me…"

"and Wallace, my mother is special to me and I want to make sure that she is taken care of the right way."

"Antonio, that is not a problem, but you have to give me a chance."

"Wallace, as long as I don't see a tear on my mother's face, then I guess we are okay; but the minute she tells me that you have hurt her, then it will definitely be a situation between the two of us. I hope that I make myself clear Wallace."

"Antonio, son, I hear you loud and clear and I promise you have nothing to worry about."

"We will see about that, time will tell, Wallace. It was nice talking to you; now I have to go and resolve something with my mother and my wife."

"It was a pleasure speaking with you as well, Antonio; and I am glad that we were able to talk to each other man to man. I must be going now. Peace and blessings to you Antonio, and all the best this season."

"Thank you Wallace, and if you ever want to go to a game don't hesitate to ask for tickets, I will hold you down."

"Thank you, and see you later, Antonio."

Antonio heads to the kitchen. "Well, have you two figured out who would tell me what my lovely wife is hiding from me?"

"Antonio honey, I am not hiding anything from you…"Just as Vikki lies to Antonio she begins to get cramps."

"Vikki, are you okay?"

"I am okay, Antonio."

"No, you aren't, so tell me now what is really going on."

"Antonio, I told you that I am okay."

"Mother, what is wrong with Vikki? I want the truth and I want it now."

"I am so sorry, Vikki, but I cannot hide this type of stuff from my son. Well, Antonio here it goes. The doctor told Vikki that she needs to be on bedrest for a month or so, but then doctor called and told her that she needs to be on bedrest longer than that; and she cannot be stressed, otherwise she will lose the baby.

Vikki, I know that you are mad at me; but that is my grandchild that you are carrying, and I want only the best for you and the baby."

"Vikki, I can't believe that you would hide something like that from me and try to harm you and the baby."

"Antonio, I am okay. I won't do anything to harm the baby."

"Antonio, my son, there is more."

"What, you have to be kidding me! What else is there, Vikki?"

"Antonio, I don't know what you're talking about."

"Antonio, that's not true. Vikki told me that not only is she supposed to be on bedrest for two months of her pregnancy, but she is trying to open up a boutique and she wants to open it while you are at training camp. I told her that would not be a good idea for her to open a boutique now, but she keeps on insisting on opening it up and she thinks that everything will be okay."

"Vikki, I am so upset right now. I cannot believe that you would try and put my baby in harm's way."

"Antonio, I would never do that on purpose, it's just that I didn't want you to always have to worry about me, so I decided to open my own store."

"Vikki, that's nice; but you can't possibly open a store and be pregnant at the same time."

"Antonio, lots of women are pregnant and run their own businesses. I'm only one month."

"I understand that Vikki, but that is the most important time in a woman's pregnancy that's the time that she can miscarry. Vikki, it doesn't matter; my mother will be here with you to make sure that you get the rest that you need. You will have to put the opening of the boutique on hold."

"Antonio, I'm not putting my opening on hold."

"Vikki, I am your husband and I said that I don't want you opening a boutique now."

"Antonio, what is your issue with me owning a boutique?"

"Vikki, I would never stop you from owning your own boutique. I just think that you need to have people working there while you are on bedrest."

"Antonio, I have a staff. I just need to be there for the opening of the boutique; and I promise you, Antonio, after that I will have your mother check and make sure that everything is running smoothly."

"Vikki, the only way I will let you do that is if my mother is there to make sure that you aren't stressing and doing everything."

"Antonio, I will do you one better. I will take over the day-to-day operations for Vikki, until further notice. Mother Cassie I don't think you need to do that; I will be alright."

"Vikki, you won't be alright and starting today you will be on bedrest; and this isn't doctor's orders this is your husband's orders, you will not be doing anything else from this day forth."

"Antonio, will you stop treating me like I'm a baby. I can take care of things at the boutique and around the house."

"Vikki, I'm not listening to anything you are saying right now. So, as of right now, I will be taking care of you until I leave for training camp. Mom, after I leave, I need you to watch over both my babies until I get some time off from training camp. After that, I will be gone for about six weeks and then I get a week off and I will be home to help take care of Vikki and the baby."

"Antonio, you don't have to do that. I will take care of myself and the baby."

"Damn it, Vikki, do not tell me what to do when it comes to you and our child.

It's quite obvious that you aren't in a position to take care of you or the baby; otherwise you would have listened to the doctor's orders."

"What is that supposed to mean, Antonio? Are you suggesting that I am an incompetent mother?"

"Vikki, that is not what I said, and you know that."

"Then, what are you trying to say, Antonio?"

"Vikki, I love you but sometimes you can be a little stubborn and want to do things your way, and I always let you do things your way; but I am pulling rank on you as your husband and I say that you will be on bedrest, and anything that you need my mother is here to help, and I will call Vanessa and see if she can stop by to help out."

"Antonio, I don't want Vanessa to take time out of her schedule to come and help me. I am not helpless; I can get around. I will be okay."

"Antonio, Vikki is in capable hands and to make sure that everything runs smoothly, Wallace has volunteered to help me out."

"Wallace has volunteered to help you with what?"

"With your wife, that's who."

"Cassie, thank you, but I don't need Wallace's help at all."

"Mother dear, that man will not be here taking care of you, Vikki or the baby. He has his own place and he can stay there. You can talk to him over the phone, but nothing more than that."

"Antonio, I am your mother, the nerve of you to tell me who can or cannot visit me."

"Mother, this is my house and if I ask that Wallace not be here, then Wallace cannot be here. I don't know him, and I definitely don't want him staying here while I am at training camp."

"Then Antonio, maybe I don't need to be here to help your wife."

"Thank you Mother Cassie, that is what I have been saying all along. I am okay, and I do not need anyone to help me right now. Why can't you guys understand that?"

"Vikki, at this point, I really don't care what you think or how you feel. My mother will be here full-time to watch you, that's final and this conversation is over."

"But Antonio…,"

"But nothing, Vikki. For the last time, this conversation is over I'm moving on to something else."

"Mother," where are you going?"

"Antonio, I have a date with Wallace."

"Mother, this will make four times this week."

"So what, Antonio. I can go out with Wallace as much as I want to. Antonio, we are not having this conversation again."

"This is it, I told you this before. I don't know why you don't understand or get it. But I don't want you seeing Wallace like that."

"And again, as your mother, Antonio, this conversation is over. Wallace will be here in a few minutes and I am definitely going to enjoy myself."

"Cassie, please get dressed and don't listen to anything Antonio is saying. He loves to bark out orders when he is mad."

"Vikki, I'm not a dog, I don't bark out orders. I want you and my mother to listen and listen well. I pay the mortgage and all the bills, so I can say what I want when I want to; and if either of you don't like it, you both know what you can do."

"Antonio, I can't believe that you are kicking me and your mother out. I'm pregnant with your baby. You know what, you don't have to kick me out. I will gladly leave and don't worry about me, I have somewhere to go. Me and my baby will be just fine."

"Vikki, where are you going?"

"Mother Cassie, I will stay with one of my friends; it beats being subjected to this foolishness that my husband is putting me through."

"Antonio, are you going to let your pregnant wife leave and not follow behind her?" "Mother, you can leave with her. Like I said, I am done with this conversation. I am going downstairs in my den to watch movies."

"Vikki, don't cry. Antonio is not mad at you; he is mad with me and he is taking it out on you. Give me a few moments and I will talk to him for you."

"Thanks, but there is no need to do that, Mother Cassie. I am gone and I might not return."

"Vikki, you can't leave like this. Something is definitely bothering Antonio, and I am going to talk to him about it."

"That's fine and all Mother Cassie; but right now, I won't subject myself to his foolishness. I hope your date with Wallace turns out okay."

Antonio returns upstairs. "Why are you still here? I told you that if you can't follow my rules then you have to leave."

"Antonio, I am leaving."

"Son I don't think that you should talk to your wife like that."

"I was talking to you too, mother."

"Antonio, I will not be disrespected. I am leaving."

"Mother, that's fine, and make sure that you call Wallace and tell him to meet you somewhere else."

"Antonio, if I want Wallace to meet me here, he will meet me here. Antonio are you going to let your pregnant wife leave and not try to stop her?"

"Mother, you can leave with her. Thank you."

Just as Antonio says this, the doorbell rings… it's Wallace. He is excited to see Cassie, that is until Antonio answers the door. "What do you want Wallace?"

"Antonio, I'm here to pick up your mother. Can I come inside?"

"Wallace, no you cannot, you can wait for my mother in your car."

"Antonio, why are you being so cruel to Wallace? Antonio what is wrong with you? There is definitely something wrong with you, your attitude is horrible."

"Mother, I am okay, I just don't want Wallace in my house. Now where is Vikki?"

"Antonio, did you forget that you told her to leave? So, she packed her bags and left you and your attitude behind."

"Well, where did she go?"

"Antonio, she went to stay with a friend. She is probably with Vanessa."

"Mother, please call Vanessa and tell her to ask Vikki to come home."

As Mother Cassie is calling Vanessa's cell phone, Vanessa receives a call on her cell phone... it's the police. Vanessa tells Mother Cassie that she will call her back because the police are on the other line.

"Good afternoon, this is Vanessa Brown, how can I help you?"

"Hello, my name is Officer Clarke, I have you as an emergency contact for Vikki Anderson. Do you know Vikki Anderson?"

"Yes, Officer Clarke, I know Vikki Anderson. She is my best friend. Officer Clarke, is there something wrong with Vikki?"

"I am sorry, Mrs. Anderson was involved in a car crash and she had to be rushed to Victor Memorial Hospital."

"Thank you, Officer Clarke, I am on my way to the hospital." Vanessa is literally shaking as she hangs up the phone with Officer Clarke.

Meanwhile, Antonio is still on a tirade; he has no idea that Vikki was involved in a serious car crash. "Mother didn't I ask you to call Vikki, why haven't you called her?"

"Antonio, I don't know who you think that you are talking too; and for the record, I called Vanessa. She said she had to take a call and would call me back; but since you are acting like a butt hole, I will call her one more time."

"Hello Vanessa, this is Mother Cassie again. I don't mean to bother you but, Antonio asked me to call you, he wants to speak to Vikki."

"Mother Cassie, I am sorry, but Vikki is not here."

"Vanessa, what do you mean she is not at your house."

"Mother Cassie, I was just on my way to the hospital. Vikki was involved in a serious car accident."

"She what! Oh, my goodness, which hospital is she in?"

"She is at Victor Memorial."

"Thank you Vanessa, I am on my way over there now. Oh, my goodness, Antonio is going to be hurt when he hears this."

"Antonio, I spoke to Vanessa."

"So, how come you didn't put Vikki on the phone?"

"Well Antonio, that's what I wanted to talk to you about. How do I say this?"

"How do you say what, Mother?"

"Antonio, Vikki is in the hospital."

"Repeat what you just said, Mother."

"Antonio, I said that Vikki is in the hospital."

"Mother, you are lying, there is no way Vikki is in the hospital. Who told you that?"

"Vanessa told me, and she is Vikki's best friend; so, you know she wouldn't lie about a thing like that."

"Mother, why would the hospital call Vanessa and not me? I am her husband."

"Maybe because you put her out and she probably thinks that you don't care about her."

"Mother, Vikki is my wife. I will always love her. I have to get out of here and go see her. What hospital is she at?"

"She is at Victor Memorial Hospital."

"Let's go."

They leave the house and Cassie lets Wallace know that she can't go on a date with him because they have to get to the hospital immediately.

"What's wrong, Cassie?"

"Wallace, Vikki was in a serious car accident, we do not have time to talk we need to get there now."

"Cassie, you can drive with me."

"I don't think that's a good idea, Wallace. Antonio is torn apart and he is in no condition to be driving."

"Antonio, I will drive."

Cassie is driving like a maniac, so much so that she gets stopped by the police.

She informs them that her daughter-in-law was in a serious car accident and that they need to get to the hospital right away.

"Hi, I am Officer Oakley. I am sorry, but I need to see your license and registration."

As Officer Oakley is speaking Antonio hands him his identification. Officer Oakley is stunned and realizes that he has stopped the number one player in the League. Officer Oakley gives Antonio back his identification and escorts both cars to the hospital.

Antonio, Wallace and Cassie are immediately taken to the Intensive Care Unit. Antonio is beside himself when he sees Vikki hooked up to breathing machines.

Wallace and the doctors catch Antonio, just as he is about to faint. Antonio now realizes that it is his fault that Vikki is in the

Intensive Care Unit. Antonio starts praying. He needs God now, more than ever. He cannot believe that because of his irresponsible behavior his wife is in this condition. Antonio will not be able to live with himself if Vikki doesn't make it. "God, please bless my wife and allow her to live and be made whole again."

Just as Antonio begins to pray the doctor walks into the room. "Hello Mr. Anderson, I am Dr. Lorenzo… "Before the doctor can say another word, Antonio wants to know the state of Vikki's condition. "Mr. Anderson, your wife did receive a lot of trauma to her body, but we were able to stop the bleeding. Mr. Anderson, your wife is going to okay, but she will have to stay in the hospital for a while."

"Oh, my goodness, Dr. Lorenzo, what about the baby?"

"What baby? I am sorry Mr. Anderson, but I was not informed that your wife was pregnant. Please excuse me, I need everyone to leave the room while I examine her."

"Sorry, Dr. Lorenzo, but as long as my wife is hooked up to that machine, I'm not leaving this room."

"I do understand, Mr. Anderson, but I just think it's a good idea that you leave; you can sit in the waiting area of the room."

"Antonio, we have to listen to the doctor, son. I know you are hurt, but let him do his job. Wallace and I are here for you. Everything is going to be okay, son, I promise you. Let's go outside and continue to pray for Vikki's healing."

Everyone leaves the room, but Antonio is keeping a watchful eye at the door. He knows that this is a critical time. Antonio's faith is definitely being tested, but he won't stop praying. Just as Antonio finishes praying, in walks Vanessa. She is crying uncontrollably; she can't believe what happened to her best friend.

Vanessa, of course, wants to blame Antonio for this because if it had not been for his attitude, Vikki never would have left home in the first place. "Antonio, you put your wife and baby in danger, and I am very upset with you. Why would you put Vikki out of the house?" Vanessa is yelling at the top of her lungs. "Answer me, Antonio!"

"Vanessa, I know that you are upset; but you will not take that tone with me."

"Antonio, I could not give two rabbits behinds about how you feel, you are going to answer my question!"

"Vanessa, it is not what you think."

"Then what is it, Antonio?"

"If you must know, I injured myself a few weeks ago; and for the first time since I have gone professional, I'm going to be out for the first three weeks of the season; and of course, I don't know what to do with myself."

"Antonio, you are supposed to talk to your wife about the situation, not throw her out of the house. My best friend is in this bed with tubes in her because of your pride and selfishness. If I wasn't a woman I might have knocked the taste out of your mouth."

Just as Antonio tries to say something else to Vanessa, Cassie and Wallace come in between the two of them.

"Vanessa and Antonio, you two are like family and I know that you are both upset about the situation with Vikki, but this isn't going to help her or either of you; so just stop it and be there for Vikki, she needs us to be a unit."

Before Cassie can finish talking to Vanessa and Antonio here comes the news reporters from every channel, they are all at the hospital. Antonio wants to know how in the world the news found out about Vikki's accident.

"Antonio, did you forget that you are a professional and well-respected athlete, so word will travel fast."

As one of the reporters begins to interview Antonio, in walks Tyrone. Vanessa asks Tyrone how he got past security.

"Vanessa, you know I can talk my way into any place."

"You don't belong here, especially after all the trouble you have caused people."

"Vanessa, I came here because I am concerned about Vikki; she is your best friend and I don't want to see her in this predicament."

"I don't believe you at all Tyrone, there is a motive for everything you do, you have never done anything because you are concerned. You are a bold face coward."

"Vanessa, I know you still harbor hate for me. Let me ask you this question. Have I not bothered you in the past six months? I am a changed man."

"If you say so, Tyrone, but you are not fooling me. I can't talk to you anymore; there are more important things to talk about and you are certainly not one of them."

"Vanessa, I really do want to stay. I know you are hurting."

"Against my better judgment, I am going to let you stay; but the minute you try to start any of your mess, I will have security escort you out with a swiftness."

"Vanessa, I promise not to cause any trouble."

As the reporter approaches Antonio to find out what happened, Tyrone snatches the microphone and begins to rant that Vikki Anderson got exactly what she deserved because she cheated on her husband with an event planner and that Antonio threw her out of the house because of her affair.

Wallace grabs the mike from Tyrone and clocks him with a mean left hook, all hell breaks loose in the hospital. Everyone is in disbelief. Wallace is immediately detained by the officers. Vanessa and Cassie are both crying uncontrollably. Vanessa is so pissed that she begins to scream at the top of her lungs. "Tyrone Tyler, I knew you were a liar! You are a piece of …, you better be lucky that I don't curse. You better be glad I'm a lady, otherwise I would whip you like a man. How dare you start drama in my best friend's hospital room. Can somebody please get this piece of trash out of my face!"

Tyrone has to be picked up off the floor by hospital personnel. Antonio has to be held back by his coach and a few of his teammates, it's taking everything in him not to beat the living hell out of Tyrone.

Antonio is asked by a reporter if he would like to respond to the allegations that were just mentioned by Tyrone Tyler. Before Antonio can utter a word out of his mouth, his teammate Juan Martinez speaks up to say something. "This man is a clown who is miserable but what I don't understand is that he is a partner in one of the top Investment firms in the country, and rich as all get up, yet he spends his time worrying about other people's lives."

Antonio screams at the top of his lungs, "I need everyone to leave now, my wife doesn't need to hear this right now. My main concern is that she has a speedy recovery. And just to let everyone know, the person by the name of Tyrone Tyler is always starting mess with people, all because he was having an affair while he was married and that's all I will say. Thank you to everyone and continue to keep my family in your prayers. Good night and goodbye."

Everyone leaves but Tyrone. He is still ranting like a baby, but he got what he deserves; he is always trying to be a man, but not the man. He is pathetic. The news reporter asks Tyrone if there is anything he wants to say. Tyrone has to make it about himself, so of course, he is going to take full advantage of this situation.

I am going to sue the city of East Hampton, this hospital and the entire League; and, of course, Juan Martinez. No one ever punches Tyrone Tyler and thinks that they will get away with it. I did nothing to provoke this situation. My lip is busted and everyone on national television saw what happened; this is going to be good; my lawyer is going to have a field day with this."

"One more question, Mr. Tyler, what does Juan Martinez have to do with any of this? He wasn't the person that hit you."

"I don't care he opened his mouth."

"All I need to know is what time this will air so that I can tell everyone to watch."

"It will be on WEHY at 6:00 p.m."

Tyrone is a major dog; he is trying to flirt with the newscaster Patrice Sparks while she is trying to do a story. Tyrone thinks that every woman wants him. He has totally forgotten about Sheila.

"My name is Tyrone Tyler you might know me; I am one of the richest black men this side of East Hampton. I am single and I know you want to have dinner with me, so here is what I am going to do. I am giving you my business card, call me when your schedule permits. I believe you will make yourself available for a dinner date with me, sooner than later. And by the way, consider yourself special because I don't give my number to just anyone. And I also know that you are going to accept my dinner date."

"Oh, you are that sure of yourself? I don't think so Mr. Tyler I don't know you and from what I have seen so far I don't particularly like you or the way you act."

"Patrice, I am shocked. You just met me and already you think that you don't like me. What is it about me that you think that you don't like?"

Mr. Tyler, I just don't like you period, point blank. Did that answer your question? And by the way, it is Ms. Sparks to you."

"My apologies, Ms. Sparks, how do I change your dislike into like?"

"Mr. Tyler, I don't like you and unless Jesus comes and sits on my shoulder and tells me otherwise, we can't talk in this lifetime or another lifetime."

Tyrone is appalled, he still thinks that he can get a shot with Patrice Sparks.

He goes as far as slipping his business card into her pocketbook, when she turns around to do something.

Patrice finds the card and angrily tries to hand it back to Tyrone. Look buster, I just told you that I do not like you and I told you the first time when you tried to give me your business card that I wasn't interested; and you slipping your business card into my pocketbook is definitely not going to help you win any brownie points with me. Why don't you just give it up? Concentrate on getting better and leaving other people alone. Have a wonderful evening Mr. Tyler." Patrice is so upset with Tyrone, she storms out of the hospital when she realizes that she still has his business card in her hand, so she rips it up and throws it away.

Patrice races back to the news station to get an edge on the story about Tyrone. Patrice arrives at the station, and in record time, she runs to get the tape to the newsroom. She doesn't want to edit the incident; she wants everyone who watches the news to see the incident in all of its rawness. Meanwhile, back at the hospital, Tyrone is giving the staff a hard way to go because he does not like what type of food he is being served; so he decides that he is going to pull a few strings and order specialty food, or so he thinks that he can do that. Tyrone has spent a lot of money to have the best of everything he can imagine in his room, but Tyrone's bubble is about to burst because hospital policy states that he cannot have specialty food in his room unless permission is granted by the lead doctor. Tyrone is totally upset. He is going off on people and what he doesn't know is that he is being recorded; this is going to make for good and exciting news.

Patrice has just finished reviewing the video footage from Tyrone's antics from earlier today this is going to be one for the records. Before Patrice can air the story Tyrone is somehow able to get through to the station and contact her.

"Well hello beautiful, how are you this evening."

"May I ask who this is that is calling?"

"This is Tyrone Tyler; you have been on my mind all day and I just had to call you."

"Mr. Tyler, do you realize that I am at work; and last but not least, how in the world were you able to get through to me?"

Ms. Sparks, I have connections and when I am interested in someone I do what I have to do to get what I want."

"Mr. Tyler, please don't call my job again."

Patrice is so pissed off that she almost curses, but she hangs up the phone in Tyrone's ear. Now Tyrone is quite pissed off, he doesn't like anyone to disrespect him; but for some reason Tyrone has kept his cool with Patrice.

Patrice says to herself, *it's going down whether Tyrone likes it or not.* Tyrone is excitedly waiting to see the story, he cannot wait. He positions himself in bed to watch this story and what a story it is. Patrice did not leave anything to the imagination. This story is going to rock Tyrone's world. He is so upset by what he just saw that he immediately calls his attorney; he wants to sue Patrice Sparks and WEHY-TV.

Tyrone uses every curse word that he can think of that comes to mind and he tells his attorney to sue WEHY for everything that he can get. Tyrone calls the station because he wants to catch Patrice before she leaves the station; but it's already too late Patrice is halfway home and Tyrone has no way to contact her right now.

Tyrone is so heated that he can't contact Patrice that he decides he is going to discharge himself from the hospital. As he is getting dressed to leave, Doctor Lorenzo is coming to check on him, but he sees that Tyrone is leaving; and so, Doctor Lorenzo tells him that he shouldn't leave because he hasn't properly healed.

"Doctor Lorenzo, I have a more pressing issue than sitting in this room for one or two more days."

"Mr. Tyler, what is more pressing than your health?"

"Doctor Lorenzo how about the fact that I was embarrassed publicly on television for the entire state of New York to see, and I don't like it at all. I need to leave so that I can restore my name. I have people that I need to sue, and I need to get back to work to make money. Every day that I am in this hospital is a day that I'm not making money."

"Mr. Tyler, I don't advise that. I think that you need to calm down, relax and let this situation die down on its own. By tomorrow, this will be old news."

"Doctor Lorenzo, right now I don't care what you advise. I just need you to sign my discharge papers. I will be okay. If this is what you want, then I will sign them. It will take about thirty minutes to get them signed and then you can leave."

Tyrone is pacing around the room; he is still angry, and he tries unsuccessfully again to reach the television station because he wants to curse Patrice out. Tyrone actually gets through to the station, but by now Patrice has already warned everyone about Tyrone and they saw his antics on tape; so, they are going to do everything in their power to make sure that Tyrone does not get through to Patrice directly. Tyrone is pissed off, he is calling the staff every name in the book, and they are secretly recording Tyrone because they are going to use these recordings against him, if necessary. Patrice is about to leave the station, and this is the first time in her three years at the station that she has asked one of the security guards to walk her to her car. It's a good thing that she did. Tyrone has decided to roll up to the station. He is so heated that he jumps out of his car as soon as he spots Patrice; and, of course, he gets in her face. It has to take more than one security guard to separate Tyrone from trying to hit Patrice. Patrice is a petite-sized woman, but one thing is for sure, she can definitely hold her own weight and Tyrone is light weight to her; but she is going to act like a professional because she knows that Tyrone is not worth losing anything. She cannot wait to tell her boyfriend what happened.

Tyrone is still screaming at Patrice. He raises his hand as though he is going to slap Patrice and that is when security calls for backup, police are everywhere. Tyrone realizes that he is surrounded and can be in trouble, for the first time in his life. Tyrone is quiet as never before; he realizes he could lose everything. Officer Scott approaches and gives his name and badge number to Patrice and asks her if she is okay and if she would like to press charges against Tyrone.

Patrice prepares to answer Officer Scott, when Tyrone tells the officer that everything is okay. "Excuse me, but I was not talking to you, I was asking Ms. Sparks if everything is alright. Can you let her answer? Sir, you look familiar, have I seen you somewhere before?"

"Officer Scott, I'm quite sure that you have never seen me before, and they always say people have a look-alike."

"I usually don't forget a face, what is your last name?"

"It's Tyler."

"I knew it, I do remember you. I came to your house about a year or so ago; your wife at the time called me because she thought someone had broken into your home."

"That's right, Officer Scott, and when I saw you I believe you told me that there was an attorney at your house who was dropping off contracts to you. Whatever happened with that situation?"

"Let's just say that things didn't work out the way that I had planned." Tyrone is scared because he doesn't know what Patrice is going to say and it could cost him a lot if she says anything.

"Officer Scott, I am sorry that you had to be pulled away from more important cases to come here for frivolous nonsense like this, but I am okay it is just a really big misunderstanding."

"Ms. Sparks, are you sure that you don't want to press charges?"

"That won't be necessary, everything is okay."

"Ms. Sparks, are you absolutely sure? Just say the word and this creep will be locked up."

"Again, Officer Scott, that won't be necessary. I just want to go home."

"Well, Ms. Sparks, here's my card; call me if you change your mind."

"Thank you, Officer Scott, and have a great day."

"You as well, Ms. Sparks."

Tyrone waits until Officer Scott leaves before he steps to Patrice. "Thank you for not saying anything to Officer Scott."

"Look Tyrone, I could have pressed charges against you, but I realized that I have a lot to lose and you simply aren't worth my time."

"How can you press charges? I didn't do anything to you?"

"Tyrone, have you heard of attempted assault? And in case you haven't heard of it, that law does exist, and you could have gotten in a lot of trouble. And you are right about the fact that you didn't do anything to me, you did it to yourself; and now you are mad because you acted like a fool in front of people which you provoked; and then, when it was aired on the news you want to fight me. You are crazier than I thought, thinking that I embarrassed you. Tyrone, get a life and get out of my face so I can go home."

"Patrice, do you know who I am? I am not someone you want to mess with. I will hurt you in more ways than one."

Patrice brushes past Tyrone and gets into her car; she slams the door, ignoring Tyrone as he is ranting on and on about nothing. Patrice speeds away. Tyrone jumps in his car, and as he is driving home he is thinking of how he can get back at Patrice and the television station.

Patrice finally arrives home, she is still so upset about what happened with Tyrone that she drops everything on the living room floor and immediately calls her boyfriend, Gabriel, and tells him what happened to her. Gabriel is beyond livid; but for the sake of Patrice, he is being level-headed and listening to what she is telling him.

"Patrice baby, I am on my way to your house now, hold that thought."

Gabriel arrives at Patrice's house, he got there in record time. He is trying to make light of the situation, but he knows this isn't over by a long shot and he will step to Tyrone much sooner than later. "Babe, why are you stressing over this Tyrone Tyler dude? He will have his day in court and remember what goes around eventually comes back around."

"But Gabriel, he was disrespectful and totally rude, and I thought that as my man you would be angry and upset."

"Listen babe, just because I'm not screaming or threatening to kick his butt does not mean that I'm not angry, I handle my anger differently. I have your back and I am with you; but right now, there is something else that I want to talk about; and it is much better than talking about that Tyrone dude, and I promise you that you will feel a whole lot better."

"Gabriel, what are you talking about?" Gabriel begins to kiss Patrice on the neck and she almost gets into it, but she stops Gabriel before he makes another move.

Gabriel is puzzled by Patrice's actions because she never pulls away from him. "Okay babe, what's wrong? This is definitely not you Patrice. Is there someone else in the picture?"

"Gabriel, are you kidding me right now? We had an agreement that we would not sleep with each other or do anything else until we are married."

"Patrice baby, I can't wait that long."

"Gabriel, it's only two more months and that will be here before you know it. You know I don't like this; but because I am madly in love with you, I am willing to give you what you want."

"Gabriel, that is why you are the only man for me."

"I cannot wait to be Mrs. Gabriel Bray." Patrice is dancing around in a sexy gown, as she is saying this. Gabriel notices that Patrice doesn't have her engagement ring on her finger.

"Patrice, I want you to explain to me why your engagement ring is not on your finger. Wait, let me sit down first so I can hear this lame excuse."

"Gabriel, what are you talking about lame excuse. I took it off because as you can see I cut my finger and I didn't have the chance to put a band-aid on it, it's been hurting me all day and my ring was irritating the cut. And for the record Gabriel I don't like you thinking that I would make an excuse, when it comes to my engagement ring. I have never taken this ring or you for granted and don't you ever forget that. Look, it's getting late and we both have to get to work early tomorrow."

Patrice kisses Gabriel on the forehead and just as she is about to walk away he pulls her closer to him. Patrice is trying her best to resist, but she can't because Gabriel is so much stronger than she is.

Patrice is five feet four inches with a mocha chocolate complexion and a pair of legs that would make every man and woman envious of her and she has a body that makes you go hmm. Gabriel is making it very hard for her to pull away; she is trying her best, but the more he kisses her the less fight she has in her. Patrice is not doing a good job she is in love with this man and she knows that she has less than three months before they get married. *What harm could it do?* Patrice gives in to Gabriel's passion, and they have a night of blissful lust and love.

Patrice wakes up in Gabriel's arms. She is smiling from ear to ear, but something doesn't feel right to her; and now she thinks that it was a bad idea, but it happened. She jumps out of bed realizing that she has to get to work. so, she immediately jumps in the shower and while she is getting dressed thinking that Gabriel is asleep she kisses him on the lips to say goodbye, He pulls Patrice closer to him and tells her that he is the luckiest man alive.

"I love you Gabriel, I will see you later tonight." Gabriel sheepishly says goodbye. Patrice hurries and jumps into her car. She has to get to work sooner than later and she makes it to the station in record time. She now knows that she can't play around like that anymore with Gabriel, as much as she wants to. Her career means the world to her and she will not mess it up for anyone, not even for her future husband.

While Patrice is at work, Gabriel takes the opportunity to get some much-needed rest; but that doesn't matter because he doesn't get the rest that he needs. And that doesn't help because he can't help but think about how Tyrone treated Patrice, and he is definitely going to say something to him about it. Gabriel is six feet three inches tall and with a honey caramel complexion. He is the top judge where he lives and in all of the surrounding areas. Gabriel is also licensed in three other states. Not only is he good looking, but he is smart, rich and a force to be reckoned with. But don't get it twisted Gabriel can hold his own when needed, he grew up in the streets.

Gabriel takes a quick shower, he just realized that he has clothes at Patrice's house. He picks out a bad navy-blue suit with a wing tipped white shirt, and some bad navy-blue alligator shoes. He is looking oh so smooth and so fine. *What a man.* Gabriel leaves Patrice's condominium and jumps into his all black Maserati and drives off, but before he goes to work, he looks up Tyrone's business address and decides to stop by and have a little conversation with him.

Gabriel pulls up to Williams, Smith, Tyler and Peterson. He parks his car right in front of the building. Most people would worry about their car being on the street in front of a hydrant but not Gabriel. He is the most prominent judge in his city, no one would dare touch him or his car. As Gabriel approaches the lobby security, he is personally escorted to Williams, Smith, Tyler and Peterson. As he approaches the reception area, the women in the firm can't help but stare at this piece of fine man. Michele has been without a man for so long that she forgets to say "hello" when Gabriel approaches the reception desk. She says in her sexiest voice, "Hello there, how might I help you?"

"I am here to see Tyrone Tyler."

"One moment, I will get him for you."

Michelle is so nervous that she can't remember Tyrone's extension and she doesn't want Gabriel to think that she is a ditz, so she pretends that Tyrone is in a meeting and politely excuses herself. Michele walks so fast that she actually has a switch that it will make a man turn and stare at, for sure, and Gabriel is no different. Michele informs Tyrone that he has a visitor by the name of Gabriel and that is all she knows. Tyrone is puzzled but he tells Michele to give him a minute and he will come out soon to meet with him.

Tyrone is upset that Michele did not find out any information about this guy. But what the heck it could be another major deal for him. Michele has never been so efficient in her life she hurries back to the reception desk, just so that she can stare at Gabriel.

Although Tyrone is a jerk, one thing is for sure, that man has a swag about himself; he can dress, and he is fine as all get up. Tyrone approaches the reception area; he introduces himself to

Gabriel. Gabriel asks Tyrone if there is somewhere private that they can go and talk. Tyrone escorts Gabriel to his office.

Tyrone says to Gabriel, "How can I help you?"

"Well Tyrone, it seems that we have a friend in common and she told me that you were very rude to her the other day, and I don't like that at all."

"Well Gabriel, does this friend have a name?"

"Indeed, she does. Her name is Patrice Sparks."

"Oh, so Gabriel, you are sweet on Patrice?"

"Number one, it is Ms. Sparks to you, and not that it is any of your business or concern, but I know Ms. Sparks very well… we are best friends. She called me the other night and explained that you raised your hands to her and that you wanted to fight her because of a story that aired on her television station, is this true?"

"Look Gabriel, I don't have to answer you and I definitely do not have to justify my actions. Just know this, that the station that she works for will be non-existent when I get finished suing the hell out of them. Tell your best friend that I am coming for her as well, and I think it would be best if you stayed out of my way."

Gabriel does not like to raise his voice, but there are always extenuating circumstances, and this just happens to be one of those circumstances. "Look Tyrone, I am not a punk and I am definitely not one to make a spectacle of myself in public, so I am going to leave you with this. Don't ever disrespect Ms. Sparks again."

Tyrone is raising his voice. "Gabriel, I know you don't think that you are checking me, because you are totally out of your mind."

Just as Gabriel is about to answer Tyrone, Mark walks in he asks, "Is everything alright in here?"

Tyrone says to Mark, "This sucker was just leaving."

"Look man, I did not come here to start any trouble. Just don't disrespect Ms. Sparks anymore." Before Tyrone can get another word out edgewise, Gabriel tells him and Mark to have a good day and politely walks out of Tyrone's office and down the hall to the elevator. He is smiling, not because he told Tyrone off in a professional manner, but because of all the stares that he is getting from the women.

Tyrone is heated. By now he is ready to run down the hall and rip Gabriel's head off. As a matter of fact, he tries to go after Gabriel, but Mark stops him in his tracks. Mark says to Tyrone, "Man what the hell is wrong with you? Where do you think you are going?"

"Mark, that punk tried to disrespect me. Who does he think he is?"

"Actually Tyrone, he didn't do anything to you. He asked that you not disrespect his friend again. What's so bad about that?"

"Mark, he had no right to say anything to me."

"You know what Tyrone, get over it. I don't get you. Why do you think you can say or do things to people and there won't be a consequence? Now I am going to say this once and for all Tyrone, stop acting like a jerk and man up. You have clients and you need to concentrate on that."

"Man, Mark, I guess you are right."

"Tyrone, I know I'm right. Now let's get in here and make these coins."

"I hear you brother, let's do this."

"I will take care of that situation later."

"That's what I am talking about, Tyrone."

Michele jumps up and coyly says goodbye to Gabriel, he smiles with admiration. "Good afternoon young lady, have a nice day."

All the woman in the office just stop and stare as Gabriel enters the elevator. All the ladies look at each other and laugh. Michele says out loud to all the ladies.

"Girls, now that's what you call ***F.I.NE***."

Gabriel jumps in his car and speeds away. He has a smirk on his face because he knows that he just got under Tyrone's skin. He knows that Tyrone is going to try something; so, he is going to be well-prepared to clap back at Tyrone the moment he tries to come for him.

CHAPTER FIFTEEN

Patrice is at work reporting the news. She is totally unaware of what went on between Gabriel and Tyrone earlier; and she won't find out what happened, at least not right now anyway. Patrice is tired from a hard day of working. She decides to call her friend and college roommate, Sheila Smith. Sheila is so ecstatic to hear from Patrice. Both ladies arrange to meet at Desire's.

This will be Patrice's first experience going to Desire's. "Now you know, once you go to Desire's you will go again and again." She is excited to meet her college roommate. Patrice calls Gabriel and tells him to pick her up about six-thirty at Desire's; she is on her way to get her hair done. Sheila can't wait to see Patrice; they are both two successful women who worked their way to the top. Sheila is so anxious and excited because she hasn't seen her friend in over fifteen years and when they finally meet face to face all that Sheila can do is cry when she sees Patrice. Both women hug each other and that's when the tears start to flow. Delicious is his usual self, but he is patient because he knows these ladies haven't seen each other in years.

Delicious personally escorts the ladies to the rear of the salon, and he wants nothing but the best for them, so he is going to style Patrice since this is her first time at Desire's. "Patrice girl, you are blessed because Delicious is giving you the royal treatment, he never styles anyone."

"Sheila, how are you?"

"I'm great Delicious, now that I have my friend here with me in the same city."

"And who is this queen that I am working magic on today?"

"Delicious, this is my friend Patrice. I'm surprised that you don't know her she is the top female newscaster in town."

"Patrice, now I remember who you are. You did a story about Tyrone Tyler and his antics in the hospital, it aired a few nights ago. What I can't understand is what made him think that he was going to get away with his foolishness?"

Delicious says with a smile "Honey I loved it. You should have stuck him where it hurts, now Patrice if you would have mentioned anything about his mistress I think I would have been done. Next time stick it to him good."

"Delicious, I guess you don't like Tyrone?"

"Patrice, I don't have anything against him personally, it's that I don't like what he did to my friend Vanessa. She was a faithful and loving wife to him, and he had an affair for five of the twelve years that they were married and then he almost got the mistress pregnant."

Patrice asks, "Delicious how do you get someone almost pregnant? Either they are pregnant, or they aren't pregnant."

"Tyrone's mistress thought she was pregnant by him until the D.N.A results proved that she wasn't pregnant with his baby. She was carrying someone else's baby. In the end Tyrone had to pay child support for an unborn child who wasn't his; and the crazy thing is that he has to pay child support until the child is eighteen years of age. Now that's what I'm talking about."

"Delicious, can I ask you a question?"

"Sure, you can, Sheila."

"So, you mean to tell me that Tyrone cheated on his wife with another woman?"

"Yes, he did! That Negro is crazy, let me tell you what he told me. He said that he and his wife just fell out of love and that he wanted children, but that his wife wasn't ready to have children and that put a strain on the relationship. I think if I saw him now I would slap the taste completely out of his mouth."

"Sheila, you have got to be kidding me."

"The only thing he is right about is the fact that he wanted children, but he didn't want children with his wife; he wanted a family with his mistress and still be married to his wife at the same time. Sheila, I can't stand Tyrone."

Patrice chimes in on the conversation. "I just met him a day or so ago and from the moment he opened his mouth I knew that I would not like him."

"Sheila, why did you have lunch with him in the first place?" Delicious asks.

"Because I felt sorry for him. I have never seen a grown man drool the way he did, it was sickening."

They all crack up at what Sheila just said about Tyrone.

"Sheila, Tyrone can drool on me any day."

"Delicious, that's just nasty."

"Honey, I can do a lot of things with a man who drools." Patrice falls out hysterically, she can't believe that Delicious just said that.

"Delicious, you make getting my hair done worthwhile."

"Sheila girl, you need to get more than your hair done." Sheila asks Delicious if he just threw shade.

"Yes, I did…," But before Delicious can get anything else out of his mouth, in walks Gabriel. For the first time, Delicious is speechless. He runs up to Gabriel so fast that he almost trips and almost knocks over some of the equipment trying to get next to Gabriel.

"Hmmm, can I serve you? You are a variety of all the chocolates that I love – caramel and butterscotch filled with a whole lot of nuts."

"Excuse me, who are you?"

"Oh, I am so sorry. I am Delicious, and I am the owner of this establishment."

"Okay, and my name is Gabriel, and I am looking for Patrice."

"Gabriel, are you sure about that?"

"Yes, I am very sure… now where is she?"

"She is in the back finishing up."

"Thank you, I will wait."

Delicious immediately runs to find Patrice because he wants to know if Gabriel has any brothers that look as good as he does.

"Patrice girl, I am ready to be your relative. That Gabriel is one hunk of a man."

"Delicious, Gabriel is straight as they come."

"Patrice, let me tell you this. When I finish with him he will screaming not to be straight." Delicious chuckles. Everyone in the back of the salon cracks up laughing. "Patrice, you know I am right. You should be finished in a few moments you just need to let your nails dry and you will be good to go."

"Thank you, Delicious. I need this beauty treatment; it has been a rough couple of days. Wait a minute who in the world is this calling me?"

"Hello this is Patrice Sparks how may I help you? Hello Patrice, this is Tyrone Tyler. I wanted to see if we could go out for dinner, I need to speak with you."

"Hello Mr. Tyler, I am trying to find out why you are calling me; and to answer your question, I am not available to meet you and I don't know how you got my number; but please do me a favor, please don't ever call me again. Have a good day." Patrice hangs up the phone, she is irritated by her phone conversation with Tyrone.

Sheila and Delicious both can tell that something is wrong by the look on Patrice's face. "Patrice, are you okay, girl? What happened? You look like you just got some bad news." Patrice tells Sheila and Delicious that Tyrone just called her asking her to go out to dinner with him, and that she is disturbed that Tyrone called her on her personal cell phone. "I would really like to know how he got my personal cell phone number."

Delicious says to Patrice, "You need to check that, as a matter of fact you need to tell Gabriel exactly what happened and how you feel about Tyrone calling you."

"No, it's okay. I don't want Gabriel to have to get involved with this nonsense, I think I can handle Tyrone by myself."

"Patrice, I just met you and I don't think it's a good idea to get involved with Tyrone and his foolishness. Someone needs to drag Tyrone into tomorrow and back. Lord knows I have tried to drag Tyrone to the other side; he won't have it, but I will break him down one day." Both Sheila and Patrice crack up.

Sheila tells Delicious that he is crazy as all get up. "Okay ladies, I love you both, but I have got to get back to my other customers."

Sheila asks Delicious, "Where is Shaniqua? I haven't seen her in quite a while."

"Sheila, guess what. I haven't seen her either. When you find her please let me know."

"Delicious, what happened to her?"

"She ran off and got married to CZ?"

"Delicious, I hate to ask, but who in the world is CZ?"

"cra-zee."

"Delicious, now you know that ain't right at all." Both ladies walk to the front of the salon to pay Delicious, when Gabriel steps up and pays the bill for both women.

Sheila tells Gabriel that he doesn't have to do that.

"Sheila I don't mind at all; you are a friend of Patrice and I wouldn't dare pay for her and act as though you aren't here. That's what a man is supposed to do."

Gabriel is looking at Patrice; he can tell by her body language that there is something is bothering her. Gabriel knows his future wife better than she knows herself. Gabriel asks Patrice, "What's wrong? And don't tell me nothing, because it is something."

"Gabriel, it's not anything. I just don't feel well."

Sheila raises her voice just a little and says to Patrice, "Don't lie to him, tell him what happened. Gabriel is your future husband and he needs to know."

"Patrice, I agree with Sheila."

"Guys, you are making a big deal out of nothing."

Gabriel demands that Patrice tells him what's wrong.

Sheila blurts out to Patrice, "If you don't tell Gabriel, then I will."

Patrice is hesitant to say anything.

"Patrice, you give me no other choice."

"Gabriel, I don't know if you know anything about Tyrone Tyler; but for some reason he got Patrice's personal cell phone number and called Patrice and he asked to take her to dinner."

Gabriel is steamed. "He did what?"

Just as Gabriel is about to say another word he looks around the salon and realizes where he is and tells the ladies in an angry tone. "Let's go," As they walk toward their cars, Gabriel tells Patrice that she is going to ride with him.

Patrice kisses Sheila on the cheek and says "Good-bye".

Sheila jumps in her car and speeds off, she is headed home. As she is driving along Highway Two Thirty-Four, she puts on the radio. She is listening to the sweet sounds of the hottest Rhythm and Blues singer in the country, none other than that of Terence. She blurts out to herself, *man Terence can blow*. She is cruising in her black on black customized Infiniti eight series. She is thinking about her love life and how grateful she is to have one because with her schedule it's so hard to have a relationship.

Mark is a dynamic man. He is tall, handsome, smart and very successful. Sheila really loves him, and she wants to marry him, and she won't let anything get in her way of marrying the man of her dreams. But, there is a little skepticism when it comes to this, especially because of what happened with their relationship back when they were in college. But people can change, and Mark is definitely a changed man.

As Sheila is cruising along, her car phone rings. She can't believe that Mark is calling her on the phone, she was just thinking about him. He is so in tune with this woman that he knows when to call if something is wrong.

"Hello baby, how are you?"

"I'm good honey, where are you?"

"I'm driving home now."

"Sheila, I need to talk to you about something. I will meet you at your house in a few."

"Okay Mark, see you in a few."

Mark can't wait to tell Sheila what happened between Gabriel and Tyrone today at the office. Mark leaves the office in a hurry; he jumps in his platinum gray Mercedes Benz ZL nine series. Mark is also rocking to the sounds of rhythm and blues sensation "Terence". He is bothered by Tyrone's antics and now he is having to meet with the other partners to let them know if anything should be done about Tyrone's erratic behavior. Mark could care less what happens to Tyrone, but he wants to have the satisfaction of taking him down, so he is going to tell the partners to give him another chance.

Why am I thinking about Tyrone and his feelings, I have better things to think about. Mark is smiling from ear to ear because he is thinking about him and Sheila. He decides that he wants to go home and change before he meets up with Sheila, he doesn't want to smell like a funk basket in front of her. So, he drives home along route thirty-three to his five-bedroom, six bath mini-mansion. Mark's house is built for a King and Queen and he cannot wait to share his home with Sheila and make her his Queen.

Mark pulls into his winding driveway in the exclusive suburbs of Moores, New York. He is dressed to the nines. He immediately opens the door and runs to the second floor and takes a quick shower in one of his many bathrooms. He realizes that he has to get to the jewelry store before it closes, he wants to get Sheila something very special. Sheila has always been in his corner, even when he cheated on her in college; and he truly appreciates her for that. She could have cursed him out and never turned back, but she stuck by him through thick and thin and that's what Mark loves about her.

Mark has just gotten out of the shower and he has changed into something more comfortable. He races down the stairs, grabs his keys off the table near the foyer and runs to get in his car. He has less than thirty minutes to get to the jewelry store. He knows that he has to put the medal to the pedal, but he has to do it within reason because if he is stopped it will be a situation.

To Mark's surprise, there isn't a lot of traffic on the highway; so, he will make it to Liam's Jewelers in time to pick up something special for Sheila. As he pulls into the lot of the jewelers, he calls Sheila to let her know that he had to make a stop and that he will be at her house in about thirty minutes. "Mark, it's okay because I still haven't gotten home just yet and it will give me more than enough time to take a shower and slip into something more comfortable."

Today is a fast food kind of day for Sheila. She stops at Janay's, a quaint Italian restaurant close to her home; and picks up some sautéed shrimp with brown rice seasoned with mixed vegetables in mild garlic and shrimp sauce. The food smells so good that Sheila is almost tempted to pull on the side of the road and eat some of it before she gets home, but she decides against it because she might fall asleep behind the wheel of the car and she might cause an accident. Sheila says to herself, *girl, just wait, you are less than ten minutes from your house.* She looks at the clock in the car and realizes that she has twenty minutes to get everything done before Mark comes over.

Sheila pulls into her driveway when she sees a car blocking her entrance. *Who in the world could this be?* She gets out of her car and walks over to the driver and attempts to politely ask them to move their car because they are blocking her. When she gets closer to the car, the driver rolls down the window. She is surprised, but anger has also set in because she wants to know how in the world Tyrone found out where she lives. Sheila asks the question "Tyrone, what are you doing parked in my driveway?"

"Sheila, I really need to talk to you right now. I have so much that's going on, and one thing for sure is that I know you would listen to me."

"Tyrone, maybe another time. Can you please get your car out of my driveway so I can go inside of my house, I have people coming over in a few moments."

"Sheila, can I call you later so we can talk?"

"Tyrone, I will be unavailable to speak with you tonight. Call me tomorrow and if my schedule permits we can talk then. Now leave, you have been here too long; and for the record, I don't know how you got my address, but don't come to my house ever again."

"I got it from Mark. Where else would I get it from?"

Sheila is seeing red she can't believe that Mark would do that to her. She is going to give him a piece of her mind when he comes to her house.

Tyrone can see that Sheila is not in the mood to speak with him, so he drives off sad and dejected, or so he wants Sheila to think that. He is thinking that she would have pity for him. Sheila is more heated now than before; she cannot believe that Mark would give out her personal information, especially to a creep like Tyrone. She is going to let Mark have it as soon as she sees him. Before she can get in the door good enough, Mark is pulling into her driveway.

He is happy because he found something that would make her smile.

Mark rings the bell; and to his surprise, Sheila is mad when she answers it. She says to him, "You have got some nerve."

Mark asks Sheila, "Why are you so mad?"

"Mark, I'm not mad I'm heated. How could you?"

"Sheila, I just got here. What in the world are you talking about?"

"Mark, why did you give Tyrone Tyler my home address?".

"Sheila, what are you talking about? I never gave Tyrone your address."

"Well I pulled into my driveway and that ass was sitting in his car waiting for me. He said that he wanted to talk to me and take me to dinner. I told him that I could not speak to him because I was having guest. I am so livid right now."

Mark grabs Sheila by the arms and pulls her closer to him. "Sheila, I did not give Tyrone your address. In all the years that I have known you, have I ever lied to you? Think about it. I know how much he makes you want to puke, and you know for damn sure that I don't like him. There has to be an explanation for what he did, and I will definitely find out, that you can bet on that."

"Mark, I can't argue with you about that, you are so right."

"Sheila it's so funny because I came here to talk to you about what happened at the office with Tyrone and now I don't think that it's a good idea to even mention it."

"Mark it's okay. What did he do now?"

"Well, it seems that Tyrone tried to put his hands on the newscaster Patrice Sparks and she must have told her fiancée about the situation because he came to the office and stepped to Tyrone.

You should have seen Tyrone he thought he was the man trying to act like he was so tough, but the minute Gabriel told him that there would be consequences if he bothered Patrice Sparks again Tyrone got real quiet and didn't say a word; but as soon as Gabriel left he was all mouth. Tyrone is a punk, for sure."

Mark I'm surprised that you don't remember Patrice. Sheila should I remember her? Yes you should, she was my roommate in college after Kayla left. Mark how in the world could you forget? Honey that's right how did I not remember her? It's probably because she is using her mother's maiden name. We called her Triece Black. That's right Sheila. Boy do I feel stupid.

"Great job, Gabriel."

"Sheila, I know what you mean. Tyrone thinks he is the man and that he is untouchable. I am so glad that another man stepped to him."

"Mark, now you know when and if I run into Tyrone he is going to tell me all about what happened, and he is going to make it seem as though Gabriel disrespected him and that he is so innocent."

"So, Sheila, now do you believe me when I said that I would never give Tyrone your address?"

"Yes, Mark I believe you and I am sorry that I fussed at you when you first got here, but you know how I feel about Tyrone and that just took me over the edge."

"Well, maybe this will help to calm you down." Mark pulls out a box from Liam's, the most exclusive jewelers on the East Coast."

"Mark, what is this?"

Sheila is speechless when she opens the box and realizes that there is a three- and one-half carat diamond ring. "Oh, my goodness Mark, what is this?"

"Sheila, what does it look like?"

"Mark, I know it's a ring, but why did you buy this?"

"Sheila, I have known you for so long and through everything I have been through in my life you have always been in my corner. Now I know that I have done you wrong in the past, but I can't see my life without you. I just need one woman and that woman is you."

Mark gets down on one knee and pops the question. "Sheila Smith will you marry me?"

Sheila is hesitant for about thirty seconds, making Mark think that she doesn't want to marry him; and then out of nowhere, she screams at the top of her lungs. While crying, she emphatically says, "Yes, Yes, and Yes, I will marry you Mark. I can't wait to spend the rest of my life with the only man I have ever truly loved."

Sheila wants to tell everyone, but she knows that she can't. "Mark, promise me one thing."

"What is it, Sheila?"

"Please do not tell Tyrone anything about this."

"Sheila, I am insulted that you would think that I would tell Tyrone anything about my personal relationship. I hate the brother and if it wasn't for you I would have taken him down a long time ago. There is one person that I would like to tell."

"And who would that be, Mark? Vanessa Brown, Tyrone's ex-wife."

"Why her Mark?"

"Sheila, because she and I have history together and you remember what happened between her, myself, and that numbskull ex-husband of hers."

"Mark baby, I understand what you are trying to do; but don't you think that she will tell Tyrone?"

"Sheila, Vanessa can't stand Tyrone and she stays as far away from him as possible."

"That might be the case for her, but Tyrone thrives on being intimidating to women."

"Vanessa is not afraid of Tyrone and she knows how to keep her personal life quiet.

When they were going through a divorce, Tyrone didn't know that she was seeing someone else right under his nose; so, I know that she will keep our secret."

Mark asks Sheila when she would like to get married. "I figure in about three years."

"Sheila, three years? I was thinking more like next year. Baby let me go I have to get home I have an extremely long day ahead of me tomorrow. Bye baby."

"Mark, before you go, I just want you to know that I love you more now than ever before and you have made me the happiest girl in the world." Mark kisses Sheila on the forehead and walks out the door and heads to his car. He turns on the engine, sits and listens to the soulful sounds of Terence, as he sings *All the Woman I Need.*

For the first time in a very long time Mark is crying but they are not tears of sadness. He is happy because he is marrying the woman of his dreams, and he is a junior partner in his firm, working towards being a senior partner. What more can he ask, for he knows that he is grateful, and he does not take his blessings for granted. As he contains his composure, he slowly backs out of Sheila's driveway onto the street and drives off. He is bobbing to the music on his radio.

After cruising on highway three forty-five on his way home he manages to get out of his car. Little does Mark know that Tyrone is sitting across from his house waiting for him. Tyrone is laying on the horn so hard and long, and he is screaming out of the window for Mark to come and talk to him because he has something important that he needs to tell him.

Mark is highly embarrassed by Tyrone. He walks over to Tyrone's car. "Man, what the hell is wrong with you?

"Mark, I need to see you."

"What is it, Tyrone?"

"Mark, I went to Sheila's house to talk to her and she basically cursed me out. Who the hell does she think she is?"

"Look Tyrone, you are a little drunk. Why don't you go home, and we will discuss this in the morning."

"Mark, I am going home; but who the hell does Sheila think she is?"

Mark wants to knock the hell out of Tyrone right there in front of his house, but he knows that he can't hit him, so he walks away steamed.

"Tyrone, go home now, and I don't want to talk to you or see you until you sober up."

Tyrone wants to knock the heck out of Mark, but he is wreaking of alcohol and he can barely stand, so the best thing for him to do is to just sit in his car and sulk and sleep because if he drives home he might cause a serious accident.

Tyrone is cussing to himself, but there is nothing else he can do. He realizes that he is not that far from Leon's, so he goes in and asks for a cup of black coffee. Tyrone notices the gorgeous waitress Myah. She smiles at Tyrone because he is a customer and she knows how to treat her customers with respect, but Tyrone has something else on his mind. Before Tyrone could say anything to Myah he throws up right on her floor. How embarrassing it is to him, but Tyrone is so nasty he will talk to a pretty woman, no matter what the situation. Myah is completely disgusted by Tyrone and his actions. She is totally turned off and just as he is about to flirt again, he has to puke again. Tyrone, being the type of man that he is, doesn't see that this is a sign to drink his coffee, get in his car, take his tail home, and sleep off this hangover so that he can be a functioning drunk at work.

Tyrone is escorted out of the restaurant by Myah, she walks him to his car because she feels sorry for him and she wants to make sure that he doesn't fall and hurt himself.

Myah takes Tyrone's car keys and opens the door and attempts to put him in his car when he tries to kiss her. It is at that precise moment that Myah slaps the taste out of Tyrone's mouth. She has never cussed anyone out before, but this is definitely one exception to the rule.

"How dare you try and kiss me. Look Negro, I am not desperate. I was trying to be nice and help you out, but now you can get in your car by yourself. You disgust me, you low down dirty dog. Get away from me and take your nasty puking disgusting self home and don't ever come to this restaurant again."

"Look you whore, you should be glad that someone wants to talk to you with your three dollar an hour making self."

"Excuse me, did you just call me something other than my name?"

Tyrone says to Myah, "Yes I did, and what about it?"

"Mr. Whatever your name is, you have lost your cotton-picking mind calling me a whore. My mother raised a lady, and as for you thinking that I make three dollars an hour I make more than you think. Why am I explaining myself to a useless self-righteous Negro like you?"

Myah doesn't utter another word. She walks back into the restaurant. She is definitely agitated by what just went down, she is sick to her stomach and tells her boss Clyde that she needs to leave. She is shaking by the experience and her boss can very well see it, he wants to know what is going on? She explains to him what just happened with a customer. As she turns around, she notices that Tyrone's car is still in the parking lot. So, she points him out to her boss. He runs behind the counter and gets a baseball bat, and then runs out of the restaurant and approaches Tyrone's car. Tyrone rolls down his window, "How may I help you, sir?"

"I ought to beat the crap out of you. I better not ever see you in this restaurant again, otherwise it will be real problems between me and you. Now get your drunk behind out of here and I mean now."

Tyrone gets out of his car. He can barely stand, but somehow he manages to get his strength to go off on Clyde because he thinks that he is an old man, but he doesn't realize that Clyde can hold his own, and he doesn't disappoint at all. Tyrone raises his hand to punch Clyde in the face when Clyde raises the bat to knock Tyrone upside the head. Tyrone has a come to Jesus moment and realizes that he better leave Clyde alone. Tyrone apologizes to Clyde for his behavior and jumps back in his car.

Tyrone slouches down and watches as Myah gets in her car. Tyrone is so-called sobered up enough to follow Myah home. He makes sure that he keeps his distance, so she won't see him following her. Myah is a beautiful mocha complexion sister; she is five feet five inches tall. Myah is an older woman, age fifty to be exact, but she looks more like she is thirty-five than fifty. No one would ever believe her age when she tells them, but she is proud of her age. Myah is single, but don't get it twisted; she can date any man that she wants to date but that's not her style. Myah has been hurt before, so she is taking her time. There is a man that is interested in her, but she knows not to jump into anything major.

Tyrone is amazed at where Myah lives; he wonders how she can live in such an upscale neighborhood such as Eons Lake, New York, and work as a waitress. Tyrone is curious, so he is going to figure out what the deal is with her.

For the first time in a long time Tyrone is not speeding, and that's because he knows if he gets in trouble with the law it can cost him his Partnership. Tyrone made it back home safely, it took him an hour to get home when it should have taken him twenty minutes or less; but that's what happens when you have been drinking.

Tyrone is still a little tipsy, but somehow he manages to open the door to his house. He plops down on his plush leather sofa and immediately falls asleep. It's the next morning and Tyrone has slept so long that he doesn't hear the phone ring. It's the office, they are wondering where he is.

There is a voice on the other end. "Tyrone, this is Mark, where are you? You have a client waiting for you." Another ten minutes have passed by and Tyrone still hasn't gotten up. Now Mark is concerned. He isn't as cool with Tyrone as most people think; but he still wants Tyrone to be okay, especially because he still wants to take Tyrone down and ruin his entire life. Mark realizes that the firm will lose a lot of money, so he stands in Tyrone's stead. He lies to the client and tells them that Tyrone is sick and that he will not be able to make the meeting, but that he knows everything that is going on and he will help them with whatever they need.

Thank goodness for Mark stepping up to the plate the meeting was successful, and he was able to get a great commission for Tyrone and himself. After the meeting is over Mark decides to go to Tyrone's house to make sure that he is okay.

When Mark arrives at Tyrone's home he realizes that the door to Tyrone's house is open. Now Mark is really concerned because he is afraid that something could have happened to him. Mark slowly walks into Tyrone's house; he is careful not to say anything or touch anything. He wants to make sure that he doesn't stumble upon an intruder; so, he basically tiptoes through the house and eventually finds Tyrone on the sofa. Mark thinks that Tyrone is dead, until he touches him, and he realizes that Tyrone has a heartbeat. Mark is glad because he cannot stand Tyrone and he wants to see the expression on his face when he and Sheila take him down.

Mark awakens Tyrone, he is still hungover. For sure, Tyrone knows that he messed up; but there is nothing that he can do about it now. He looks around and asks Mark, "How in the hell did you get inside of my house?"

"You left the door wide open, so I walked in and wanted to make sure that nothing was missing. So, Tyrone I guess this is why you missed your meeting?"

"Mark, what are you talking about? I didn't have a meeting today. My meeting is Friday. Umm Tyrone, today is Friday' but don't worry about a thing I took care of it."

"What do you mean you took care it?"

"Tyrone, I called you several times and you didn't answer, and the client was waiting for more than forty-five minutes. I tried to stall as much as possible, but I couldn't hold them at the office any longer; so, I had to step in and handle the meeting. Don't worry; they are going to do business with the firm, thanks to me. And my commission was sweet."

"Hold the hell up, Mark! What do you mean, *your commission was sweet*?"

"Tyrone, did I stutter?"

"You blew the deal and I stepped up and worked my magic so now the commission is mine."

"Mark, you have lost your damn mind. Don't play with me I want my commission and it better be on my desk when I get to the office."

"Tyrone you better get up out of my face, otherwise there will be a situation in here today and I am sure that you don't want to get hurt in your own home."

"Like I said, all I know Mark, is that my check better be at the office when I get there, that's all I'm saying or else."

"Or else what Tyrone? You know what, I just came here to see if you were okay, now brother I don't care. I have to get back to work."

"You heard me, Mark."

Mark whispers in Tyrone's ear, "Brother I don't take to kindly to idle threats, watch who you are talking to man. Don't let this three-hundred-dollar suit fool you. I will get thuggish on you."

Tyrone attempts to push Mark, but Mark blocks him before he can push him.

Mark tells Tyrone this means war and before Tyrone can utter another word out of his mouth Mark walks away. Tyrone is trying his best to provoke Mark to fight him, but Mark is doing his best to ignore this ignorant fool.

Tyrone does his best to make his way upstairs, He jumps in the shower, he is still ticked off that Mark thinks he is going to get his commission. As soon as Tyrone jumps out of the shower he runs to the kitchen to get some coffee and runs back upstairs to get dressed for work. Tyrone sets a record in getting dressed, he didn't have to iron anything because he pulled clothes out of the closet that he had picked up from the cleaners two days ago.

Tyrone is so ready to get into it with Mark that he almost forgets to lock his doors. He really doesn't care if the door isn't locked. Right about now, all he wants to do is punch Mark in the face.

Tyrone jumps in his car and speeds to his office, he just misses getting caught by the police. He makes it to the city in record time and he feels that everything is going his way. He arrives at work, looking good as always. He parks in a nearby parking lot and struts to his office.

Tyrone struts pass Karen the receptionist, he is truly smelling himself. Karen smiles and greets him. He responds surprisingly in a nice tone. "I am fine, Karen. Good to see you."

Michelle is surprised that Tyrone is being nice, because he usually doesn't have anything good to say to her at all. She is thinking to herself something feels weird. Tyrone walks his happy tail straight into Mark's office. He doesn't care that there is a meeting going on, he wants to get to the bottom of things, and he wants his commission check or there will be problems with Mark.

Tyrone walks into Mark's office and immediately goes off on him. "Tyrone, can't you see that I am in the middle of a meeting? What's wrong with you?"

Tyrone stands in front of the whole group and says loudly, "this so-called man, whom I thought was a friend, went behind my back and stole my client right from under my nose and then had the nerve to steal a four million dollar commission that was owed to me."

That's when the Board of Directors (Williams, Paul and Thomas) decided to make their presence known. "Mark is there a problem with what he is saying?" Mark lets them know that he has a serious problem with Tyrone.

"Mr. Williams, Paul and Mr. Thomas, here is what happened. Due to Tyrone's lateness and his reckless behavior in not answering multiple phone calls that were made to his house this morning, I had no choice but to help a client whose business we were trying to get, but because they had been waiting for so long and they could no longer wait for Tyrone to answer his phone, I was told by one of the other senior partners to assist the clients. Because of this, they let me know that I should be entitled to the commission."

As much as Mark wanted to say something to Tyrone in return, he decides to keep his mouth closed, because he knows that sometimes silence speaks volume. Mark calmly walks to the door and says to Tyrone "Have a nice day."

Even though Mark didn't respond to him the way that he wanted him to respond you can tell that Mark is steamed and he knows that he has to stay calm because he knows that Tyrone's demise is going to happen sooner than later.

Tyrone is stunned by Mark's actions. He really doesn't know what to think, but Tyrone is so arrogant that he thinks that everything is okay with his behavior and he doesn't see that anything is wrong with the way he acted. Tyrone is going to make this about Mark and how bad Mark treated him.

Tyrone is seething, he cannot make sense of what happened because he now realizes that he made a total fool of himself in front of the Board of Directors; and because of his antics, chances are Tyrone will no longer be a Partner. Out of nowhere, Tyrone walks back into Mark's office and apologizes to everyone. "Mark you are right, you deserve the commission. I want to thank you for helping me out."

Mark is stunned by how nice and how calm Tyrone is. With Tyrone, it's usually the quiet before the storm. Tyrone gives Mark a high five, and he says good-bye to the Board of Directors and heads to his office. Tyrone is a sneak, so he is definitely up to something. He is trying to figure out when and how he is going to seek revenge on Mark.

Mark knows that he needs to watch his back, but he really doesn't care about Tyrone's antics. Mark walks to Tyrone's office and apologizes to Tyrone and wants him to know that he is more than willing to share the commission with him.

If looks could kill Mark would have been killed, brought back to life, and killed again. Tyrone is more than pissed off, but he is trying his best to play it cool. Mark is also trying to play it cool, but he knows how to handle Tyrone.

Tyrone is about to curse at Mark when his phone rings. Believe it or not, it is Sheila, she isn't calling Tyrone because she likes him she is calling him because she knows that he acted a fool the other night when they went out; she is looking for an apology from him.

Whenever Sheila calls Tyrone he becomes a shy little boy. He changed his mood; he is very happy to hear from Sheila. "Well good afternoon Sheila, it is such a pleasure to hear such a wonderful voice as yours."

"Thank you, Tyrone. I was calling you to talk to you about the other evening."

"Sheila, what about it?"

"It went left, your behavior was horrible."

"You think so Sheila, well that's your opinion. Sheila why are you calling me?"

"Tyrone, I thought you would be a man and apologize for the way that you acted, but now I see that you have a lot of growing up to do. Do me a favor I need you to lose my number and never call me again Tyrone, I hope that I have made myself clear."

He is hurt by what Sheila just said, but he will never let her know. He wants to tell Sheila off; he is so frustrated as all get up.

Mark doesn't want to give him his commission and now Sheila wants him to apologize for nonsense. "Sheila, I have to go."

Before Tyrone can get the words out of his mouth, Sheila has already hung the phone up on him. She slams the phone down in his ear. Tyrone calls her a "bitch."

It takes everything and then some for Mark not to slap the taste out of Tyrone's mouth. "Tyrone you must be out of your mind calling a woman out of her name. How would you feel if someone called your mother that? You would be ready to beat a Negro down."

As much as Tyrone doesn't want to speak to Mark he has to agree with what he says. "You're right Mark, that was not cool. I will call Sheila and apologize for calling her out of her name."

Even though Mark could care less about what Tyrone really thinks, he is going to be the bigger person and keep the peace for now, but this isn't over by a long shot.

"Tyrone you know what, I have been thinking about it and you know what I am going to do? I am going to give you the commission, it's your client."

Tyrone asks Mark if he is absolutely sure. "Yes, I am sure, I want you to have it." Tyrone's mood has totally changed.

Mark tells Tyrone, "I will go and get the check now."

Mark is smiling as he walks to his office. He can't wait to see the look on Tyrone's face when he sees the commission check. Mark walks back to Tyrone's office and hands him the commission check. Tyrone looks at the check and throws it back at Mark in disgust. Tyrone says to Mark, "I think you have the wrong check."

Mark says to Tyrone, "Brother I have the correct check and why are you so mad?" You said the commission check belongs to you, so I'm giving it to you."

"Mark you could have kept this."

"Tyrone, I don't know what you are complaining about you got a commission check for twenty thousand dollars, it's better than nothing."

Tyrone says to Mark, "This is bull crap. What the hell can I do with twenty thousand dollars?"

Tyrone tells Mark that he is going to contact the client and tell them that they gave him the wrong amount for his commission. Mark tells Tyrone that he doesn't think that would be the wise thing to do. They might not give you anything. "Oh, trust and believe me, they are going to give me my money or there will be hell to pay, believe that."

"Tyrone, just stop it, you aren't going to do anything to anyone."

"Watch me, Mark."

Tyrone proceeds to call the mystery client and attempts to chew the client out, when all of a sudden Mark grabs the phone and puts the caller on hold. Mark then begins to light into Tyrone. "Tyrone, you are a partner in a very large and exclusive firm. Do you think that it's worth it to lose your partnership for a measly twenty thousand dollars? Believe me when I tell you it's not worth it. So, you might want to think about it before you say anything that you will regret later. If you don't want the twenty thousand dollars then return it to the client."

Tyrone apologizes to his client and then for some reason he calls Sheila. She picks up and asks Tyrone, "Why are you calling me? There is nothing that I need to say to you but goodnight and goodbye," and she abruptly hangs up on him again.

Tyrone isn't going to give up, so he calls Sheila again, and again she does not answer the phone; so, he decides that the only way she will respond to him is through text. So, he sends her a text message and apologizes for calling her out of her name.

Sheila receives the text, but she dares not respond to Tyrone because that would only start more drama and she is sick of it. Five minutes have passed, and Tyrone is blowing up Sheila's phone again, he is repeatedly apologizing to her thinking that this will solve the problem between him and her; but the only thing that it's going to do is to draw a wedge between the two of them.

Tyrone is literally stalking Sheila; she is more disappointed than she is petrified. She has to turn her phone completely off so that she does not have to see his text messages. As soon as Sheila cuts her phone off Mark calls her repeatedly. He is concerned because she is not answering and that's not like her, she always answers Mark's calls. Mark decides to leave the office so he can check on Sheila. He tells his assistant, Victoria, to take messages and if anyone calls for him tell them that he had to leave because he has a family emergency.

Mark doesn't want to admit it because he is a man, but he is worried that something has happened to Sheila. He is also upset because he doesn't know where she is, so he decides that he is going to her office, whether she likes it or not. Mark is still trying to contact her, but she is not answering. He rushes to her office so fast that he breezes right past the receptionist. Mark bursts into Sheila's office, while she is with a client. "I'm sorry Sheila, can we talk?"

"Sure, we can." Sheila excuses herself from her meeting with her clients. "Mark is there something wrong?"

"Sheila, are you okay? I have been trying to reach you and you never responded."

"I apologize for that Mark, but Tyrone has been harassing me by texting me every five minutes. I had to turn my phone completely off."

"Sheila, you need to report him that's stalking."

"Mark, I have better things to do."

"Sheila, if you don't do something he is going to continue to stalk you. Sheila, let me handle it for you, turn your phone back on. I will handle Tyrone for you, I promise that he will never harass you again." So, Sheila turns on her phone; she looks at her phone and realizes that she has over one hundred text messages from Tyrone.

Mark is infuriated by this, so he decides to take matters into his own hands. He decides to respond to Tyrone. "Sheila go back to your meeting and by the time that you finish meeting with your client I will have taken care of the Tyrone situation for you."

Sheila raises an eyebrow. "Mark, I know that you aren't afraid of Tyrone and I also know that you will make sure that he never calls or texts me again; but I want to make sure that you don't get into any trouble with your job. Mark, trust me when I tell you that Tyrone is not an issue to me, I can handle him. Plus, I want Tyrone to continue to think that everything is okay between us, this way it will make it much easier for my case against him."

"I am not the type of person to seek revenge on anyone, but I want to take Tyrone down. He really deserves everything that he gets, and I can't wait to see the look on his face.

Sheila kisses Mark and tells him that she loves him. "Baby, I have to get back to my clients. Let's have a quiet dinner at home tonight. That's my girl. I will be over later, and wear something sexy."

"I got sexy for you Mark, now let me go."

"Girl, you just don't know what you do to me."

Just as Sheila says this to Mark, Tyrone has texted her again, but he is steamed. Sheila ignores him again and runs back into her meeting; she apologizes to her clients for leaving but she had an emergency.

Mark responds to Tyrone as though he is Sheila. "Hi Tyrone, how are you?"

"Sheila, why the hell haven't you returned any of my text messages?"

"Tyrone, I have been extremely busy. Is there something that you needed?"

"Sheila, what is your problem? All I was trying to do was apologize to you."

"Tyrone, I saw your message and I accept your apology. I am with a client now and I cannot talk to you."

"Sheila, I want to see you so meet me tonight for dinner."

"Tyrone, are you asking me or are you telling me because you and I don't have the type of relationship that you can tell me what to do."

"Sheila, I'm not telling you anything. That was my way of inviting you to have dinner with me, so that I can show you that I am a human being and not the monster that most people perceive me to be."

"Tyrone, let me think about it and if I decide to have dinner with you I will text you either way."

"Sheila, that's enough for me, but I hope it's not too late."

"Tyrone, I just said that when and if I decide what I want to do I will text you; as I said before, I have a meeting." Mark is loving this game that he is playing with Tyrone. Two grown men playing little boy games.

Sheila has finished her meeting and is surprised to find out that Mark is still in her office. "Mark, what are you doing here? I thought that you would have gone by now."

"Sheila, I decided that I didn't want to wait until we got home, I wanted to see if you would have dinner with your favorite fiancée now."

"So, does this mean that you don't want me to wear anything sexy?"

"Baby girl, you will have the opportunity to do that when we get home and I can't wait to see what you have in store for me."

"You ain't said nothing but a word; give me fifteen minutes to shut everything down."

"Oh, by the way, I played a cat and mouse game with Tyrone."

"Mark, what in the world are you talking about?"

"Don't get mad, but while you were in your meeting, I pretended that I was you and I texted Tyrone."

"Mark, what did you do?"

"Baby, I told him that you have been busy and then he invited you to dinner and I told him that you weren't sure and that you would text him when you have decided as to whether or not you wanted to have dinner with him. So, now you have made up your mind and you will not be having dinner with him, and when you tell him that you won't have dinner tonight, let him also know that you will not have dinner with him in the future."

"Mark, why did you do that?"

"I know that Tyrone is a pain, but I needed to handle the situation with Tyrone the way I felt was best for me to handle. Sheila you are my fiancée and I wanted to make sure that you were okay, and that he didn't try to harass you anymore."

"Mark, that's why I love you and I do appreciate what you did, but you better pray that this doesn't come back to bite us both in the behind."

"Sheila baby, trust me it won't now all you need to do is tell him that you can't make it to dinner tonight. Are you ready to leave? I have a surprise for you."

"Mark, give me a minute, I have to respond to Tyrone."

"Tyrone, this is Sheila. Thank you for the dinner invitation, but I will not be able to make it to dinner with you tonight, and as of this moment, I don't think that it will be a good idea to have dinner with you in the future. Have a great evening."

As soon as Sheila sent the text message to Tyrone she cut her phone off immediately so that she doesn't have to be bothered with any drama that will happen with him once he sees the text message.

And of course, Sheila is right. As soon as she cut her phone off Tyrone is calling and leaving message after message in hopes that she will answer him. He wants to know why she doesn't want to have dinner with him, the crazy part is that Tyrone doesn't get it. He was an embarrassment when they had lunch together, but he continues to think that everything is okay, and that he has done nothing wrong. But Sheila can't worry about Tyrone she has a man that is waiting to take her to have a wonderful dinner and other treats and she can't wait. She calls Mark from her company phone and lets Mark know that she is on her way out to meet him in the reception area.

Mark laughs lovingly. "Sheila, that is so cute that you would call me and let me know that you are meeting me, while I am sitting in your waiting area. Woman that is why I love you. It's the small things that you do that have my heart captured. I'm waiting for you."

Sheila has packed up and is leaving the office. She and Mark head to the company garage and they jump into Mark's custom made black on black Maserati and take the twenty-minute drive to his house.

As they are driving along, guess who decides to call Mark on his car phone? You guessed it, Tyrone Tyler, President of the Real Creep Squad. "Hey Mark, how are you?"

Mark hates to talk to Tyrone for anything, but he is being nice until it's time for the go-down. "I'm good, Tyrone."

"That's nice to hear. Mark, the reason that I am calling you is because it seems like Sheila is trying to avoid me and I don't know what to do. She said that I messed up when we had lunch together, but Mark you know it wasn't that bad. I can admit that I might have said something, but it seems that she is holding that against me."

Unbeknownst to Tyrone Sheila is listening to every lie that he is telling Mark, and she is hating him more and more with each lie that he tells.

"Tyrone I am sorry but there is nothing that I can do about that. If Sheila doesn't want to be bothered with you, then I guess you will have to let it be."

"Mark, now you know that I am not the type of man to give up so easily. I like Sheila, but I'm not going to keep playing games with her. I can step to any other woman I want, but I am trying to be patient with her."

"Tyrone, I don't know what to tell you. I can't talk to you right now, maybe we can talk in the morning. I am on my way home." Mark doesn't normally lie but he doesn't want him showing up where he and Sheila are having dinner; and one thing is for sure, Tyrone will show up just like that.

"Mark, I can deal with that, but I am going to give it one last shot with Sheila and then the game is on. Mark, now you know you can't stop a real playa."

"I hear you Tyrone. Well Tyrone, like I said before I will see you at the office tomorrow. Peace my brother. Goodbye Tyrone."

Sheila is beyond pissed, but she is not going to let what Tyrone just said get to her, because she is spending a romantic evening with her future husband. "Honey, I can't believe what Tyrone just said to you. I know that I said before that I wasn't sure if I wanted to be bothered and take Tyrone down; but after hearing what he just said baby, I am one hundred percent behind you… let's do this."

"Sheila, I am so glad that you are on board with this. Let's play this fool and take him down."

"I am with you all the way Mark, but can you please do me a favor? Can we come home instead of having dinner, all I want to do is go home so that we can have the pleasure of taking care of each other."

"Now that's what I like to hear, Sheila baby. I am all yours."

As they enter Mark's estate she turns her phone back on; she figures by this time that Tyrone has gotten the message that she doesn't want to be bothered with him. But not Tyrone, he just doesn't get it. Now guess who decides to call Sheila, none other than Tyrone. He doesn't know that Sheila heard everything that he said to Mark when he called him on his car phone. She is about to let Tyrone have it, but Mark mouths to her be nice; so, Sheila picks up the phone and tries to be as nice to Tyrone as much as she can possibly be to this character.

"Tyrone, I am busy. I can't talk to you is there something that you want?"

"First of all, Sheila, you say "hello" when you answer a call."

"Tyrone, you called my phone. I really don't have to say "hello" to you. Be glad that I answered your call; again Tyrone. what is it that you want? I am busy and I have company over, and I don't have time to talk to you."

"Sheila, I know that you aren't playing me with another man, when you know that I am trying my best to make you my number one girl." As soon as Tyrone says that, Sheila drops the phone. She can't believe how bad this "Negro" is lying.

"Tyrone, I don't understand why you don't get it. I have company and I am not about to have a conversation with you. I will talk to you another time, have a good evening."

Sheila hangs up the phone so hard in Tyrone's ear that he can actually hear the phone vibrating.

He is steamed and he is getting fed up with the things that Sheila is doing to him. *This trick is crazy; that is the last time that she will hang up the phone on me. I will call her tomorrow and her behavior better improve or this situation will only get worse for her.*

CHAPTER SIXTEEN

It's a crisp cool Autumn Friday morning. Mark and Sheila leave home together headed for work after a romantic evening the night before. Both of them are smiling from ear-to-ear as a couple in love should be. Mark knows that he has to deal with Tyrone when he gets to the office. Mark drops Sheila at her office. They both give each other a kiss before Sheila leaves the car. She is still bothered by Tyrone's behavior, but she also reminds Mark to keep his cool when he talks to Tyrone.

"Baby, I can't stand that man and I know that you don't want me to be anywhere near him; but Mark I want to go to dinner with him so that I can get more ammunition on him."

"Trust me Mark, I don't want to be around him; but I have to do what is necessary to help win this case against him. Mark baby, Tyrone is so disgusting that he makes me puke."

"Baby girl, I understand what you are saying; but don't worry, everything is going to work out in the end."

"Give me a kiss. Eww that kiss on the cheek was boring, I want some real suga."

"Excuse me, I was trying not to give you my cold; but if you want my cold, then I am going to give you two lips of brown sugar with an added dose of a cold.

They both laugh. Sheila steps out of the car in a navy-blue one-piece form fitting dress that hugs every inch of her body.

Mark is smiling from ear to ear because he knows that Sheila is his and only his. Mark rolls down the passenger side window and yells out and says to Sheila, “Girl you better stop, otherwise neither one of us will be going to work.”

Sheila turns around and says lovingly to Mark, “Boy you better stop, or I might have to take you up on that offer.”

“Baby girl, you ain’t said nothing but a word.”

Sheila walks back towards the car. “Boy, if I didn’t have this deposition in an hour you would be in a whole lot of trouble.”

“Girl, I love the way that sounds; but unfortunately, I have two new clients that I am meeting within an hour, as well; and of course, I have to deal with Tyrone, but, he is so easy to handle, it’s not difficult to throw out trash.”

“You are right about that, Mark.”

“Baby, I love you. I will see you later.”

Sheila turns and walks away. Girlfriend has a mean walk; she has a switch without having to switch. Just as Mark drives off, a stranger comes over to her and gives her a compliment, she smiles giddily. She knows that she is fierce, and she also knows that she can turn heads; and Sheila can have just about any man she wants, but she has a lifelong partner in Mark, and she will not do anything to mess that up.

Sheila makes it to her office of Smith, Johnson and Brown. It is conveniently located at Three Thirty-Three East Mountain Street on the thirty-third floor with a view that will take your breath away. Before Sheila can put her bags down, she gets a call; but she doesn’t answer it because she is meeting with her assistant to talk about a deposition that she will be having in about forty-five minutes. As much as Sheila tries to ignore the phone, the caller keeps ringing her phone and they won’t stop. Sheila finally decides to answer the call. “Hello, this is Sheila Smith. I am currently in a meeting; please leave your name and number and I will get back to you as soon as I can.”

"Sheila this is Tyrone and I need you to hear me and hear me clear. I don't know who you think you are, but let yesterday be the last time that you hang up a phone in my ear, otherwise…" and again, before Tyrone could get the rest of the sentence out of his mouth, Sheila hangs up on him and she immediately cuts her phone off.

Tyrone is now beyond pissed he tries to call her again and he begins to leave a very vulgar message on her voicemail. When he realizes that he can't get her on her personal phone he tries to email her. She is beyond livid because she didn't give any of her personal information to him.

Sheila is trying her best to prepare for a meeting, but she can't get Tyrone's antics off her mind. She doesn't want to call Mark and tell him that Tyrone is harassing her because she knows that Mark will lose it and go off on him, so she is going to do her best to handle this on her own. Sheila is flustered by Tyrone's actions but she knows that she can't let his behavior consume her; so, she continues to prepare for her meeting; but one thing is for sure as soon as she finishes her meeting, it's going to go down… she is going to let Mr. Tyler have it.

Just as Sheila finishes getting her papers in order for her meeting, the phone rings. At first, she jumps because she thinks that it's Tyrone, but then she realizes that he doesn't know where her office is located, so it can't be him. She picks up and she has a sigh of relief when she realizes that Mark is the caller.

"Hey Babe, it's me, Mark. I have been trying to contact you for the past thirty minutes, are you okay?"

"Yes, Mark, I am okay."

"Sheila, are you sure?"

"Mark, can we discuss this later? I am preparing for a meeting with a new client. As a matter of fact here they come now. I'll see you later honey."

"Okay Sheila, love you, love you too, Mark." Sheila hangs up with Mark, and she walks to the reception area to greet them.

"Hello, my name is Sheila Smith."

"Hello, Ms. Smith. I am Ethan Townes, and this is my wife Brie Townes."

"I like my clients to call me Sheila, it makes the relationship more intimate."

Ethan and Brie Townes own some of the most successful businesses on the East Coast.

They have a private and elite school named after them. They also own a very lucrative real estate investment firm, and they are part owners of one of the most successful sports team there. They are inquiring about legal services and they know that Sheila is the best in town, when it comes to a lawyer. Sheila is able to practice various types of law, contractual law, sports law, corporate law and defamation law. That is why it is so surprising that Tyrone doesn't know anything about her, but he will find out about her sooner than he wants to know.

Ethan and Brie Townes are happy to meet Sheila, but they are hesitant because they think that Sheila is a rookie in the business. Sheila has to school them and let them know that she has been practicing law for well over twenty-five years, which makes that hard to believe because she doesn't look like she is in her early forties; Sheila looks like she is twenty five or twenty six years of age.

After two hours of talking and crunching numbers and looking over contracts and listening to Sheila speak, Brie and Ethan decide that they want to retain her services. They realize now that there is no one better than Sheila Smith. Sheila hands the Townes a piece of paper and she tells them that it is a survey and she would like them to fill it out before they leave. "The survey is to just let me know if I am doing a good job and what areas I need to improve on."

Brie Townes tells Sheila that she is great and that she gets five stars, and that she will recommend all her friends to her. Sheila is humbled by the kind words from her new clients, but she is tired, as well. At this very moment all she is thinking about is her bed and how fast she can get to it.

The Townes begin to pack up their belongings. They are excited as they leave because they are about to make history again by building the tallest and the hippest hotel there will ever be. They thank Sheila and leave. Sheila politely closes the door behind them. She walks over to a big plush chair and takes off her shoes. Just as she closes her eyes to relax the phone rings; she decides that she isn't going to answer it. She again attempts to close her eyes to relax and again her phone rings. Now she is mad because she can't believe that someone would be interrupting her naptime. She looks at her phone and realizes that Mark has been trying to reach her; she is hesitant to speak with him, but she realizes that this is a call she has to take.

Sheila returns Mark's call and she puts up a front. Hey baby, how are you doing? How is my beautiful queen? You didn't answer the phone when I called you. I know Mark, I was in a meeting with some new clients and it was quite intense; but the good thing is that they retained my services.

Just as Mark is about to say something else to Sheila, he hears her breathing heavily on the phone. He yells out to her at least two times before she decides to answer. "Baby girl, you need some rest I will be there in about fifteen minutes to pick you up."

Sheila turns Mark down. "Baby, you don't have to do that I can drive myself home."

"Sheila, I am not taking no for an answer you can't drive in this condition."

"Mark, what condition is that? I am perfectly okay."

"Sheila, you are not okay; your falling asleep on the spot is not good, especially if you want to drive home."

"Mark, sleeping because you are tired is not a condition."

"Sheila, actually it is it is called sleep deprivation. It doesn't matter, I am coming to get you and I don't care what you say. I'll be there soon. I don't want my wife falling asleep behind the wheel and getting into a serious car crash."

"But Mark…"

"But nothing Sheila, I am already in my car on my way to your office… see you when I get there." Mark is so upset with Sheila that he hangs up before she can say "good-bye".

Sheila hangs up the phone with Mark and begins to start packing so that she can go home. Before she knows it her phone rings again and thinking that it is Mark she decides to answer her phone, only to realize that Tyrone is on the other end. She is upset, and you can tell by the sound of her voice when she answers the call.

"Hello Tyrone, how can I help you today?"

"Sheila, it seems like you are not too happy to hear from me."

"Tyrone, I am trying to leave, and you caught me at a bad time, and I really don't want to hear from you."

"Sheila, you are so rude."

"Tyrone, I am not the rude one, you called me and yet you didn't know how to say 'hello' on the other end and you thought that I was going to be 'miss nice girl'. Tyrone is there something that you want?"

"Well Sheila, I wanted to see if you would have dinner with me tonight, but by the tone in your voice I don't think that I want to have dinner or anything else with you for that matter."

"Tyrone, thank you so much for not wanting to have dinner with me, because I feel exactly the same way about you. So please do me a big favor."

"Oh, so now you want a favor from me. What is the favor Sheila?"

"Tyrone, please get off my phone and don't call me."

Tyrone is livid, but before he can say another word out of his mouth Sheila has turned her phone off as she finishes packing up for the evening. Tyrone is seeing red, but he knows that this is how Sheila is. She can't stand Tyrone, but he doesn't care. He wants to make Sheila his love interest and he will do everything possible to make sure that happens. But, there is one thing, or shall I say there is one person who is standing in the way of all of this. Tyrone still has feelings for Kayla, even though Kayla can't stand him either.

Tyrone is a 'good for nothing' Negro who thinks that he is God's gift to women and that every woman he meets wants him, including Kayla. Yes, I do agree that Kayla fell for the okey doke in the past, but that was before. This time around, she will not let Tyrone get under her skin, ever again. Tyrone is going to try his luck again with Kayla, so he decides to call her, He is positive that she is going to answer him. Tyrone dials Kayla's number and to much of his surprise Kayla doesn't answer him; so, he decides that he is going to give it another try and as luck would have it someone picks up Kayla's phone. But to the surprise of Tyrone, he hears a man's voice on the other end. He says hello and quickly hangs up, thinking that he has the wrong number. So, he tries again for the third time and again there is a man's voice on the other end of the receiver. This time, instead of hanging up the phone, Tyrone says, "Hello, this is Tyrone."

"Hello," the male caller says, "is there something that I can help you with?"

"I'm sorry, I was looking for Kayla Jones, obviously I have the wrong number."

"Brother, you have the correct number, this is Kayla's number. By the way my name is Lawrence, she asked me to answer your call. We are having dinner now; she will have to get back to you later."

Tyrone can't believe what he just heard, a man's voice on Kayla's phone. Tyrone is beyond livid. He wants to step to Lawrence, but he is going to hold what he has to say until he meets with Kayla. Tyrone has emotional problems because as soon as he hangs up the phone with Kayla, he tries to call Sheila again, and again he thinks that he can win Sheila over. Well, he has another thing coming. This time around, Sheila totally ignores him. As she is preparing to leave, Mark calls her and tells her that he is on his way up to her office. Sheila is clearly upset because she is tired of the nonsense with Tyrone and she didn't want Mark to come to pick her up.

Mark knocks on the door to Sheila's office. She answers, but with an attitude.

"Hey baby, what's wrong, you don't look to happy to see me."

"I am sorry Mark; I am just a little bothered. I had a long meeting and I am tired, and upset because I told you that you didn't have to come here."

"Sheila, you are my future wife and I really don't care what you think I should not do. When it comes to you, I am going to bend over backwards. And you know good and well that you are happy to see me."

Sheila lovingly says to Mark, "Baby, you are so right, I am glad you are here." Mark helps Sheila pack and up to leave. As they close the door and turn the lights out they hold hands. While they are in the elevator, once they reach the indoor garage, Mark makes the executive decision that they will take his car home and that Sheila's car will stay parked in the garage until the next day.

"Mark, how will I get to work if I leave my car here?"

"Baby, now you know that I will drive you to work. Stop asking so many questions, let's get out of here. I am tired and all I want to do is snuggle up with my baby. I don't want to talk to anyone on the phone, just the two of us fooling around trying to make a baby."

Sheila is surprised at what Mark is saying to her, she knows that he is in his feelings, but she is also in her feelings too. Mark is the man of her dreams and she is happy that they are finally going to be married. They jump into Mark's car and take the fifteen-minute drive home. They are listening to the soft and soulful sounds of rhythm and blues sensation Terrence; the traffic is smooth, and they are in their own little world. Mark is trying his best to sing tenderly to the sounds of *My Woman.* Sheila is all smiles. She closes her eyes and lets her mind take her away. She is in her feelings when she opens her eyes and realizes that she and Mark are already home. She doesn't want to get out of the car, but she knows that she has to, plus her bed is calling her name real loud.

Mark helps Sheila out of the car and lovingly escorts her to her house. Sheila is exhausted and all she wants to do is to go to sleep. But Mark has other ideas about this evening; he is definitely not in the mood for sleep, at least not right now. Mark can't wait to get Sheila in the mood, she is going to be surprised. In the bedroom he has rose petals spread across the room with a box that is filled with lingerie. As far as Mark is concerned, it's going to be on and popping. Sheila tells Mark that she is tired and all she wants to do is go to sleep. He completely ignores her and continues to lead her upstairs into the bedroom, but he has to make sure that she is completely blindfolded.

"Mark, what are you doing?"

"Sheila, just go with the flow."

"Mark, now you know that I am tired, and I really don't like surprises."

"I think you are going to like this surprise."

Mark lovingly guides Sheila to the bedroom, as she is standing in front of her bed he makes sure that she is not peeking, and he tells her that he is going to count to three and then she can open her eyes.

"One, two, three, now open your eyes."

Sheila is completely stunned; she can't say anything. After a moment or two, she finally says, "Oh my goodness Mark, this is beautiful. You did this for me? I can't believe it."

"Sheila, you are my queen and you deserve this and so much more."

Sheila says to Mark in a sweet but sexy voice, "I am not tired anymore."

Just at that time, Mark presents Sheila with a box.

"Mark what is this?"

"Woman, you ask too many questions, open it up and see what's inside." To Sheila's surprise she finds the sexiest of all sexy piece of lingerie in her favorite color blue.

As she is examining it, Mark is saying to her, "I can't wait for you to put it on so that I can take it off."

Sheila busts out laughing hysterically.

"What's so funny?" Mark asks Sheila. "Oh, so you think what I said is funny, thanks for nothing Sheila."

"Mark, why are you making a big deal out of this? I didn't laugh at what you said, I laughed at the way you said it. You sound country as all get up. How about I do something special for you Mark. Now I need you to close your eyes." Sheila goes to the bathroom and slips on the sexy piece of lingerie that Mark purchased for her. And what a piece of lingerie it is. "Okay Mark, now you can open your eyes."

Mark is tongue-tide; he doesn't know what to say or what to do. "Girl, you look sensational. I am speechless, I am glad that you are my wife." He gets off the bed and gently takes Sheila's hand and leads her to the bed. Mark lays next to her and lovingly strokes her hair; she is loving this. Just as Mark is about to go in and plant a kiss on Sheila's lips, her phone rings.

Mark is heated, he says in an angry tone. "Unbelievable, you have got to be kidding me."

Sheila is livid as well; she can't believe that Tyrone is calling her while she is trying to get her groove on. She totally ignores the call, but as you well know Tyrone is not the type to give up, so he calls again; and again, Sheila can't believe that he is calling her. Mark is furious he wants to know who in the world is calling Sheila.

"Honey, please don't be mad, but it is Tyrone. Let me answer it, because if I don't he will keep calling my phone."

And of course, Mark is more than pissed, but he has a trick and a treat for Tyrone that he will not like. Mark answers Sheila's phone.

"Hello, I am looking for Sheila, by the way who is this?"

Mark replies sarcastically, "This is her man, and don't call my women's phone anymore. I hope that I have made myself very clear. So, brother hang up this phone and have a good day."

"Who the hell is this?"

"What part of don't call my woman's phone don't you understand, my brother?" Mark hangs up the phone; he knows that Tyrone is pissed off and that's exactly what he wanted to happen. Mark wants to see if Tyrone is bold enough to call back again.

And of course, you know that Tyrone doesn't care what Mark just said; he immediately calls Sheila's phone again. He wants to find out who is answering Sheila's phone. Tyrone says to himself, *so Sheila wants to play these type of games, knowing that I am interested in her. If I don't catch her today I will definitely catch her at another time, and she is going to have to explain herself to me. She ain't nothing but a stank slut and I know that she doesn't think that she is playing me. She has another thing coming. I can't wait to get to the bottom of this and then I am going to show her who the real player is.*

Mark let's Sheila know that they need to speed up the process on taking Tyrone down. He wants to do it now more than ever before; the takedown is going to be awesome. Sheila is usually the levelheaded one, but she is so sick of Tyrone and his childish behavior that she is totally on board with taking Tyrone all the way down. "Mark, honey, let's not talk about Tyrone anymore; this is our time. He is irrelevant and totally unimportant."

Mark and Sheila make it a point to get down to business; and I don't mean regular business, I mean the it's time to get your groove on grown folks' type of business. What a way to end a night, rose petals and being with the one that you love. Mark is in his glory because he knows that he messed up once with Sheila and he will not make the same mistake twice. Come hell or come high water, he is going to make Sheila his wife sooner than later.

After a romantic night of passion and Sheila being in the arms of Mark they both wake up smiling. Mark is so ready for, not only round two, but round three and round four; but he knows that he has to get to work he has three important meetings and two of them are with new clients. Oh, and he also has to deal with Tyrone telling him about how bad Sheila is treating him.

Mark kisses Sheila on the forehead and heads toward the bathroom to shower and prepare for the day. Mark slides into a Nathan Pierce original double-breasted navy-blue suit, with wing tipped navy blue shoes. Not only is Mark sharply dressed, but he is looking good as well. Mark is fine as all get up with a brain and he is Junior partner in his firm. But, after he finishes bringing Tyrone down he just might have to fill Tyrone's spot of being a full-fledged partner. He knows that he has to keep his cool when he reaches the office because he doesn't want to blow anything.

Sheila has to get to the office as well, but not before she stops and sees Delicious for a beauty make over, and boy does she need it. Mark lovingly kisses Sheila on the forehead as he makes his way out the door to his car. She is smiling from ear-to-ear because she can finally say that she has a good man who makes her happy. Mark jumps in his car and heads to the office, before Sheila could get out the door her phone rings; she is hesitant to look at it because she thinks it's Tyrone. As she turns her phone around she realizes that it's Mark calling her. She answers in a worried tone, "Mark, honey, is there something wrong?"

"Sheila why must something be wrong? I wanted to call the woman that I love. Is there something wrong with that?"

"Mark, there is nothing wrong at all. You don't know how much that made my day. Honey, I have to go, I need to stop by Desire's to get beautified."

"Sheila, you don't need to get any more beautified than you already are."

"Mark, that's why I love you."

Sheila and Mark both blow each other kisses over the phone and then proceed to hang up. Sheila grabs her bag and proceeds to leave her house, she jumps in her custom made blue on blue Infiniti the double xx series. She looks fantastic, as always. She rushes to get to Desire's because she knows that if she doesn't get there early enough, it will be jammed packed. Women come from near and far to get styled by Delicious; he is an incredible stylist, even on a bad day Delicious can make a woman look better than good.

Sheila arrives at Desire's in record time, she walks into the salon looking fabulous as always. She has on a form-fitting two-piece Natalie Pearce double-breasted suit, with matching pumps and purse. Delicious is glad to see his friend and he lets her know that she has about a fifteen-minute wait. Sheila is okay with that because it gives her time to check her emails and to go over things with her wedding planner; she is making an appointment with the bridal shop to begin her journey of picking out wedding dresses. Just as she is about to finalize her on-line appointment, her phone rings and yes, you guessed it; Tyrone is calling her… this fool just doesn't give up. Sheila doesn't want to answer this call and against her better judgment she answers it anyway.

"Yes, Tyrone, how can I help you?"

"Sheila is this really you?"

"Yes it is, Tyrone, is there something that you want?"

"Sheila, I don't know what the attitude is about, but you need to fix it."

"Boy, I don't know who you think you are talking to, but my name is not Vanessa and I am definitely not the one."

"Hold the hell up, Sheila. Did you just try to come for me, because if you did you have another thing coming. I will rip you to shreds piece by piece."

Sheila is so angry; she can't believe that Tyrone is disrespecting her like this. Sheila loses it in a nice way and simply says to Tyrone, "Go to hell, you punk." I'm just beginning to come for you; now have a good damn day, and don't ever call my phone again. "She hangs up before he could take another breath to say anything more to her. By the time he realizes what happened, his number has been blocked and she had turned her telephone off and put it deep down in her pocketbook.

Sheila is so upset she is almost in tears. Delicious walks over to her, he can see in her face that something is wrong. "Girl, you look horrible what happened that quick?"

"Delicious, I was just on the phone with Tyrone and he literally cursed me out, I know that Tyrone can be rude at times, but he was beyond rude. He was disrespectful to the point that I had to block his number; he can't ever call me."

"Sheila, I am so sorry. Do you need me to handle it?"

"Call him so that I can give him a piece of my mind, although my mind isn't the only thing that I want to give him a piece of. Delicious you always seem to put a smile on my face just when I need it the most."

"Girl, come with me. I am going to make you look fabulous, all I want you to do right now is to forget about… you know… what's his name and concentrate on yourself. Are you sure that you don't want me to handle Tyrone for you; because, Sheila, when I get finished with him your phone won't be what he will be calling, he will be calling the name Delicious."

"I can't with you Delicious, now you know good and well that Tyrone is not that type of man."

"Sheila, but I am that type of man."

"… and what type of man is that Delicious?"

"Whatever type you want me to be. The type of man I really am is an 'eye-candy' type of man."

"Why is that, Delicious?"

"Sheila, it's because I like to keep my eyes on the candy; as a matter of fact, my eyes aren't the only thing I want to keep my eyes on when it comes to some candy. Come to think of it, Sheila, they shouldn't call it eye-candy, they should call it my candy, because after I finish they will be saying that's my candy." Everyone in the salon cracks up laughing hysterically.

"Delicious, you are completely out of control."

"Sheila, you look good", and just as he says that, in walks Vanessa and Vikki. "Well, look who we have here, the double-mint twins. I haven't seen you two in about a month. Vanessa, you look like you need emergency treatment; and Vikki girl, I don't know what to say about you."

"Delicious, you always think that my hair isn't looking good."

"Vikki, that's because it doesn't look good. You look like a combination of a Brillo pad and steel wool."

"Delicious, I don't look that bad."

"Vikki your hair is so rough that if I tried to run my fingers through it, I might slice my hands."

"Delicious, you are not right, just make me look good."

"Vikki, I am going to have to perform a miracle."

Delicious escorts Vanessa and Vikki to the back of Desire's and as they approach the sink to get washed they both notice that Sheila is there. "Hello ladies, how are the two of you?"

"Sheila, it's good to see you, do you remember my friend Vanessa Brown?"

"Yes, I sure do. You are the ex-wife of Tyrone Tyler."

"Yes, that's me. How are you Sheila?"

"Vanessa, considering that your ex-husband is a total butt hole, I am doing great."

"Okay, what happened now?"

"Sheila, please let me tell the story because you won't tell it correctly. I know you don't want to hear this about that fine specimen which is your ex; but he is in love with Sheila but, she is engaged to his nemesis and Tyrone totally disrespected Sheila to the point that she has cut off all contact with him. But I am into recycling even men."

Vikki asks Delicious what he is talking about? "Girl let me just say this. All I need is about five minutes with Tyrone and he will be singing like the commercial, *I'm loving it*. And he will be loving it for sure."

"Eww Delicious, that's just nasty as all get up."

"Vikki, there is nothing nasty about anything when it comes to me." Just as Delicious is about to say something else, to Sheila's surprise, in walks Mark. Delicious turns around and smiles and says to Mark, "Well, well, well look who we have here, the one and only M and M with peanuts. I think I just hit my payday. Mark have you ever heard of the saying…?"

Mark interrupts Delicious and asks him, "What saying?"

"The one where I get to say, "Sometimes you feel like a nut and sometimes you don't, today is your lucky day, Mark, because I feel like feeling a nut."

"That's my cue, Sheila, it's time to go."

Vikki, Vanessa and Sheila crack up hysterically. Sheila tells Mark that Delicious is harmless, he just likes to spice up a day.

"Now Sheila, why are you lying to this fine specimen? It's not a day that I like to drive up, I mean spice up, I have some other things in mind."

"Okay, enough already, Delicious. What in the world is your real name, because I know that your mother didn't name you Delicious on purpose?"

"Mark, my name is Lavell."

"Well then, enough already, Lavell. Ladies I hope you all have a great day, but I am here to pick up my sweetie, Sheila. Wait a minute, aren't you Antonio Anderson's wife?"

"Yes, my name is Vikki Anderson."

"Well, hello Vikki. How are you?"

"I am great Mark, it's good to see you. Vanessa says to Mark. How is the job?"

"Things are good."

"Mark, this is me. I know that it's not easy working with Tyrone, he is a piece of work."

"Ha ha Vanessa, you know your ex-husband very well, he is more than a piece of work."

Delicious is over in the corner telling Sheila that she needs to let Mark know what happened with Tyrone, but Sheila doesn't want to say anything because she knows Mark will be livid. Delicious tells her that she must tell him because if he finds out from someone else it's not going to be good for Tyrone at all.

"Delicious, I understand what you are trying to say, but it's not the right time. I will explain everything to you at a more appropriate time and location. Just trust my decision. Mark will get the chance to curse Tyrone out; and when he does, everyone will have the chance to see it firsthand."

"Okay Sheila. I won't say anything this time, but if Tyrone messes up again I am definitely going to mention it to him. Tyrone might be fine, but he is a punk for the way he treats women."

Mark is curious about what Sheila and Delicious are discussing in the corner, so he makes his way to where they are. He immediately knows that something is going on, because as soon as he gets there both Sheila and Delicious stop talking; and anyone who knows Delicious knows that when a fine man is in his presence, he has something to say.

"Hey Sheila, baby, is everything okay with you?"

"Mark, I am fine."

"Sheila, I know you are fine. I asked you are you alright and don't lie to me because I know you and I know when you are okay, and when something is bothering you."

"I promise you, Mark, nothing is bothering me. I am just a little tired. Can we go home?"

Sheila and Mark begin to walk towards the door, when Sheila tells Mark that she wants to say good-bye to Vanessa and Vikki. "Ladies, it was a pleasure running into you, let's get together and have a fun-filled ladies' night."

Both Vanessa and Vikki tell Sheila that it's a deal and that she should set it up. Vikki tells Sheila that she needs to get out more, but with her being pregnant it's hard and Antonio is so overprotective he wants to know her every move.

Vanessa explains to Vikki that it's Antonio's first child and he just wants to make sure that everything turns out okay. "Can you blame him? You just need to realize that you have a husband who cares about you. But you also have a husband who loves you above all else, but right after God, so enjoy it."

"Vanessa I guess you are right. Speaking of this, my wonderful man is calling now, excuse me while I talk dirty to Mr. Anderson."

Of course, Delicious has to put his two cents into the conversation by telling Vikki that he wants to talk dirty to Antonio, "As a matter of fact, I want to do more than talk."

Vikki has to ignore Delicious so that she won't laugh at him. Vikki tries to talk sexy to Antonio, but she realizes that she can't say what she wants to because she in a public place; so, she whispers and tells Antonio that she loves him and that she will see him soon.

"Vikki I can't wait to see you."

"I can't wait to see you either, baby."

Vikki thinks that Antonio is getting ready for the new football season; but he is surprising her, he is actually at home waiting for her to arrive. Vanessa is in on the plan. Finally, after Antonio sends the message to bring Vikki home, she and Vanessa leave the salon, looking like America's next top hair models.

Delicious makes sure to say good-bye to Mark. "Excuse me Mark, are those nuts Almond Joy or Snickers?"

Now Mark is angry. "Sheila, let's go and I mean let's go, not now, but right now. I don't want to be here another minute."

Delicious tells Mark that it will only take him a minute. "Oh, by the way I need everyone to check out my website, it is called amansnutsarethebest.org. Let me repeat it in case you didn't understand, and I need everyone to listen, especially you, Mark. I'm going to say it nice and slow for you a man's nuts are the best."

Sheila tells Delicious that she has had enough. "On that note, it's definitely time to go. Mark, let's get out of here."

"Yes, baby girl, let's blow this place."

"Mark I have something for you to blow and it isn't the salon."

By now Mark is so mad and disgusted that he leaves without saying another word to anyone, especially Delicious. Mark is sweating profusely; he is running so fast to his car that he almost knocks a woman down to the ground. He turns and apologizes, after he realizes what he almost did. Sheila is close on his heels she is laughing hysterically at Mark.

"Sheila, what the hell are you laughing for? Nothing is funny."

"Mark, why are you so mad? You know good and well Delicious is harmless and he is not interested in you or any of the men that the women date; he is in a committed relationship. He likes to bring joy and laughter to the day."

"Sheila, he doesn't bother you and make you feel uncomfortable?"

"Mark baby, he's not supposed to make me feel uncomfortable. He is someone that I got to know and if you get to know him, you will find out that he is cool, and he has a lot of connections."

"Sheila, there are just some people and some things that I don't want to be connected too, Delicious and Tyrone are the two people, and Delicious is by default."

"Mark, I'm sorry that you feel that way."

"Mark, let's go home; and trust me, there is nothing to be uncomfortable about." Mark is still mad, but he is slowly coming around. He has something special set up for Sheila and he hopes that she is going to enjoy it. He is quiet on the ride home. "Mark baby, are you sure that you are okay? You are quiet."

"Believe me, everything is perfectly okay. Sheila, I just want to get home and relax."

"Mark, I feel the same way."

"And by the way, I have something special for you."

"What is it, Mark?"

"You will see when we get home."

What Sheila doesn't know is that Mark has planned a romantic evening for the two of them. Mark is getting more and more nervous because he doesn't know if Sheila will like what he did. They approach their home; and as they get out of the car Mark blindfolds Sheila, she is suspicious and questions Mark. "What in the world are you doing and why am I being blindfolded?"

"Sheila, just trust me and go with the flow."

"Alright Mark, but I don't like it."

Mark carefully escorts Sheila inside, and when they get inside he takes off her blindfold.

Sheila is speechless, "Oh my goodness, Mark, this is fabulous. I can't believe that you did all of this for me."

"Baby girl, there is plenty more where that came from."

"Everything looks fabulous."

"And I prepared it myself."

Sheila laughs at Mark. "Sheila, I don't know why you are laughing, I don't see anything funny."

"I'm laughing because you don't cook Mark, but you prepared it. How is that if you don't cook?"

"For the record, I called in a favor and had all of this delivered and I prepared it by putting it on these plates and making everything look good. "They both crack up laughing.

"All that really matters is that you thought enough of me to do this. Mark you are an incredible man and I am so blessed to have you in my life. I can't wait to be your wife,"

"And Sheila, I can't wait for you to be my wife.

"I have waited for this long enough, we will be husband and wife."

"Woman, you don't know how happy you have made me." Just as Sheila is about to respond to Mark, her phone rings. "Who is this?"

"Sheila don't answer that."

"It's my office."

"Don't answer it."

"But honey, suppose it's important. Myah never calls me."

"I don't care, this is our time. Let her leave a message."

"Honey, I guess you're right. Finish telling me again how much you can't wait for me to be your wife."

Mark is whispering sweet somethings in Sheila's ear when her phone rings again, and again it's Myah. "Mark, I have to take this call… it's Myah calling again."

"Nope, I will handle it."

"Baby, please don't be rude."

"I'm not rude, I will handle it." Mark answers, "You have reached the phone of Sheila Smith leave a message and I promise that she will call you back before the night is over; however, she is with her future husband and they are enjoying each other."

"Well I must say that you did a fantastic job; but I just know that something is important, otherwise she wouldn't call again."

"Well, baby girl, we aren't going to find out because I am going to turn the phone off; this is your time and I don't want any more interruptions. You are going to enjoy this time. Sit back and relax."

They are both enjoying each other's love, but Sheila is still concerned that Myah is calling, because something is going on and she really needs to speak with Sheila. She is going to do her best not to think about work tonight. She is going to enjoy all the love that Mark has to offer her. Mark turns the light off. Ah yeah, it's going to be on and it's going to be popping and I mean adult popping.

CHAPTER SEVENTEEN

A woman's intuition is never wrong, so Sheila takes her phone and goes to the study and calls Myah. Sheila is right, something was important. It seems that Antonio Anderson is in her office; he is livid, he was served with documents. It seems that Tyrone has pressed charges and there is a warrant out for Antonio's arrest. He has to turn himself in, in the next twenty-four hours. Sheila tells Myah to tell Antonio to stay put and that she will be there in about thirty-five minutes.

Sheila knows that Mark is going to be upset with her because this was their time together and now she is going to have to leave him alone for a couple of hours to take care of something that probably could have waited until the next day. Mark, of all people should understand; but she knows that he isn't going to be a happy camper. Sheila walks back into their bedroom and Mark can already tell by the look on her face that he isn't going to like what she is about to tell him, but he is going to listen anyway.

"Baby please don't be mad, but I called Myah. I know you told me not to, but I needed to know if it was something important, because she kept calling and texting me, and it is very important. Antonio Anderson is at my office; he is facing assault charges."

"Sheila baby, that isn't good, and it's weird because Antonio doesn't seem like the violent type. Every time I have seen him or spoken to him he was very nice and levelheaded. Antonio isn't the type to fight."

"Mark, you truly won't believe who is accusing him of assault."

"I have no idea, because everyone likes him."

"Well, not Tyrone Tyler."

"Wait a minute, you have got to be kidding me."

"Tyrone has pressed charges against Antonio for assault and battery."

"Sheila, when did this happen?"

"Baby, I don't know. Let me get to the office and I will tell you everything, once I get there."

"Go ahead and keep me up to date. I will be here if you need me."

"Thank you, that's why I'm glad you are my future husband." She and Mark kiss on the lips; and she immediately runs and jumps into her car.

Sheila arrives at her office and apologizes to Antonio. "Now let me read this. Tyrone is claiming that you assaulted him while he was in the hospital and then had it aired on National Television for the world to see."

"Sheila, that is not the truth. I need an attorney to represent me and you are the best."

"Antonio, I would love to do this, but I can't. It would be a conflict of interest because I am representing you in another case against Tyrone. However, I have a friend, Lawrence Mills, who is very capable of taking on your case. I will call him now."

As Sheila is speaking with Lawrence, she is briefly explaining to him about Antonio's situation.

Antonio is on the phone with Vikki, trying to deflect from answering any questions. He doesn't want her to know anything about what's going on; he doesn't want anything to stress her out and cause her to have the baby earlier than necessary. Before he can get another word in edgewise, she asks Antonio, "Who is that woman that I hear talking in the background?"

Antonio has never lied to his wife before but there is a time and place for everything, and this is the time. "Honey I don't know who that woman is I am in a public place; she is talking to someone on her phone.

No sooner than Antonio says that, Sheila calls out to him, "Antonio, I need to see you." Vikki is steamed. "Antonio, I thought you said that you didn't know who that woman was. Then, why in the world was she saying that she needs you? Antonio is she your mistress?"

"Woman, what in the world are you talking about? Do you think that I would be talking to you on the phone if I was having an affair? You should know me better than that."

"Antonio, what are you not telling me?"

"Vikki, I love you and only you; but I have to hang up now. I am being summoned. I will fill you in later, love you gotta go." Antonio hangs up on her because he knows it's going to cause an argument between the two of them.

Sheila informs Antonio that she spoke briefly to Lawrence and that he will be more than happy to take on his case. "Sheila, are you sure about him?"

"Antonio, Lawrence and I went to school together. We were the tops in our class. I was the Valedictorian and he was the Salutatorian. He has won all of his cases. Antonio, put it this way. Lawrence is the male version of me in the courtroom. We got you." As soon as Sheila speaks, in walks Lawrence. Lawrence is six feet four inches tall, lean but muscular. When a woman sees Lawrence, it's sure to put a smile on her face, and Sheila is no exception. Lawrence greets Sheila with a kiss. She is happy to see him; this is a good friend of hers. She always feels a little tingly when Lawrence is around. She tries not to have those feelings, but it's without fail.

"Lawrence, I would like to introduce you to Antonio Anderson. Antonio has to turn himself in because a person in the name of

Tyrone Tyler is pressing charges against him for something that he did not do. Antonio will explain everything to you."

"It's great to meet you Antonio. I hope you don't take offense, but has anyone ever told you that you look like the running back Antonio Anderson? He is my absolute favorite player."

"Nice to meet you Lawrence, I am the Antonio Anderson that you speak about."

"I am truly honored to represent you and believe me you won't be sorry."

"I'm sure you are good; Sheila speaks highly of you. She just informed me that you were second best to her in school and that you are a male version of her."

"I wouldn't put it like that, but I can do the darn thing."

"Well Lawrence, since you are a fan of mine I will make sure that you get tickets to one of my games... please be sure to bring the family." Lawrence can't stop thanking Antonio enough.

"Lawrence, I am glad that I am in a position to help." As Lawrence and Antonio are sitting down and talking, in comes some unwelcomed guest in the form of the Police Department.

"Good evening, my name is Officer St. Claire, and this is my partner Officer Mitchell. We are looking for Antonio Anderson."

"I'm Antonio, officers, is there a problem?"

"We have a warrant for your arrest, but we wanted to speak with you before we did anything. We wanted to talk to you about these charges being filed by the complainant named Tyrone Tyler."

Antonio tells the Officers that the charges against him are false and that he never laid a hand on Mr. Tyler. "And, just to let you know that I am telling the truth, I want you to see this recording of the entire incident. As a matter of fact, my attorney Lawrence Mills will be handling any questions or concerns that you guys might have."

Mr. Anderson that won't be necessary and we are sorry to have bothered you; it's not your fault that Tyrone Tyler is a jerk. Antonio asks the officers, “What happens next?"

“Actually sir, nothing. We will let Mr. Tyler know what happened if he comes to us and asks us.” Officer St. Claire encourages Antonio to have a great season.

“Thank you, and because of your kindness towards me I am inviting both of you to a future home game. We appreciate that and we are sorry to bother you. Have a great day everyone.”

As the officers leave, Vikki calls Antonio, “When are you coming home?”

“Honey, I don't know. I'm in a business meeting.”

“Antonio, are you sure it’s just a meeting and nothing else? How about this, I'm going to text you the address and you can meet me yourself and you will see that I am not cheating on you.”

Vikki gets to Sheila's office in record time. She is not feeling the best, but she wants to get to the bottom of Antonio's behavior. When she finally arrives at Sheila’s office, she is surprised and embarrassed to find out that Antonio is telling the truth.

Sheila greets Vikki with a hug, “Hey girl, how are you and the baby?”

“Sheila, we are great.”

“Vikki, what brings you here?”

“My husband told me to meet him here. By the way, where is he?”

“He is in the conference room with Lawrence.”

“Sheila, who's Lawrence?”

“Vikki, that is something that Antonio needs to tell you. By the way, it was good seeing you and congratulations again. Have you picked out any baby names?”

“Yes, and Sheila, Antonio is so overprotective. It irks my nerves sometimes.”

"Vikki, let him baby you and the baby; you have a good man."

"You are so right. Thank you for your prayers. Sheila, maybe we can do lunch soon."

"Vikki, call me tomorrow and we can schedule a time."

"You got it, now let me get my husband."

Vikki walks in on Antonio's meeting with Lawrence. "Hey baby, how are you?"

Antonio gives Vikki a kiss and introduces her to Lawrence.

"Hi, I'm your husband's attorney."

"Attorney! Why does my husband need an attorney?"

"Vikki we will discuss it when we get home."

"Antonio, we will discuss it now why do you need an attorney?"

Antonio doesn't want to tell Vikki about what happened, but this is something that he can't keep from her. He doesn't like to lie, but he has to tell her the truth. "There was a warrant out for my arrest."

"An arrest warrant? Antonio you aren't a troublemaker. Who would try to tarnish your character?"

"Tyrone, that's who."

"Wait a minute, what did Tyrone do?"

"He told the Police that I hit him two months ago."

"Two months ago, I was in the hospital and you never laid a hand on him. Tyrone is sick he needs some special help. I can't wait to fill Vanessa in on this mess. What are we going to do?"

"Vikki, you aren't going to go anywhere near Tyrone. You are carrying my child and if he does anything to you or the baby, there will be a real warrant for my arrest. As a matter of fact, I don't want you talking to Vanessa about this either."

"But Antonio, she is my friend."

"Vikki, I don't care. I said to stay away from Vanessa and Tyrone. Do I make myself clear?"

"But Antonio, Vanessa is my friend and she can't stand Tyrone."

"Vikki, just stay away from them and that's that."

Lawrence suggests to Antonio that he file a suit against Tyrone for defamation of character. "Antonio, Tyrone is going to wish that he had not messed with you."

By now Vikki is aggravated with Antonio. She is going to keep quiet, but this isn't over by a long shot. Vikki pretends that she isn't feeling well so that she can get away from her husband.

"Vikki, baby, are you okay?"

"No, I need to go home."

"Honey, I will be finished with my meeting with Lawrence in about twenty minutes."

"I can drive myself home. Bye honey, I will see you when you get home. Lawrence it was great meeting you."

"And to you as well, Ms. Anderson."

Vikki leaves; but before she speeds away in her car, she calls Vanessa and tells her that she needs to speak to her."

"Come over, I am home."

Vikki takes the fifteen-minute drive to talk to Vanessa; she is happy to see her friend. "Girl, look at you. Pregnancy looks fabulous on you."

"Well, thank you, my friend. How is that husband of yours, Mr. Brown?"

"Vikki, Kevin is great, and we are officially with baby."

"Oh, my goodness Vanessa, I am so happy for you."

"Vikki, are you okay? You don't seem like yourself."

"Vanessa have you ever had something to tell someone, but you swore you wouldn't tell?"

"Vikki what in the world are you talking about?"

"Vanessa, Tyrone is trying to have Antonio arrested for assault and battery charges."

"Vikki, you have got to be kidding me."

"Vanessa, it's the truth. I left Antonio with his attorney strategizing their next move."

"Vikki, Tyrone is unbelievable. I hope Antonio sues Tyrone for everything he's got maybe that will teach him a lesson, but then again that won't stop Tyrone."

"Vanessa, there is one other thing, I'm not supposed to tell you what Tyrone is trying to do to Antonio, but you are my best friend and I needed to talk to you."

"Don't worry Vikki, your secret is safe with me."

Vikki thinks about it and decides to change the subject. "Vanessa, is Kevin excited about becoming a dad?"

"Well, he doesn't know yet."

"What do you mean he doesn't know yet?"

"I haven't told him because I just found out today and I want to make sure that the mood is right. I have something in mind. I'm just filled with emotions, especially because we had a miscarriage the first time."

"Vanessa, I'm sure that everything is going to work out for you and Kevin. I have a great idea. Why don't you have a baby announcement dinner and invite only close friends; I think that he will love that. That's Antonio calling me now. 'Hi honey, how are you'?"

"Vikki, where are you? I am home and you're not here."

"Well I stopped by to see a friend; I will be home soon. Love you. Vanessa, let me go; my husband is calling me. I told him that I was going home and for him to be there before me is not good. Antonio is such a worry wort he always wants to know where I am, I can't breathe without him questioning me."

"Vikki, I don't think he is a pain like you say, you're pregnant with his first child and he just wants to make sure that everything is okay with you and the baby. That man loves you so much, Vanessa, I know he does."

"Let me go, I will speak to you later, love you so much girl."

"Okay Vikki, call me when you get home."

"Will do, Vanessa." Vikki jumps in her car and makes her way home as soon as she can. She knows that there is going to be a situation with Antonio, but she will be able to handle him. She manages to make it home, but she is in no mood to be bothered with him. Her feet are swollen, she has a headache and she isn't feeling good. When she arrives home, Antonio has greeted her with six dozen blue roses. *To the love of my life I am forever yours.*

"Aww Antonio, this is why I love you so much. It's the little things that you do that make me smile so much. Vikki places the roses on the coffee table in the living room.

Now that looks wonderful. Don't you agree, honey?

"Now let's address the elephant in the room."

"Antonio, what in the world are you talking about?"

"Vikki, don't play stupid, don't act like you don't know what I'm talking about."

"I honestly don't know what you are talking about. Why weren't you here when I got here, and what friend did you go see?"

Vikki is going to try her best to worm her way out of this question. "I went to see a friend and I stayed longer than I had anticipated. "She immediately changes the subject. "Now, what do you want for dinner?"

Antonio steps in front of his wife, "Woman, don't lie to me where were you?"

"Antonio, I just said that I went to see a friend; so please stop asking me where I was."

"Hold up Vikki, what is going on? You don't normally act like this."

"Antonio, I can't believe that you are questioning me about where I was, you have to give me some breathing room."

Just as Vikki says that her phone rings, it's Vanessa on the other end. "Hello, hey there, how are you?"

"I am fine. I am sorry I was supposed to call you when I got home, but I haven't had the chance to relax. I made it in safely and now I'm having a slight disagreement with my husband."

"Are you okay?"

"We will be fine. Can I get back to you later? Thanks a bunch."

Vikki hangs up and Antonio has a strange look on his face. "Vikki, who was that?"

"That's the friend I went to see, and they were checking to see if I made it home alright."

"Wait a minute. Is Vanessa the friend that you went to see, after I told you that I didn't want you to see her?"

"Antonio, Vanessa is my best friend and no matter what, she is always going to be my friend; and I can see her when I want. You have no right to tell me that I can't see my friend."

"Vikki I have every right; I am your husband."

Antonio should have never said that to Vikki because she is in a great deal of pain. "Oh no, please God, no."

"Baby, what's wrong?"

"I am going into labor; it's too soon for that. Call the ambulance, Antonio."

"That will take too long, I am going to take you myself." Antonio rushes Vikki to the hospital. No sooner than they get on the road, they are stopped by the Police. The Officers approach Antonio's car; his window is already down. "Is there a problem, Officer Sharp?"

"Sir, do you realize that you were speeding?"

"Yes, but my wife is in labor."

When Officer Sharp bends down to look inside the car, he realizes that he is talking to Antonio Anderson. He immediately returns to his car and escorts them to the hospital. They arrive in record time and Vikki is rushed to the maternity ward she is in labor. Antonio calls his mother and Wallace and tells them to get to the hospital because she is about to have the baby. They get there as soon as possible.

Cassie calls Vanessa and tells her to get to the hospital because it's time for the arrival of baby Anderson. Everyone makes it to the hospital in the nick of time. They are excitedly awaiting the arrival of baby Anderson. What Antonio and the rest of the crew don't know is that during her birth there was a complication and the doctors are not sure that Vikki is going to make it. This is a hard task, but Antonio must be informed. Everyone is talking and out comes Doctor Johnson.

"Hello Mr. Anderson, I am Doctor Johnson."

"Hello Doctor Johnson, how is Vikki and the baby?"

"You have a healthy six-pound nine-ounce baby boy."

Antonio is gleaming with excitement. He gives Wallace a high five, he hugs his mother Cassie and he even hugs Vanessa; she is Antonio Junior's Godmother. Antonio turns to Doctor Johnson to say thank you, but he realizes that something isn't right. "Can I see my wife and the baby now?"

"I'm sorry, but there were some complications during the pregnancy and we aren't sure that she is going to make it."

Doctor Johnson I don't think that I heard you?

What did you just say to me? Doctor Johnson are you telling me that my wife could die?

"Mr. Anderson, I'm not saying that. I'm just saying that she is not doing well right now."

Antonio is beside himself; he doesn't know how he can make it if he loses Vikki.

"Doctor Johnson, I need to know what happened with my wife."

"Mr. Anderson, as you know your wife was not supposed to be stressed because it could possibly do damage to her. Vikki has a heart condition and the less stress she has in her life the better. And with her having a high-risk pregnancy, we wanted to make her pregnancy as easy as possible. Something triggered this. Do you have any idea what could have caused this?"

They can't believe it. *Vanessa just spoke to her about an hour ago. What could have happened that fast that Vikki is in such a dire condition?* "Antonio, what did you do to my friend? Why is she here?" Antonio ignores Vanessa, but she wants to know what's going on.

"Yes, I know what caused it." Antonio is beside himself because he just had a disagreement with Vikki and he knows that this is what triggered her being in the hospital. Antonio is upset with himself because he knows that the disagreement he had with his wife could have been avoidable.

"You knew that there was a chance that something could happen to her and you got mad with her and let your ego get in the way because she wanted to stop by and let me know what Tyrone was doing to you. She thought that I could help. She also said that she was only trying to help you and she didn't think that you would be mad at her, once you found out it was me; but no, you had to make a big deal about it and now look what happened. Antonio you better hope for your sake that my friend pulls through this. As much as I want to punch your lights out, I'm going to calm myself down and just walk away from you."

"Doctor Johnson, can we see Vikki and the baby?"

"Yes, you can, but only for a few moments. She is very weak now and we need her to get her strength built up."

Antonio walks back to the waiting area and lets the gang know that they can see Vikki, but only for a few moments. It's at that very moment that Antonio pulls Vanessa aside and lets her know that he wouldn't do anything to purposely hurt Vikki.

"Antonio, I know you love your wife, but you need to know that I am for you and Vikki always. So, anytime she needs to talk about Tyrone, just know that I am the best person. I know him like the back of my hand, and I can help your case more than you know."

"You're so right, but let's talk about that later. Right now, we need to be strong for Vikki."

Antonio, Cassie, Wallace and Vanessa are escorted to a private maternity ward. Antonio's eyes begin to fill with water as he sees his son for the first time. He is overcome with joy when the nurse hands Antonio Junior over to him. Tears begin to flow from his eyes, as well as Cassie and Vanessa. How handsome is Antonio Junior. Antonio doesn't want to let him go, but he also wants to see his wife. "Vanessa, since you are AJ's godmother, would you mind holding him for me?"

"Antonio, I would be honored, but you have to do me a favor."

"What is that Vanessa?"

"When you stop by to see Vikki, please give her a kiss for me. She is my best friend and I wouldn't be the woman that I am without her."

Antonio assures Vanessa that he will do that. This is a walk that he doesn't want to take, especially because he now realizes that he caused his wife to be in this predicament. Antonio is shocked to see his wife hooked up to machines. He breaks down uncontrollably, he is beside himself. Antonio knows that the most important thing that he can do is pray for his wife. He is praying for a miracle. He cannot bear not having Vikki in his life; she and baby Antonio are his world. "God, please heal my wife. I can't do this without her and my baby. I'm trusting in you to work out a miracle."

No sooner than Antonio prayed, Vikki opened her eyes. She is staring at him, and she squeezes his hand slightly. He calls out to the nurse to come to the room because Vikki is awake. He is crying tears of joy because God answered his prayers. Antonio showers Vikki with kisses, he whispers softly in her ear, “Hey beautiful, I am so glad that you are still with me. I don’t think that I can function, if you aren’t here. How are you feeling, are you okay?”

Vikki is too weak to speak, so she just nods her head up and down. Antonio lets her know that she gave birth to a baby boy.

Vikki is overjoyed. All she can do at the moment is cry. She tries to talk to Antonio because she wants to apologize to him.

“Baby, what are you apologizing for? You didn’t do anything. I need to apologize to you. I was so hell bent on you not talking to Vanessa that I caused you to go into labor earlier than expected. Baby I love you more now than ever before.”

Vikki whispers to Antonio, “I love you so much”.

“Baby, I am leaving. I am going to stop and see little Antonio and then I am going home, I will be back tomorrow bright and early. Rest well, my beautiful queen.” Antonio kisses her on the forehead and leaves. He walks away and stops to see his handsome baby boy. There is nothing like a father’s love for his son, and Antonio loves his son. He speaks to his son in only a language that the baby will understand.

Antonio has left the hospital and takes the long drive home. He is in a quiet but thankful mood. It’s going to feel strange with him being home in that great big house alone, but he also knows that he has to be strong for Vikki and Junior Anderson. He arrives home and is tired as expected he would be. He is just trying to make it through the night.

It’s a bright sunny morning in August. Antonio is up bright and early, getting dressed. He will be heading to the hospital soon. He receives a call from Sheila and Lawrence, they are both on the phone. "Hey dude, I'm just calling in to check on you, and to update you. I have filed a counter suit against Tyrone, and I am sure that he is going to be livid once he sees it. We have to wait for him to answer the counter suit. Antonio, when can you come into the office?"

"Lawrence I don't know when I will be able to sit and talk with you, my wife is in the hospital in Intensive Care."

Sheila screams out, "What happened?" There were complications during the pregnancy, Junior Anderson is great, but she is in Intensive Care. She woke up, but she is still weak. Please keep us in your prayers.

"Antonio, I am so sorry, you don't have to worry about coming to the office. Take care of your family; and as your attorney, I will take care of whatever you need. I will call you if I need anything from you. We have your back."

"Thank you guys. I will speak with both of you later."

Antonio arrives at the hospital. He is shocked to find Mother Cassie and Vanessa already there. "What are you guys doing here?"

"That's my best friend and Godson; and I am going to make sure that they are both okay."

"Now son, did you think that I was going to have my one and only daughter and grandson in here and not check on them. You are part of me and so are they."

"Actually, I am glad that you guys are here." Mother Cassie hands Junior over to Antonio so that he can hold him. Antonio lights up when he has his baby in his arms, and Junior has the biggest grin possible, he can't see his dad really clear, but he knows who he is and is comfortable being wrapped up in his father's big strong arms. "Hey, you two, me and the baby are going to go and visit Vikki for a while, we will see you when we come back."

Antonio and Antonio Junior take a nice little walk down the hall to see mommy.

Vikki is doing better. She isn't hooked up to tubes anymore; but she is still weak, and she is hungry as all get up. She does manage to sit up when she sees her husband and her son. Antonio hands Junior over to Vikki. This is the first time that she is getting to hold the baby. She is overjoyed; she is crying and happy, all at the same time. Antonio wipes the tears from her eyes. "Baby, I'm here and you are okay and so is our son."

"Honey, I'm hungry."

"Okay, I will get you something to eat, but not this nasty hospital food. Is there anything particular that you want?"

"I want a nice burger and fries."

"Vikki you don't eat food like that, are you sure?"

"Antonio, I am very sure."

"Okay, I will find you what you want to eat." He walks over to Vikki and kisses his son. He doesn't want to leave, but he wants to grant his wife's request.

Antonio goes to the waiting area to meet with Mother Cassie and Vanessa. "Hey guys, Vikki is up, and she is hungry. I am going to get her something to eat. Can you guys keep her and the baby company until I get back. I'll show you her room." Antonio escorts Mother Cassie and Vanessa to his wife's room. "Hey baby, are you up for company?"

"Sure Antonio." Mother Cassie and Vanessa surprise Vikki; she is so excited to see them.

"I'm leaving, text me if you want something else to eat. I will be back soon."

All the ladies laugh and cry together. They are so happy to see each other, but sad about the circumstances. In walks Doctor Johnson. "Hello ladies, it's good to see you all. I'm sorry to interrupt you."

Mother Cassie asks Doctor Johnson if there is a problem.

"Actually, there isn't. I'm just checking on Mrs. Anderson to see if she is well enough to go home tomorrow. It's a miracle that she has improved as much as she has."

"Doctor, it's not a miracle that she has improved. Do you believe in the power of prayer? We are a praying family. I had no doubt that she would be better."

Doctor Johnson has run a series of tests and listened to her heart all while Mother Cassie and Vanessa were in the room. "Mrs. Anderson, you are doing quite well, and I am going to discharge you tomorrow; but you have to rest and take care of yourself and that handsome son of yours."

"Doctor Johnson, as her mother, I promise that we will make sure that she and my grandson are well taken care of when they leave the hospital. I will be there to help out as long as she needs me."

"That's great, and with help like that I am sure she will be back to normal in no time. See you ladies later."

Vikki is happy that she gets to go home. "Hey, let's not tell Antonio just yet. I want to surprise him."

Antonio texted his wife to let her know that he is on his way back from getting her food. Little Antonio is sleeping comfortably on his mother.

Even though Vikki is excited to see everyone she wants to get a little more rest. "Hey guys, can you take the baby. I want to get some more shut eye before Antonio returns with the food."

"We would be happy to watch the baby; we will sit here and be quiet." Vikki hands the baby to his godmother, Vanessa. He cries for a second, but then he calms down as Vanessa sings softly to him. She has a great voice.

Vanessa looks wonderful holding her godson. In walks Antonio. He stops and records this moment, all the women in his life. He catches all the women off guard, his son knows when he is around because as soon as Antonio got closer to him he opened his eyes and when he doesn't see his dad he begins to cry. Vikki immediately awakens. Antonio walks over to Vikki and gives her a great big kiss on the lips and then proceeds to feed her. "Antonio honey, I'm not a baby I can feed myself. As a matter of fact, I have to pump in a few, I need to feed the baby." Everyone leaves the room so that Vikki can have a privacy.

Antonio cannot believe the strides that his wife has made in such a short time. If he didn't believe that God is able, he surely believes it now. His faith was surely tested, and he definitely passed.

Antonio doesn't want to let his son go, but he knows that he has to, it's feeding time. Antonio brings his son to his mother so she can feed him. Antonio looks at his son and says to him, this is my future "Football Hall of Famer".

"Now honey, he might not want to be a baller. How about a future lawyer?"

"Nah, Vikki when we have our daughter she will be the attorney, she is going to negotiate all of Junior's contracts."

"Honey, he isn't a week old and you're already planning out what you want him to do. When he gets older he will decide what his career will be, and we will support him."

"Yeah honey, I guess you're right."

"Antonio, I'm trying to feed our son, can you give me five minutes."

"Vikki, I want to witness this. It's such a beautiful thing to see my wife breastfeeding our baby."

Antonio walks to the door he is just about to tell the women to come in and eat when Vanessa asks, Antonio do you think that it's okay for us to come inside to eat while Viki's trying to breastfeed the baby that's a sacred time and I don't think she wants us to be around.

"Vanessa, you might be right but let me ask her and see what she says."

"Baby girl, do you have a problem with Vanessa and my mother coming in to eat while you are breastfeeding AJ?"

"Antonio, normally I would have a problem with it; but because they are family it's okay this time."

"Okay baby, I understand. I will let the ladies know."

Antonio steps out of Vikki's room for a second to let Mother Cassie and Vanessa know that it's okay to come in and eat. They all step back in the room and begin to eat. Everyone is excited about the strides that Vikki is making; so much so that when she finishes breastfeeding the baby, Antonio takes him and holds him in his arms. He doesn't care about not eating, he is in his own little world.

As soon as Antonio is about to utter another word, in walks Doctor Johnson. "Hello Mrs. Anderson, how are you doing?"

"I'm doing okay, Doctor Johnson."

"Well, Mrs. Anderson, if I must say so myself, you are looking quite well; and it's short of a miracle that you are up eating, talking and feeding your baby."

"Doctor Johnson, it's no miracle at all, it's God."

"Mrs. Anderson, I can't argue with you on that, you are absolutely correct."

"Well, I came to let you know that I have some news for you."

Antonio asks, "What is it, Doc?"

"Mr. Anderson, I explained to your wife earlier that her vitals were up and that she was doing better. She is cleared to go home; but we just want to keep her until tomorrow, just to be one hundred percent sure."

"Doctor Johnson, that it is great news. I can't wait for my wife and baby to be home where I can take care of the both of them."

"Soon, Mr. Anderson."

"Doctor, you have been so helpful to me and my family. Please call me Antonio and if there is anything that I can do please let me know."

"I didn't want to ask, but can I have your autograph for my son?"

"Doctor Johnson, I'll do you one better. How about tickets to a future game? You pick the game and they are yours."

"Really? Oh, my goodness, my son is going to be so excited. You are his favorite player."

"No worries, Doc. I will be happy to do this for your son. As a matter of fact, I have to go to training camp next week, bring him by."

"Thank you, Mr. Anderson... I mean... Antonio, and all the best to you and your wife."

"Antonio, where are you going?"

"Baby, you will see."

Antonio leaves and texts Vanessa and Mother Cassie to meet him outside. They both leave, but one by one. They don't want Vikki to start worrying. After about twenty minutes of being alone, she realizes that no one is coming back; so, she continues to eat. By this time, the nurse comes and takes baby Anderson back to his room. Vikki is sad because she doesn't have anyone around her at the present time. She literally cries herself to sleep.

Vikki awakes. This is the day that she and her son are able to go home, and she can't wait. She slowly gets out of the bed and proceeds to the bathroom and washes herself and brushes her teeth. She is preparing to leave the hospital and take her son home. She is still a little weak, but she won't let on. She also has to be strong for Junior and she dare not tell Antonio this because he will never go to training camp. As she is finishing getting dressed, she walks down the hall to get Junior. She is so excited. She is handed her son, and she then walks back to her room. Standing in her room is Antonio with a dozen blue roses, and clothes for the baby.

"Antonio, I already have a baby bag prepared for him with all his clothes inside."

"Baby, I know; but I couldn't help myself. Can he please wear this?"

"Okay and guess what! You have the honor of washing him up and getting him dressed. But, I will put his pamper on him; you haven't quite mastered that just yet." They crack up laughing, especially because they know Vikki is so right in what she is saying.

As they are getting the baby dressed Vanessa and Mother Cassie show up they are excited to see Vikki and Junior go home. They both shower Vikki with gifts.

"Aww, you guys are the best. I'm so ready to leave this place. Can we go, Antonio? The baby is getting cranky because he is hot, I am hot as well. Your mother doesn't want to be here, and I'm sure that Vanessa is ready to go."

"Honey, you have to be discharged, that will take hours. You know how slow the doctors are." But they have a surprise in store for Vikki. Her discharge papers are ready; they are going to bring them to her, and once she signs off on them she and her family can head home.

Antonio, with the help of Mother Cassie and Vanessa, have coordinated a baby shower for Vikki. All of the players' wives are at the house; Sheila is also there, but she can only stay long enough to greet Vikki and the baby. Delicious is on his way, he can't miss this; and believe it or not, Kayla was invited but only because she is going through some things.

Antonio makes sure that everyone is safe in the car. As he is preparing to leave the hospital, a young boy and his mother stop and ask for his autograph. Antonio can tell that the mother has fallen on hard times. He does something incredible for them both. He stops a hospital employee and asks them for their assistance.

"Here is some money. I need you to get them some food and I need you to set them up in a hotel room for a week, after which I need you to get all of their information. I want to do something special for them, but don't let them know anything. Thanks."

Antonio jumps in his car and heads home with his family in tow. Any other time he would be driving really fast; but today he won't because he has precious cargo with him. They finally arrive home. Vikki has no idea that there is a house full of people in her back yard, waiting to see her and the baby. Vanessa pretends that she hears a noise coming from the back of the house. She insists that Antonio comes as well. Antonio takes the baby from Vikki and tells her to stay put. Antonio, Vanessa and Mother Cassie walk to the back of the house leaving Vikki standing alone in front of the house. She expects one of them to come back to the front of the house to tell her that everything is alright; but none of them do that, so she takes it upon herself to see what is going on.

She is calling out names, "Vanessa, Mother Cassie, Antonio! but, no one is answering. She is becoming increasingly nervous because no one is responding to her; and she is even more concerned because Antonio has the baby. She slowly walks to the back of the house and what she sees is amazing. "Oh, my goodness!" She is in tears; she can't believe that all these people are here for her and Junior. "Antonio you scared the heck out of me, I thought something happened. Antonio, where is AJ?"

"He is with my mother, upstairs. She took him up to his room so that he wouldn't cry while we were trying to get you back here. They will be down in a second. Baby, I hope you are happy."

Vikki says to everyone, "I am so honored, I thank you all for coming here today. I'm overjoyed, I'm so happy to see all of your beautiful faces. Please eat and enjoy yourselves."

Mother Cassie hasn't had too much time with the baby, so she decides that she is going to show off her first grandson. Antonio is pleased that everyone is enjoying themselves.

Sheila has to go she has a case that she is handling, and she has to appear in court in the morning. "Congratulations to both of you, what a handsome baby you have. Antonio I will speak with you soon."

It's a good thing that Sheila left because fifteen minutes after she left Tyrone appeared at the shower uninvited. After ringing the bell numerous times and not getting an answer, he heads toward the back of the house. "Antonio, I know you are in here because I see that car, and I hear music coming from your house. You might as well come and talk to me and let us settle this like men."

Vikki notices Tyrone and she confronts him. "What in the world are you doing at my house? Get the hell out of here!"

Meanwhile, Antonio is in the house with the baby, putting him to sleep; so, he doesn't know what's going on.

Vanessa summons him to come downstairs immediately, and he asks her what's wrong. "It's Vikki, she is trying to get my ex-husband off your property, but he refuses to leave."

"Here, hold your godson."

"Antonio, please don't do anything stupid. Your son and your wife need you."

"I promise that I won't do anything."

Antonio is heated. "Tyrone, what the hell is your problem? Why are you at my house?"

Before Antonio can utter another word, his teammates have all stepped to Tyrone. They all know what happened the last time, and they are not going to let anything happen to their friend and brother.

"You Negroes need to get out of my face, this is between me and Antonio. Antonio you are a punk and a liar, you make people think that you are so nice, but I know the truth."

Vikki asks Tyrone, "What in the hell are you talking about?"

"Vikki, get the hell away from me before I slap the taste out of your mouth."

That did it; Antonio is on fire. He is about to light into Tyrone, once and for all. "Negro you have lost your mind, talking to my wife like that. You got two seconds to get out of my yard, or you will see how much of a punk I am. One, two…" Antonio raises his fist to hit Tyrone, but Lawrence grabs his hand and tells him that he is not worth it.

"Take him to court and settle it that way."

Sam, a teammate of Antonio, escorts Tyrone away while Tyrone is still popping off at the mouth.

Antonio follows him, "Didn't I tell you to get the hell off my property?" Wallace steps in front of Antonio because he knows that Antonio will lose everything if he touches Tyrone and he definitely doesn't want that. Meanwhile Mother Cassie calls the police. They arrive in record time when they find out that the call is coming from the residence of Antonio Anderson. Tyrone doesn't realize that the police are there; he is still going off at the mouth.

By this time, Wallace has taken Antonio into the house to try and calm him down. Officer Mitchell and Officer St. Claire are trying to assess the case. They are escorted into the Anderson residence, as quickly as possible. Wallace wants to make sure that they speak to Antonio before they say another word to Tyrone.

They realize that this is a sensitive matter and they are going to do their best not to let on that they know what's happening. Officer Mitchell speaks with Tyrone and asks him to remove himself off the property; otherwise he will be removed by force.

Tyrone is still popping off at the mouth. It's at that time that the police handcuff him.

After realizing that he could end up in jail, that's when he decides to shut his mouth and begins to listen to them. "Sir, Mr. and Mrs. Anderson don't want to press charges; they just want you to get off their property and never come back."

Tyrone has to have the last word. "This ain't over by a long shot, Antonio. I'm only leaving because I don't want to embarrass you in front of all your people and because these officers are making me leave."

Antonio is using a lot of self-control right now. His main concern is his son, what would he be teaching him? Actually, he would be teaching him to defend himself, when suckers like Tyrone step to him. Vikki is crying, she is relieved that nothing happened to her husband. She and Junior would not be the same without Antonio.

"Hey everybody, let's go back to the backyard!" Antonio is embarrassed by what just transpired. "I'm sorry that you guys had to see that, but I need you all to do two things for me. The first thing I need everyone to do is to pray for me and my family; as I will continue to pray for each and everyone here. I am so grateful for all the love and support. The second thing that I need everyone to do is to eat up and enjoy the rest of the evening." Junior is sleeping comfortably.

Antonio wants to give a special thanks to Wallace for being the voice of reason. "Wallace, you are a good man and I'm glad that you are with my mother, and as long as she is happy then what you two have is all good with me."

People have eaten and drank and had all the fun they could have for one night. Vikki is so exhausted that she doesn't have time to open all the gifts that she has received. She just wants to get into the shower and go to sleep. She tells Vanessa to spend the night and that she can sleep in the guest room and go home in the morning. Vanessa obliges because this will give her more time to spend with her godson. Mother Cassie and Wallace decide to spend the night as well; but they stay in the guest house, which has four bathrooms, three bedrooms and two Jacuzzis. It looks more like a mini mansion than a guest house.

Antonio, Wallace, and a few of Antonio's teammates have finished cleaning. They have put all the food away and put everything else back in place. After every person has gone, Antonio goes to check on his son. He walks into his bedroom where Vikki is sound asleep. Antonio knows that he won't be getting any loving tonight; but he is not mad at all. He knows that they can't do grown people's things tonight, ...but, maybe next time. He kisses Vikki on the forehead and slips into the bed next to her and immediately goes to sleep. Antonio is snoring so hard that it sounds like two trains colliding.

CHAPTER EIGHTEEN

The sun is shining brightly. Antonio Junior is crying uncontrollably, and Antonio can't figure out why his wife has not gone into his room to comfort him. He turns over and realizes that Vikki is not there, he begins to yell out for her; that's when he realizes that she is not in the house. He immediately gets to Antonio Junior to see what's going on with him. Antonio Junior stops crying, as soon as he hears his dad's voice.

Just as Antonio carries his son back to his room, Mother Cassie comes upstairs. "Mother, where were you? Didn't you hear the baby crying?"

"Antonio, he was asleep, and I was washing his clothes. I have only been away for five minutes. I didn't know he was going to wake up. As you can see, I was on my way back upstairs to check on him."

"By the way, mother, have you seen Vikki? It's not like her to leave, and not text or call me, or even leave a note."

"I have not heard from her son. Why don't you call her on the phone?"

"I guess you're right." Antonio calls his wife but to no avail. "She's not answering."

"Antonio, son, let me try her." Mother Cassie tries as well, and she did not get an answer. "Let me take my grandson downstairs to the living room and feed him, you go back to sleep and I will let you know when Vikki calls."

"Why hasn't she called back?"

"Antonio, it's only been five minutes."

"But mother, where could she be that she can't pick up her phone?"

"Maybe she is at the hairdresser under the dryer."

"Maybe you're right. I'm really tired, mother, and I'm going to do what you said I should do earlier, get some rest."

Mother Cassie takes the baby and leaves and lets Antonio get some rest. Mother Cassie is worried because Antonio is right, Vikki would never leave and not call or text. She finds a card with Delicious' name on it and decides to call him, only to find out that he hasn't seen Vikki since the baby shower; but he promises to call if he happens to hear from her.

It's been over and hour and still no word from Vikki. Mother Cassie doesn't want to alarm Antonio, but at this point she has no choice. But before she does that, Wallace comes and greets her with a big kiss. "Hey, sexy lady, how are you?"

"Wallace, I'm alright considering."

"Considering what, Cassie?"

"Considering the fact that my daughter-in-law has been missing in action all morning. No one has heard from her. Antonio and I have called and texted her numerous times and no answer. She wouldn't leave and not let someone know where she is."

"Cassie, have you called all of her friends?"

"Yes, we did, and none of them have heard from her. Wait a minute, Wallace, we forgot to call Vanessa. She is Vikki's best friend; she would know something; at least I hope she would know something." Cassie calls Vanessa, but her phone goes straight to voice mail.

"Cassie, I pray that everything is okay." Wallace and Cassie continue their conversation. Ten minutes later Cassie receives a call from a private number she usually doesn't answer private calls; but this time she does and it's a good thing because it's Vanessa.

"Vanessa, thank God you called me back."

"Mother Cassie, is everything alright?"

"No, it isn't. Antonio and I have been trying to contact Vikki for more than an hour and she has not contacted either one of us. We have tried everyone, Vanessa, have you heard from her?"

"Yes, Mother Cassie, I have. Vikki is with me; she is in the hospital and that is the reason why you haven't heard from her."

"Oh, my goodness, is everything okay?"

"She was sick since she left the hospital the other day, so she asked me to come with her. The doctors are running tests on her; they want to check and make sure her heart is okay."

"That's good to know. I will let Antonio know."

"Mother Cassie, Vikki would like for you not to say anything to him because he is a worry wort and she doesn't want that; she will be home in a few hours."

"I guess she will tell him then."

"Now Vanessa, you know I shouldn't be keeping this from Antonio."

As soon as she said that, Antonio walks in the living room and says, Keep what from me?"

"Oh, nothing son."

"Too late, mother."

He grabs the phone from her; but it's too late by then. Vanessa has already hung up. "What secret, mother? Vikki is with Vanessa, and what else?"

"Vikki is in the hospital. That's why you haven't been able to contact her; she can't use the phone while in the hospital."

"Vikki is in where? What the hell is going on? Why didn't she tell me?" And he does exactly what she said he would do, worry. "Mother, can you watch the baby while I get dressed?"

"Son, where are you going?"

"I'm going to the hospital to be there with my wife."

"Antonio, she is fine. They are just running some tests; she will be home soon. Relax and let me fix you something to eat, please hold your son while I whip up something."

Wallace asks Antonio if he wants to watch a game. "Nah, I'm good, Wallace."

"Antonio, I think it will get your mind off things for a while."

Antonio says in a hesitant voice, "I guess you are right, Wallace."

Vikki knows that Antonio is going to be livid with her; but she doesn't care, she did what she had to do.

After doing a series of tests on her heart, Doctor Johnson lets her know that everything is okay. He told her that she was still a little weak and that she needed to have more food in her system. "Go home and let your family take care of you. Promise me that you will eat and relax."

"I promise you."

"Good, now go home and take care of your handsome son."

"Vanessa, let's get out of here, I am hungry."

"Me too, Vikki." As the two women leave the hospital, they drive until they come across a new restaurant called Liam's. "Let's try this."

"Vanessa, this place is packed. How come we haven't been here before? There isn't a restaurant that we haven't tried."

Walking towards the ladies is this five feet eleven inches of pure muscle mixed with dark chocolate hottie. "How can I help you ladies today? My name is Thomas. I am the owner of this establishment and I wanted to come over and personally introduce myself."

Both ladies might be married, but they aren't dead, and they can look, and he is something worth looking at. Both ladies say "hello" at the same time. "I'm Vikki and this is my friend Vanessa. This is quite a charming place that you own." Vikki asks Thomas how long his establishment has been open.

"I have been here for about three months. I have another location on the West Coast that is very successful, so I decided to try and see what happens here."

"Well, it's a great spot and we will come back again."

"Vanessa, what are you ordering?"

"Vikki, I think I want a salad. Thomas can you please bring us both a salad, but I would like baked salmon and macaroni and cheese. And we would like Iced Tea with a twist of lime."

"My pleasure, ladies. I would be happy to oblige."

Vanessa looks at Vikki and says, "Girl he is fine."

"I know what you mean. It's a good thing that Delicious is not here, otherwise he would be trying to take his clothes off."

Vikki can hardly breathe because she is laughing so hard, but she knows that Vanessa is absolutely correct.

Speaking of the devil, guess who's on the other end of Vikki's phone… none other than Delicious. "Well hello Delicious, how have you been?"

"Vikki, it's been a while since I saw you, just wanted to see how you are doing?" "Delicious, you just saw me yesterday at the baby shower."

"Girl, you are so right; but you still need to get your hair done. By the way what are you doing?"

"I'm out with Vanessa. We are at Liam's, but I don't know how long we are going to be here."

"Okay, tell Vanessa 'hello' for me. Talk to you both soon."

"Vanessa, Delicious said 'hello'. Can you believe that he was calm on the phone, no jokes."

"Vikki, Delicious calm? Yeah, that's not normal."

Delicious looks up where Liam's is located and decides that he is going to show up there unannounced to meet the ladies.

Delicious has gotten to Liam's in record time. He just wants to be nosey, and of course, he sashays into Liam's like nobody's business. All of a sudden, Vikki looks up and all she can say is, "Oh my Lord, what is he doing here?"

"Vikki, who are you talking about? Girl please tell me that Tyrone did not just walk in here."

"Nah Vanessa, it's not your ex-husband, it's Delicious."

"Vikki, why is that fool here?"

"Vanessa, I can't answer that question; but we will find out because here he comes."

"Hey ladies." Both ladies welcome Delicious to their table.

"Delicious, Vanessa and I want to know what in the world are you doing here?"

"I needed my friends."

"Delicious, I'm sorry what happened?"

"My boyfriend, Kenny, broke it off with me. He said that he doesn't want to be in a relationship. Girls, can you believe that I gave that man the best three years of my life, and he breaks it off so suddenly. I don't know how I'm going to get over this."

The ladies do their best to comfort Delicious, but to no avail. That's when Thomas comes over to their table to personally bring the women their food. *Why in the world did Thomas do that?* Vikki tells Delicious to behave. He totally ignores her. "Well hello, scrumptious."

"Hello, my name is Thomas. I am the owner of this establishment. What would you like to eat?"

Delicious gets up out of his seat and glides over to Thomas and says, "How about you?" Thomas is mad, "Man, if you don't get away from me, I will hurt you."

"Sir Thomas, that's exactly what I hope will happen."

By now, Antonio has called Vanessa on the phone. He is calling because she never reached back out to him to let him know about his wife. "Hi Antonio, Vikki is fine I am with her now; we are actually at Liam's eating. She will be home soon."

"Vanessa, why did you tell Antonio where I was?"

"Vikki, calm your nerves. Antonio has never heard of Liam's and he doesn't know where it is, so you will be fine."

"Vanessa, I guess you're right."

Thomas asks Delicious again, "Have you decided what you want off the menu?"

"Is there any way I can get you on the menu?"

"There isn't."

Delicious says sarcastically, "Alright Thomas, in that case just give me a steak…well done…with a baked potato and salad. That should hold me over until later this afternoon. Vikki how are you doing? And what are you two doing on this side of town?"

"Delicious, I wasn't feeling good, so I had to get a checkup to make sure that everything is okay."

"So, why did your husband call?"

"He was looking for me. I left the house early this morning, I called Vanessa and she came and picked me up. Delicious, you know that Antonio is a pain. I love my husband, but there are somethings that I have to keep from him. He would have driven everyone in the hospital to drink."

"Vikki, now you know you ain't right."

"Delicious, Vikki might not be right, but she is telling the truth." As she is talking to Delicious and Vanessa, in walks Antonio. Vikki says to the both of them, "What in the world is Antonio doing here?"

"Girl, you are lying he's not here."

"Vanessa, I know who and what my husband looks like. That's Antonio. "And of course, he can spot Vikki in a crowded place, no matter where that crowded place may be.

Antonio walks over to where his wife and friends are sitting. He is not too pleased with Vikki because she left the house without telling him anything. As mad as Antonio is, he is not the type of man to make a scene. He sits down without saying a word.

"Hello Antonio, hello Delicious… I mean Lavell… how are you?"

"I'm okay, Antonio. "There is silence for a second or two. "So are you going to address the elephant in the room?"

Before Antonio could answer the question that Delicious asked. Thomas walks over with Delicious' food. Thomas and Antonio make eye contact, they are happy to see each other. They give each other a brotherly hug. "Thomas, my dude, what are you doing here? So, this is where you work?"

"No, my brother, this is what I own. Thomas I heard so much about this place, I had no idea that you were the owner. I will make sure that all my teammates and friends patronize this place, we will definitely support you. Thomas this is my wife, Vikki, and her best friend Vanessa and Delicious."

"So, we've met Antonio, he is an interesting person."

"That, he is."

"I'm in the room, guys."

"How much is the bill, Thomas? I will be paying for everything."

"Would you like to sample what's on the menu?"

"It's cool, I don't want to put you out of the way."

"Antonio, for you, there is nothing that I won't do. You have supported me and had my back when no one else would and you believed in me. When I said I wanted to open a restaurant, you didn't hesitate to loan me the money that I needed."

"Thomas, my man, I was just glad to help a brother out. You are a good guy.

Now look at you, you have two successful restaurants open. I couldn't be more proud."

"Antonio, please sit down and enjoy I'm going to whip up something very special for you."

"Wait! You are fine as hell and you can cook, owner of two restaurants and not married. And Antonio, you are a famous and rich athlete, I could get two for one. Forget Snickers, I'm going to call it something else. Dark chocolate and milk chocolate, that's just delectable with nuts added on."

Vikki angrily tells Delicious, "Enough of your antics, sit down and keep your mouth closed."

"I'll do you one better; I am going to leave. I have to get back to the shop. Vikki, call me later to schedule an appointment because you look busted and disappointed. Vanessa don't you laugh because you look like the brush and comb missed you. I will see you both tomorrow."

"Where did you guys meet him?" Definitely feeling uncomfortable. Thomas, Delicious does that to every man he meets, but he is harmless. He owns the hottest hair salon in town, people don't know this, but he is about to open up another location. Delicious may get under your skin but the brother can lay some hair down. He is the best. I don't trust my hair with anyone else but him."

"Well, he can stay on that part of town and I will stay over here."

"Thomas, thanks for everything. This food is the bomb. How much is the bill?"

"Antonio, it's on the house."

Antonio is appreciative of the gesture; but he is not about to get a meal for free, no matter who it is. Antonio gives Thomas a business card with all of his information on it.

"Make sure you call me, Thomas, we need to get together before football season starts."

"I will make sure that I do that, and it was good seeing you Antonio… I really appreciate you."

As they are leaving the restaurant Antonio hands the Maitre'D an envelope with one thousand dollars in it. "Please make sure that you give this to Thomas. I will call later to make sure that he received it."

"You got it, Mr. Anderson. I will walk it over to him right now." The Maitre'D hands Thomas an envelope.

"What is this?"

"I don't know, I was just asked to give this to you."

Thomas is dumbfounded. He can't believe that Antonio did that; but then again, he can believe it because Antonio is a standup type of man.

As they leave Liam's, Vanessa takes the long thirty-minute drive home. Antonio thanks her for always looking out for Vikki. As Antonio and Vikki drive off, he begins to light into her about not letting him know that she was sick. "Vikki, how could you do this to me? Do you realize that I almost lost you and when I finally get you and the baby home, and I hear him crying uncontrollably and I don't see you in the bed next to me, and you are nowhere to be found in the house… do you know what went through my mind? Only to find out that you were at the hospital. Please don't do that ever again, I don't care how tired that you think I will be, wake me up. I don't care what time of the day or night it is. After God, nothing is more important in my life than you and Antonio Junior."

"Antonio, I apologize for having you worry about me. It won't happen again." Vikki is being cooperative because she doesn't want to get into a heated discussion with him, at least not now. They finally arrive home. Mother Cassie, Wallace and Antonio Junior are waiting to greet the both of them. Junior was crying until he saw his daddy; now he is all smiles. He loves his mommy and daddy and he is always joyful when he sees the two of them.

"My lovely daughter, how are you? Where have you been? We were all worried about you."

"Mother Cassie, I wasn't feeling the best, so I called Vanessa and she came and took me to the hospital. Mother Cassie I have already been yelled at by my husband. All I want to do right now is love on my baby and my husband."

Wallace tells Antonio that he needs to talk to him. "Okay Wallace let's go into the living room and sit down. Wallace what's wrong?"

"Antonio, son, there is nothing wrong. The reason I wanted to talk to you is because I wanted your mother's hand in marriage, and I wanted to ask you."

"Wallace that's so noble of you. Sure, you can marry my mother. She seems happy and as long as you make her happy, then I am okay with it. So, how do you plan on proposing to her?"

"Antonio, I haven't decided that yet, but it will be soon. I also need your help picking out a ring."

"Wallace, I am not the right person for that, you might want to take Vikki with you."

"You are probably correct. That does require a woman's touch."

Vikki walks in on the conversation. "Wallace, what requires a woman's touch?"

"Picking out engagement rings."

"Wallace, are you going to propose to Mother Cassie?"

"Yes, and I need you to go with me to pick out a ring."

"When do you want to go shopping? Wallace this is going to be so much fun."

"Vikki, I was wondering if you had time today."

"If my husband doesn't mind watching the baby, we can go now."

"Vikki, you know I don't mind watching our son. Go and have fun ring shopping, I'm going to enjoy spending time with my son."

"Let's go Wallace, before my mother-in-law starts asking questions."

"Yes, let's do this now."

They sneak out the side door so that Cassie doesn't see them leave… she can be quite nosey at times. They are able to drive away without incident, and of course there you have it. As soon as Wallace and Vikki drive off, in walks Cassie into the living room where Antonio and the baby are. She is excited to see them, but she notices that Vikki and Wallace are not around. "Antonio, weren't Vikki and Wallace here a little while ago? Where did they go?"

"Mother, Vikki had to run an errand and Wallace volunteered to drive her to where she was going. They will be back soon."

"Son, that's great, this will give us time to talk."

"Mom, is there something wrong?"

"Not at all. I am blessed. I have a great son, and daughter, a grandson, and a man who loves me."

"Speaking of that mother, does Wallace really make you happy?"

"Antonio son, yes he does. I couldn't have asked for a better man."

"Okay mother, there is something else on your mind. What is it?"

"I will tell you, but you have to promise not to worry about me."

"What is it mother?"

"I went to the doctor and they found a lump in my breast."

"Mother, what are you saying?"

"Antonio, I'm going to be okay. We have to think positive. I have to go to the doctor's office on Friday to get a second opinion. Will you pray for me?"

"I will do better than that, I will go with you."

"Antonio, you don't have to do that. I will be okay."

"Mother, I know that I don't have to do that; I do it because I want to do it. You sacrificed everything to take care of me and to make sure that I didn't lack for anything. You might think I don't remember, but I will never forget all the times you were with me when I was sick and in the hospital; and when I was injured, you nursed me back to health. I love you and there's nothing I wouldn't do for you."

"Antonio, you are the best son a mother could ask for. Whatever you do, I don't want Wallace to find out about this; because if he thinks that something is wrong, he will worry. You know what, son? He reminds me of you."

"Now mother, you know you're wrong." They both laugh.

Meanwhile, Vikki and Wallace have found the perfect ring for Mother Cassie. Vikki takes Wallace to Liam's, where she gives him ideas on how and where to propose. They are sitting at a table when Thomas comes over to greet them. "Hello Vikki, how are you doing? Twice in one day and who do we have here?"

"Hi Thomas, this is my future father-in law. We were just discussing when and where he is going to have his engagement party. Well Vikki, that's a no brainer, you guys can have it here. Today is Thursday is Friday evening okay."

"Young man, that sounds great. How much?"

"Mr. Wallace, how about eight hundred dollars? We will provide everything… music, food, desert… you just bring the people. About how many people do you plan on having attend the dinner?"

"About forty people."

"Wallace, I didn't know that you knew that many people."

"Vikki, I don't know that many people. Most of them are people that you, Antonio and Cassie know. However, I do have one or two close friends that I would like to invite."

"Then invite them, make the arrangements; and Antonio and I will make sure that they get here Friday evening. This is going to be so much fun. Wallace leave everything to me and Vanessa, we are going to make you proud."

"Vikki, I am glad that you are my daughter-in law, now let's order something to take home with us."

"That's a good idea, Wallace; but I need to call Antonio and let him know that everything is okay. Hi baby it's me. Wallace and I are at Liam's. We have the ring, and we secured Liam's for the dinner." Vikki could tell by Antonio's response that something is wrong. "Honey, are you alright?"

"Vikki, I am fine."

"Antonio, I am your wife and one thing we promised is to never lie to one another, so tell me what it is."

"Vikki, this is not your problem; this is something that I have to deal with."

"Antonio, you are so pig-headed. Stop it, I am your wife and we should be able to handle things together."

"Okay, I will tell you if you promise not to get crazy on me."

"I promise, Antonio. Now, what is it?"

"My mother has to go to the hospital on Friday, they found a lump on her breast."

"Honey I am so sorry, but you know that your mother will be okay. The engagement party will be on Friday. Wallace has a few friends that we need to pick up, and Vanessa and I will handle all the decorations."

"Vikki, did you just hear me tell you that my mother is going to the doctor's on Friday?"

"Honey, I heard everything you said, and I understand that your mother isn't at her best but, you have to believe that she is going to be okay; and maybe this will take her mind off of things."

"I guess you're right, honey."

"Antonio, where is Junior?"

"He is with your mother-in-law in the den watching television."

"Honey, let me go. Wallace and I are on our way back from Liam's, we will be there soon."

Vikki hangs up with Antonio. She and Wallace leave the restaurant they are excited about Friday, but she is also thinking about what Antonio has told her on the phone. She doesn't want to alarm Wallace because he is just like Antonio, a worry wort.

"Wallace, I am so excited for you and Mother Cassie. This is going to be a night that she will never forget."

They finally arrive at the house, and they are about to go inside when Vikki stops Wallace and tells him to walk back to the car with her.

"I just remembered you can't go inside the house with this bag from Liam's. You have to do something with it, because you know Mother Cassie is nosey as all get up and she will find the ring."

"I tell you what, give me the ring. I will put it in my purse, and I can hide it in my room. How does that sound?"

"Vikki, that sounds like a plan and a good one at that; and please, whatever you do, don't let Cassie know that I agree with you about her being nosey." They both laugh.

"Wallace, I promise that I won't say a word. Honey, we're back. Where are you?"

"Here I am honey."

"Here where, Antonio? Why are you whispering?"

"I'm in the den with Junior and he just fell asleep." They walk back upstairs together. "So, Wallace, how did it go?"

"Antonio, you are right. Your wife can pick a ring. And Liam's is fancy. I think Cassie will like it. By the way, where is my future wife?"

"I believe she is somewhere upstairs."

"Well, let me go look for her. I know she has a ton of questions to ask me; but I am able to take care of her."

"Wallace, you do that."

"Antonio baby, how do you feel about Wallace being a new addition to the family, because you couldn't stand him when he and your mother first started dating?"

"Wallace has turned out to be a standup sort of guy."

In walks Mother Cassie with Junior on her arm, he is crying.

"Mother, I thought you were upstairs? Wallace was just up there looking for you."

"I was upstairs on the phone and I was on my way down here. I decided to take the back way, and I wanted to check on my grandson. I heard him crying, so I didn't want him being by himself… so here we both are."

"Thank you, Mother Cassie. Aww, what's wrong with mother's baby? Let me take him and feed him, I will be back shortly." Vikki leaves and here comes Wallace.

"Now Cassie, my love, how did you get here? I was just looking for you."

"I'm sorry, but I came through the back way. How did everything work out?"

"Fine." Wallace, Antonio and Cassie are sitting in the den relaxing and chatting when Antonio's phone rings… it's Lawrence.

"Hello Lawrence, how are you today?"

"Antonio I wanted to warn you. Tyrone did an interview on KCC sports show and he accused you of doing some crazy things. I just wanted to give you a heads up because the story is going to air in about fifteen minutes. Don't worry Antonio, we have a great case against him for slander. I am going to sue him as well as Sheila, and when we both get finished with him, he won't know what in the world hit him. We are going to sock it to him every which way but loose."

"Lawrence, good looking out. I'm not worried about the lies. He is a miserable punk."

Antonio's phone is ringing off the hook. First Lawrence, then he received a call from Mark; and then as soon as he hung up with Mark, he gets a call from Sheila; and Tyrone is on the phone now. Antonio can't believe this Negro called his phone.

Antonio picks up; but before he can say anything Tyrone is going in on him. "You punk, you tried to ruin me; but I have the last laugh. Once this interview on KCC Sports airs in a few moments, you and your football career will be dead as a door nail."

It's taking everything inside Antonio not to get out of character and curse Tyrone out. "Tyrone, get the hell off my phone and don't you ever call me again, or you will be sorry." Antonio is steaming. He hung up the phone on Tyrone, not letting him get another word in edge wise. He is so mad that he throws the phone down.

"Antonio, what's wrong, what just happened?" He doesn't respond immediately to his mother. He turns the television to KCC Sports because he wants to see what Tyrone has been saying about him that is not true; and of course, Antonio and his family are stunned by the accusations that Tyrone has said about him. Vikki walks in on the tail end of the story; she is completely taken off guard by this.

"Antonio honey, what are we going to do about this?"

"Vikki, you aren't going to do anything about this. Your responsibility is to take care of our child and that's all I need you to do. As a matter of fact, I don't want any of you to do anything. I will handle this situation in my own way."

"Son, I don't want you to do anything that will jeopardize your career. Cassie, we don't want him to do anything that will jeopardize this family. Tyrone Tyler is not worth it. Lawrence is going to hit him where it hurts."

Antonio is so angry that he starts yelling at the top of his lungs. "I love you all, but I got this, and I will handle this the way I want to handle it. Now if you can all leave the room, I need some time to think about this whole situation."

Antonio immediately calls Lawrence. "Hey Lawrence, it's time to take this fool down; but before we do that I need to go to KCC Sports and clear my name. He has defamed my character and now I am going to shred his name, reputation, his character and him by any means necessary."

"Antonio, promise me that you will allow me and Sheila to handle this."

"Vikki, I'm not in the mood to deal with you right now. I just need you to take care of our son. Honey I got this."

The next call Antonio receives is from Patrice Starks. She had an encounter with Tyrone that was very unsettling, so she will do everything that she can to get Antonio on her show. Antonio tells Patrice that he would be more than happy to sit down and talk to her, so that he can clear his name.

"I can be at the station at seven o'clock tonight. Thank you." Antonio knows that he has to keep calm and let this play out; but one thing for sure, Tyrone better not cross his path, or it's going to be a situation that Tyrone won't like.

Antonio prepares for his interview. He is very quiet as he is getting dressed. He has not uttered one word to anyone in the house, he wants his mind to be focused. He calls Lawrence on the phone and tells him to meet him at KCC Sports Station.

Both Lawrence and Antonio arrive at KCC Sports at the same time. They both meet with Patrice Sparks to hash out last minute questions. Patrice assures Antonio that he has nothing to worry about. “Antonio, just answer the questions and nothing more and you will be okay. You got this. The studio is set.” Patrice has started interviewing Antonio. He is calm, cool and collected; he is open and honest about everything.

Out of nowhere, Tyrone decides to make an appearance he is screaming at the top of his lungs and trying to tell the world that Antonio hit him for no reason, and now Antonio wants to sue him. He is yelling at the top of his lungs that he feels disrespected by the authorities because they didn’t arrest him. Tyrone is making a complete fool of himself. Antonio is doing everything that he can to keep his composure.

After about a minute of trying to get Tyrone off the set, Antonio invites him to sit down and man up about these accusations. But of course, that’s not Tyrone’s style, he is more of a talk crap and run kind of person. He has made himself look like a total fool in front of millions of people. Patrice questions Tyrone about his accusations. “Tyrone, is there anything that you would like to say while Antonio is here? We would all like to hear what else you want to talk about.”

“Patrice, I don’t have to say anything to you and I definitely do not have to say anything to this punk. The whole world will know the real deal about Antonio when I win my lawsuit, and I promise you that he will no longer be the people’s favorite athlete. They will see that he is a fake.”

“Once again, Tyrone, is there anything else that you need to talk about? If not, then please leave the station.” It takes a minute, but Tyrone leaves without incident. He is yelling off camera, "This ain’t over Antonio, you can’t lie your way out of this!”

“Antonio, is there anything that you would like to say?”

“Patrice, I want to thank you for inviting me to KCC Sports and attempting to hear my story. I appreciate you and the fans.”

The phones start ringing like crazy. All of the callers support Antonio. There are a few fans outside the station with signs that read "We Love You Antonio Anderson". You are the best athlete there is.

Antonio leaves KCC Sports and stops and signs a few autographs before he gets in his car and heads home to his family.

CHAPTER NINETEEN

Antonio leaves KCC Sports, and he takes a moment to reflect on what is happening in his life, while he turns his car on and puts on the seductive and soulful sounds of Terence. He realizes how blessed he is; he has a great family - a caring mother, a second father in Wallace and an awesome wife and adoring son. They are the reason he didn't want to jeopardize and pick a fight with Tyrone. Lawrence phones Antonio on his car phone.

"Antonio, I just got off the phone with Sheila. We both agreed that Tyrone has to be taken down sooner than later. We will talk about it later. Get home to your wife and son and get some rest. By the way, Antonio, good job tonight. I know that Tyrone was trying to get you to get out of character, but you held your own. It takes a real man to do that."

"Lawrence brother, I appreciate you. We can talk tomorrow."

As soon as Antonio finishes his call with Lawrence, Vikki calls; she wants to make sure that everything is okay. "Baby girl how are you and Junior?"

"Antonio, I'm worried about you."

"Vikki there is nothing to worry about, I am okay. I'm on my way home now. I will be there soon, give Junior a kiss for me. Love you."

"Love you too, Antonio."

Antonio decides to stop and get some roses for his wife. He finally arrives at home; he is tired from all the stupidity that has happened with Tyrone. All he wants to do is give his wife a kiss and the two dozen blue roses that he purchased for her; and he can't wait to take a shower and hold Junior.

As it would be, Wallace wants to talk to Antonio about the engagement dinner. "Wallace, my man I forgot all about that."

"Can we talk about it tomorrow?"

"Sure, and by the way, where is my mother?"

"She is asleep, she said that she wasn't feeling well."

"Wallace, I think you should hit the sack as well; you need all of your rest for the dinner tomorrow."

It's all quiet in the Anderson household. Junior is fast asleep in his dad's arms. It's a bright sunny Friday morning. Vikki is already awake; she is in the kitchen preparing breakfast. Junior awakens his father with his crying. He immediately changes him. Antonio brings his son to his mother. "Baby, it smells good in here."

The aroma is so good that Wallace and Mother Cassie wake up; they both head straight to the kitchen. "Vikki, this looks good, sit down and let's eat."

"So, Wallace do you have anything planned for today?"

"Vikki, I am going to relax for a little while and then I have to run some errands."

"Wallace, we would like to go with you."

"Baby I'm sorry, but I can't go."

"Antonio, I wasn't talking about you, I was talking about me and Junior; and I want him to see his godmother."

Antonio responds lovingly, "Well, excuse me. It's alright because I am going out with my mother; we haven't had the chance to spend any time with each other, and today would be a great day to do that." He winks at his wife, because he knows that the engagement dinner is this evening. Everyone dresses and leaves to go about their business, but they all know that they need to be back in the house by seven o'clock, so that they can ready themselves for the dinner.

Antonio takes Cassie to the doctor's. He is very nervous, but he is going to pray for the best. He is trying to be strong for his mother. The nurse comes and escorts Cassie to the examination room, she tells her to change and the doctor will be right with her. Cassie is scared because she could potentially have cancer.

Doctor Sanders comes into the examination room; she talks to Cassie and then runs a series of test. Afterwards, she tells Cassie to get dressed and sit tight while she reads the results. Doctor Sanders walks into the examination room; she sits down and begins to talk to Cassie. "Cassie, this is short of a miracle; the lump in your breast is totally gone. I believe the results will confirm that. I will have a definitive answer when the rest of the results come back." Cassie lets out a yell so loud that Antonio can hear it. He tries to run to the Doctor Sanders office to comfort Cassie, but they will not let him go to the room.

He can't stand the wait. Finally, after about fifteen minutes Cassie comes from the examination room to the waiting area. Antonio jumps up and runs to his mother. "Are you alright?"

"Son, I am fantastic. The doctor told me that the lump is totally gone, and the other tests should confirm it. I don't have cancer, Antonio; this is one of the happiest days of my life."

"Mother, that's fantastic news, now let's go out to get something to eat."

"Antonio, we ate already; let's just get some coffee."

They run over to a quaint bakery called Page's Exquisite Bakery. They talk about everything, including Wallace. "Mother, I never said this before, but I think Wallace is a good man and I'm glad that he is in your life."

"Antonio, I don't know what bought this on, but I am so happy that you have accepted him. I like everything about that man."

"That's more than enough information, mother. Let's change the subject. I know, I want to treat you to get your hair done. Maybe you and Vikki can both go. I'll take care of it. I will call her soon."

Meanwhile, Vikki and Wallace stopped to pick up Vanessa and take her to Liam's so that she can help her decorate for the engagement dinner tonight. Vanessa is excited because she also gets to see her godson and spend some time with him.

Antonio calls Vikki and tells her that his mother wants to get a makeover and he was wondering if she can take her. "Honey, I would love to take her, where are you?"

"We are at Page's Bakery on Velda Street."

"Antonio, we will be there in a few."

Vikki tells Wallace that she can no longer assist him in decorating because she has to meet Antonio and Cassie. "Vanessa, can you go with me to meet Antonio and his mother? He wants me to take her to get a complete makeover and I want him to watch Junior until we get back."

"Vikki, now you know that Antonio can't handle Junior for all of those hours; he will go crazy."

"Vanessa, I know, but he has to learn and now is as good as any; plus, Wallace will be there with him."

Vikki and Vanessa both jump into Vikki's car; they take the fifteen-minute drive to Page's Exquisite Bakery. Antonio is so impatient he has called Vikki's phone eight times in the past ten minutes wondering where she is. He finally decides to call her car phone. "Hey babe, where are you?"

"Antonio, we are on our way. Give me a few minutes, we will be there soon. Vanessa, do you see what I have to go through? One thing for sure is that he loves me, and I can't wait until the season starts so that I can have some peace." They both crack up laughing. Junior is in the back seat; he has fallen asleep.

They arrive at Page's Exquisite Bakery. Vanessa is holding Junior, he is sleeping comfortably in her arms; that is until he hears his father's voice. Then he slowly opens his eyes and realizes that daddy is there, and he grins from ear to ear.

"Cassie, how are you? You are looking more and more beautiful every time I see you."

"Vanessa, I am doing well. And I must return the compliment, you are certainly a rare beauty."

"Antonio, I am leaving Junior with you. We will be gone for about three or four hours do you think that you can handle Junior without me?"

"Vikki, I am your husband… I got this. You and mother go and enjoy yourselves. And Vanessa, you too. I'm taking Junior home; he and I are going to have a good time together."

"Like I said before, we are going to be gone for about three or four hours."

"Honey, here is my credit card I will see you when you get home. I have Wallace to help me." He kisses Junior and leaves. Antonio straps the baby in the car seat, and they head to pick up Wallace from Liam's.

"Cassie, we are going to take you to the best place there is to get a makeover. Everyone goes to Desire's. Let's go."

Cassie gets in the car with Vikki, and they drive to Desire's. Once they arrive, they are immediately taken to the back. Delicious is in rare form. He wants to be the one who handles the women's hair.

Cassie likes Delicious' salon. "Well, who do we have here?"

"Delicious, this is my mother in-law… her name is Cassie. She needs a makeover."

"Vikki, you are right about this. Let me see what I'm working with."

"Miss Cassie, you have a beautiful head of hair, but you are going to need intense work done to it. I am going to give you a treatment to make your hair healthy, but you must continue to see me."

Meanwhile, Antonio stopped by Liam's to pick up Wallace so that they can go home and get an hour or two of rest before they get dressed for the engagement dinner. "Wallace how are you going to get my mother out of the house?"

"Don't worry about it, Antonio. I have this. I want everyone to be at the restaurant at seven thirty; I am going to get her there by seven forty-five. I am so excited… I am getting engaged to the woman of my dreams."

Wallace tells Antonio that he will drive so that Junior can enjoy being held by his father. "Thanks for that man, but he has to be strapped in his car seat. I love this boy. I can't wait to have another one."

"Antonio, you and Vikki deserve it. I'm so happy that she pulled through. Now is everything else okay?"

"Wallace, what are you talking about?"

"You know, the situation with the guy who was attacking your character. What's his name, Tyrone Tyler?"

"Well, I am countersuing him, and I have two great attorneys. I don't want to seem disrespectful, but can we talk about something else?"

"Antonio, this is not the way to your house."

"Wallace, I know; we are going to Nona's. I need to pick up something for tonight.

Okay Wallace, now that we are here, is there something that you like?"

"Antonio, what are you doing? Wallace you are getting engaged to my mother, so I want to do something special for you. Pick whatever you want and it's yours; price is no object."

"Antonio son, I can't have you pay for this. I will give it back to you."

"Wallace, you will do no such thing. This is for you."

Vikki is calling on the phone. "Hey honey, how are you and the baby doing?"

"We are okay, we are at Nona's picking out something for Wallace for tonight. After that we are going home so that we can rest up for tonight. How is my mom?"

"Antonio baby, she looks fabulous. Delicious did his thang, as usual."

"Well, I don't want to keep you on the phone too long. See you soon."

The ladies look fabulous as ever. Delicious escorts them to the front of Desires. In strolls a sexy mocha chocolate hunk of a specimen. Delicious stops dead in his tracks and says to Lawrence, "How many licks does it take to get to the center of a tootsie pop?"

"Excuse me, who are you?"

"I'm whomever you want me to be."

"I want you to be out of my face."

"I'm moving, but you will be back again."

"Look, I'm here to see someone and it definitely ain't you."

Vikki greets Lawrence, "What are you doing here, Lawrence?"

"Actually, I came to check on you."

"What are you talking about, Lawrence?"

"Well, I know that Antonio was upset about the situation with Tyrone and I just want to make sure you are alright."

"We are okay and that was nice of you to check on me. Oh, where are my manners? Lawrence, this is my mother-in-law, Cassie, and this beautiful woman over here is my best friend Vanessa, and the ex-wife of Tyrone.

"I'm sorry about that, Vanessa."

"Lawrence, no need to be sorry; it's the truth. Tyrone is a butt hole."

"And, before I forget, this is Delicious."

"Vikki, what did you say his name was?"

"This is Delicious, he is the owner of this establishment. He can be a little abrasive, but he is very sweet. I promise you Lawrence, he is not interested in you, he just doesn't know what to say at times. He has no filter at all, but he does have a heart of gold."

"Vikki, thank you for the introduction."

Delicious sashays over to Lawrence, "You still haven't answered my question, how many?"

"The answer is none. Now, I know it's time for me to leave. Ladies, have a wonderful day."

"Aren't you going to say good-bye to me?"

"Bye David."

"David? Who's David? The name is Delicious."

Vikki looks at Delicious and cracks up. "You have got to stop scaring the men off."

"Girl, you know I'm just having fun. Vikki, can I speak with you for a moment?" Vanessa and Cassie tell Vikki that they will wait for her in the car.

"Delicious are you alright?"

"Vikki, I'm good. I just want to know what time we need to arrive at Liam's for the engagement dinner."

"Delicious, please be there at seven thirty, we want Cassie there at seven forty-five."

"I will be there with bells on."

"Delicious, please don't wear bells." They laugh because they know Delicious would do that. "Delicious, love you; but I have to go. We have to get something for this evening without Cassie becoming suspicious."

"Bye girl."

Vikki tells Vanessa that she is stopping at Paola's Glamour Designs. "Ladies, let's go."

Cassie is inquisitive. "Why are we stopping here?"

"Because we are trying to help Vanessa pick out something nice for an event that she is having tonight."

"Cassie, I would really like for you to come. It will be at Liam's and it starts about seven forty-five. Vikki will be there."

"I would love to come, Vanessa, and thank you for thinking of me."

Vikki tells Cassie to pick out anything she wants; so, she decides on a black form- fitting evening gown. "Mother in-law, you look good. Wait until Wallace sees you.

"Excuse me, that's Antonio calling me."

"Hey baby, we are on our way back home."

"How is Junior?"

"Baby, he is okay, but I'm not, he is crying. I changed him, and I tried to give him a bottle, but he doesn't want that kind of food."

"Antonio, I am about fifteen minutes away." The ladies make it home in record time.

Antonio, is relieved to see his wife; he knows that he can't feed him the way his wife can. "Baby, can you wake me up in thirty minutes. I must get some rest."

Everyone is preparing for tonight's celebration. Vikki is so tired that she falls asleep with the baby in her arms they forget that she is even in the house. It's almost seven o'clock and Antonio realizes that he has not seen or heard from Vikki. "Has anyone seen my wife and my son?"

They searched all through the house only to find out that she was in the den. Antonio quietly takes Junior from her so that she can prepare. He whispers lovingly in her ear. "Baby, you have to get up and get dressed; everyone is waiting for you."

Vikki jumps up and prepares to get herself together; she makes it in record time. Once they realize that they are not going to get to Liam's by seven thirty they just decide that it is best if they all go together.

Vikki finally gets it together she looks sensational. Cassie, Vanessa, Antonio and Wallace don't look too shabby either. The only person missing is Kevin; but that's okay, he is going to meet Vanessa at the engagement dinner.

They arrive at Liam's. Wallace jumps out of the car to pretend that he has to go to the bathroom. He wants Cassie to wait in the car until he comes back because he wants to escort her inside. He knows good and well that he isn't going to escort her anywhere. Antonio is going to wait for the cue to bring her in. Vikki pretends that she has to go to the bathroom, as well. Everyone is scattering as fast as possible. Vanessa goes in, as well, because she has to pretend that she is hosting this dinner.

After about ten minutes, Cassie tells Antonio is worried because Wallace didn't come back yet. Vanessa calls Antonio and tells him to bring Cassie inside the restaurant. "Okay you guys, lets' go." Antonio walks his mother inside Liam's. He opens the door, and everyone screams "surprise!".

"Oh, my goodness son, what is going on? Antonio, my son, why are all of these people here? I thought this was a party for Vanessa."

"Mother, this is for you."

"Antonio, what are you taking about?"

Wallace comes from behind the crowd. He gets down on one knee and asks Cassie if she would do the honor of being his wife. She is in shock and she is in tears, and Wallace says to her, "I understand the tears, but you know my knees hurt."

Cassie cracks up, laughing. "Yes, yes and yes I will marry you." That's all Wallace needed to hear.

Everyone is dancing and having a great time. The best time of the night is when Cassie and Wallace share a dance together. But the most memorable time of the dinner is when Cassie makes a speech in front of the entire crowd and tells them that she is overjoyed because earlier in the day she went to the doctor and they told her that there was no sign of cancer.

The crowd went wild and everyone turned up the volume even more. They danced and ate the night away with the exception of Vikki; she had to leave because she had to feed Junior. She kissed everyone and left.

As Vikki arrived home, Tyrone had come to her home. "Tyrone, why are you at my house? I am trying to put my child to bed." When she attempts to close the door, Tyrone sticks his foot in the door and tells her that if she ever closes the door on him that he will slap the taste out of her mouth. Normally, Vikki doesn't let anything, or anyone bother her, but there is always an exception to the rule, and this is definitely an exception.

"Tyrone Tyler, if you don't get your damn foot away from my door, you are going to find out what it feels like to have my foot in your behind. Now get the hell out of here and learn how to be a man. Oh, that's right you don't know what it's like to be a man, because you aren't a man; you're a punk, and that's too good for you."

Vikki is so upset; but she knows that she must calm down she has a baby in the house, and she needs to be okay for him. Once she feeds him and puts him to sleep, she calls Sheila because she wants her to know what just happened. "Sheila, where are you?"

"I'm at the office preparing for a case. Is everything okay?:"

"No, it's not. I don't want to worry Antonio, but I had a visit tonight from Tyrone."

"Vikki, what did he say?"

"Not too much of anything. We exchanged words; actually, I exchanged the words and told him to get away from my house."

"Sheila, is there something that can be done about him harassing me and my family?"

"I am building a case against him. Don't worry, it will all come to a head sooner than later; you just have to trust me. I'm finishing up another case and then I can totally commit to bringing Tyrone Tyler down."

"Take care of that handsome son of yours, relax, and we will speak soon. And whatever you do, you cannot mention anything to Tyrone, or anyone that he knows, that I am your attorney. When I get finished with Tyrone, he won't know what happened. He is going to be pissed off with the outcome and he will probably try to sue me and make a spectacle of himself, but that's okay. I am definitely up for the challenge."

"Thank you, Sheila. I appreciate what you said, and I am feeling a little better. Let me go Junior is crying."

Vikki runs upstairs to Junior. He is soaking wet; she changes him, and he immediately goes back to sleep. It's about twelve midnight and the gang is still enjoying the engagement dinner. Vikki wishes she could have stayed; but mommy duties call.

Vikki is finally able to get some rest, but it's not much; she still can't shake what Tyrone did. She knows that she can't tell Antonio because he will be livid, and he might hurt Tyrone, for sure. Antonio, Cassie and Wallace arrive home about one thirty in the morning. They had a wonderful time and Cassie is still in awe of her ring.

Antonio takes a shower and falls asleep next to his wife. It's six o'clock on a bright sunny Saturday morning. Vikki is up and excited about the day, she calls Vanessa. She wants to go shop and talk to her friend about what her ex-husband did, while they were enjoying the dinner.

"Vanessa, it's me, Vikki. I know that you are tired and that you are probably asleep, but I wanted to know if you want to go shopping with me. I have some tea that I need to spill and I'm sure that you will love to hear what happened last night."

"Hello Vikki, I'm sorry that I didn't pick up, but I was in the shower. I would love to go shopping with you and to find out about the tea. Let's get together about twelve noon; we can meet at Liam's."

"Okay Vanessa, see you at twelve."

By this time, Antonio is awake. Vikki wants to know why he is up this early in the morning. "Didn't you and your crew come in about one thirty this morning? I can't believe that you aren't sleepy."

"Honey, I can't believe that I am awake either, especially after coming in at one-thirty in the morning. Vikki I must tell you the engagement party was cool; you outdid yourself with everything."

"I have to get back to my routine; you know that I have to report to camp soon.

I'm going to go running and then I am going to hit the gym. I will see you when I get back."

"Okay, husband of mine." Vikki is about to give Antonio a kiss, when Junior starts crying. "Antonio, I'm sorry."

"Honey, let me get him. You had to leave the dinner early last night so that you could stay with our son, it's only fair that I do this."

Antonio loves his son and he loves to hold him every moment that he can, and Junior loves it when his dad holds him in his arms. It's like papa bear cuddling his little baby. Antonio doesn't want to let him go. "Baby, don't forget that you are supposed to go training."

"I know, but I want to be here with my son."

"Honey, that's fine. You can spend as much time as you want with him, after you finish training."

"So, we never got the chance to talk about how the dinner went last night."

"Vikki, it was great. Wallace and my mother were happy. It was a special night and they were surprised to see so many of their friends. Wallace couldn't contain himself when my mother said "yes" when he popped the question. They had so much fun. I'm glad that my mother found someone special in her life."

Vikki is not herself and Antonio notices it, but he isn't going to say anything to her just yet. He will talk with her when he gets back from training. One thing about Vikki is that she doesn't do a good job of hiding her feelings.

As soon as Antonio leaves, Vikki calls Vanessa and reminds her that she will meet her at twelve noon. Vanessa is excited to meet with her friend she wants to know if Vikki is going to bring the baby with her. "No Vanessa, he is going to stay home with his grandparents. They need to spend more time with him. He can stay with you and Kevin when Antonio and I have our date night."

"Girl, hang up so I can get dressed."

Vikki leaves instructions with Cassie and Wallace; she lets them know that she should be back in a couple of hours. She will be with Vanessa if they need her. Junior is in his own little world; he is smiling at Wallace because he is making silly faces.

Vanessa and Vikki meet up at Liam's and of course Thomas is there to greet them. Vanessa asks Thomas, "Do you also own Liam's jewels?"

"Yes, I do. Why do you ask?"

I didn't know if it was by accident that your restaurant and jewelry store have the same name. I actually shortened the name of the jewelry store; it's called Liam's Fine Jewels."

"Would you ladies like to order something?" Vanessa tells Thomas that all she wants is a salad. Vikki decides that she is going to have the same thing.

While they are waiting for their food, Vikki gives Vanessa the tea. "Well Vanessa, you know that I had to leave the engagement dinner early so that I could feed Junior. I made it home safely. I put him to sleep and just as I was going to lie down myself, the doorbell rang. I thought it was a neighbor coming over. When I opened the door, your ex-husband was standing there."

"Vikki, are you sure?"

"Vanessa, I think I know Tyrone. I asked him why he was at my house? I told him that I was trying to put my baby to sleep and when I attempted to close the door Tyrone sticks his foot in the door and tells me that if I ever close the door on him again he would slap the taste out of my mouth."

"Vikki did you call Antonio and let him know what happened so that he could put Tyrone in check?"

"Vanessa, now you know that the minute I say something to Antonio he is going to flip out on Tyrone. He will beat Tyrone like he stole something from him and gave it back to him and stole it again."

"Vikki, I see what you mean, but you still need to tell him. You don't want him to find out what happened from the idiot. I'm mad as hell that Tyrone would say that to you. I wouldn't normally say this, but Tyrone needs to be stopped, sooner than later. Sheila is the right person to do the job."

"Speaking of Sheila, I called her and told her what happened. She is going to add this to the long list of charges that she is going to file against Tyrone. Honestly Vanessa, I really hope that his happens soon."

"And why is that, Vikki?"

"Your ex-husband needs to see and feel the pain that he has put others through.

He needs to know that it's not about him."

Thomas delivers the ladies' food in the middle of the conversation. Vanessa is hanging on Vikki's every word. Antonio calls looking for his wife. "Hi honey, I'm having lunch with Vanessa. I will be home soon."

"Vikki, why didn't you say something?"

"Honey, we can talk when I get home." She hurries Antonio off the phone because she doesn't want him to ask her anything else. Vanessa that's not the way to do it, I will eventually tell Antonio maybe while he is away."

"Very funny, Vikki. You better not do that to your husband. Enough about Tyrone, he can't have any more of my energy."

"Well, as you know, it is my two-year anniversary with my husband, and I wanted you to be the first to know that we are expecting again. Kevin will be so happy. I didn't think that I would ever get over having a miscarriage. I just knew this was the end of my marriage, but Kevin was great. He loved me beyond what I expected. And because of that I want to do something special for him. Nothing has changed, Vikki. I still want you and Antonio to be the godparents."

Girl… Vanessa, you don't have to ask. Antonio and I would love it. Girl, let's get out of here and do some shopping."

Vikki pays the bill and they leave Thomas quite a tip. He tries to return the tip; he thinks that it's too much, but Vikki is not having it. "Thomas, take the tip and leave me alone."

"I can't let you do this; you are leaving a five-hundred-dollar tip for a twenty-dollar meal."

"Bye Thomas, enjoy your day. The food was sensational."

The ladies drive off and are enjoying a day of fun and shopping. Vikki finally arrives home and she needs help with all of the bags that she has. She spent at least ten-thousand dollars. Antonio is happy to see his wife. "Baby, I'm so glad to see you."

"I'm glad to see you, as well. Now where is my son?"

"He is with his grandparents; but he is a little irritable because he needs to be fed."

"Mother to the rescue." Cassie, Wallace and Junior are in the movie room. Junior is getting excited now that he sees his mother, because he knows that it's time to get fed. While Vikki is feeding Junior, Antonio wants to know if everything is alright with her, because she didn't seem like herself. She lies to Antonio and tells him that everything is okay. She wouldn't dare let him know what really went down, and she knows that her secret is safe with Vanessa.

As Vanessa heads home to her husband, her ex-husband Tyrone calls her on the phone. "Tyrone, why are you calling my phone? I am no longer your wife. I need you to lose my number and don't call it ever again. I told you that before; I shouldn't have to repeat myself. Please let this be the last time that I tell you that. If you call my phone again, it will definitely be a situation and one that you might not like."

If Vanessa was standing next to me I would choke the living life out of her. She has lost her cotton-picking mind. He decides to call her back, but she doesn't answer. "Vanessa, this is Tyrone. If you ever talk to me in that manner again, I will hurt you. I don't know who you think you are; but I'm not the one you want to go toe to toe with."

Vanessa can't believe that Tyrone left that message on her voice mail. She is upset, but she lets him think that he got over. She tells Kevin what happened as soon as she gets home. He wants to know where Tyrone lives; he wants to go and beat the living pulp out of him. Vanessa pleads with Kevin not to do anything to him. "Vanessa, what is wrong with you? Your ex-husband just disrespected you and you don't want me to say anything? Why not? Well, I'm waiting for an answer."

"Kevin, I'm pregnant. Tyrone is irrelevant to us. We need to focus on our family."

"Baby, you are right. Are you serious, you are pregnant?"

"Yes, I'm three months. I wanted to wait because we have been through so much with the miscarriage. I didn't want to say anything until I was well into my first trimester. Are you mad?"

"Vanessa, what would I be mad about? You made me a happy man. I can't wait for our child to come into this world. I want at least four children."

"Really? Too bad, three kids are enough for me. Boy, move and let me cook dinner. Kevin runs upstairs. He calls Antonio. They don't talk much, but he always gives Kevin good advice.

"Hello this is Antonio Anderson. How may I help you?"

"Hey brother, this is Kevin, Vanessa's husband. Long time, don't hear from."

"Hey Kevin, how are you?"

"Antonio, I need to talk to you. Is there somewhere we can meet?"

"You can stop by my house… it would be great to see you."

Kevin is getting dressed when Vanessa comes upstairs, and asks him where he is going? "I'm going to meet up with Antonio, he is a cool brother and we haven't talked in a while."

"Kevin, promise me you won't go to Tyrone's house and beat him up."

"Vanessa, I promise you. I got you."

Kevin is tempted to step to Tyrone, but he promised Vanessa, so he is going to keep his word. He is listening to the one and only Terence. He finally makes it to the Anderson Estate. Antonio is so happy to see Kevin. "Come on in, let's go to the movie room and sit and talk."

Before they can get there, Vikki runs into him. "Oh, my Lord, Kevin, how are you? What are you doing here? I thought you would be home with your wife and baby."

"Baby? What baby?"

"Honey, Kevin and Vanessa are expecting, and I am so happy for them."

"Man, that's great. This is Antonio Junior, my little man. He and my wife are my world."

"Kevin, are you guys hungry?"

"Nah, I'm good."

"Okay, it was good seeing you."

Vikki knows her husband, she decides that she is going to whip up something for them anyhow, and she was right. As soon as she brings the food to the movie room, their eyes light up; they act like they haven't eaten in months. Kevin waits until Vikki walks out of the room to talk to Antonio.

"Antonio, I need to talk. There's this dude that I need to step to. He disrespected my wife and I don't tolerate that at all. I want to go to his house and punch his lights out, but I promised Vanessa that I wouldn't."

"Kevin, how can I help? Do you need me to talk to him?"

"I don't think that would be a good idea Vanessa would kill me if she knew that I got you involved."

"It's okay, brother. What is his name?"

"It's Vanessa's ex-husband, Tyrone."

"Kevin, I wish I could help you with that one, but I have a case against him, and I can't touch him. Believe me brother you know I would handle him. Here's what I can tell you. Leave it alone, things have a way of working out for you. Believe you me, Tyrone is going to be in for a rude awakening. Let the brother say or do what he wants; payback is coming after a while."

"That's why I like talking to you; I am going to get good advice when we get together."

"Hey brother, how about a barbecue this weekend? I want you and Vanessa to come over."

"Antonio, if your wife makes this chicken again, then you've got a deal."

Kevin heads home to Vanessa; she is patiently waiting for him. "Kevin, did you go to Tyrone's house?"

"Vanessa, I told you that I wouldn't, and I kept my promise. I went to see Antonio and Vikki; they have a handsome son."

"Kevin, did you stop along the way?"

"Vanessa, I can't believe that you don't trust me. Have I ever lied to you?"

"Vanessa, what is this about?"

"Honey, I received a call from Tyrone, telling me that you came to his house and tried to step to him, but he had to shut you down."

"Vanessa, it takes fifteen minutes to get from our house to Antonio's house, I left his house at seven-thirty."

"What time is it now?"

"It's seven-forty. There is no way I can leave Antonio's, and get across town and back home in fifteen minutes.

"Baby, I am so sorry for not believing you. I can't believe that I allowed Tyrone to try and take me there."

"Something is wrong with that Negro; I can't believe that he would lie like that."

"You don't know my ex-husband. He is up to something and I am going to find out what it is."

"Vanessa, you will do no such thing. Let me handle your ex-husband and to make you feel at ease there will be no violence."

Meanwhile at the Anderson Estate, there is a knock on the door. Vikki answers the door, only to find out that it's Tyrone again. "I thought I told you yesterday to get the hell away from my house.

Now move!" This time, Vikki doesn't give Tyrone an opportunity to say another word. She slams the door in his face with a swiftness and this time he doesn't have a chance to stick his foot in the door.

Instead of Vikki telling Antonio what just happened with Tyrone, she calls Vanessa to tell her what he did. "Vikki, this is the second time this week. You need to tell Antonio otherwise Tyrone is going to think that he can do a pop up any time that he wants."

"Not now Vanessa, maybe tomorrow. I need to sleep on it."

Vikki can't really sleep because she knows that she needs to let Antonio know about Tyrone's antics. She decides to go downstairs to the den, so she picks up a book and begins to read. After about ten minutes of reading, she finally falls asleep. It's early in the morning, and junior is fussy.

Antonio is flustered because he doesn't see his wife; that is, until she appears. "Baby where have you been?"

"I was in the den; I came upstairs when I heard the baby crying."

"Vikki, are you sure that you are okay? You seem a little off your game."

"Antonio Anderson, I am alright."

"If you say so, then I have to believe it." Antonio knows deep down inside that something isn't right with Vikki. But, he is not going to pressure her; he knows that she will eventually tell him what's going on.

"Antonio, I didn't want to mention this to you, but I haven't been feeling the best. I have another doctor's appointment, but I am going to put it on hold. I need to make sure that you and Junior are okay."

Before Antonio can get a word in edgewise, Wallace and Cassie make their way to the dining area. They want to let Antonio and Vikki know that they want to elope, and they don't want to wait.

"Mother, you want to do what?"

"We want to elope, and we are going to do it tomorrow and we need the blessing from the both of you."

Wallace asks Antonio to be his best man, and Cassie wants Vikki to be her maid of honor.

"Wallace, I would be honored to be the best man. So where are you going to elope?"

"We have settled on Las Vegas; we think it would be a great get away for us all."

"Wait, I can't go. Did you forget that we have Junior? I can't take him on a plane for that long and I don't want to take him to Las Vegas to a chapel. That's just too much for a little baby. We have to come up with something else."

Vanessa calls in the middle of their conversation.

"Hey Vanessa, how are you? What's wrong?"

"Girl, let me tell you what Tyrone did."

"Oh Lord, what happened?"

"That negro threatened me. Something is seriously wrong with him."

"What did your husband say?"

"He wanted to go to his house and tear him apart, bit by bit; but I told him not to do it because we have more serious things to concentrate on like making sure that we have a healthy baby boy or girl. And then Tyrone calls me to tell me that Kevin went to his house and actually beat him up, he sent pictures. You know that I was really upset with Kevin because I really thought that he was trying to boss up on Tyrone and knock his lights out. Girl, enough about Tyrone, he is a manipulative liar. He needs Jesus and I am serious about that."

"Vikki, you ain't never lied about that."

"Vanessa, I have a question to ask you. If you say "no" I will understand. Wallace and Mother Cassie just informed me and Antonio that they want to elope tomorrow in Vegas, but I don't want to take junior. Do you mind watching him for a couple of days. We are leaving in a couple of hours; we should be back in about a day or two."

"Vikki, I would love to watch my godchild and I'm sure that Kevin feels the same way. This will give us a chance to practice."

"Thanks, I will pack a bag and I will bring him over on our way to Vegas."

While Vikki is packing, Antonio tells her that he wants her to see the doctor while they are in Las Vegas. They drop Junior at Kevin and Vanessa's house and then they head to the airport on their way to Las Vegas. As soon as they arrive they check into their hotel and look for a chapel for the impending nuptials.

The four of them celebrate and walk along the strip, just enjoying each other's company. They realize that time is getting late, so they head to their hotel rooms and prepare for the nuptials.

Wallace is nervous, but excited. Antonio takes him aside and comforts him and tells him that everything is going to be alright. "Wallace, you are marrying the woman of your dreams, your friend and your soulmate. If you just remember that, you will have a wonderful marriage.

"Thanks for that advice, Antonio."

Cassie walks in and she is looking absolutely stunning. All Wallace can say is "WOW". The whole experience takes a total of twenty-five minutes. *We now welcome Mr. and Mrs. Wallace Haynes.* Both Wallace and Cassie look like they have just gotten married for the first time. They are overjoyed and love each other so very much.

They enjoy a night on the town, dinner and dancing, Vikki is feeling a little tired. So, she goes to the room to rest. Antonio is very concerned about her. Morning has come, Antonio takes Vikki to the doctor to find out what is wrong with her. They immediately run tests on her. After about thirty minutes of tests, the doctors come out to see Vikki. They take her to the back, and they inform her that she is pregnant. Vikki is stunned, she doesn't know what to say. She is happy but she is a little sad, as well, because she doesn't want another kid right now. Antonio will retire if he finds out she is pregnant. She loves her husband, but he can be a pain in two people's behinds. She doesn't want to tell him, so she tells the doctor that she prefers it if he tells Antonio what's going on and he obliges.

Vikki walks out with Doctor Albright. By the look on Antonio's face, he thinks that something is seriously wrong with his wife because she doesn't say one word to him. Doctor Albright breaks the news, "Well, Mr. Anderson, your wife is just fine... nothing serious. Oh, by the way, get ready. You're going to be a father again."

Antonio is excited, he can't wait to have another child. He lets Wallace and Mother Cassie know that they are going to be grandparents again. Both of them are happy about the situation.

"Antonio, my son, that's great."

"Mother is there something wrong? You don't look happy. You just married the man of your dreams. I would think that this would be a blessing."

"I'm overjoyed, just thinking of where I want to live."

"What are you talking about?"

"Antonio, your family is growing, and you know that Wallace and I are going to need somewhere to live."

"Mother, I don't know what the issue is. We have two guest houses; you and Wallace can live in one of them."

"Antonio, are you sure?"

"Yes, I am sure."

"Are you sure that Vikki won't mind?"

He summons Vikki. "Baby, do you have an issue with my mother and Wallace living in one of our guest houses?"

"Not at all. I would love to have them both here. And I know that they want to be close to their grandkids. Mother Cassie, you and Wallace can help me with the children."

"I love you both so much, that was a load off our backs. Antonio this is good. You are going to need backup for people like *what's his name* who acts like he is stupid."

"Who is *what's his name*?"

"You know, the guy that is always starting trouble."

"Oh, you mean Tyrone Tyler, yes he is a sucker."

"Can we all get ready to get home and not talk about him?"

"Okay, we need to take some pictures."

To the surprise of everyone there, Delicious is in Las Vegas on vacation. "Well who do we have here?"

"Delicious, this is Wallace. Leave him alone. I need you to be on your best behavior."

"Vikki, I'm insulted. I would never say anything out of pocket to your father-in-law. I was talking about this young fine thing right here. Hello there, I love Vanilla Chocolate and mixed nuts, now that is a wonderful combination."

Wallace can't believe what Delicious just said. "Does he always act like that?"

"Yes, he does; but he is harmless. He is more than harmless, he is ridiculous. Wallace, he just likes to laugh and enjoy life. Why are you sweating what he says? You might be uncomfortable talking to him, but he will have your back. Get your mind out of the gutter, not like that. He can handle his own. Don't let him bother you. Let's pack and get ready for our flight home."

Vikki has contacted Vanessa; she is checking on Junior. Vanessa lets her know that the baby is okay. "We will be home tomorrow, Vanessa. Thank you so much for everything. You don't know how much this means to me. The trip was amazing. I have a new father-in-law and a new mother-in-law. And I have some more tea for you; but that's something that we can talk about at another time."

Antonio, Vikki, Wallace and Cassie all arrive home. They are all smiles. They have picked up Junior; but Vikki doesn't want to say anything yet to Vanessa about her pregnancy.

Sheila tried to call Antonio, but he didn't answer, so she is going to try him again in about fifteen minutes. Sheila needs to get a hold of Antonio because she has news for him, and she needs to let him know. After about the third attempt, she is finally able to get in contact with him; but there is a bad connection when he answers the phone. It must be important because Sheila is calling him again; and again, she can't get him.

He tries to contact her. "Hello Sheila, this is Antonio. We are playing telephone tag with each other. Please call me back when you have a moment."

"Hello this is Antonio. How may I help you?"

CHAPTER TWENTY

"Hello Antonio, this is Sheila. I want to let you know that we have a date set for the case against Tyrone. It's two days from today. There is no need for you or Vikki to be there. Get ready for training camp."

"Hey baby, I just got a call from Sheila, they are trying Tyrone's case in two days. Now, I don't want you doing anything to stress yourself. I need you take care of you and the baby and my mother will be here to help you while I'm in training camp."

"I'm a big girl, Antonio. I can't believe that they got a court date so soon. I cannot believe that Tyrone would do this. But then again, it's Tyrone. Why wouldn't I believe it? Can you believe that he was trying to get back the alimony that Vanessa was awarded? What a coward he is."

"Tyrone needs some serious help. And he really thought that Vanessa was going to give him back the money, now that's funny."

Sheila calls back. "By the way, Antonio, please let Vikki know that I am going to include what Tyrone did the other night as a part of the case."

"Thank you Sheila, I will let her know." Antonio is steamed because not only did Vikki hide something from him, but she hid something major. Antonio yells at the top of his lungs, "Vikki Anderson come here!"

Vikki rushes to her bedroom. "Hey honey, what happened?"

"Vikki, is there something that you want to tell me?"

"Antonio, what in the world are you talking about? I was with the baby, and Mother Cassie was in his room."

"Vikki, don't play me like I'm stupid. What don't I know?"

"Antonio, I don't know what you're talking about."

"Vikki, are you sure about that? There is nothing that you need to tell me?"

"Antonio, there is nothing that I need to tell you." She goes to kiss Antonio and he pushes her away.

"When you are ready to tell me the truth then we can sleep in the same bed together; otherwise I'm going to stay in the guest house. Vikki, I can't believe that you are standing in my face and lying to me."

Vikki is upset. "Antonio, you are losing it."

"Okay, let me say it this way, since you seem to have selective amnesia. Was there a situation that occurred the other night with Tyrone?"

"Oh that! Well it wasn't anything major, and you were at the engagement dinner for your mother and Wallace; and by the time you came home, I had already handled the situation, so that there was no need to say anything."

"Vikki, you are my wife. I could care less how unimportant you think a situation is; I should know what's going on. Now what the hell happened?"

"Tyrone basically told me in a nutshell that if I ever close a door in his face again he would slap the taste out of my mouth."

"He said what? And you thought that didn't warrant me knowing. For Tyrone's sake, he better be glad that I didn't know what happened. It's okay, I am going to step to him."

"Antonio, why are you letting him get to you? His case is coming up in two days. You can step to him then; but in the meantime, I am sorry. Babe I promise not to keep anything from you especially when it comes to Tyrone."

"That's fine, but Vikki you are my queen and I won't tolerate anyone disrespecting you. I don't care if it's my mother, our child, anyone, and definitely not that character Tyrone. I am always going to have your back." Tears are flowing down Vikki's face. "Baby, stop crying it's you and me forever, together, always. We are in this together. When someone disrespects, attacks or does anything to hurt you or Junior, it's as though they hurt me. Woman, I love you and I am your protector, friend, lover, and husband, and nothing will stop me from doing that."

"Let me wash up and get dressed and we are out of here. Go get Wallace and mom and get dressed, we are going to have family day. We are going to Liam's for breakfast."

Vikki calls everyone together and tells them to meet downstairs in an hour. "Antonio wants us to spend the day together as a family."

"Vikki, can you believe that this is the first time that we both stayed home from church? Antonio, it feels weird."

Cassie walks into the room, she notices that both Antonio and Vikki stopped talking as soon as she appears. "Did I interrupt something? You two stopped talking when I came in the room."

"Well mother, let me say this, "I was trying to do something with my wife."

"Oh oh, my bad, son. Have fun, but remember we need to be downstairs in an hour."

Antonio laughs and Vikki is a little embarrassed. But what can she do? She loves spending time with Antonio in more ways than one.

What a day. They had so much fun that when they arrive home Junior is knocked out in his father's arms. Antonio puts him in his crib and he never wakes up. Junior has had a long fun-filled day with mommy, daddy, poppa and nana.

"Whew, I am tired. Antonio, aren't you tired yet?"

"I am tired, that's why I'm going to jump in the shower and get some rest. No nookie tonight, Vikki."

"So, what are you trying to say, Antonio?"

"Babe, I have training tomorrow and you know that I have to be on my best behavior."

"Antonio, that never stopped you before. What's so different now?"

"Before, I was just practicing and working out and playing sporadically; now it's down to business training camp and then pre-season; and then it's time for the season to start. I know you want your man to have a good season, now don't you, babe?"

"Yes, I guess you're right. It's no fun getting denied from my husband."

"Aww baby, I got you when I have my bye."

"Your bye, what is that?"

"That's when I have a week off. It's going to be on and popping."

Everyone gets a good night's rest. Junior is up; he is growing bigger and bigger by the day. Vikki puts him in the bed with her; she needs to get some more rest. She hasn't told Antonio yet, but her boutique will be officially open in a week. He isn't going to like it, but he will have to deal with it.

She is a woman who wants to have her own, she doesn't want to rely on her husband for everything. Antonio has already left the house to train. She calls Vanessa and tells her to meet her after work, she has a surprise for Vanessa.

"Vikki, I love surprises."

"Oh, by the way, Vanessa, did you hear that Antonio's case against Tyrone is set for tomorrow?"

"Girl, I heard. I took the day off just so I could be there."

"Vanessa, this is one case I would love to be at; but Antonio won't let me go, and Sheila said there is no need to be there. Antonio postponed training camp for another day or two, just so that he can make it to the case. I am going to support my husband and he can get an attitude if he wants; but I will be there."

"Vikki, what about Junior?"

"Oh, that's not an issue. I already asked my mother in-law and my father in-law if they will watch him while we are in court and they were ecstatic."

"Okay let me get off this phone so that I can finish this work. I want to be out on time, and I will see you about three o'clock."

"Vanessa, I will text you the address to where we are going to meet."

"Great, see you later today."

Vikki is so excited about the opening of Anderson's, her new boutique. This is something that she can finally call her own. *Let's see how Antonio will take it.*

Antonio comes back home from training. "Antonio, we need to talk. I promised you that I would not hide anything from you, and I don't want you to find out from anybody else. Well, here it goes. I will be having a grand opening next week for my new boutique that I am opening."

"Vikki, when did this happen? I thought you decided against opening a boutique."

"Antonio, you decided against me opening a boutique; you know that this is my passion."

"Vikki, I don't think that's a good idea."

"Oh, so you don't think that I can manage a boutique?"

"Honey, I never said that, I think you will be a great owner and manager. All I am saying is give it a few months; wait until Junior is a little older and then do it. You need a suitable babysitter."

"Antonio, your mother is available."

"Vikki, she and Wallace just got married, they are going on a honeymoon; and as newlyweds they want that time to be with each other not taking care of a baby."

"Antonio, they had their honeymoon in Las Vegas. Mother Cassie already agreed to help me out."

"Let's talk about this after this case is over because if we talk about it now it's going to end up in an argument. We don't need to argue over something that we can sit down and discuss with clear minds."

"I appreciate that, Antonio. I'm still going to have my grand opening next week."

"Vikki, I said 'no'."

"Antonio, it's too late. I have already invited people and the press to come; baby, please support me on this. I will get someone to manage the store for a few months."

"Okay Vikki, I will be there for your grand opening."

Meanwhile on the other side of town. Tyrone received court papers: *Anderson vs. Tyler.*

Antonio must be crazy, *trying to sue me for what? When my attorney gets finished with him, he is going to wish he had paid me. I'm calling my attorney now.*

"Hi Greg. What the hell is going on? I just received papers that I'm being sued by Antonio Anderson for thirty million dollars. This has got to be a joke."

"Tyrone it's not a joke. You don't have to appear in court. I can handle everything for you; don't worry. By the way do you still have the photos of incident?"

"Yes, I do Greg, I will send them over to you as soon as I finish with a meeting that I am going to."

"Then, we are good. Relax and I will call you tomorrow telling you that you won the case. Enjoy your day."

"Thanks man, I knew I could count on you. But I want to come so that I can look at Antonio's face when he has to pay me thirty million dollars, plus interest. This is truly going to be epic. Antonio won't know what hit him."

"It truly is, Tyrone. This is going to be good. Just remember, Tyrone, that you are not to say anything to anyone, not even friends. The fewer people that know about this case, the better it is for you and your case."

"Alright Greg, you have a good day. Thank you and good-bye." *I need to call Sheila and tell her what's going on. She isn't going to believe this foolishness. Plus, I can talk to her confidentially.*

"Hello Tyrone, I'm in a meeting. Are you okay?"

"No Sheila, I am not okay. Can you believe that Antonio is suing me for defamation of character, and he wants thirty million dollars? Who the hell does he think he is? That Negro has lost his mind. My attorney is going to eat him and his attorney alive. He is going to put them both to shame."

"Tyrone, you need to calm down. Look, we can talk tomorrow."

"Sheila, you always know what to say to me. I'll let you get back to your meeting and maybe we can go to lunch tomorrow. I don't think that will work; I have a meeting until about four o'clock."

"Okay Tyrone. I'm sure that everything will work out alright." She actually feels sorry for Tyrone because she is going up against his attorney who is basically a rookie compared to her and she is going to eat him alive. When she gets finished, Tyrone and his attorney will both be crying.

"Hey Mark, it's Sheila."

"Baby girl, I know who you are."

"Well, I just wanted you to know that Tyrone's court date is set for tomorrow at two o'clock. I hope that you can make it."

"I wouldn't miss it for the world, I will be there with bells on. It's about time that someone knocks him off his high horse. I can't wait for the take down and the shake down. It's going to be on and popping. Sheila, I will call you back, Tyrone is coming toward my office."

"Alright, and if I don't speak with you later today, I will see you tomorrow." After she finishes her call with Mark, she immediately calls Kayla. "Hey girl, are you busy?"

"Not at all… what's up?"

"I have some great news that I think you will want to hear."

"Please tell me what it is."

"Well, you will be happy to know that Tyrone's case is on the calendar for tomorrow at two o'clock."

"Sheila, I will be there, sitting in the front row. I'm clearing my schedule right now. I'm so sick of his nonsense. Girl, I hope you stick it to him good. I want to see the look on his face when you appear as Antonio's attorney."

"I don't like to see people go down, but I am so sick of Tyrone and all of his antics. Maybe this will teach him to leave people alone. He has made a spectacle of others for far too long; now it's time for the tables to be turned."

"Sheila, I am proud of you girl. I know you will do a fantastic job."

"Kayla, is everything okay? You sound strange."

"Girl, I am just sleepy. I will call you back when I wake up."

"If you are free later on, maybe we can go to dinner, Kayla."

"Sheila, that would be great. Bye for now, Sheila."

This is the law office of Lawrence Gray. Please leave a message after the beep and I'll be sure to return your call as soon as possible. "Hi Lawrence, it's Sheila please give me a call back at your most opportune time."

Lawrence calls Sheila about fifteen minutes later. "Hi Sheila, I got your message.

I am sorry I was on a call. What's going on, my friend?"

"Well, Antonio's case against Tyrone is on the calendar for tomorrow at two o'clock. I hope that you can make it."

"Sheila, I wouldn't miss this case for the world."

"Great, I look forward to seeing you tomorrow."

"Lawrence, I would like for you to be the second chair on this case because you are representing Antonio in another case."

"Sheila, I would love to be a part of this case. I want to call Antonio and let him know that I will be there, as well. I have his case on the calendar for three o'clock so it will be quite a day for all parties in involved; especially Tyrone Tyler, he is going to be hit with a double whammy. This is going to be a precedent for him."

"Hey Antonio, this is Lawrence. I want you to know that your case is on the calendar for tomorrow right after your first case with Sheila, both of them will be open and shut cases. Enjoy and get some rest and see you tomorrow. Sheila said that you didn't need to be there. That was for her case; but for the case where I am representing you, I need you there; it should not be longer than thirty minutes."

"Thank you, Lawrence. I appreciate all that you have done for me, thus far. Antonio, there is no need to thank me… we got this. Enjoy your day."

"And the same to you as well, Lawrence."

"Antonio, who was that on the phone?"

"Vikki, it was my other attorney, Lawrence; he called me about my second case. He is representing me on my defamation case, and Sheila was representing me on another, but both cases involve Tyrone."

Tyrone just called Sheila. "What is it, Tyrone?"

"Sheila, what's with the attitude?"

"No attitude, Tyrone." She lies and says to him, "I'm just tired and you interrupted my sleep."

"Sheila, I'm really sorry about that I didn't mean to awake you out of your sleep. I will call you tomorrow and we can we go out and celebrate."

"Celebrate what, Tyrone?"

"My case against Antonio, the one where he punched me. My attorney already guaranteed a win against Antonio he said that I didn't need to be there because it was an open and shut case, or shall I say a total slam dunk."

"I'm happy for you, Tyrone. You must have an awesome attorney that he can guarantee you a win before your case even goes before a judge. I would love to know his name. Yes, he is the best. His name is Greg Boyd he has been an attorney for four years."

"Tyrone, don't forget that Antonio will have a good attorney as well."

"Greg will sweep the floor with Antonio's attorney. Greg is a pit bull in the courtroom."

"Tyrone, I'm happy that you are confident in your attorney and I would love to finish this conversation with you, but I must get some sleep. I have a very busy day tomorrow. I have one more call to make. 'Hey handsome how are you'?"

"Sheila, I'm good, it's been quite a while since we have spoken. Greg, I know but I have been busy. So, Greg what have you been up too? Just missing you. Greg, now you know…"

"Sheila, I know that I am a day late and two dollars short." Now, you know if things don't work out between you and Mark, I am here for you. I have always wanted to be in a committed relationship with you."

"So, are you ready to represent Tyrone Tyler?"

"Baby, I'm ready as ever. You are the only person I don't mind losing a case for… especially when I'm getting paid five million dollars to do so."

"Good night, baby."

"Good night, Greg."

The day has finally come, and everyone is anxious. Tyrone arrives thirty minutes early; he is pacing the floor. He has called Greg at least ten times, and each time Greg has told him that he is on his way. Tyrone has called Greg so much that he had to turn his phone off. He is trying to get last minute documentation and he is looking at the photo that Tyrone sent him. Greg has to crack up himself because he knows that this is a losing case, but he will do his best to present it before the judge.

Tyrone is panicking because it is 1:50 in the afternoon and he still hasn't seen his attorney. As he is waiting for his attorney he sees Antonio, Vanessa, Kevin, Wallace, Cassie, Delicious, Patrice and Mark step into the courtroom, but he hasn't seen his attorney. He is pissed off because he can't believe that Patrice is there.

He actually sends a message to her telling her that she better not record any part of his case; otherwise she and KCC Sports will be sued for everything.

The bailiff comes and addresses Tyrone and lets him know that it's time for his case to start. "Thank you, but my attorney is not here as of yet."

"Mr. Tyler, your attorney is already in the courtroom."

"Oh well then, let's get this case started."

Tyrone may be a creep, but you have to admit it that he is one fine piece of specimen. He is a head turner. He walks to the front of the courtroom and sits next to his attorney and his team.

Greg steps up to present his case to the honorable judge Sterling Eady. He shows the pictures that Tyrone sent him showing that Antonio did not hit him; but in Tyrone's psycho mind he is saying that Antonio hit him. He has convinced himself that something happened when it actually didn't happen.

It takes Greg all of fifteen minutes, if that, to present his case against Antonio. Sheila is quiet as a button, but she is a pit bull when she has to present a case; and this one is no different. Tyrone's mouth drops open when he sees Sheila. He can't believe that she is Antonio's attorney. She begins to present her case; but unlike Greg, she has so much more evidence and photos and eye-witness testimony that she presents her case before the honorable judge Sterling Eady, for thirty minutes.

After she has presented her evidence, the honorable judge Sterling Eady adjourns the case while he deliberates. Tyrone is upset with Sheila. "Sheila what the hell are you doing? How in the world can you represent Antonio after what he did to me?" Sheila wants to retaliate verbally but she is not going to say anything to him.

Tyrone is floored when he finds out that Sheila, his so-called love interest, is representing Antonio. *How can this be, she is a sports agent? She won't win.*

After much deliberation from the honorable Judge Sterling Eady, the verdict comes back. Tyrone has been found guilty and it turns out that he is the one who must pay Antonio Anderson; and he has to pay him dearly to the tune of thirty-five million dollars, plus Sheila's attorney fees.

Now this is just the first case that was presented. Lawrence is presenting the second case of the afternoon in which Tyrone claims that Antonio punched him in front of people on national television. Greg did everything he could, but he can't win anything when it comes to Sheila and Lawrence.

"Sorry Tyrone, but you lost the case. The judge ordered you to pay Antonio fifteen million dollars for extortion and ten million dollars for defamation of character. So, in total you have to pay Antonio Anderson fifty million dollars."

"Greg you have got to be kidding me. I paid you five million dollars and you lost both cases what good are you? I could have represented myself and won. Fifty million dollars down the drain."

"Tyrone, I know that you are upset right now, but I forgot to tell you that you also have to pay Sheila's attorney fees, which total five million dollars."

"You have got to be out of your mind if you think I'm paying Sheila five million dollars. This whole thing was a farce."

"Tyrone, so what did you say about your attorney being a pit bull, and that he was going to sweep the floor with Antonio's attorney? It looks like I did the sweeping."

"Sheila, you stink bitch."

"Wow Tyrone, and you wonder why you lost the case."

"And by the way, Greg is an ex-boyfriend of mine."

"Greg, you are her ex-boyfriend? I ought to knock your lights out. You deceived me."

"Tyrone, how many people have you deceived throughout the course of your life? Do I need to run it down to you?"

"Get out of my face, Greg, with your nonsense and learn how to be an attorney."

"Tyrone, so I heard you lost. Great now you see what it feels like to lose something."

"Mark, what are you rambling about? I never did anything to you."

"You're still pretending like you didn't do anything or steal anything from me. Let me refresh that memory of yours. You stole my girl."

"Mark, what girl?"

"You said that you and Sheila were friends."

"I'm not talking about her. I'm talking about Vanessa. Do you remember, she was my college sweetheart? You lied and told her that I cheated on her and I had a baby with someone else. Tyrone, that was you. She broke it off with me because she actually believed you. I did everything I could to win her back, to no avail. It took some time and some years later; but one day it was going to happen. I promised that I would pay you back some way, somehow. I'm glad that Sheila won the case. This plan was set in motion from the day she stepped into the office."

"Sheila, congratulations girl. I knew you could do it."

"Kayla, what do you mean, you knew she could do it? How do you know Sheila?"

"Sheila is one of my best friends. I knew all about your dates with her, and how you acted a fool in the restaurant. Did you really think my friend would date you?"

"So, you all came here to do what?"

Antonio asks Tyrone a very important question, "Who's crazy now, Negro? You lost your case, you lost your mind, you lost your ex-wife, you lost your mistress, you lost your love interest and you lost your money. By the way, Tyrone, you are on the news, smile for the camera. I guess that partnership is over. I can't wait to see what the headlines say tomorrow. *Tyrone Tyler loses case against the People's favorite athlete Antonio Anderson.* Patrice did you get this?"

"Yes, Antonio, I got it all. I am going back to the station so that I can air the story. KCC Sports will be the first to get this."

"Patrice, you must not have gotten my message from before. You better not show one minute of the trial; otherwise I'm suing you and KCC Sports."

"Tyrone, do not threaten me."

"Patrice, it's not a threat… it's a promise."

"Didn't you just lose two cases in one day; do you want to make it three cases? I can make it happen. Tyrone, grow up, give up. You always want to blame everyone else for what you did. This is all you. The sad part is that you haven't learned your lesson. You will continue to do the same thing."

"Vikki, to hell with all of you."

"That's where you will be going. Tyrone you were all talk. Cat got your tongue? All I know is this, 'If you ever threaten my wife again, they will have to peel me off of you."

"Antonio, go for yours." *Why did Tyrone say that?* Antonio stepped to him and he was about to put his paws on him, when Wallace grabbed his hand.

"Antonio, this scum bag isn't worth your time."

Before Sheila leaves, she hands Tyrone her bill. "Tyrone you have forty-eight hours to pay my attorney fees, and you have one week to pay what Judge Eady ruled on today; otherwise you will be in contempt and you will be jailed."

"I have to get back to work; I don't have time for this."

"Tyrone, now I know you don't think that you have a job anymore. You lost your partnership a long time ago. It was because of me that the other partners agreed to let you stay on as long as you did, they wanted to fire you long ago. I guess now they have a reason to release you from your duties. You are a fierce investment banker/broker, but it was your personal life that took you down. How does a man go from making fifty million dollars a year plus commission to almost nothing?"

"Mark, screw you and Williams, Peterson. I can find a partnership anywhere; I have skills."

"But your personal life is in shambles; and until you get it correct, nothing else will go your way.

"Tyrone, I feel sorry for you. You would have had one person in your corner, but you tried to get back the alimony money that was awarded to me. I lost all respect for you. I guess you will never get a woman, a woman doesn't want a broke man."

"And you actually thought that I was interested in you. You don't know what it's like to have real love, you try to destroy everything and everyone that comes in contact with you. You are a poisonous snake, sneaking up to suck the life out of folks. But look at what happened? You got your life sucked out of you."

"Sheila, the hell with you; I'm not paying you a dime."

"Tyrone, I bet you will."

"Sheila, I bet I won't. It will be a cold day in hell before I give any of you any of my money."

"Tyrone we will see about that, you really don't know who you are dealing with."

"Don't get it twisted, I can hang with the big boys, and I will take you down again."

"Tyrone, you still haven't seen the light. I will be your love interest all day long."

"Delicious, I will beat you so bad that you will never want a man again. Now get the hell away from me and don't you ever disrespect me again."

"Tyrone, screw you. Oh, that's right you need someone and something to screw; and from what I heard you need a magnifying glass to see it."

Everybody waves good-bye to Tyrone and walks away with big smiles on their faces.

Tyrone looks at his phone and calls Myah, hoping that she will talk to him. She picks up and realizes that it's Tyrone; and she hangs up on him. When he calls back, her manager picks up and he tells Tyrone that if he ever calls his employee again, he will have him arrested for harassment.

Tyrone realizes that he has nothing left. He walks out of the courthouse, puts on his shades and jumps into his car and drives off into the sunset alone, jamming to the sounds of Terence.

Everyone meets at Liam's for a Victory party. Antonio says his speech. "As you all know I am leaving for training camp tomorrow, but I needed to say "Thank you" to everyone for making this possible. Sheila, Lawrence and Greg, you are all fabulous attorneys; and I want to thank you for everything. But most of all, to my wife, Vikki. I am the man that I am because of you. I love you more than words can say. Just take care of Junior and our new addition. I will be home soon. Let's celebrate!"

Patrice calls Antonio and tells him that she is about to air the case on KCC Sports. He asks Thomas to turn on KCC Sports so they can watch the case on television.

It turns out to be the highest rated court case in history.

Delicious calls Tyrone and surprisingly he answers. "What do you want, Delicious?"

"Tyrone, you lost your ex-wife, and your mistress, I am willing to be your love interest."

Tyrone hangs up on Delicious without saying a word.

Vikki says out loud, "No one says it better than Delicious." Everyone cracks up laughing.

ABOUT THE AUTHOR

Sharyn Paige was born and raised in NYC.

She published her first romance novel entitled: "Don't Play If You Can't Pay". **"Ex-Wife, Mistress and Love Interest"** is the second installment.

Sharyn is single, and a member of East Ward Missionary Baptist Church.

CPSIA information can be obtained
at www.ICGtesting.com
Printed in the USA
LVHW051431170520
655842LV00003B/142